UNSPEAKABLE BEAUTY

Georgia Carys Williams lives in Swansea. Her short story collection *Second-hand Rain* was shortlisted for the Sabotage Short Story Award and longlisted for the Edge Hill Prize and the Frank O'Connor International Prize. She has a doctorate in creative writing from Swansea University. *Unspeakable Beauty* is her debut novel.

UNSPEAKABLE BEAUTY

Georgia Carys Williams

PARTHIAN

Parthian, Cardigan SA43 1ED www.parthianbooks.com
First published in 2024
© Georgia Carys Williams
ISBN 978-1-914595-42-4
Editor: Susie Wildsmith
Cover design by Emily Courdelle
Typeset by Elaine Sharples
Printed and bound by 4edge Limited, UK
Published with the financial support of the Welsh Books Council
British Library Cataloguing in Publication Data
A cataloguing record for this book is available from the British Library
Printed on FSC accredited paper

For my nan

who told me to never give up.

You do not understand my love of dreaming,
For you have never dreamed; you cannot see
The wonder of a bird with white wings gleaming,
The breathless beauty of a wind-swept tree!
– Myfanwy Haycock, 'Taskmaster'

PROLOGUE

When you say your dreams out loud, they're brought to life for others to kill. That's what Mam always said. *No one believes a seed will become a flower until they see it bloom. Some people will need to see it happen a hundred times and even then, they'll have their doubts.*

I wish it wasn't true, but it only takes a whisper, and next thing you know, your dream – in all its delicious detail – is running wild in the mind of a stranger who can't wait to put a pin in every arm and leg of your idea and watch its entire body squirm as it stretches for answers.

Over time, if you're not careful, your dream will become so small and unrecognisable that there'll be nothing left to pine for, just a flicker of a fleeting thought you once had. *It was a stupid idea anyway*, you'll say, almost convincing yourself, but the uncomfortable truth is that something within you, months, years or decades later, somewhere deep down, will feel as heavy as the whole world but as hollow as a wooden Russian doll.

Dreams kept quiet, however, are as light as leaves; limitless. You needn't worry about those. They make you feel invincible. You can do anything, be anything. There's no need to work out all the hows and whys first; you're wise enough to know that if you did, you'd never summon the energy to execute your plan.

So, to look after your dreams, you need to hold them close to your heart and keep your lips sealed. When someone steals your dream, they sort of steal you too.

For as long as I can remember, my dream was to be something extraordinary.

Part One

SECRET HAVEN

Melody and I had known each other since the beginning. We were born at the same hospital, with only a day and three beds between us, me following her lead as I *sautéd* into my second world. My skin was a bit bluer than it should have been, so together with Mam's love for flowers, I was named Violet. Once I turned the expected colour again, and once we saw our mothers – all eyes and clouds of pink – we knew we'd be swaddled with them forever. After we left the hospital, we stayed only three homes apart, on the long road that rests not far from the edge of the Common.

I lived with my mam and dad on a smallholding in our ivory house, and Secret Haven was our back garden, but it was much more than that. It was a quiet, magical place they had created – all by themselves before they'd even met me. Dad had laid the earth and Mam had planted the scenery, so together, they'd made sure it was a place where the very roots of all our dreams had enough space and light to come to life. Over the years, as the trees took guard and Mam's flowers bloomed, Secret Haven became more and more secret as well as beautiful. Mam said that was around the time I arrived, *finally,* after fifteen years of them dreaming me up.

At Secret Haven, Melody and I took the name of our world dead seriously, pressing our fingers to our lips and speaking in low voices whenever we discussed it at school. Our secrets were always shared so delicately – through the graze of fingertips, the rub of shoulders, our foreheads resting ever so gently against one another's, with eyes closed, so any thoughts could float freely – without being watched. We didn't realise back then that not all secrets are good, that some people's secrets are just too dark to speak of.

That didn't matter at the time. We spent so many of our days dancing at Secret Haven that it was almost the only place we knew. It was, after all, where we first learnt to point our toes, *plié* across the clover, lasso clouds from the sky and *pirouette* just to see how trees could twirl – before we even knew it was called ballet. It was where we learnt to collapse dizzily in the daisies just to gracefully get up and start all over again.

Secret Haven smelled of home; a mixture of cut grass, thirsty flowers and chicken business. And I was so glad it was *my* home, snaking all the way back from the ivory house with its cottage windows and sloping, charcoal cap, and then right to the end, where there was a hedge so high that we couldn't see anything beyond it, which Mam used to laugh was her plan all along, so nobody could snatch us away.

But one late summer day stays with me more than others, rises to the surface like a bruise: changes colour depending on how I'm feeling.

I was nine years old. Everything was a flickering yellow and the rain had been hushed away beneath the twinkling blue sky. I remember how still everything felt, far from the bustle of Mam and Dad's barn shop and the cluck of hens, just opposite our Wendy House, as I – in my daffodil-yellow swimsuit – dangled on my swing under the tree of greengages, staring at my bony ankles and knobbly knees while I waited for Melody.

6

Some people may have found the place unsettlingly still, too comfortable a bubble, but I knew of the life that was brought to it whenever Melody arrived.

I remember gazing – one of those extra-long gazes – at Secret Haven, lengthening my neck and adjusting my head to frame everything in the best way, and then blinking to take a snapshot with my eyes. *Perfect.* That image is always the first one that creeps into my mind.

There was Mam, entering the shot in her paint-splashed summer dress, with a watering can in one hand, secateurs in the other, and her amber eyes reflecting the whole garden in sepia sunlight. Mam belonged outside, in the physical world, so at home with earth on her hands and petals in the ends of her chestnut hair as it fell over one of her shoulders every time she leant forward and then back, the odd, silver streak breaking free.

Mam always meant business; it was in the movement of her strong, freckled arms, the restful rhythm of her footsteps, something so sure, so the world moved with her, shadowed her, even, rather than her moving with the world. I suppose, in a way, she'd grown herself at Secret Haven too.

Melody was late and my feet were beginning to fidget.

'You know she'll be here soon, don't you?' Mam said with a smile, bending to fill the bird bath. 'She always is.'

I nodded, feeling the same smile bloom between my cheeks. It was true. Melody had been there almost every day so far that summer. Mam certainly had a way of breathing life back into everything, while Dad especially – found joy in her atmosphere, taking in her light, so they could duet in their own little photosynthesis. Me and Melody were similar.

I focused on a Painted Lady dancing around the border of heather, the strange stiffness of its black-and-orange wings gliding towards one flower and then the next. Dad had told me how they only live several weeks, so I couldn't help but wonder if the twitch of one of its fragile wings was because it was near death or just curious.

While Mam's back was turned, I swung like a pendulum, stretching my legs to urge time forward as best as I could, swinging so high that I could see right over the hedge. With each sweep, I could peer down into Dad's fields where all sorts of root vegetables were growing, and there was the long line of Mam's greenhouses, where she brought every flower and plant to life. School wasn't far from home and ballet was just the other side of the Common, a name I still didn't understand being given to such an unusual and lonely-looking place, with nothing common about it at all. Further on from that was our town. I could see it all from the swing, and if I looked right past the Common, far in the distance was the gargantuan tongue of the sea, a place that seemed to happen all on its own, just drifting in and out whether we were there or not. I wondered if one day, it would poke right out and swallow us all.

But no, everything stayed perfectly in its place. So, I took the opportunity to stand up on my swing, with feet turned out and hands clinging to the rope either side. I lifted one of my legs behind me with a pointed toe. *Look at me, on the edge of everything. If I can balance here, I can balance anywhere. If I lift my arms, I could even fly!*

That's when I heard thunder above me, the crack of wings whipping at the air. A formation of geese was in full motion, a giant V of triangles in the sky.

'Vi-vi! Down here!'

I jumped out of my butterfly-skin and my wings shrunk into arms again. I fell onto the swing-seat with a jolt that shot right up my spine, then slowed down and allowed my legs to flop back and forth like those of a puppet as I returned to land.

'Did you *see* that?' Melody's sun-bronzed hand hid a gasp until she saw I was okay. There she stood, glowing – as always – wearing one of her oldest leotards, magenta with gold stars, and cradling at least six dolls tightly in her arms as she looked up.

'Yes! Where do you think they were all going?'

'Perhaps they're arriving,' Mam said, adding an 'and be careful, you!' as she exited our scene.

A butterfly of freckles fluttered across Melody's short nose and pudgy cheeks as she smiled after Mam. *Is it possible to miss someone when they've only just got here?* I was glad the future had finally arrived. Her buttery hair was twirled into two buns on either side of her sparkling head, double the fun of my lonely one. I was usually much paler than Melody, with the dull dishwater hair of a mouse and a fringe that always tried to cover my eyes, but lately, even I had begun to yellow from the scorching hot summer.

'I'm ready,' I shouted, then jumped down and pressed play on Mam's old CD player in the Wendy House. *The Nutcracker* music burst out of the saloon door while Melody lined the audience of dolls up on the bench and rushed to join me on our green palladium. We would do everything Ms Madeline taught us at ballet class last week, just as we did every week, drawing fists towards our hearts.

'This is someone in love,' I shouted, becoming the teacher,

9

'this is someone sad and tearful,' as we rubbed our eyes, 'ballet is about *acting,* and we can feel whatever we want to feel!' Melody laughed at my serious, Ms Madeline-voice, as we both *pas de bourréed* across the grass and I blew my fringe out of my sight again. 'Be whatever you want to be; I want to see your dreams come true,' she screamed, sprinkling blades of grass and limbless daisies over my head, and laughing straight afterwards. Being worried wasn't something we felt the need to practise.

That's what I most loved about ballet; being able to be anything so freely, to play someone different from the 'quiet Violet' I was at school. In ballet, life was limitless. Friendships were limitless. Vi-vi and Dee-dee were forever because our world had a beginning and end that only we decided.

During our performance, on one of our lefts and one of our rights, the back of the ivory house cast a shadow over a third of the lawn, and just the other side of that dark line, we danced and danced and danced, perfectly warm in the bright sunlight. Secret Haven was our whole universe and it was just the beginning.

If we forgot anything, I just whispered, 'Dee-dee, it's like this,' or Melody shouted, 'Vi-vi, it's like that,' and then we carried on, attached – by strings – to the sky. For us, there was only that land, with its perfectly green grass, and that sliver of light in each other's eyes. Melody's glistened like sapphires and she said mine were like peridots. Together, we were precious.

We were as innocent as dolls to each other; arms were just arms, legs were just legs and clothes were just clothes. She was just my Melody, who I'd always known, and when I was the one to play dead, she was always the one to save me.

When the shadow on the lawn drew over us, we knew our time was up, that the whole sky would change – *until tomorrow.*

I ran to turn off the music, noticing – at the same time – that Melody's mother was standing near Mam at the back door, so tall and pointed towards the sky that she was already altering something in the air.

'To be honest, it's been on the cards for months,' she said, nodding her severely parted hair.

'Well, it's good of you to come round,' I heard Mam say.

And there was Melody, already standing alongside them with her head down, its two buns sticking up like ice-cream cones.

I ran over too, trying to meet her eyes again, but for the first time ever, she wouldn't look at me.

Mam wrapped her arm around my shoulders and gently squeezed. 'Violet, love,' she said, 'something quite important is happening. Melody and her family are moving house tomorrow...'

At first, I pictured our Wendy House. We'd just refurbished it, pinned new Margot Fonteyn posters to the eggshell blue walls for some famous ballerina inspiration, added a vinyl floor and some curtains, so nobody could see in... Then I remembered the other house, the supposedly real one. *How could they possibly move the whole house, with all their lives still inside it, and our lives all around it?*

'Melody's mum has been lucky enough to find a new job, so they're moving away to be a bit closer to her work,' Mam added. She was trailing off into some explanation, but I didn't recognise the name of the place she mentioned, I didn't remember Melody telling me about this and I didn't understand how this was 'lucky' in any way whatsoever, especially not for me. I wished somebody had warned me about how big the world was going to be. Secret Haven suddenly felt so small, and it was getting smaller by the second.

'We only surprised Melody with the news this week,' her mam said, looking at mine, 'you know how it is, Haze…'

As Mam threw her hair back over her shoulder and puffed out some air, I wondered if she really did know.

And when Melody started to cry, I found it hard to look.

Her mam eventually came down from the sky to put an arm around her and carved the best smile she could. Still, she looked so stiff as she stood there, all in grey, ready to knife through anything she found a bit too pleasant. *What is she wearing? Some kind of office blazer and trousers? On a day like this?* I'd never seen such a dull flower before. Supposedly younger than Mam, she looked so many years older… No, my mam was a multicoloured artwork all of her own, wearing mustard wellies and gently blowing a ladybird from the inside of her elbow. My mam was a sigh of relief.

'Melody, darling,' she said, edging her daughter forward, 'why don't you give Violet…'

Give me what? What could possibly…

Melody took a few deep breaths before wrapping her arms right around me, tighter than she ever had before. The chunky pads of her digits said they weren't letting go. *I suppose none of this is Melody's fault.* I wrapped my arms around her too, rested my head upon her cushiony shoulder, closed my eyes to properly take in the coconut smell of her suncream and the way those stray ringlets of hers brushed my neck. *This isn't acting, not this time.* For many seconds, we stood like that,

12

twins after all, never more than three houses away. And that's when I wanted to cry too, needed to explode like the seeds of a dandelion at the mercy of Melody's breath.

But I didn't cry.

Instead, I found myself unpeeling Dee-dee and pushing her whole body away. It wasn't her fault, I knew that, and yet, I whispered,

'How could you not tell me, Deeds?' I looked at her again. 'Were you *never* going to tell me?' My voice cracked and it seemed to cause the deepest splinter between her eyebrows.

She bowed her head and reached out to hug me again.

'Don't do that,' I whispered, but a loud whisper, 'stay away,' and then I crossed my arms, not wanting to be taken in again. That blue sky above us all could have been any colour; if it was as black as a crow, it made no difference to me – to any of us.

'Oh, Violet,' said Mam, as her eyes sussed out mine, 'this isn't like you.'

But who am I now?

'There's no need to worry, dear. I'm sure we'll be back someday, won't we?' Melody's mam said, looking down at my shrunken twin with her beady blue eyes. 'Well, we'd better go and carry on with our packing…'

That's when Melody's shoulders gave way and her sniffles turned to sobs.

'Okay, well, thanks for coming to see us,' said Mam, 'Gosh, we'll really miss you – I know this one will,' nudging me, 'but we hope everything goes okay with the move, don't we?' she nudged me again. 'Keep in touch. *Please* keep in touch.'

'Ohhh, of course we will.'

Melody raised her chin with some hope, took a deep breath

and then became inconsolable, her blotchy face streaming with tears. She collected her dolls from the bench before her mam grabbed her hand and dragged her away from Secret Haven. Sometimes I wished she wasn't her mother at all.

I wanted to shout, 'We'll be okay, Dee-dee, we'll see each other tomorrow,' only this time, we wouldn't, and I was worried about how we'd ever dance together again – how I'd ever dance again.

'You'll be fine, love,' Mam said, quickly turning to me and cradling my face in both her brambly hands. 'You'll be fine, I'll make sure of it.' She looked me straight in the eyes, and then planted a kiss on my forehead, right where my fringe had parted thanks to the heat. 'Come on,' she said, 'come inside and I'll get us a nice glass of that iced lemonade I made.' Then she turned to go into our ivory house.

Dad had turned up in his usual blue jeans – frayed at the knees – and a striped shirt with the sleeves rolled up to his elbows. He was beginning to mow the lawn as though the whole world hadn't changed, and I couldn't bear the noise. I was worried about what I'd said to Melody; tormented by it.

Mam used to say words were like toothpaste, *once you've said them, you can never squeeze them back into the tube.* Now, I tried to gulp down every one of them. *Stay away,* I'd said, *stay away,* but I felt the vowels stick to my throat as I stood there, watching our green dance theatre go up in dust.

THE NAKED FACE OF THE MOON

This day had crafted hours into years. I'd aged since Melody had said goodbye, I must have, our summer holidays seemed as though they'd only been imagined. *What will happen to our games?* I wondered, *and our thoughts? Will they all travel back to the mysterious place where they came from? A place built from the intertwining strands of us over the years – scraped knees and broken nails and bee stings and giggles and jinxes and snaps and hands and feet and faces, and Vi-vi and Dee-dee – will they be forgotten?*

I heard doors being slammed as I wandered past the landing window. Through it, I could see Melody's car struggling to reverse off their drive. Yes, there it was, gaining pace as it passed us, heading towards the Common, as peaceful as ever beneath the naked face of the moon, and then it was gone. They were gone.

There, under the faint light from the lamp post, was the roof of Melody's house; I couldn't quite believe there were no people underneath it. It must have still been warm from their last-minute arguments, from Melody being shouted at for pouring too much milk into her cereal bowl, and Polly their dog, barking if anyone other than Melody's mum tried to touch her pom-pom-shaped coat. But now it sat empty.

I wanted something to happen, anything – a shock of lightning, a galloping pony, a scream because none of it felt right, nothing should have been that quiet, but still, nothing came.

Even one of my Russian dolls on my bedroom windowsill had turned her back on me.

THE RED-HAIRED GIRL

I was standing at the bottom of the stairs, still in my flamingo pyjamas and slippers when a long-legged red-haired girl blazed through the house as though she'd been there a million times before. She kicked off her shoes, *chassé* down the hall, *jeté* up the stairs and split-ran across the landing while our mothers spoke together. They were clueless of their surroundings and the show this girl with pigtails was suddenly putting on for me, whose hair fell more like rats' tails upon my shoulders after just waking up...

She nosed in and around the rooms of our ivory house, in and out of *my* bedroom, and I began to panic as she seemed to gravitate towards the final room, my special room, the dance room. That was when I really felt my blood boil.

'No, please. Don't!' I said, trying to flatten my morning-fringe with one hand, but this stranger was turning the doorknob, pretending not to listen.

'No—! My – Mam's – dolls' house is in there!'

'A dolls' house?'

I wanted to kick myself for saying the wrong thing. The girl's glassy eyes lit up as she threw open the door and faced the white four-storey home in all its ornate glory.

'Oh my God, I *love* dolls' houses!'

And I'm not sure why I stood so still while she breathed it all in, harassed the delicate, painted faces of each figure, examined the bottoms of each little table and chair with its spindly legs, and crouched in absolute awe of the miniature creation.

'This is *so* good. I've never seen *any* like this before.' Her eyes were wide as she turned to me, but I sent her the sullenest face I could, hoping that if I closed my eyes for long enough, she'd leave. The longer she crouched there, the less the dolls' house belonged to Secret Haven, to me – or Mam.

'It's not to be played with,' I mumbled, 'just looked at. It's my mam's…' but she just laughed in disbelief, tugging at its side-windowsills, and stroking its black roof.

'Why would dolls not be *played* with? That's the whole point! You're so silly…' Her eyes rolled.

It felt like she was playing with *me*, and it hurt; it hurt more than any of the week before, or maybe it was because of the week before, I wasn't sure.

'Wow, look how much better this looks over here,' the girl was exclaiming, but I couldn't look.

She poked around a little more, swapping bathroom and living room furniture, removing shoes and shawls from the women, and not putting anything back as it was found. She was finding every possible way to dull its shine with her own vision until there was nothing of Melody, Mam or me left anywhere inside. She was stealing its story; stealing me.

Then, she started looking through the attic windows in wonder and asked, 'Does this come off? It would be easier if the roof came off. There'd be more room to play.'

As she was about to try, I shouted,

'Stop it! *Please!* Stop it *now!*' Still, my voice wasn't as loud as I wanted it to be, and it was trembling like jelly as I shut my eyes again.

18

But it was too late. When I opened them, the red-haired monster had upturned the whole house and its insides were an unrecognisable heap on the rug.

The girl held two hands over her mouth and nose when she looked up and saw my tears. She started to pick things up, all in the wrong order. *Useless.*

'Bobbie? BOBBBBBBIIIIIEEEEE?' Her mother was calling her from the front door, so she gave me one last 'oops' look and then scarpered.

'Bobbie's mum brought some old dance outfits for you, Violet! Isn't that lovely?' Mam shouted to me after shutting the door behind the intruders' noise. 'They're very pretty and she said the only reason they're getting rid of them is because they're too small for Bobbie now.' But I didn't respond. *How could I possibly dance without Melody? And why would I want anything that's belonged to such a show-off? Pfft.*

Mam's footsteps reached the landing where I was still standing. 'Oh, Violet. What happened?'

'I don't know,' I said, feeling the lump rising in my throat.

'Why did you let her in here?'

'But I didn't. I didn't let…' I shrugged my shoulders as the tears filled my eyes. It was all my fault.

'Well, you'll have to clear that up and put it back just right. You really need to look after your things, Violet. Is anything broken?'

I hoped not but it certainly felt like I was, like a storm had swept through me and taken down everything in its path. That's what happens when someone walks in on your world – uninvited. I slumped against the wall and let the tears roll down my cheeks.

Those dolls had watched me for years. They didn't say a word, but I knew they paid attention. One stood with her toe over the edge of the second floor and a hand upon her hip. I waited for her to gallop side to side, which of course, she didn't. They were all dusty, too, their hats had doubled in height and the furniture was layered with what had become extra cushions, all the bold-coloured fabrics of them faded from terracotta to yellow, from blue to green.

Slowly, I began to save each figure from the massacre, where shoes had flown across the room and left dolls' arms raised as though trying to reach them. I patted down their hairstyles, replaced their hats, and made sure they were all back in their starting positions on the floors where they'd stood for years. Still, they looked different since their trauma. They looked *at* me, as though I was the one who'd viciously uprooted them.

'I'm sorry,' I whispered, still shaking a little as I twisted their faces away, not wanting them to see me in such a state, 'just for a while.'

I stomped towards my bedroom, greeted – as always – by the huge poster of Margot's perfect ballerina pose and immaculate face, smiling at me from the wall. I tore it down and shut the curtains on Secret Haven for good.

AS BRITTLE AS *PAPIER MÂCHÉ*

All week someone kept yanking me out of one nightmare and hurling me into another, changing the scenery in the blink of a stage curtain, leaving parts of me behind with each act: a hand here, a leg there, one on the Common and one in the sea, and what could I do about it?

Finally, I was back in my bedroom where my Russian dolls stared at me from the windowsill like mute choristers. Their big navy eyes smiled above rosy cheeks, all of them dressed in violets, with parted yellow hair; a gift from Mam after my first ballet exam. She had hung a kingfisher-blue costume – a hand-me-down from the red-haired girl – on the wardrobe door, where it taunted me with sequins that glittered in the sun.

I'd been on good terms with summer for years, but now, we were unhappy with each other. Its glare made it impossible for me to shut my eyes. There was the sound of swallows. I watched their silhouettes, shadow puppets; I imagined their red throats diving at me, and then, *squawk*, they were only spindles of light flying through the gaps in the dusky pink curtains, stalking the glass with golden beaks. That was Secret Haven trying to get in, but it wasn't allowed, not on the first day back at school, maybe not ever.

When I stood up, everything looked the same but felt different. *Do I have company? Has someone followed me from one of my dreams?* I shook my pillow upside down, but not even a moth fluttered out, and neither did Melody.

The floorboards creaked beneath my feet, and it struck me that our house was as brittle as *papier mâché*. It looked sturdy from the outside, but it felt as though, say I was to knock at the surface a bit too hard, it would tremble, and, say I stepped too far forward, I would fall – slippers and all – through all the paint and scrunched-up newspaper, and straight into another planet. I would fall through to the earth's centre, where Dad said it was too hot for anything to survive. He'd said before that the earth was burning up more and more every day, and so we needed to look after the sky, to make sure we didn't pollute it with unnecessary matter. The trouble was most things mattered to me.

My green check school dress was sitting upon the wicker chair, with my cardigan around its shoulders as though someone was already wearing it. Mam must have crept in last night. She did that kind of thing for Dad and me sometimes, mapped out our worlds. I often found abandoned socks moved by the time I woke up, and the glowing petals of my bedside lamp switched off. A few weeks earlier, I'd woken up to Mam looking at me from the bedroom door, much quieter than she usually was; she was just standing there, not even whispering.

Once I'd slid my dress over me, I ran to brush my teeth.

'Violeeeet, are you nearly ready?' Mam was shouting upstairs. 'There's toast on the table for you!' I ran back to my room to steal the smallest Russian doll from the windowsill and nestled her familiar face inside my sleeve before I raced downstairs.

Walking to school with Mam instead of Melody made my stomach hurt but I was glad Mam was there. As we strolled up the road, the sun needled through the air around us, and a snapshot of the house before we'd left it stayed in my head; a flash of the door slamming before Mam had rushed off and I'd followed. Abandoned cups of tea would drink themselves up in their own time, and a tower of strawberry jam jars, which Mam must have stirred up overnight, waited to be stacked at the barn shop. As we made our way up the sloping road, there was no car in the driveway of Melody's house.

Mam kept a strong hold of my wrist. She knew I was thinking of Melody, but she kept her head high for both of us. I imagined Melody starting at a new school that morning. It felt as though I was too. When she was in my class, the teachers had often sat us at the same table, so we'd smile across at each other whenever we could, and no one else would know what we were thinking. I had no idea where I'd end up sitting now; I'd hardly spoken to anyone else.

Our feet were at the playground before we knew it, where hundreds of small strangers swarmed around the tarmac. None of them were the shape of Melody and I seemed to have frozen to the spot. The size of school suddenly looked so enormous that my chest blew up like a balloon. *If I explain everything, just to Mam, it might all feel better.* But I couldn't. I sensed myself stepping back as I watched the schoolchildren. There was a sheet of glass between us; they were characters on a television screen, and my ears were turning down the volume. I knew it was just a playground, but it felt like an auditorium. If I closed my eyes, maybe I could escape altogether. My heart was growing larger and larger inside me as I heard Mam say,

'It must be lovely to be back here with everyone!'

My stomach tumble tossed. 'I don't want to go,' I mumbled.

'Now, don't be silly, love, of course you do, you love school! You'll soon make new friends.'

But how? I'd never had to do it before. I'd always known Melody. Mam was chatting to some of the other mothers; something about summer being gone in a flash... She managed to knit friends like gloves, and she'd made so many gloves, there weren't enough hands to wear them all.

'I can't!' A lump the size of the largest Russian doll rose in my throat. As the crowds of children swirled around in front of us, I edged behind Mam, but she immediately moved out of the way.

'Come on, now, love.' She knew me too well, and when people know you well, you run out of choices. In the distance, we saw lines of shouty children forming at the bottom of the playground, a teacher at the end of each one.

'Go on then,' Mam nodded towards the queues of children, 'off you go!'

She planted a kiss on my cheek, took the soggy, uneaten slice of toast from my palm and handed me my school bag, not allowing me to say any more. I heard the crunch while she turned around, leaving me no choice but to run over to one of the lines. I stood at the very back, behind Frederick, a fidgety boy whose light-blonde curls moved like rice pudding. He wasn't talking to anyone either. I looked down at the gravel and imagined Mam dropping the breadcrumbs along the way as she walked home. If she ever lost me, she could find her way back.

I kept an eye on Frederick as he hung his coat and backpack

up in the cloakroom, and I followed him follow the other children towards our new classroom.

'That's right, everyone; choose your own seats for now,' said the teacher. 'We'll see how it goes for the first few weeks and think about moving around later on in the term.'

I watched Frederick pick a seat in a corner at the back, and I sat next to him. We didn't look at each other and we didn't say anything about him not being Melody. The varnished desk was cold as I folded my arms, and as Frederick scribbled alongside, his elbow invaded my space.

The morning grew around me. Through the window, the clouds looked whiter; the day was puffing out, then inhaling again. *If I sit still forever, will I miss anything?* Everything felt larger than usual, even the wooden seat I was sitting on. I drew it as close to the desk as I could, and with every chance I got, I glanced at the watch on Frederick's wrist; the strap was bright green and yellow, one of those watches that had little illustrations along each strap to help you to tell the time. It was a whole three hours until lunchtime, but at least it was the same time wherever Melody lived. I wondered if she was sitting at her desk, feeling lost like I was. I picked up my new rough book and wrote *Violet & Melody, BFFs* on the inside cover.

I found it strange that no one mentioned Melody's disappearance; commented upon how tragic it was that we were cut right down the middle, that her mother had completely ignored the tall hedge, scooped her out of Secret Haven and left a Melody-shaped crater everywhere I went. *How will you survive?* They should have been asking me. *Who will you be without her?*

'Best friends forever,' I mouthed under my breath.

Frederick's foot nudged mine, but I ignored it and continued to stare through the window at the sunny playground, at the fence beyond it, at the road beyond it and the hills behind that, and the fickle sky. *You can't colour in a landscape like that with crayons. Just how far away is Melody?*

'Violet!' A voice made me jump. It was Mrs Treadwell. 'Will you look this way, please? There's nothing more interesting out there.' But I felt sure she was wrong. I saw her long, bony face, all beak and all directed at me. I wondered what kind of bird Dad would say she was. *A rook, perhaps, with that glossy, black plumage of hair.*

She was talking about water, how it begins in the sky, in a large puff of cotton wool. Her hands formed fists and cracked open to fall like rain. She was describing how the rain lands in streams, and the streams join up to rivers, where the water begins to meander before it splurges out into the big blue sea. I couldn't help but imagine that happening to tears after they've rolled down your cheeks.

I was amazed, hearing how rivers flow through so many towns and cities. It sounded like a very watery world, the way all of us drift past each other in our own little bubbles, about to collide and not knowing when. *If Melody stands in the river, and I do, perhaps our feet would be in the same water. It would be just like when we both used to look up at the moon from our bedrooms.* I wished I could tell Melody to find out where her river was, and to dip her feet in it right now!

At the lunchtime bell, Frederick merged with the crowd and then disappeared again. I walked outside not knowing where to go. There was an old stone bench at the edge of the playground, so I sat down and watched some kids playing football and other games, but I couldn't see Frederick anywhere. While my feet dangled, they started practising their ballet point.

'Not now,' I whispered, 'not anymore.'

Back in class that afternoon, there were no more questions about rivers, but there were plenty of others that came like currents in the rising and falling sea of arms. My elbows didn't move from the desk, and Mrs Treadwell didn't look in my direction. *Mam will be here soon. I'll tell her everything.* Whenever I pictured Mam, if she wasn't with me and Dad, she was looking after Secret Haven, gently pruning leaves and inspecting flowerheads, speaking to them in her low, calm voice, or helping Dad at the barn shop and breaking out into a loud laugh with the odd customer. That made me wonder what else she did when I wasn't there. I guess I could never know for certain.

At quarter past three, Mrs Treadwell told us to pack our books away inside our desks, and I could already see the rusty red pick-up truck through the window. There was Mam, swinging open the door, jumping out and walking towards the school gate in her long, purple summer dress. The fact that I'd soon be sitting alongside her made me feel homesick. I willed the moment closer to me with magic. *Maybe I could will myself away from the next few days at school just as easily...*

CAN YOU LOVE SOMETHING THAT FRIGHTENS YOU TO DEATH?

I'd taken a stand; no ballet ever again, and I'd ignored Secret Haven for days. Melody and I usually went together but without half a duet, a stage is empty.

Mam found me wrapped under the covers like a marshmallow at 11am. I tried to roll the torn Margot poster under my bed as soon as I saw her, but her eyes darted straight towards the gap on the turquoise wall.

'Violet, what's gotten into you?' She perched on the end of my bed and for a moment, I thought I might have a chance. 'You're being ridiculous! You love Margot, and I hope you know you're going to ballet whether you like it or not. You don't want to miss the first class of the new term.' She'd already stood up again. Her hands were on her hips.

'Mam, Melody's…'

'I know how you're feeling love, but put your ballet clothes on now, please, or you're going to be late. Simple as that.'

I knew she'd stand there until I was dressed, so I started rifling through the drawers. I ignored the blue sequined outfit; it felt wrong to be in such bright colours under the current circumstances. Instead, I put on the plainest leotard I could find – a black one with white tights and a pink elastic belt around my middle. I could mourn in style. Margot would have. Still, it wasn't going to be the same without Melody.

'Right, face the mirror,' Mam said, with bobby pins pursed between her lips, a hairbrush in her right hand and a bobble over her wrist. *Surely, I can't go to ballet feeling this way. I don't think Mam gets what it'll be like for me.* I slumped down in front of my dressing table for her to whip my hair up into a bun. 'Don't you look at me with those big green eyes,' she mumbled as I peered out of my puffy lids. 'Gosh, just like your father's, they are.' The face looking back at me had already paled since Melody had left and taken all the colour with her. I'd have preferred not to see it. 'When did this hair start to get so long?' Mam yanked the hairbrush through all the mousy knots, so the ends managed to reach just below my collarbone. 'Anyway, you're a beautiful dancer, Violet. It's the thing you enjoy the most, isn't it?' She didn't wait for an answer. 'You have to go. Don't you dare let Melody stop you!' *But she doesn't understand,* I told that face looking back at me. When I didn't smile, it appeared narrower. *It's not Melody's fault, it's just that I've never done anything without her. I don't know if I'd enjoy it without her, I just don't know who I am all of a sudden.*

Outside, even the sky seemed stretched to full capacity, the air around us threatening to pucker. The pick-up truck yawned whenever we climbed into it. Dad insisted it was tired from the sun just like he was, which would explain why it gave up every now and then. *Hopefully, it's had enough today,* I crossed my fingers, *and I won't have to go to ballet.*

'Come on, love,' Mam said, winding down the windows so the clumps of dried mud catapulted off the glass. She tapped the dashboard, 'be good to us today. Our Violet has to get to ballet class!' She flashed me a wide smile that fell before she started the engine.

'I didn't tell you earlier love,' she said, 'as I didn't want to make you nervous, but Ms Madeline has something *very* important to share with you today!' She rested her hand on mine before reaching back to the gearstick. 'Don't worry, it's very good, but I think she should tell you herself.'

Part of me thought Melody might be there to surprise me, but part of me had also learnt to leave dreams behind.

I'd never known the Common's true name, just that it had always been quiet, like me. Not many people seemed to acknowledge it, that mysterious piece of land spread along either side of the main road, but I'd always been drawn to it – its stillness, its silence. There had been so many weeks of uninterrupted sun that the Common was solid like clay, fringed by scorched gorse, thirsty heather and dried-up ponds. Wild ponies were circling, scraping their hooves against the dirt, probably wondering when everything would change back to how it was before. So was I. *Where do they come from, anyway? And where do they go?* I'd have to ask Dad. It looked so incomplete, like the scenery of an abandoned performance.

As the truck gained momentum, Secret Haven became a speck through the rear window. We could see the blush-red of the new housing estate on the other side of the Common, and the vague, pointed shape of the ballet building in the distance. When we stopped, the truck sighed. As soon as Mam had wound its windows back up, she stole my hand and rushed us along the busy road.

Ms Madeline's School of Dance was a distinctive old chapel. We strutted along the black and white chess tiles of the empty corridor and that's when I realised we were very late.

'It's all through expression,' shouted Ms Madeline from the

dance room as we reached the studio door. 'Remember, this is for an audience. You always have to tell a story!'

The fact the music was already playing made me want to cry. I hadn't been late for ballet my whole life! I followed Mam to the closed door. I did love ballet but I really didn't want to be there alone. *Can you love something that frightens you to death?*

Mam barged in, leaving me to peep around the corner behind her. There, clear as the afternoon, was the slender but imposing Ms Madeline, dressed in her long, black skirt, which was wrapped around a purple, long-sleeved but low-back leotard, with her customary black bun, sunken at the back of her head. Her hands were a clapping metronome to the ballet steps before her as she slowly strode left and then right, and then… One of her dark eyes spied us straight away.

Mam nudged me. 'Go on, love.'

I tiptoed closer, trying to ignore every dainty bunhead that turned towards me. Mam slid my dance bag from her shoulder and handed it to me. Everyone else's were in little heaps alongside the wall; all the socks rolled into shoes and T-shirts with the arms still in. And there, in a line along the *barre*, was a rainbow of stretching gazelles, only, the mirrors all around the room made everything look much larger than it really was, so there were four times as many heads, arms and legs.

Mam and I stood there for what seemed like forever. The longer I stood, the more scared I became, and I found my mind stepping out of the dance room, running down the stairs and ending up in yesterday, back at Secret Haven. But Secret Haven wasn't even the same since Melody left. Mam's figure was blurring back into view alongside me. I didn't yet have the power to disappear whenever I wanted to.

'Come and stand by me at the front, dear, once you're free to join us!' Ms Madeline said, seeing me dither.

I unfolded my black ballet shoes like liquorice, slid them on and ran towards the *barre*. The bang of the dance room door behind me meant Mam had gone and taken away the opportunity to crawl back to moments ago. I blinked twice to stop myself crying, clenched and unclenched my fists, then looked up and caught up with the other dancers.

'Good girl, Violet. Lovely point,' Ms Madeline said, raising one of her heavily powdered eyebrows, and I knew that while my foot was as curved as a cashew, the moment before – me being late – was forgotten; I was good again.

'Okay girls, now move to the centre and pair up for some free dancing,' Ms Madeline said. 'Let your imaginations run wild, that's why we do this!' She said 'we' as though she danced as much as we did, and I hoped that was the case. 'Just let yourselves go!'

The other girls all found partners and for a moment, forgetting how everything had changed, I searched for Melody. She hadn't turned up after all. Instead, I saw myself spinning in the mirror, ghostly white in my black leotard, grieving. I lifted my arms into a *port de bras* and closed my eyes. *Melody will always be with me,* I thought, as I let the music carry us to a faraway place, until all the other girls disappeared.

'Wonderful, Violet!' Ms Madeline's voice made me jump out of my skin. 'I think you're ready to attend the older girls' class.'

As I looked up at her, her eyes lit up.

'You're already dancing just as well as some of them. So, if you're happy to join them, next time you come, make sure you turn up an hour later.'

She winked so only I could see her. Maybe Ms Madeline understood what I was going through. She had lost a dancer too.

'Right, now, cool down before you all leave, girls.'

I pressed my forehead against the cold, tiled floor and closed my eyes, allowing every muscle to find its own way of expanding within me. Melody and I used to do that before class started; practise our stretches together. I wandered into our usual corner and found my usual space on the floor.

Oo! The floor is freezing, Melody would have said, flinching as though we were inching into the sea together in February.

I rolled my eyes and laughed; she said the same thing every week. Sometimes, we whispered about how long Ms Madeline's hair would be if it was ever let loose from its bun, and we imagined it travelling across whole countries and continents. I slid into the splits, where I threw my arms as far in front of me as I could, and stretched my chest as far across the floor as it would go, waiting for Melody's ice-cold fingertips.

I thought about what Ms Madeline had said. I either moved forward or I remained alone. *Maybe I could still be like Margot...*

MIST

Sunday morning, just as I did every week, I put on some jeans and went for a walk to find Melody. My feet tiptoed away with themselves before I arrived at her empty driveway and remembered I had nowhere to go.

It bewildered me what could change overnight. The air felt unsure of itself and so did I. As I was outside, I decided I might as well keep going. The trees either side of the road looked cold, some of their leaves were forgotten at their feet and they seemed to shiver a little with a breeze that blew whenever it felt like it. The ground crunched like ash: autumn had arrived all at once, as everything had lately.

Someone else arrived too. A sound escaped one of the bushes; a *rrrr* not too far from my shoes. When I looked more closely, I heard rustling and there, I saw them: two marbled jade eyes looking back at me. A tiny paw. And then another. I loved the way it looked at me, with a little sympathy somehow. *What do you know, kitty?* Hypnotised, I found myself slowly blinking at the kitten until she blinked back. Her ears were like tiny roofs, and her whole face, so fluffy, with leaves for hair, pounced at me. But I didn't mind. As she clawed at my jeans, I stroked her messy grey, squirrely body until she let go.

'Have you been looking for Melody too?' I whispered, following her, and making sure to stroke the back of her warm, collarless neck whenever she stopped to check I was still there.

She seemed to purr at every touch. Maybe she didn't belong to anyone; maybe she was like the wild ponies on the Common. She followed me up the drive and around the side of our ivory house, and through the squeaking gate that startled her when it swung shut.

'Come here, kitty,' I said quietly, and as I kicked off my trainers at the back door, her paw padded the air for a while as though to check the room for any bad energy. She *piquéd* the terracotta tiles and finally leapt over the threshold. Then, she ran her fur along every shoe on the mat, and the edge of every cupboard and chair leg in the kitchen. I considered how I'd have no choice but to keep her a secret; make her a home in a cardboard box, feed her chicken while my parents worked outside, but as I shut the back door, Mam strolled into the kitchen with her nose in the air.

'That's one skinny kitty,' she said, hand on one hip as she rested on the worktop, with an amused look on her face. The kitten froze, ready to turn around, but her eyes stayed focused on this human she'd never met. Within seconds, Mam was as hypnotised as I was, and she couldn't help but smile. She took a saucer from the table and began pouring some cream from a pot in the fridge. Still, I could see that the kitten was nervous; one of her ears twisted independently of the other and she stood stiff as a brush as the unknown hands placed the dish in front of her and said, 'not too much. Just a little treat.'

She shivered as Mam leaned over us both to watch her enjoy.

'Oh dear, look at her. You'd better watch out. Cats don't ever leave once you start feeding them, you know?'

'That's fine with me,' I said, grinning.

The kitten didn't move a hair at first; her tail stood firmly on end behind her while she purred. She already had a strength about her, I liked that, treating the scenery with caution. Mam took a large step back, looked me deep in the eyes and mimed,

'You can do it. Go on...'

I looked into those jade eyes, frozen like gemstones. I leaned forward, ever so gently, so my denim knees didn't scratch loudly against the floor, and I ducked my head a little and pretended to drink. It only took seconds for the kitten to imitate. She lapped up the cream with her pink tongue.

Once she'd finished every drop, she stood up straight, looked up at me, and began to wind her body back and forth in a figure of eight around my ankles. I kept still, eyes closed for a bit. *I can do it. This is how you make friends. Mam was right.*

'Nice to see you smiling again, love.' She stroked the top of my head as though I was a kitten too.

Dad muddily appeared in the doorway; the odd leaf needing to be raked from his short wave of grey hair, and his tawny face still squinting from the sun. He was carrying a bedraggled birdhouse under one arm; I remembered him nailing it onto the fence years ago, but birds didn't seem to flock to it. I could tell from its soggy insides that it needed to be either fixed and spruced up or thrown away altogether. Mam walked straight into the living room, I followed her in, and the kitten followed me.

Mam was searching. She was lifting the sofa cushions and slapping them back down, before doing the same with the rug in front of the fire, determined to find whatever it was. When Dad walked in, and eventually lifted his chin to look at her, I could see – as Mam threw her hair over her shoulder – that it was an argument she'd been looking for, been shoehorning into shape for that particular moment. The empty birdhouse sat in Dad's arms, with wood-tags hanging from it.

'You're always fixing things,' Mam announced to him from the other side of our living room, 'fixing, fixing, fixing.'

'You're always breaking them,' Dad said, more quietly, before turning to walk straight back into the kitchen. He was right, now I thought about it. Most of the things he'd ever fixed, Mam had been the one to break: drinking glasses, furniture, garden ornaments, and yet Dad seemed to enjoy fixing them. Looking around, there were many parts of our house that needed repairing; it had always been that way, from the chairs at the kitchen table that were duct-taped together, to loose floorboards, to the attic door that was always open to the Bogeyman.

'We'll just buy a new one!' Mam had flown into the kitchen now, easy as a cuckoo since the door handle no longer worked. She'd continue like this for a while, dancing back and forth. I followed her from room to room, without stepping into her air. Mam always needed to keep moving.

In a brief interval, as I was about to go upstairs, Mam dropped her hand upon my shoulder. Her face was splintering with news.

'I almost forgot to tell you, Violet,' she said, and I could feel a flutter high up inside my chest, 'we had a phone call from a certain someone while you were out!'

Not that I needed to guess who. I didn't feel as excited about it as I thought I would.

'Melody's mum said it's been an exhausting time, but Melody would love to speak with you,' Mam talked on and on and I found my ears tuning out. Then she started laughing, as though my face was the most hilarious thing on earth. 'Oh, I bet Melody misses you too, love.'

Still, for the first time in my whole life, I didn't know how Melody felt. I didn't know how I felt. I couldn't place her, couldn't guess what she might have been doing right then, at that precise moment, couldn't even picture her home, never mind catch up with the thoughts inside her head.

'Well, I told her you'd ring her back tonight, okay, love? You'd like that, wouldn't you?'

I nodded, worrying about where the words were supposed to come from when I'd pick up the phone. She used to be so close that we could speak through plastic cups. *What is there for me to tell her now?* I felt ashamed I hadn't visited Secret Haven, or maybe she wouldn't want me to, I didn't know! *But what should I tell her if she asks what I've done?* I'd been to ballet without her, and I'd sat next to Frederick at school. Worst of all, what if she told me all the things she'd done or hadn't done? Either way, I was going to be upset.

In the kitchen, Dad sat hunched over the table, continuing to hammer away, holding each nail between finger and thumb, now and again using his wrist to nudge his glasses back onto the bridge of his nose. He was adding a front wall to the birdhouse, one with a much smaller door, only a bit larger than a spy hole for the birds to squeeze their puffy bodies through. He wouldn't buy a new version, no matter how often Mam told him to. Dad loved recycling; he was always making something out of nothing.

Mam was staring at him with eyes budded open now, willing her husband to look up at her. I could see even more amber in them when she was angry.

'Well, we can't go worrying about everything breaking all the time,' she said, with her hands on her hips, 'afraid to touch this, afraid to touch that. Next, you'll be telling me I'd better not collect the eggs from the henhouse.' Her hands took turns to claw through mid-air and recoil. I looked around for the invisible audience. 'Can you imagine what life would be *like*?'

We didn't answer her; we didn't think Mam needed answers. She looked almost envious of the attention Dad was giving this task; the way he bent down, eye-level with it, yet another object bound to fall apart. I thought about how I quite enjoyed collecting the eggs in an empty ice-cream tub and picking tomatoes from the greenhouse. Then, I imagined Mam's eyes rolling off the table and smashing so liquid honey poured onto the floor tiles.

Whilst they argued, neither of them stayed still, especially Mam. She used space like a bird flapping its wings. I watched her, the way she moved with such expression.

'It's like talking to a brick wall,' she said.

Dad's stubbly chin rose as he bit his bottom lip and watched his bird ruffle her feathers. I thought of the wall he was building outside, and how reliable it was, how much time he'd quietly taken to build it, every stone so solidly glued to the next, and all because it was Mam's idea.

I ran upstairs and the kitten bounded after me. I rushed to put something on to drown out the noise coming from below. As I collapsed on my bed, I could still hear Mam whipping at the air with her tongue. Her dance would continue for a while.

Tchaikovsky's *Sleeping Beauty* began to play and I thought about when I'd last listened to it. *A few months ago, with*

Melody? Now, it floated around the room, and I let it, whilst daydreaming about the romance of it all.

I could still hear Mam and Dad's voices beneath my feet, but through the ceiling, they were too blurry to pick apart, just echoes without words. I could have been in my own world under my duvet. It was strange that our house had belonged to other people in the past, with its walls so thick that anything could be hidden between them, whole people stored within walls. I imagined Mam as a young girl, just like me, tossing and turning in her sleep, thinking of the future, and feeling safe.

My parents were properly shouting downstairs now, and I could hear everything again.

'*You can't grow flowers if you keep fiddling with the soil!*' This was one of Mam's sayings; she had many and that one stuck like treacle to the brain.

Dad was different, this moment would become part of him for a while, hang on like a loose button he'd end up stitching more tightly to an old shirt. 'Objects have experiences, just like people,' he said, loudly, channelling a louder human than him. 'Not everything is ruined just because it's acquired a scratch or two.'

There it was. I knew he'd say something of that sort. He was sure of his words, *very* sure of them. It made me wonder why he didn't speak more often; he must have had whole stories in his head, stored like fireworks ready for when the right moment struck.

I waited for an explosive retort, turning down Tchaikovsky just in case.

But the kitten already seemed to have had enough of it all

and was darting through the small gap in the door, looking at me as though I should follow.

'Kitty, where are you going?'

As I crossed the landing, everything went quiet downstairs. No shouting. No words at all. *Has Mam still not said anything back? Did they run out of breath?* But then I heard Mam and Dad burst into laughter at exactly the same time.

Dad had been right about this one, and Mam had secretly wanted him to be. Mam got restless with too much silence, so she'd created a performance where their voices could be heard.

You have to rebuild – just as I had with the dolls' house – you always have to rebuild as a family. Each room in our ivory house had an experience within it, and the small room, alongside my bedroom, belonged to me.

What would someone see if they were looking in through the window, poking around? Well, they would have seen a little room with a ballet *barre* that a father had fixed to the wall when his little girl was just four. They would have seen a tall mirror in the corner, framed with golden feathers, standing there so the little girl could watch herself turn into a swan. In the opposite corner of the room, they would have seen the four-storey dolls' house unplayed with yet facing outwards – with pride – passed down by the girl's mother.

They would have seen that little girl, Violet Hart, re-entering her room through a pair of green eyes, and seeing its sad emptiness while it stood unused. They would have seen her running out of the room and then returning with a rolled-up poster of Margot Fonteyn – her favourite ballet dancer – in a white tulle outfit against a black background, baring her soul to the world, and they would have seen her tape it to the wall opposite the *barre*.

They would have seen her slowly reacquainting with the *barre*, stroking the smooth, white painted wood, remembering how at home she felt there, gazing through the window at the wild Common, catching the glimpse of a bouncing hare, and lifting her left arm into a *port de bras* above her head. *You are my partner now,* she said to the *barre*, pleasing her legs with a *plié*, and moving smoothly between first, second and third position, making sure her arms curved along the same lines.

They would have seen her realising that if she was to enter the big ballet class, she would have to practise and never again try to stop her pointed feet mid-journey. They would have seen her feeling the floor with her toes, *chasséing* away from the *barre* to move straight into the centre of her dance room and looking up at the soulful face on her rehomed poster.

They would have seen her bending down to the little kitten and saying its name: Mist, in the hope it would continue to follow – or lead, and always be longed for.

And I saw it all too. Just as Dad said, objects hold memories and so did that room. So did I. Maybe Mam had been waiting for us all to explode? Together, Mam and Dad had stopped me from falling apart.

I decided it wasn't a bad idea to speak to Melody – if she wanted to.

MAM

My face and Frederick's squashed up against the window as we watched breaktime wither away in diagonal rain. Somewhere beyond the pane, I saw summer and Melody's smiling face gradually dissolving. The playground was as dull as the Common and the sky hung grey without any stage lighting; a world put to waste. I couldn't stop thinking about something Ms Madeline had said. *Wouldn't it be a shame for ballet to have no feet? For no stories to be told this way?* I'd soon tell Mam I'd decided what to do.

We continued to stare in case the playground came to life again. *Watery dancers will spring from the ground any moment now...* Still, nothing happened. I nudged Frederick's elbow and freed the Russian doll I'd been keeping up my cardigan sleeve, looked him deep in the eyes and handed it to him. He was in awe as he held it; big blue eyes popping out of his head. They were *as blue as cornflowers*, as Mam would have said. They were as round as them too.

'Wow,' he said, 'that's cool,' and I thought the same, from behind my hand, so he didn't notice me staring, not that he would have; he was often in his other world, too. He tried to twist the doll into two halves. I watched his face wrinkle up, his mouth pulling to the side as his long fingers reached up past his forehead to scratch at his curls. His hair jiggled all together as though it was a wig.

43

He puffed out both his lips. 'It won't open.'

Frederick wasn't disappointed, just confused.

'No,' I said, 'she'll never open. She holds the secret.'

He handed the doll back to me with a sideward smile on his face, content again, and I hid the doll back up my sleeve.

'Let's go outside,' he whispered.

Frederick edged slowly out of the classroom, giving me a chance to follow him. As I did, I saw more of his image colouring itself in. He lifted his arm like this. He turned his head like that. He yanked his coat from its hook in the cloakroom and draped the hood of it over his head but didn't put his arms in properly. I stole my bright yellow coat to do the same and we flew around the schoolyard together, leaning our heads back as far as we could, tongues out to taste the raindrops. We were in costume! I imagined we were onstage, unable to see through the fog of a cloud machine, spinning and spinning, only the audience were all the children behind the windows. I laughed as he chased after me, and surprised him by chasing him back. We didn't care that we were drenched, and we didn't care if Mrs Treadwell saw us. Sometimes, there were important things to be done.

While we twisted and turned like fairground waltzers, Frederick shouted,

'Violet?'

And I shouted, 'Yes?'

'Do you think you'll be my friend?' He was out of breath and smiling from ear to ear.

I laughed and swerved between imaginary children. I wasn't sure what it was like to be someone's friend. I only knew how it felt to be a sister, a twin. I imagined Frederick waiting for my gate to click open so he could run right in, but he didn't need to visit Secret Haven anyway. When I saw his pleading face, I immediately shouted back with the biggest grin I could find,

'You already are!'

Frederick might have been the happiest thing I'd ever seen. Just looking at him, I knew I wouldn't need to bring the little Russian doll to school anymore.

The rest of the day, Mrs Treadwell showed us to the library, so we could sit far away from the rest of the class and think about what we'd done. It was a proper treat. All I could think about was how the classroom had seemed enormous that morning, but Frederick had magically made it shrink by the afternoon. He was extraordinary! I couldn't wait to tell Mam about how I'd made a friend, a *real* friend. I was desperate to tell her about my plan to move up to the next ballet class too. I knew she'd be so proud!

*

Mam won't be long. I slouched against the outside of the honeycomb school fence and watched children pouring into their parents' arms; bags swinging at their sides. I watched them all climb into cars then drive away until the road was empty.

The school felt strange with the crowd gone, and I felt less invisible. I looked down and saw my bare knees shivering above my long socks. My summer uniform suddenly seemed inappropriate.

I heard a group of big kids approaching from the big school

in the distance and I heard big words I didn't know the meaning of. Some of them made me flinch and feel like I'd done something bad. It sounded like there was a whole universe where people spoke a different language. A passing group of girls who noticed me by the fence smiled, and it made me slouch smaller. I wished Mam would hurry up.

The sky was as deserted as the playground, only the odd blackbird jetted across every now and then, or a hungry seagull. I copied the sound – a long, bitter screech – and flew around using my arms like wings. 'No elephant feet,' Ms Madeline had said, and I'd tried to become a flamingo instead, like a proper ballerina. When I stood by the fence again, I noticed the lollipop man looking at me and smiling. It always felt like someone was watching.

As I gave up thinking about anything, a car horn beeped right in front of me, and I could see the familiar coppery text that read *Harts' Barn Shop* on the side of Dad's dirty-white delivery van. There was Dad, sitting calmly behind the wheel in his usual grassy attire. He didn't have the same sense of time as most people; you could tell he was in a different place inside his head. He didn't smile as I ran to the other side, but he did give me a nod. Mam would have given me a hug, but Dad stayed right where he was.

'Alright, Vila *bach*?' he asked. The van was stuffy inside and smelled thick with poultry. As I looked through the dusty windscreen and nodded, I saw the lollipop man walking home in the distance, his lime clothes brightening as the sky dimmed.

'Where's Mam?' My words sounded sulkier than I'd meant for them to.

'In the truck,' he said. 'Gone to buy a few things for you. Something about them running out of stock. Belt up, love.'

Dad always played classics in his van; Simon and Garfunkel or The Platters, I can't remember the names of the others. On this occasion, it was Simon and Garfunkel and they were singing about Mrs Robinson. He sang so quietly that I wondered what he even got from joining in. I could only hear the quiet chirp of his voice at the beginnings and ends of the chorus.

The thing about good music was that we didn't need to talk, which always happened on Mam's journeys home. Everyone needs different sometimes. I wasn't sure which I preferred as I looked through the window, seeing the dullish green Common roll past, the fastest I'd ever seen it move as Dad sped up and rain pricked the windscreen, *tip-tap, tip-tap*, as though something was finally about to happen there!

Dad and I walked into the house through the back door, and I used one foot to push the other shoe off.

'Want some toast, *bach*?' I don't think he knew what else to do.

'Yes, please.'

I watched him cut two slices from a crumbling loaf, one for him and one for me. Once he'd slathered the toast in butter and Mam's strawberry jam, we sat down together at the kitchen table. He sniggered at the TV and even more when he knew I was laughing too, but whenever we caught each other's smiles, we looked away. Then the phone rang and I wondered if it was Melody. *Maybe she's trying to call again and I'll get the chance to speak to her after all.*

'Most likely your mam,' Dad said and I sighed with relief. 'I'll bet she wants to remind me to do something,' Dad said, standing up and seizing the phone. 'Hello?' I could usually tell if it was Mam on the other end of the line because Dad tended to hold the handset a few inches from his face because of the volume. This time, he pressed it tightly to his cheek and his eyes closed while he listened.

'Yes, this is her husband,' his smile faded like the sun. 'I'll be right there.'

His eyes stayed closed, and without a goodbye, he let the phone spring on its wire.

'I've got to go and see your mam for a while,' he said, somehow looking at me without using his eyes, and already slipping his boots on again. I wanted to ask, *are you okay?* But I didn't.

'Can I come?'

'Yes, you can,' he said, remembering that I had to; I wasn't allowed to stay home alone yet. 'Come on then, best grab your coat.' He fumbled with the keys and tried to turn the wrong one in the door.

Soon, we were back in the van and my laces were damp and undone beneath my feet. Dad forgot to put music on and it didn't seem right to mention it, so I sat in silence, waiting for him to speak, if he wanted to.

'Mam's been taken into hospital, Vila,' he said eventually, 'so we're going to make sure she's okay.'

'Oh,' I whispered, not looking at him. I had a feeling he didn't want me to.

'Gets too stressed, she does,' he said, but I didn't understand what he meant; why that had anything to do with her being at the hospital. She hadn't needed to go to the shops *that* much. It wasn't urgent enough to get stressed about.

'Gets too stressed,' he said again, and I hoped he wouldn't keep saying it.

*

'We're here to visit Hazel Hart,' Dad said to the A & E receptionist sitting proudly behind glass.

'Right, okay, just follow the red line on the floor and speak to the next receptionist you meet at the end of the corridor.'

The bleach and rubber gloves smelled so heavy as we walked in that it made me feel sick, but I was also a little curious. Something about hospitals was fascinating, the way they pieced people back together again and magicked away their illnesses. I didn't know Mam hadn't been well; she wasn't the type to fall apart.

I needed to tell her about my day, once we made sure she was fine of course; she always asked me about school. The red line was turning around corners like an unsure snake and we eventually found ourselves at another desk.

'Uh,' Dad's voice trembled, so he coughed to disguise it, 'we're here for Hazel Hart.' He usually called her Haze, but he was speaking to two people behind a desk, both busy typing at their computers. One of them was a male doctor who guided us back to the red line that must have gone on for miles. Without saying anything, he led us further. I was well-versed in following the red line by this point, it made me wonder how enormous the hospital must be and how many people there were to visit, how many families went trudging in and out every day, all freshly fixed and ready to return to being teachers or gardeners or builders of walls.

We wound around a corner until the red line eventually came to an end where there were a few sets of grey double doors. Outside one of them, a different doctor was standing dead still, his stethoscope limp around his neck. He was extremely tall with a shiny bald head; he must have had to duck whenever he walked through those hospital doors.

As we got closer, the doctor approached Dad.

'Mr Hart?'

'That's right,' Dad said. 'Edward Hart. Ed. Here for Haz-el...'

'Do you mind if I have a word with you alone?'

A nurse had grown out of the bleachy air and was standing by the doctor's side, smiling through her teeth as though she wanted to steal me. She walked closer, about to try, and Dad let her, turning his back, and listening to what the tall, bald doctor was whispering to him.

Within seconds, something was different. I couldn't quite pinpoint what it was, but everything other than the tall doctor seemed to collapse. I saw the colour drain from Dad's edges as he doubled-up; his hands pressing more deeply into his face, but the doctor continued to talk. 'If you'd like to see her...' And then the nurse was stooping, too, with her hands on her chunky knees, so her thick-skinned face looked directly into mine. I hated it, people being that close. Only Mam was allowed to see into my world, or Melody.

The nurse ushered me over to a leathery beige wheelchair that must have been used a thousand times over the decades, while Dad and the doctor stood to one side, and I could only see the back of them. Dad looked so unexpectedly short. I'd never thought about it before. It must have been the way he was crumpling, and the way his shoulders were beginning to shake as though he was fitting; he was wrapping his arms around himself to try and stop it, but he couldn't, and he didn't look at me, not once. *Are you okay?* I wanted to ask, needed to ask, but didn't. The tall doctor walked over to me and let his arm drop a whole mile, just for it to land upon my shoulder. It was heavy, a big hand that could collect whole human beings.

'Would you like a drink of water?' he asked. 'Your dad will be back in a moment.'

Dad pushed through the double doors with his elbows and then disappeared.

He came back out of the room only minutes later, and he looked as though he was making a point of trying to stand up straight again, to keep my world as big as it was before. But he looked different. His glasses were in his hands and his face was a blotchy, radish-red like he'd been out in harsh winds. His arms weren't shaking anymore.

'You want to see your mam, don't you?' he asked, nodding so I didn't have to. He must have known I needed to speak to her. He took my hand in his. 'Well, listen, Vila. Your mam had an accident.' Hearing the word *Mam* so often was strange, as though she wasn't really Mam at all, but Dad was struggling to get his words out and he was pressing my hand between each one. His was rough with callouses and a hundred times the size of mine. 'Vila, she isn't going to be okay,' he said, taking a deep breath. 'Do you understand?'

This was where I stopped understanding. *If I say yes, will Mam not get better? Is this all up to me?* His huge hand was trembling, and it made my shoulders tremble. I wasn't sure if

I'd be able to control them.

The tall doctor gestured to lead us through the grey double doors into a private room where no other patients were. This was nicer for Mam, I imagined, although she did love to talk to people.

Dad and I followed the doctor inside, their steps a few before mine, and there, in front of us, under the dim hospital light and a chalk-green sheet, was someone I'd never seen before, someone who wasn't Mam at all.

It was nice for the woman to have her own space, I would have wanted my own space in there, too, but she only looked a bit like Mam. There she was, lying on the bed with her eyes wide open, startled by light, as though two fuses had blown at the back of them, and she looked cold, too, lying alone like that. I was convinced she wasn't Mam. Not *my* Mam.

'I'll leave you alone,' said the doctor, but I still didn't understand; doctors usually helped. Instead, I watched him duck under the door frame as he left the room, and I turned back to this woman, who, if she was Mam, hadn't been tucked in very well. I could see her knobbly fingers, still green beneath the nails, from all her gardening, and the veins that used to look like turquoise tree veins or the coastlines on a map, had blurred into the rest of the skin, losing their definition, so her whole hand looked a bluey shade of grey. On her fourth finger was the plain-gold wedding ring, as solid as ever, and sitting in front of it like the shining head above a strong collar, was the eternity ring that Dad had given her only last year.

Dad's hand let go of mine, and he was holding the strange

woman's hand instead, rubbing his thumb across gold and stone. It felt like something magical was about to happen. He ran his thumb across her whole hand, pressing those veins, warming them up as he would with dead batteries. I wanted him to pull back the chalk-green sheet, just to make sure it was Mam, you know, for definite. I knew those were her arms, the same freckles dotted all over them, but they looked more prominent than usual. She looked ghostly pale.

I still wasn't sure what Dad had meant. I'd heard of people being unwell and ill for a very long time, but I'd never heard of them not getting better, not unless they were really old. Mam wasn't old, she was younger than Dad and it was me who she was always worrying about. *Wrap up warm or you'll catch a cold,* she always said, and I always tried my best to listen.

'Her heart stopped beating.' Dad was trying words again, and looking right at me, but I could tell he didn't believe them himself. 'It was beating, and then it stopped,' he said. 'She was in town.' Then, he stopped, seeing my face understand it all at once. I knew where she was. I looked at the nurse, who had somehow appeared in the corner of Mam's hospital room. I wished she would go away.

'Your wife dropped these when it happened. I'm terribly sorry, Mr Hart,' the nurse said, but she was looking at me, and I could see from where I was standing, that inside the bag was the peach of new ballet tights and the pink of new shoes, the ribbons squashed around them like entrails and the satin, cleaving through the plastic like bone beneath skin. My stomach felt sick again; fright. *Don't be silly,* Mam should have been saying, but it hurt more than ever being there, and I was afraid it would never go away. I snatched the bag from the nurse at once, imagining her dusty fingerprints all over it. Reading my mind, she disappeared from Mam's room as quickly as she'd entered it.

Dad must have needed proof that the woman was Mam, too. He pulled the blanket right down to her waist, and there she was, maybe the doctor was right. I could see that scar, like a skewed cross near the centre of her chest, and she was in exactly the same clothes she'd been wearing that morning when she'd left me at the school gate: a long, navy dress with tiny, pink blossoms all over it, a bit like confetti. Someone had taken her socks off, too. I didn't know who, or why, and I doubted Dad had noticed but it was just so strange, her toes were bare as anything, peeking out of the bottom like that.

She's a stranger, she must be. Where's her favourite coat, the aubergine one that I sometimes hide behind? Shouldn't she be wearing it? Where is it? Her hair was the same chestnut colour with silver streaks, but there was nothing alive about it, not a strand blowing back and forth with a breath or a turn of the head. The real Mam was always moving. I'd never seen her face that still before. I stood by her side and kissed her cheek. It was already turning cold on my lips.

Dad had been silent for so long that I wasn't sure he'd intended to say anything, but he said those words again.

'Her heart was beating and then it stopped, just,' he tried to breathe in, 'stopped.'

If Dad had been the one lying there, Mam would have been shaking him back to life, but he wasn't doing that, *why not?* He was looking at her as though he had no power at all. I wanted them to argue about it, consult each other about what was going to happen next, but none of that happened. She didn't flutter around or squawk, and he didn't think of anything profound to say. No, *there* Mam was, a Sleeping Beauty through all of it. And yet, she wasn't. She wasn't, well, she wasn't *home. Perhaps if Dad kisses her, she'll wake up?*

Dad was standing over her, looking into her eyes just as I had been. His head hovered above hers for a while as though giving her one last chance to say something, *just in case* – and there, he did it, thank God – finally kissed her left cheek, and then her right. He kissed her forehead, whispered something I didn't understand and then, just as I waited for her to say something, Dad used two fingers, *oh no*, to shut her eyes.

Just like that. Gone.

I wanted Dad to fix her, *please fix her,* but he didn't even try.

THE MIDDLE OF NOWHERE

When we got home, we already had a gift waiting for us. There, laid across the doorstep, was a head torn entirely from its body other than a thin, bloody string that connected the two. The pink nose and tail had turned grey, and a glassy, black eye looked out at me.

Dad stepped over it, almost kicking the whiskers. He left his keys hanging in the back door, ringing against the glass, before he disappeared into another room. The sky was grey behind me; thick and determined not to move again. I locked the door behind us. *No one should leave themselves open to what's out there.* Through the glass, I couldn't see Mist anywhere, only the fog of my own breath steaming up. She must have been searching the night for something. I left the dead outside, in two parts.

The house seemed different, the furniture barely there. I didn't see the living room as I walked through it, or the stairs as I walked up them. Along with everything else, they were dissolving, leaving only outlines. Upstairs, my bed was the only thing I recognised; its quilt drawn up by my own hands that morning. It was the only thing I could think about sinking into, and as I closed my eyes, I hoped to be drawn down and down and down into some black hole, and all the way back through the afternoon: the hospital, the Common, standing outside school, waiting, the classroom with Frederick, then –

whoosh – back to the playground, back with Mam. All would dissolve. There she would be, smiling, talking; always talking. I would go further and further back until I was right back at the beginning, settling inside her womb, vacuumed inside via the belly button, and I wouldn't be shifting. I wanted to stay there for as long as I could, trying my very best not to tumble.

Dad must have been doing the same, going to a different country, where it was dark and everything including us was invisible. I suppose we wanted to visit Mam for a while, in that place of blackness no one knows about, and the only way we could reach her was through sleep, through forgetting everything, stepping out of the world, escaping. I wanted to find where Mam went once the lights were out. We, the three of us, wanted to be together.

*

It could have been hours, days or even weeks until I finally woke up again, and breath came back. My body was heavy and light at the same time, and as I rolled onto one side, it felt as empty as the Russian dolls shut away behind the curtains. I'd had another nightmare.

It was the same nightmare once I was awake, or very similar. I could feel it in the air, affecting me, just like the last line of a ghost story. How could I know if I was in the right world? Everything was pitch-black, only my body was tucked in as tightly as a mummy in front of me. It didn't seem at all like our house.

As I pulled the curtains open, I expected to be in the middle of nowhere, thrown out to another galaxy and floating away in space, but no, there – as always – was the Common, highlighted by a long necklace of distant streetlights through the trees. I let the curtains collapse together again, and I curled into as tight a ball as I could, wishing I was tucked up in one of Mam's black, velvet jewellery pouches, poking my nose right into the corner where no one would be able to see me. But sleep wouldn't take me again. I couldn't seem to find any gravity.

Instead, I unwrapped myself, tried crawling out of bed. The springs squeaked beneath my elbows and knees, and as I stood on two feet, my body catching up with me, the bedsheets fell behind me like paper. There was that hollowness again; as an instrument, I'd have been a woodblock.

I could just about make out the cube of my room and its rectangular door, the crack at the side not showing the usual strip of light. The landing was dark. There wasn't a light on in the whole house. The door made no sound when I opened it, but as I took my first step, the floorboard beneath it groaned. This house was stapled together no better than Mrs Treadwell's classroom displays.

I crept downstairs, not knowing what I was afraid to disturb: the creatures hidden in silence? The peace? Mam would have said it was too dangerous to walk down the stairs like that, holding on to an invisible banister. *Never mind*, I pushed the living room door open and fell into more darkness, felt myself sinking back into an armchair. *Come, sleep, please come and take me away.*

Us away. There was something else in the room. I could hear the whimpering in the corner. *If only we could put the light on! But we need the dark to bring us closer to her.* There was a

58

shadow, it was crouching. *Is it her? Mam? It can't be Mam, she doesn't cry, does she? Maybe she's come back and doesn't know where she is! I'll tell her she's in the right world. I'll tell her.*

But if it was Mam, she would have spoken, not left me sitting there like that, afraid to move again. I could feel myself shaking. My eyes were growing used to the dark. They were opening like long tunnels, and I could see the living room shaping around me. There was a silhouette of Dad, doubled-up as he had been at the hospital, curled over; he couldn't help it, he couldn't control his cries; he needed to be sick. It was like a sound I'd heard before, on television, of dogs at night, wolves – but as a little light crept in through the window, the howls didn't get any quieter. If anything, they bellowed, and I saw that he was on his knees, with his head bowing down into his hands and coming up every now and then as he bit at the air to collect more breath. There didn't seem to be enough breath for everyone.

'Dad?' I whispered, 'are you okay?' The creature looked up at me, but his eyes didn't seem to see anything. His paws were scrambling across the carpet as though something was buried beneath. He let out another wail, and his head fell completely. It was the loudest I'd heard Dad in my whole life. I wanted to lead him back into the other world, the one where Mam sorted everything out, helped us, told us what was best to be done, what was right, what was perfect. But I couldn't.

I was beginning to wonder if me being there was making him sadder, so I ran back upstairs as fast as I could, to my room, where the door was open to everything just as I'd left it. But when I tried to sleep again, I felt even worse than before, and like the largest Russian doll of all: a big Violet in a small world, or a small Violet in a big world, I didn't know, and I wondered how many other kinds of worse were in the making.

Before daylight came, there was a knock on my bedroom door that made me sit up straight.

'Better get yourself ready for school,' said Dad's voice, muffled by a cough.

He'd gone before I had a chance to say anything back. *Okay, so we're going to act the same as usual? I can do that.* I was afraid to argue, anyway; I didn't want to upset him, and I wasn't too sure of the game rules when someone disappears off the face of the earth. I put my uniform on, which was as creased as a jigsaw puzzle since everything that had happened, and I went down to the kitchen. Dad was on the house phone, one call after another, but he wasn't saying much.

'Won't need you this week,' he mumbled, 'yep, shop'll be closed,' he took a deep breath, 'thanks, think I'll manage. Yep, tell them all. Thanks, will let you know.' I saw him swallowing hard. 'Will do.'

There was no toast waiting for me, so I chose some cereal from the cupboard and sprinkled it into the bowl just as Melody would have, but I didn't like milk, so I ate some of it dry and left most behind. *Russian dolls survive fine when they're empty, as long as they have each other.*

Dad's mobile started ringing too, and he took the next call outside. I got up, slipped my feet into my shoes and waited for him. Then, I saw him leaning on one of the fences in our garden and looking up, trying to alter the grey sky. Who knew how long he would stay there for, or who he was talking to?

I hovered for a while, but he didn't look at me when I waved, so, for the first time, I walked to school by myself. It was quite cold, and my hair blew everywhere in the wind, leaving my fringe impossible to flatten. My hands were turning blue because I wasn't sure where Mam kept all our gloves. The journey was much quicker than usual; Mam and I used to practise times tables on the way. Instead, I just zig-zagged, exploring the space where she might have been, slowly spinning around every now and then, just to check. After I crossed the troll bridge over the brook, I was sure someone was following me, which made me feel safe. *It's Mam, looking out for me.*

When I arrived at the school gate, I stopped and waited for a while as I would have with Mam; I preferred pretending. This was where she handed me my backpack and gave me a kiss. Now, our rituals must have been caught in the air somewhere, so, I stood there just to watch everything. I was better at that. It seemed wrong that the children were swarming around the playground just as they had the day before. It seemed cruel of them.

An arm hooked around mine.

Frederick.

'Violet,' he whispered, his way of hello.

So I was in the right place. And there was his mother walking a few metres away, her face down as she searched her handbag, probably for car keys. She wasn't smiling as much as she had been before. I didn't know why.

Frederick made sure his milky face looked at me until I looked back; his cheeks were turning a bit pink in the cold. He showed – just me – a gentle smile, both lips tucked in and puffing his cheeks out like hamster pouches. I wondered if he knew. Not everything, but something. We didn't say anything as we caught the end of the school line as it walked into class, but our arms stayed linked until the very last moment.

I found school hard to believe: the sounds, the smiles, the activities, the schoolwork, it was mostly the same as before. The only thing that seemed at all different was me. It was the way I walked around; I didn't mean to do it, but I felt as though I was drifting somehow, always a second or two behind everyone else, catching up. Even when Frederick chased after me at breaktime, he caught me straight away and I'd already forgotten we were playing. I felt like my wings didn't work.

Mrs Treadwell kept her dusky eyes on me more than usual during the rest of the morning and I wished she would send me to the library again. I could see her head flicking from left to right from her desk at the front and poring over the rest of the children, just so she could see me. I would have hidden inside my desk if I could.

At lunchtime, as Frederick ran ahead of me again, I realised I was actually quite small compared to the whole playground of people. I looked down at my uniform, buttons overlapping at the bottom because I'd rushed that morning, and I ran around and around in circles with Frederick like we were two puppy dogs. One circle ended and another began, I didn't quite understand why we were doing it, but I just ran and ran and ran.

It was when I fell that I crumbled. Frederick and I were running our ninth circle and I tripped right over my own feet whilst crossing the tarmac. There was no need for it to have happened, not really, but not only did I cry, I wailed and whimpered like a cub. All the children in the playground froze at once, their heads tilting and their hands ending up on my shoulders until I found myself melting; they pressed me further into the tarmac with each touch. The fall had peeled a few layers of skin away and abandoned them on the ground.

The dinner lady, all-in-blue, helped me walk to the nurse's office, a tiny room near reception. It was very messy as though I was the first to visit it in a while.

'This is Violet,' she said, 'she's in Mrs Treadwell's class.'

'Right, flower, let's check that knee for stones,' was the first thing the nurse – also all-in-blue – said, getting up from her seat and dusting her skirt with her hands. No fuss. The dinner lady ushered me towards a narrow, leather bed in the corner, which had boxes covering half of it. I dangled my legs over the edge.

'Three stones! Collecting them, are you?' she asked me, smiling with diamond-shaped eyes.

I shook my head.

The dinner lady shut the door as she left. The nurse pulled each one out with a pair of tweezers that I hoped she wouldn't later use for her eyebrows, and dropped them onto a blue paper towel.

'Now for the magic cream,' she said, smoothing it onto my knee. The smell was warm and bodily, and I shouldn't have liked it, but it was unusually comforting; it lingered in the air. I cried the whole time she did it.

'There we are. All done.' The nurse sighed and looked up at me as though to say I should leave, so I jumped down onto both feet. As my knee straightened, it pulled on the open wound, which felt cold and soggy. I didn't want to move but the tears kept making it difficult to say anything.

'Why are you still crying, little one?' I liked how she spoke to me. 'It doesn't hurt too much, does it?' Her face became serious. It hurt an awful lot, everything did. But whenever I tried to talk, my quick breaths were interrupted, and I couldn't keep calm.

'I'm just going to have a word with Mrs Treadwell for a moment, flower. I think perhaps you should go home.'

'No, no, no.' I got out between breaths. I didn't want Dad to panic; I didn't want to be another bad phone call. I didn't want yesterday to happen again. We were supposed to be pretending!

It was too late. She'd left the room.

While I waited, I could hear voices mumbling from the office on the other side.

'Right, oh dear,' the nurse said. 'Oh, bless her.'

And then a different lady spoke.

'Hello, Mr Hart?'

I was picturing Dad rushing in from the garden with his work clothes on, muddy gloves picking up the handset. I was panicking so much inside that I worried I'd run out of breath. I sat on the bed again, rocking back and forth. 'Yes, I think you'd better come and pick her up straightaway. She's okay, but she needs to be home. With you.'

When the red pick-up truck arrived at the school, my heart sprung up out of habit. I whispered, *stop*. I was looking at everything through a different window to usual, but part of me still waited to see the flicker of Mam walking towards me. For a few seconds, I wasn't sure whether it was dust on the glass, but I realised it was just Dad's unshaved face as his body walked him towards us. *Left, right, left, right.*

'Was wrong to have let you go, Vila *bach*,' Dad said when the truck's door closed again, and I could see that his eyes were all pink and puffy. He'd even forgotten to put his glasses on. 'You'd better have this week off.' He let out a sigh. 'Won't work too much, either. Got the funeral to sort out.'

Dad cut the beginnings from a lot of his sentences, which usually meant he left himself out of them. I tried to stop my lip from quivering so I could speak, but nothing came out.

As we arrived back home, I saw a sign in Dad's wary handwriting. It said, *Harts' Barn Shop: Closed until further notice*. I suppose we'd forgotten what parts to play since our lead role had gone.

I cried even more once we were inside. It poured out of me as soon as I shut my bedroom door. There had always been something about my bedroom that did it, opened me up, ever since I was a toddler; I became all body and no brain. I'd cried in that room the most, of all rooms, straight into my fluffy, turquoise cushion, so no one would hear me. It must have known all my secrets.

'What are you going to do when something really bad happens?' Mam used to ask me.

'I can't help it,' I'd say, struggling to breathe.

This time, though, it had happened, and I'd ended up in the same place as usual, with nothing to do at all. I sat up and slotted all the Russian dolls inside one another on the windowsill. Their Mam smiled back at me.

Dad and I didn't speak much for a few days. To anyone. I sat around our ivory house, willing Secret Haven to grow around me. But it didn't. Dad wouldn't let it. Instead, he tried to keep it the same as it always had been. He ignored the chickens' clucks of questions, keeping his lips sealed beneath the growing stubble that shadowed his face. There was only so much one person could do; there was only so much energy someone like him could have. I just watched, as he followed his paths.

I stood, sat, laid down and watched over all that Dad moved around me. There was a constant flow of visitors bringing cakes and casseroles 'to keep us going', which Dad would push aside. 'Don't know what we're gonna do with all this food, Viola, *bach*,' he whispered. 'Only you and me. Only ever been you, me and your mam. Small family, we are. Three only children, you see. No brothers, no sisters.'

I could see that Mam had left her marks, her dents, her fingerprints. She was everywhere, and in the smallest of things; the folds in our clothes, the scent in the air, the way the mugs had been stacked haphazardly in the cupboard. There were her marigold wellies by the back door, pointing outwards, ready to go. We didn't want to tidy her up; we wanted to keep her calamity there so she was alive, so her paths still existed. Without them, where was she?

The house itself felt like a shell. I traced around the edge of it, noticed how thin the windows were, just one glaze with wood all chipped around the frames. *Maybe it's made of papier mâché after all? Maybe I could topple into nowhere and cause no ripple at all? I'd just fall through the other side of meaninglessness.* Maybe I was a shell, too.

I thought Dad may have felt the same, the way he drifted around, doing things as though they had no bearing on anything, and yet he kept doing them, I didn't know why. Our God had disappeared, and she had abandoned us for a better land, forgotten how we would struggle to cope without her, just humans on green and blue, with nothing to worship afterwards, no structure, no plan, and nowhere else to go.

Outside, in the garden, it was cold. Dad must have fiddled with the sky after all because I could see a bit of sun peeking through. Bunches of flowers had been laid to rest outside the barn shop. Dad said he wasn't surprised; Mam knew lots of people. Still, she'd always said, *as soon as you pick flowers, they begin to die.*

I laid my body flat on one side of the wooden picnic bench and stretched my arms above my head. The planks creaked on my side without Melody lying opposite to balance it out. I felt oddly relaxed right there, the way you do after you've cried for hours or days, a comfortable kind of exhausted that stops you from wanting to move.

That was when Mist found me. I felt her first, just her head pushing against one of my dangling hands. And when I didn't flinch, but opened my eyes, I saw her upside down, doing a curious hop closer to me, her four legs as stiff as wire, as if to say,

'Hey! Look at me. Look at me *properly!*'

When I still didn't move, she ran to my side and leapt completely onto my stomach, already much heavier than she was before. She began to lick my hair, just the wispy bits beneath the temples, where my head caved back in. Soon, she was licking my face until I found it impossible not to smile because her tongue prickled like cut grass with every stroke. I wondered what Mist's mam had been like, and how many kittens there were. *Do they all move in the same, elegant way?* I don't know why, but I imagined Mist killing me just as she had killed the mouse. She would lick my bones, bury them somewhere in the garden, and I would do nothing to stop her.

I went inside to get a saucer of cream and then placed it in front of her, just like Mam had done.

MY ENTIRE LIFE

I finally got to see Melody again, but not in the way I'd imagined. There she was, standing at the back of the chapel. I gave her a look to let her know there was a space right next to Dad and me, but she stayed where she was, a small gap between her and the open door. Her hair was different; its wispiness must have flown away, so it was flatter and darker. It was held back by a black hairband. The girl had her eyes, only, they gazed as though she meant to look at everything she saw, rather than buzzing about like dizzy bees, the way they used to.

It might have been that she looked like her mother, who was smiling more than I'd ever seen her do. It seemed strange to do that then, right there, in a place filled with sad people dressed in black. I wanted to wave at Melody, but everyone stood up, and it made the ground creak beneath us all. I knew we should have been looking straight ahead, but every moment I could, I kept my eyes on Melody and her mother, I had to; they were standing beside each other in matching black clothes, as still as bowling pins. Melody's coat was made of the same, thin black wool and there wasn't a crease to be seen in either of them. Time must have stretched Melody because she was a lot taller, and almost as slim as I was. *Wobble*, I wanted to shout at her, before poking her in the ribs just as I used to at Secret Haven. I wanted her to stumble and laugh but she'd remain standing, telling me to stop being so silly, I knew she would. Her eyes were still staring straight ahead. She wasn't even twitching. *Why doesn't she want to see me?*

The chapel doors closed.

'We'll begin with a hymn,' the vicar announced. He'd been talking for a while, but I mainly saw rather than heard him. He was dressed in white robes that quivered around him like a ghost, his body somewhere underneath. His face was still, too, but he was comfortable inside it, I could tell, so much that I wondered if he might be what death looked like if it ever came in person. He glided away and an Order of Service with Mam's face on rustled in my hands. It said she 'of Secret Haven,' as though her home was a little mystery. I liked that. The pages stirred very slightly from left to right with the chapel draught, and the boom of an organ being played stole the silence around us. There it was, at the far right, a man sitting at three keyboards. I watched his left foot pedal from left to right and the fingers that followed. I'm sure they had more joints than they were supposed to as they spidered up the keys. It was strange that his job was to play along with death. Funerals must have been like concerts to him.

I wanted to know what Melody thought, but when the singing began, I found it more difficult to turn around. There was something about the music, and the words, that tore into me. My mouth opened but not a sound escaped as a chorus of voices around Dad and I, belted out how we felt.

As the voices rose higher and higher, I began to feel icy, and I was sure that if I looked at my hands, they'd be blue. I felt sure I was beginning to fracture. If any sound was to come out, my voice would completely smash. Beside me, I heard

Dad's voice joining in, gentle but so powerful that it didn't sound as though it came from his body. I heard it rip right down the middle but before the next verse, he was back to who he'd been all week. One look at Mam, just lying there all boxed-up and his voice had disappeared.

I looked at the floor. Then at Mam. Then at the floor, while more hymns passed by like peculiar dreams. A woman was wailing from one of the pews on the other side, but I had no idea who she was. I could hear Dad lifting tissues to his sore nose and, when I looked at his face again, it was so pink that I wanted to link arms with him, hug him, or something. I felt like I should. But the second his black sleeve accidentally touched mine, his cry turned into the teeth-chattering kind, drew inwards and didn't stop. I kept my head down.

*

After the service, Melody edged her way over to me from the other side of the vestry, where taller people stood between us. Her hair, so long that it almost reached her waist, didn't even flicker as she walked. She was a true ballerina. There she was, smiling at me. But it wasn't her smile. It was the smile someone must have told her to bring, or drawn upon her, the same smile that everyone seemed to be giving us, moulded out of clay. A man pushed his way behind her, and as I stood up from the seat I'd been hunched over on, Melody was nudged towards me and finally, we were almost nose to nose.

This is it, the closest we've been for months. And for a second, we didn't know what to do. We stood there, not saying anything. All I could tell so far was that Melody didn't smell of summer anymore, but of soap and perfume. I think I was waiting for her to speak first, to open that smile of hers and swallow us both back into the past. The thing was, it hardly opened at all, just stretched wider as her words escaped, so her eyes pinched more at the sides, just like a grown-up's. *Why is she changing so quickly?*

'How are you doing, Violet?'

That was when I knew, for definite, that things would never be the same again. It was the first time she'd ever called me by my proper name, like that. *Violet.* Only Mam did that. Even though Melody was just an inch away, there may as well have been miles or even countries between us. Her voice was so soft and unfazed, as though it didn't have the energy to get to me.

I felt my shoulders shrug, just once, with no words at all.

When an elderly lady I'd never met before came up to me, the hundredth person to place a hand upon my shoulder and enforce another one of those odd conversations, I let Melody and her smile disappear, her strange hair and height tiptoe across the room back to her smiling mother.

Melody had escaped for a second time. I'd wanted to tell her how I'd hoped to cry again, right there on the spot, in front of her. Instead, I'd just stood there, studying the new shape of her face but it had been too painful to take in all at once. I'd wanted to hear her laugh, only I didn't know how to create it anymore. I was afraid she'd forgotten that feeling where every single thing was hilarious, and we didn't need to ask any questions. We'd have needed to build all that again, just like our Wendy House at Secret Haven, a house I'd thought had half belonged to her. Only it was all cardboard now, it must have been because it fell this way and that way as every season knocked against it, and Dad and I were just trying to stay on our feet. I wished Melody would tell me how she managed to stand so still. I wanted to whisper to her, *please wobble, just once.*

When Melody and her mother left, after having a single cup of tea between them, I couldn't bear to think about it anymore. The afternoon was becoming blurrier and more tea-filled. The last slices of cake disappeared from the buffet table, and so did the people giving their final condolences to Dad. Distant family once again became distant.

I watched the ballerinas – led by the dark and spectral Ms Madeline – filing away, their pink skirts swapped to black just for that day, and when the vestry was empty other than Dad, me, and some chapel people, we took a walk together, side by side. The hearse was long gone; it might have even been already carrying its next mother or father.

'You won't remember Mam's parents, Vila *bach*,' Dad said, 'you were very young when they passed, but they adored you when you were born. Everyone loved you. Sadly, you never met mine, but they would have loved you too, almost as much as your mam did – and that was an awful lot – more than anything.'

As we passed the wreaths, so many of them, all laid for Mam, we took in every card attached. They said they'd miss her, some said they were sorry, some said she was in a better place... *How can there be a better place than Secret Haven, with us?* As I noticed the largest wreath of all, the one clutching Mam's favourite photo of the three of us, without her there to see it, Dad put his arm around my shoulders.

'Let's go, Vila.'

Had I seen a glimmer of the real Melody somewhere? Just for a second? It wasn't the same, I knew it wasn't. You see, Melody and I didn't live in the big world, we lived in the small one, where a giggle or hiccup was what mattered, or a fleeting thought or remark, and boring stories, and picking blades of grass for no reason but to drop them with the other hand, or *pirouettes* and *pas de chats*. That's what it was, I didn't feel like I could tell Melody about those little things anymore. We weren't meant for talking as adults do, about what we were doing with our lives, conversations that catch up on hobbies and happenings. We were meant to see each other's sighs. We were meant for the yawns, the sneezes, the tears that are hidden once you enter the big world. We were meant for tight closeness that no one else knows about, for noticing freckles changing on the other's skin.

Melody was half of me, maybe more, but Mam was my entire life, my home. After the finale, I had nowhere to go.

A MOMENT FOR YOU
TO LOSE YOURSELF

The world looked different through a balloon. This one was blue, and I'd written 'Mam & Violet' on it in black marker pen. There was a blue me in the reflection, fringe and all, but the face more shadowed as it morphed narrower and wider as I held it in front of me by a thin string. I was small. I was miniscule. I looked at the smudged fingerprints and waited. I saw my breath making the image foggy, and then, the world, all at once, let go of my hand and we floated right up to the sky.

I watched it glide, blue into blue, and then blue into all the other colours of all the other children's balloons, which they'd written numbers on for charity. It only takes a moment for you to lose yourself if you let it happen. In the centre of our school field, I was left to wonder where I would go, and just how small I would become, until there was no air left inside me to give me any shape. I imagined being tangled in the branches of foreign trees, or sinking to the ground, just to be trodden on.

All our worlds were flying high in the sky, clusters of coloured balloons above our school. Frederick's world was yellow, just like his hair, and it blended in with the streak of gold sun that was trying to throw us some light. The worlds were whizzing up in one group and just as they were at the last point where we could see them, they detached themselves, red after green after yellow after pink after blue, world after world after world. We hoped they would fly far away, overseas, I suppose to another country, and that someone would pick them up and hold them in their hands. I wasn't meant to, but I'd attached a scrunched-up piece of paper to the string. It asked Mam if she'd like to come back from that place above the clouds.

I could see Mrs Treadwell's bloated lips moving, and her eyes were as round as pool balls, but I could no longer hear what she was saying. Frederick was a few metres away, gazing at the heavens, but I only found an empty blueness and suddenly needed the ground beneath me.

When he saw me, he jumped, and started running over. There, he knelt beside me on the grass, where I must have sunk. He unpeeled my fingertips from my ears and just put one arm around my shoulders as he looked up and waved goodbye to the balloons.

'Whatever's the matter, Violet?' he asked, with his face huddled only a whisper away from mine. But I didn't know what to say. I just noticed how weird it was that all around us, in the grassy gaps between children's feet, even the daisies had clasped their petals right around their faces. And even in the warmth of Frederick's arm, and in the tangerines on his breath, I felt my chest puffing up like a sad songbird, and I found myself wondering when we would all go bang.

THE SUGAR PLUM FAIRY

Other than the nutcracker I'd placed at centre stage of the mantelpiece, Christmas passed our ivory house without checking in on us. Dad changed the TV channel every time a festive film showed up, so we ended up seeing only ourselves in the black screen, a sad audience in the dark living room.

Dad spent the season sprawled across the settee and I hid in the corner of Mam's winged armchair, petrified I would soon see right through myself. I wrapped a long stretch band around one of my feet: *pull and point, pull and point,* before swapping to the other. *You need to be strong. Slow but strong.* Time had stretched over centuries in the three months since Mam left, and I seemed to have left myself behind too.

Every now and then, Dad got up and walked around, yawning and stretching as though he believed he'd been sleeping, before collapsing in his original place and closing his eyes until the next time. His hair grew faster as the weeks went on, higher above his head and thicker over his face, threatening to close in on him entirely.

New Year spat snow at the glass and slowly fell in long party strings. We stayed locked inside our empty globe as crystals swirled and melted into a flat sheet of undisturbed icing around the house. The phone rang but most of the time, Dad didn't answer. I began to hope someone would knock on the glass to ask how we were doing, or even try to tip us upside down. *Anything!*

That's why I decided to peek inside the bag the nurse had handed us at the hospital that day; the bag Mam had dropped when she was taken away from us. It had been sitting on a side-table in the corner of the living room ever since, and I hadn't dared to open it. But this day was different. This day, I *needed* to open it, and while Dad's eyes were closed, I realised I had a right to. It was meant for me after all.

I tiptoed to the corner and clasped the bag tightly to my chest before I rushed back to the chair, ready to witness the last things Mam had held in her hands... I opened the bag and the new pair of tights unravelled on the floor. I slipped on one of the beautiful satin shoes, *perfect size twos* and admired my ankle. But they weren't the only items in there... There was also a shiny maroon leotard, the colour the girls wore in Grade Four! *Oh, Mam.*

'Dad? Dad? How did Mam know? How did she know I was going to join the higher class?' I tried to take a breath as I stood there, looking down at his exhausted body, his flannel shirt-collar folded the wrong way beneath his snoring beard. *Never mind, Mam must have guessed what my decision was when she'd heard Tchaikovsky playing that evening. You're even here when you aren't. But hang on, this also means Ms Madeline may have been waiting for me to turn up for weeks! What if I lose my place?*

I burst into my abandoned dance room, and beneath the layer of dust, I found even more secrets. A new clothes rail ran along the wall opposite my dance *barre*, packed with all the costumes I'd worn to shows at Ms Madeline's over the years; all delicately draped from pink, satin hangers. There at the front, was the blue, sequined costume that originally belonged to the red-haired girl. I hadn't even noticed it had made its way from my bedroom! I suppose the whole house had been so dark lately, and yet, it suddenly looked so dazzling, just when I needed to shine.

Underneath the clothes rail was my very own vanity case. I unzipped it to find a hair kit including a selection of hairbands, bun nets, bobby pins, bobbles and a giant can of hairspray.

On the windowsill, sat a small, rectangular wooden box I hadn't spotted before. When I opened it, I found a little friend; a dainty dark-haired ballerina twirled to *The Dance of the Sugar Plum Fairy* on the very tips of her toes, with her arms in *port de bras*. Below the ballerina, in the tiny space where perhaps a bracelet would go, was what looked like a folded-up grocery receipt. As I opened it, tears crept into my eyes. Mam's handwriting looked back at me.

Our little dream,
Violet,
Always hold on to yours.
Love, Mam xxxxxxxx

Seeing Mam's curved letters made my stomach hurt. The way her first few words were in blue ink and the rest in black was so normal, so alive, as if she was right there!

I opened and shut my dream box, winding up the ballerina each time. *Wow. Maybe Mam will pop back up one day too. Maybe she just needs winding, so she can become a new version of herself, with an even wider smile, shinier skin and a brighter look in her eyes than when I last saw her… Maybe she's just waiting for the next act?*

From that moment, I decided I'd keep the box permanently open, just so the Sugar Plum Fairy could breathe. The dance room was so full of life, so full of Mam's energy and I couldn't help but smile for the first time in what felt like forever. *My Mam's looking after me, even now.*

Since it was Saturday, I removed one of my old, white ballet skirts from a hanger and fastened it around my waist before I stood in front of the mirror, lifted my arms into a high *port de bras* and smiled. I opened my eyes as wide as possible and raised my flat, mousy eyebrows under my overgrown fringe until my whole face looked as bright as Margot's when it was lit up in wonder at the world. My new tights were a little wrinkled around my calves, more than normal, but I'd soon grow into them. That was probably Mam's intention. There was a whole life I need to grow into.

The shoes were a perfect fit, and Mam must have requested for the ribbons to be stitched onto either side of each heel, so they'd be ready to wear. Until then, I'd always worn elastics, but these ones were much prettier, and I knew just how to tie them; the ribbons crossing over each other at the front of the ankle and then around to the back before tying them on the inside of each calf. I used a little hairspray to fix the knot. *Practice makes perfect. Perhaps I could still make the new class?*

I ran downstairs towards the back door, grabbed Mam's woollen aubergine coat from the hook and threw it over me. It still smelled of her favourite perfume all around the collar. *Perfect Moonberry!* My favourite lately, too… It was okay, I could brave the cold in Mam's hug, which reached right down to my ankles. I slid my ballet shoes straight into my boots, about to hop outside.

'Dad?' I called, 'Dad. I'm going to dance...'

His doggish snores escaped the living room, just a little down the hall. He found it difficult to sleep these days, so, I shut the door behind me, took some of Mam's coins out of the marmalade jar on top of the cupboard, slid the key beneath one of my heels and I began to walk with my dance bag over my shoulder. I was doing just what Mam would have wanted me to!

Within a minute or two, I was at the Common. There it was, the same as always, but on foot, it felt like you could fall right off the edge of the other side, wherever that was. The sky above it was darkening to a deep grey, and I could no longer see the birds. *Are there places to hide in the sky?* I walked along the curve, keeping close to the edge where the road met boggy ground and I looked across to find no ponies, none, and the odd car whizzing past faster than it was supposed to.

The Common was prickly cold but I was wrapped up by Mam and finally able to just breathe. Still hearing *The Dance of the Sugar Plum Fairy*, I spun and jumped, I *relevéd, frappéd* and threw my arms into fierce *port de bras* before doing *tendu* after *tendu*, ending in different *arabesques*. I *chasséd* as though I was on an iced swan lake and it even started to snow a little. I felt like a real swan, swimming on a lake of tears. *I'll dance upon our sadness for Mam! I will! I'll dance!* When I finally saw Ms Madeline's in the distance, I split-ran across the frosted grass, I *piquéd, sautéd* and *jetéd* all the way there, making the

Common feel just a little more alive, just a little more magical. *I'm here, Mam. I'm here.*

I finally reached the road where ballet was. *Not long, now.* There was the old chapel with its low windows, bars around each one, to stop us from leaping through the glass. A man was standing at the side of the pavement opposite, lost in a puff of smoke. I looked at him, just quickly, then wrapped Mam's coat more tightly around me. I wanted that breeze to return, a gust of wind, anything to disrupt the moment. *Almost there.*

By the time I ran into the building, I was so excited that I shimmied between a group of whispering mums in the foyer and hearing the familiar patter of ballet shoes along the marble tiles, I burst through the swing doors of the dance room without saying anything, even to Ms Madeline, and found a place at the *barre*.

I hadn't realised nobody else was standing there yet.

'Ah, Violet!' Ms Madeline's voice echoed towards me from the front of the room. 'Lovely to see you've made your way back.' It did feel a little like that. Looking out, I saw that a group of girls were practising their *pas de chats* in a line at the centre. Ms Madeline had told us the previous year that this meant 'step of the cat' so I couldn't help but picture Mist pouncing through the air with them.

I smiled back. Ms Madeline's hair was always pulled back so tightly from the centre that every one of her facial expressions was genuinely forced, which had always made her hard to interpret.

'Right, girls, chop chop. Everyone follow Violet to the *barre*, so we're ready to begin.'

That's when the red-haired girl who had upturned Mam's

dolls' house all those months ago burst through the door with only a second to spare. I couldn't believe it. She looked even taller and thinner than before, and her ringlets were clipped up into the chunkiest bun I'd ever seen. She threw her bag down beside me, and then bent to change into her ballet shoes.

'Oh my gosh, I am *so* sorry,' she said, and I assumed she was talking about being late, but instead of turning to Ms Madeline, she turned to me. 'I am *so* sorry about your mum, Violet. It's totally awful!'

I flinched as all the bunheads turned towards me. Bobbie's big blue eyes seemed rounder and continued to stare into mine. *How dare she act as though she knows me, or like she cares.* This obnoxious girl had no sense of discipline and was far too loud. *How does she even do ballet? And what's everyone been saying about me?* I felt my whole body shrink as I hunched my shoulders and tried to disappear beneath my fringe.

Ms Madeline's hand flew towards the pianist, who immediately started playing a slow, delicate tune I hadn't heard before, and I was supposed to follow the girls ahead of me. *Demi-pliés, pliés and grand-pliés right down to the floor this time – I can do this.* The music was peaceful. I let myself sink into each bend, comforted by having something to hold on to.

As I faced the *barre*, I heard the leathery squeak of Ms Madeline's jazz shoes approaching me.

'There's absolutely nothing to be nervous about, dear,' she said. 'You dance beautifully. You'll fit right in.'

Her icy, twig-like hands pressed my shoulders down and snapped them back.

'Relax, dear,' she said as one of her rings glistened like a tiara. 'You're allowed to lose yourself here.'

I wondered if she knew what it had been like at home for me lately. *Does she lose herself in dance too?*

The red-haired girl was chatting away to the girl on the other side of her, who was looking up and trying her best to ignore it.

'Bobbie! Please leave Marie alone!'

That brought me a genuine smile, but as we entered the centre of the room for *Allegro*, I realised that this girl somehow danced even better whilst talking, it kept her in rhythm! She was the only ballet dancer I'd ever seen who expressed every huff and puff, and her face turned blackcurrant after each *relevé*. However, she was strong, and her moves were impressive. She might have even been the best one there. There was passion in everything she did. Sometimes too much. She wasn't the kind of person I wanted to be friends with. She insisted upon nattering to us all as if she wanted us to forget which steps we were on.

'Okay girls,' Ms Madeline said, 'now stay in the centre for some free dancing.'

Without a moment's thought, the red-haired girl started doing split-runs diagonally across the room. Her back leg was as bent as a spider's, but Ms Madeline said, 'Well done, Bobbie – that's the way! Everyone, look at Bobbie! See how she's free!' And we all joined in, one after the other, leaping across the imaginary river running through the room. We jumped as far as we could, even if it hurt. There were fifteen of us, all taking turns, and when it was my turn, I leapt for my life. When I approached land, Ms Madeline winked at me. Then, she clasped her hands together.

'This is our last 'free dancing' session for a few weeks

because we'll be using this time to practise the performance for all your parents soon. So, just enjoy!'

That tug in my stomach yanked even harder. I saw the girls flock around a magic trunk alongside Ms Madeline's table, where they pulled out silk-coloured scarves as big as wings. *Just a moment.* I tried to take a deep breath and bowed my head to hide my eyes. I was glad my fringe was growing longer since the last time Mam had cut it. A clammy hand rested on the top of my back, just where it joined my neck. I turned to the blushed face of the red-haired girl and for the first time, I heard her whisper.

'It'll be okay,' which calmed the gallop in my chest. She gently handed me one of the coloured silk scarves from Ms Madeline's magic ballet trunk, which I had never seen open before. 'A purply-blue one, to match your name.' She nodded with an excited smile until I nodded back.

I watched her wrap her sage-green scarf around her like a cocoon and fly through the air like leaves in a breeze. I joined in as she tugged the scarves between us, so we were connected by butterfly wings. Together, we twirled them, and I held on tight until the red-haired girl flew towards another ballerina, and another, so all different girls twirled in and out of an amazing embroidery. *Bobbie* – who I really hadn't wanted to be friends with.

When Ms Madeline let us leave, we burst through the swing doors, one after the other.

'See you on Wednesday, girls,' she said, not looking up from her table.

I looked towards the fresh air again and had almost

forgotten how I'd got to dance that day. On a whim, I suppose? Part of me felt like Mam had taken me, just like before.

I was ready to turn the corner to walk towards the Common when I saw Dad pulling up in his delivery van just halfway up the empty road where all the other ballerinas had disappeared. He looked taller for a few seconds, his whole body sitting up straighter than usual. He sunk more comfortably as I jumped in.

'Vila,' he didn't look at me, 'please don't ever do that again. Been looking everywhere for you. Thought I'd lost you too. God knows how you got here, but I'm not alright with it. Not alright at all.'

He was angry, I could tell from the sudden narrowing of his eyebrows, but the sigh that came from him... It was sad. We both were, but I'd needed to make Mam proud.

ANA

I measured time by Mam: the time she existed and the time she didn't. School happened to me almost every morning and afternoon, whether I liked it or not, and the rest of the time, I either danced or thought about dancing. Don't get me wrong, I did everything else I needed to at school; the writing, the drawing, the adding and subtracting, the nodding and listening – I didn't feel like talking much – all while I stayed close to Frederick.

After school, I sat with my legs in splits either side of me on the living room rug. I leant forward with my face resting on my hands, watching old film footage of Margot on our family laptop. Dad was outside, checking on the greenhouses after abandoning them for too long, but never mind, Margot was the ideal company; so quiet and yet so passionate. Even if the spotlight wasn't on her, she could light up a whole theatre. Mam used to light up a room. One day, I wanted to do that too.

The house phone rang. It was often ringing, and Mam would usually have been the first to answer. I wouldn't dare answer and Dad was often outside, so this time, it rang and rang. I pushed my headphones more cosily around my ears, turned up Margot and became absorbed again. In the corner of my eye, I saw a shadow stepping into the kitchen. Dad was there after all. The shadow kicked off his boots and soon, the phone stopped ringing.

What wonderful costumes Margot got to wear. There, she was dressed in a blush *tutu* with a rose-red underskirt to match the rose that sat proudly in the centre of her lace, white bodice. A feathered tiara rested in her jet-black hair and her eyes burnt with a depth of both happiness and sadness; a raw beauty, as Mam would have said.

But I could still hear Dad, louder than usual, and having a longer conversation too. I wondered what it was about. It didn't sound like work. Nothing about vegetables, flowers, or money. And then I heard my name. He called me Vila, even to whoever was on the phone, *so it couldn't be anything awful, could it?* I turned Margot down, just for a second, watching her spin in a wondrous silence.

'Of course, yes, understand why you're concerned,' Dad said, 'will try my best but I can tell you, if she's anything like me, Vila won't talk if she doesn't feel like it. What's the rush, anyhow? She lost her mother less than six months ago, for Christ's sake.'

Is it Mrs Treadwell? A teacher had never phoned the house before... *Oh no, it isn't Ms Madeline, is it?* I hoped not. I thought everything had started to go so well again, in dance, at least. Whoever it was, I felt uncomfortable. I'd never thought of myself as being like Dad, *but then, Mam did used to mention it, didn't she? 'Cut from the same cloth!'*

'Yes. Everything will be fine. Thanks very much for calling,' Dad said, sighing as he hung up. He looked over to me and gave me a little nod to say that whatever it was, he'd dealt with it, and I could get back to Margot.

She spoke to me from other worlds, so many magical worlds.

*

When I next turned up at school, before I even sat down, Mrs Treadwell told me a counsellor was visiting and they'd like to chat with me in the afternoon. I wasn't sure why, and it made bees buzz around my stomach. I just wanted to go home. Instead, I sat alongside Frederick, smelling the bananas in his hair, wondering what the counsellor was going to say.

Lunchtime didn't feel like a break at all. Eventually, Mrs Treadwell, all in navy, collected me from Frederick, walked me towards a room at the end of the corridor, just alongside the toilets, and knocked the door.

'Violet's here to see you, if you're ready, Sacha?'

'Yes. Come in, lovely,' said a young voice from inside, with an accent that seemed to chassé around each word.

Mrs Treadwell hovered a little, then nudged me into the room and closed the door as she left. I soon saw that the counsellor's face was very young. Her olive cheeks gleamed within the frame of a candyfloss-pink hairstyle that was longer on one side than the other, with an angled fringe slyly revealing the glint of a nose-stud. Her bright, opal-gaze made me wonder if even I looked older than her, with my chapped lips and red eyes from all the punctuated sleep. She ushered me towards the empty chair, which another little girl; a *doll,* was sitting calmly alongside.

The doll was less than half my height, and I could only see the back of its yellow hair, bobbed beneath its ears, each strand combed perfectly into place. Its shoulders looked unusually narrow, perhaps it had been given the wrong ones, and its neck was so thin that it would have done nothing to stop its moon-sized head from rolling away.

As I got closer, I noticed how enormous its eyes were behind the flat, peekaboo fringe cut too much like mine, and they were peeled open like the roundest of radishes above a smile that was *actually* from ear to ear, so big that its lips were close to tearing at the corners. It had that look of amazement at the world going on around it, but there was something eerie about it. I smiled as I stepped alongside; tilted my head a little to look at it, but I knew not to expect it to do the same.

'Great. You get to meet Ana,' Sacha said, standing up and smiling almost as much as the new girl.

And…? Who is she? What is she? And why is she even here?

'Well, aren't you going to say hello?' Sacha's words had a softness to them.

I raised my hand up to wave and take a closer look at the new girl as I sat down. I could see she looked a little ragged, an outside-doll, as Mam would say, but she was also very well-made; her skin had been tugged back and forth over the years, so a suppleness had been left on the surface from the life she'd led before.

'I've heard, Violet, that you've been through quite a lot lately, and may be having some difficulty talking about it?' Sacha asked, 'so, I'm here with Ana – to see if we can help.'

Her dimples were the first blemish I'd witnessed in her dewy face.

Sacha crossed to our side of the room and picked up the doll with one arm, so its legs flopped like wind chimes beneath it. All at once, she stuffed her hand inside its back before she could be stopped! I saw its mouth open, close, open, close, taking over her whole face. It was alive after all.

'Hello, Violet. It's very nice to meet you,' the doll said, holding out her hand, but I couldn't stop thinking that this was the strangest thing I had ever experienced. Ana's doll eyes were as dark as midnight; she even had the purple shadows painted into the delicate creases of skin underneath, and they were a little transparent just like the shadows of real people, the ones who didn't sleep properly – like Dad!

I let her hand drop into my palm; felt the ice-cold mould of her tiny fingers. They were horrible hands. And there was her mouth, blood-red and varnished, highlighting the cracks as though she'd been out in the cold. It opened and continued to talk to me.

'Good morning, how are you today?'

Does the doll have an accent too? French, maybe?

'She's yours, now. You try,' Sacha said, dumping Ana onto my lap. My face felt even stiffer than Ana's must have, as though the skin wasn't even mine to stretch.

Sacha took my hand and placed it flat on the doll's back.

'Now, Violet. Lovely Ana is here to help you. If you don't always want to speak, Ana can say it for you.' She was smiling at us both.

Does she think everyone's lovely?

My fingers, panicking, found a long slit inside the doll's back, where the spine should have been, and I slowly slid my hand inside. After a second or two of searching, I found, buried, what must have been a heart. There it was, an oval pump that I clenched inside my fist all at once, squeezing the rubber until I felt some movement, and finally saw the doll's

91

face changing, her mouth opening wide as she took a big gasp of air, and slamming shut when I let go. I continued to press and let go, press and let go, so Sacha and I heard the squeak of the creature's mechanism, but not a word escaped her.

'Hello, Ana,' Sacha said, but those big eyes didn't turn in their sockets and her smile was as wide as before. The three of us waited for many moments for something to happen but all she did was stare...

As Sacha swept her fringe to one side, I noticed her smile creeping away.

'Now,' she coughed and lifted the doll away from me, 'can you tell me what's going on with Ana, Violet? I am worried about her.'

I held my chin up and drew my eyebrows together as though to ask a question.

'You know, she doesn't seem to talk. I am concerned that she is not very happy.' My stomach began to hurt. 'Do you know *why* she will not talk?'

I shook my head.

'Okay,' she said. 'Well, can you tell me how she is feeling?'

I shook my head again. *I don't even know Ana!*

'I see. Well, where are her words?'

I quickly pointed at Ana's feet.

'Is that because she is sad?' Sacha asked.

I nodded again.

'Well, when she is happy, where are her words then?' Sacha's hands were on her hips.

I looked at the doll's fleshy arms that flew out of the white, puffed-up sleeves belonging to the purple pinafore she was wearing. I pointed at her throat. Looking at Sacha, I expected her to be a bit happier with me, but her whole face had lost its luminosity.

'Okay,' she said, 'okay.'

She nodded a lot and then patted the doll on the back and placed her back on the chair. 'Well, in that case, I hope Ana feels a lot happier soon,' she said, showing a hint of her dimples, 'but we mustn't expect too much of her for now, isn't that right?' Then she patted me on the back, too, and moved to the other side of her desk. 'You can take Ana with you, Violet,' she said as she handed her to me in a carrier bag. 'She'll help you so much at home, I'm sure.'

Does she really think a doll is going to help me and Dad? I thought of Dad pottering around Secret Haven, about the way we both tiptoed across the margins of our old lives. There was so much that couldn't be said with sentences, words, even. And when they were uttered, they could be dangerous; allow terrible things to happen, like death. At the same time, there were no words I could have said that would bring Mam back.

Sacha, the doll and I sat there in silence. I could hear people walking past the door and I wanted to leave.

'Don't worry,' Sacha said as I finally stood up, 'keep her as *long* as you like.'

As soon as I was outside the office, I stuffed the creature headfirst into my backpack, but she was so big that it was impossible to zip up. She felt as heavy as one of the nursery children, so I had to lug her alongside me. Still, I moved towards the school gate as fast as I could. I had to get out of there. Thankful for the sight of our rusty pick-up truck in the distance, I flung open the passenger door, heaved my backpack into the footwell and jumped in.

'Did everything go okay today, Vila?'

I looked down at my backpack. The doll's legs were hanging out and folding right over. The feet were grubby, as though they had walked miles all on their own.

'Um, yeah. Fine, thanks. Just warm.'

I wanted to squash the feet back inside, but I didn't want to bring too much attention to her, so I took my duffle coat off and let it fall somewhere near my shoes.

'Oh, good. That's good…'

As soon as we reached home, I ran upstairs, threw the creature onto the wicker chair in the corner of my bedroom and made sure she was facing the wall. Her legs flew open in a v-shape and she sat up unusually straight. 'Violet,' I imagined her saying while laughing into her chunky, mucky hands. 'Ohhh, Viiii-o-leeet?' I hoped she wouldn't count to ten and then come and get me. *What a horrible thing to have to sleep next to at night.*

'No, we should never expect too much,' I found myself whispering to the window. There, the other side of Secret Haven, was the Common, as still and unpromising as always.

THIRTEEN

'Come on, Violet. Need to leave now if we're gonna get there by four.'

Dad was waiting at the bottom of the stairs for me, keys in hand. He was right. I'd longed for this day since I'd first learnt to curl my toes. I was so excited – then nervous – then excited – that morning, that my breakfast had worked its way down the sink, and I couldn't eat any lunch. Neither could I find anything I needed from my bedroom. It had seemed to shrink in recent years, while its insides had grown into messy mounds of leggings, bra-tops, skirts and jumpers that covered all available surfaces. How it had happened, I wasn't sure, and I couldn't seem to do anything about it.

There! Draped beneath a pair of creased jeans, Ana sat in her corner, grinning, and clutching my ballet tights beneath one arm. Her hair was laced with layers of dust and a cobweb masked one eye. Such a wide and unfathomable eye.

'Give that back,' I screamed, and as I snatched my tights from her wrinkly fingertips, she tumbled to the floor, still smiling as she landed upside down with her bruised feet there for the whole world to see!

'I was meant to send you back years ago – and I should have,' I yelled, unable to help it. There was so much stuff that felt out of my control lately. 'Mam would have said you were just another dust-collector!'

I lifted the inconsiderate creature by her collar and put her back in her place. 'Sorry,' I whispered, stopping as I noticed the crack in her face; a mouth dropped open with shock. I realised this was the first time we'd spoken for a few years. It's just, she'd watched me the whole time, so she knew what this day meant to me. *How dare she try to sabotage that. Why hadn't I sent her back?*

*

After more than two hours of driving, we finally arrived at the street we'd been looking for; a long line of colourful buildings with shops beneath. I could hear Dad's knees uncreaking behind me like an artist's mannequin as we searched for the dance shop I'd heard so much about.

The bell rang a superfluous hello as we walked through the door. The room had walls of clothes that no one was wearing, and I wondered how busy the shop ever was, since we were the only ones in there. On any remaining wall space, there were pictures of girls and women outdoors, wearing everyday dresses with *pointe* shoes instead of boots, sandals, or stilettos, and they were all looking up to the sky, in search of something. *Ballet outdoors.* Dad and his excessive hair couldn't have stood out more in such a place, so I took the lead in what we looked at, and he followed. That was me acting. Dad probably didn't know how reserved I was at school. With his hands almost completely in his pockets and his long, burgundy jumper sleeves, he had no arms.

'Nice to meet you in person, Miss Hart.' I turned around to check the voice wasn't speaking to someone else, someone more refined, but only Dad was there. The lady at the desk finished scribbling on a slip of paper and took gentle, turned-out strides across the room to shake our hands. She was so long and graceful that I doubted she ever moved a thing out of place.

'So,' she said, 'it's a big day for you, finding your first *pointe* shoes.'

I nodded.

'We'll start with the pair we think suits best. What size are you again, Violet?'

I didn't think I'd ever told her, but I raised my four fingers and a thumb like a starfish in the air. 'Right, well, I have a whole heap of boxes ready – if you'd like to sit down, we'll start.'

Nervous, I shuffled over to the seat.

'Posture, Violet!'

I already felt my backbone thickening and I began to wonder if there was a Ms Madeline everywhere, in every city and country, all waiting to shout at a student like me.

The lady folded her skirt just below her knees and sat at my feet, taking a tape measure out of her blouse pocket. 'Hmmm, right,' she said, pouting her lips. She strode to the back of the shop where there were shelves and shelves of pink feet, hundreds of them, in all different sizes, each with the same, square toes. The lady took a selection of feet and strode back to me.

I tried on one slipper after another, and while the lady knelt, I had a chance to look at her face properly, the elegant silver head propped above an elegant frame, her clavicles jutting out in a sophisticated way above her black, wrap-over cardigan.

Up close, her face was wrinkled but the wrinkles didn't move, they were stubborn in their position above her eyebrows. Her brown eyes were heavily made up, and I wondered if they were even real. Even her face was disciplined. I wanted to ask her; *do you still dance?* But I couldn't, and anyway, we seemed to have finally found a shoe style that fitted both feet properly. I slipped my toes into toes, my feet into feet, and left the lady to pull the drawstrings.

'Right, put yourself in front of the *barre* and stand in first position, facing the mirror.' She gestured towards the back of the room with an open palm and I took my first steps, feet turned out and trying not to let the blocks knock too hard against the polished floorboards.

'Right, now do a *plié*,' she said, once I was settled in my place, the shelves of hundreds of pink feet surrounding me.

I nodded and the lady ended up gliding over and shuffling onto her knees again, poking around my feet with every slight change of position, then squeezing at my heels.

'That's it, Violet, now *relevé*,' she said, looking up, and I felt my feet pushing past a *demi-pointe*. There I was, doing it, becoming taller than absolutely everything. My toes didn't exist anymore, they were just a foot, not even that, but an extra-long leg with a misshapen hoof poised upon the end. If my arms had turned into them too, perhaps I could have galloped around the room.

I saw myself, just Violet, wearing a sloppy, lavender jumper over cropped jeans and tights. *Did Margot ever look this … casual?* I rose higher, feeling the invisible line Ms Madeline had always talked about, that line that runs from the bottom of your tailbone, right up to the top of your head and even higher, *an extension of you,* long enough for someone to hold on to and move you around like a puppet, your body stiff as a corpse beneath the strings. Not being able to help but raise my arms into *port de bras*, I stood on tiptoes for as long as I could, feeling my insteps stretch downwards, my legs never-ending. *I'm finally en pointe.*

'Boy, doesn't that hurt?' Dad said, biting his lip; the only words he'd uttered since we'd got there.

'That's right, Violet. Good girl,' said the lady. 'It will hurt for a while. How old are you?'

'Thirteen,' I said, quietly, worried she would take my new shoes away.

'Oh. I see. Very good.' She seemed impressed. Well, with more practise, you'll hardly notice the pain.' She pursed her lips, not requiring a response. 'There's no beauty without pain, Mr Hart,' she added, turning her big, dark eyes towards Dad. Maybe she'd looked like Margot in her day. *How old is she?* You could never tell with ballerinas; they seemed to live forever.

I lowered back onto my heels and smiled at Dad. He already knew that nothing good came without hard work. We'd always been on the same page about that. Dance wasn't work for me. It was all I thought about, leaping out of the dark wings of a real performance.

'Well, I think we've found our pair,' the lady said, with a glint in her eye.

As we left, the bell rang again, witness to me leaving with my new feet in a box, with ribbons I'd need to stitch on myself.

'Oh, and Violet, dear,' the lady said, raising her voice to be sure we heard her, 'please *don't* let the pain get to you. You have the head and the body perfect for a ballerina.'

I made sure to smile back at her as the door swung shut behind us. *Don't worry*, I wanted to say, *you have no idea how much my heart is in this.*

On the way home, I watched unfamiliar places sail past the window; clocks turned into faces, planes turned into birds, birds became v after v after v. *Violet,* they all called, *Violet!* The truck was even quieter than usual, or it would have seemed so to an outsider. They would have only heard the engine running, the change of gear, the breath of a father and a daughter silenced by the memory of someone who was deeply needed. We didn't have to say it out loud, we were both thinking of Mam.

When we reached the halfway mark, Dad pulled over in a lay-by and we came out of our daze. 'Brought us something to fill our bellies on your big day,' he said, while yanking a giant cooler bag from the backseat, straight onto his lap. Dad removed a brick of foil from the bag and slowly unwrapped a doorstop sandwich, just like the ones Mam used to make. 'This'll do, won't it?'

'Definitely. Thanks, Dad,' I whispered, taking my first bite.

We sat together quietly at the side of the road, as dusk crept over the truck's dashboard. Foil rustled on our laps as we chewed over thick slices of ham and cheese, tasting the Worcester sauce Mam used to add for sweetness. If I closed my eyes, we could have been back there, with Mam, all those years ago; just the three of us, with only Secret Haven to worry about.

'She'd be awful proud of you, mind, Vi,' Dad said, nudging my arm as I opened my eyes. 'As long as you're careful,' he added, reading my mind and speaking Mam's words. Someone had to.

Dad poured tea into Mam's mug, the one with the grazing cow and a little chip along the rim. The last one she'd drank out of. 'Don't want any more, do you, love?'

'No, I'm fine, thanks, Dad.' I watched him bottle-up our moment and zip it into the bag.

As we got moving again, he hummed along with the radio while I continued to watch the ups and downs of the landscape fading further into the darkness, all so different to the flatness of the Common. From the light of passing cars, I noticed how tired Dad's eyes were, softly aching in their corners as he blinked slowly behind big, thick glasses. I'd have done anything to see those lines disappear, to help him smile – truly – again. As cats' eyes led us home, I held on to Mam's mug for the rest of the journey, long after its heat had disappeared.

WHAT HAPPENS TO GIRLS

A thunder of fur leapt across my chest. There was no stopping Mist, now nearly four years old, from becoming the wildcat she was destined to be. I'd dreamt about the famous ballet, *Don Quixote*. Or, rather, he'd dreamt about me; invented me, fallen in love with me and then let me disappear into the big world again. Mam used to say, *dream big but be careful not to breathe too much life into your dreams or they'll be the death of you.*

Oh, but what it must have been like to dance with a partner, a real partner; *can you imagine? To feel their hands, so stable as they loop around your waist, ready and waiting to catch you as soon as you fall from a pirouette on the very tips of your toes...* Only Margot would know. You can't *pas de deux* without a partner. They become your foundation, and yet, I felt like I would crumble at the sight of any boy who wasn't Frederick!

Only then did I realise that my toes were still pointed and my arms were in a *port de bras* that framed a jaw-aching smile. And I was outside! Grass was prickly beneath my fingertips and the scent of the lilac bushes tried to soothe me back to sleep. As I yawned and stretched, *zzzzzzz*, something zoomed straight past my ear and jolted me upright.

I opened my eyes to a tapestry of colour; the lawn was covered with baby-faced daisies and buttercups, separated by the odd shot of violet weed, and framed by primroses running along the edge. I was the anomaly, stemmed by too-short pyjamas and rooted by bare bunions. *What on earth am I doing?* Mist went to sniff at her new meadow, checking for poison. To me, the air – alongside chicken business – smelled of green sweetness; of growth. I knew where I was, and for a moment, I pretended Secret Haven was the same as it had always been. Mist's ears poked up like morning petals. Her jade eyes had found a sparrow. Her tail waited, a fluffy pendulum in the thick summer air. A whole life can change with a single *pas de chat*.

The *zzzzzz* got louder as though it wanted to break out of somewhere. Then I saw Dad.

'Oh, Vila, *bach*! What on earth are you doing out here?'

I suddenly noticed the grass stains all over me and looked back up at him.

'You had me so worried,' he was rubbing his forehead, 'couldn't find you anywhere. Anything troubling you?'

I shrugged. It hadn't been until now. Sleepwalking had never led me outside in the past. Secret Haven looked so beautiful in the morning, it was true, but what about the night itself, the very lonely night that had happened without me knowing? I'd heard of sleepwalkers visiting the strangest of places: throwing themselves – completely naked – into ice-cold lakes, crossing railway tracks and motorways, or climbing pylons, all before returning the very same night, somehow unscathed. What about that moon in the sky, which I'd always thought someone could just poke their hand right through? What if that someone had grabbed me from the dark?

'I've been setting up a beehive, Vila *bach*.' Dad's eyes were excited.

I imagined the bees shaking hands with the petals and

whistling as they flew past the butterflies. Secret Haven was the perfect place for bees.

'I've never been very good with flowers, you know, not quite like your mam, but now I've got my bees,' he said, strolling towards his shed. Then, he unbolted the door and came out with a large, solid crate in his hands. 'All in here, they are, all ready for helping us out with some honey for that shop of ours,' with the first proper smile I'd seen on his face for months. 'Perhaps you could help us out a bit more in the shop sometime too, *bach*?'

I pursed my lips and pushed my cheeks out like petals, and then his eyes were on the bees again. At the same time, I felt them buzzing around in my stomach, stings making me twinge, but I wasn't sure why. There was nothing to be nervous about. Dad and I had found a quiet rhythm in our world over the past few years since Mam had been stolen. We performed at different times; me in my dance room and him in Secret Haven; a real secret to me lately. We sometimes crossed over, dropped peacefully in and out of each other's scenery, closed the curtains and then began again.

That's what was so enthralling about ballet. You learn the steps and you know the story enough to tell it. You practise them over and over until you know it by heart from beginning to end. You dance so automatically that your body dances without you even guiding it, and that's when you enjoy it the most. You feel safe in your own freedom. You forget everything else. My stomach felt like a hive… *Why is it twitching like that?*

There were questions I wanted to ask Dad; lots of them, but seeing him there, at peace for the first time in a while; his green eyes a little less tormented in the sunlight, I pushed my words back into the wings.

It was time for a quick change, ready for school. I glided out of our ivory house, floating through the air with every step. I was *en pointe* and I couldn't wait to tell Frederick.

When I arrived at registration, the whole class had split right down the centre. The boys were being sent to another room while the girls whispered in each other's ears and laughed. Frederick looked over his shoulder at me with that awkward, sideward smile of his, and I fell into our cosy corner. I'd forgotten we were different.

Within moments, a woman we'd never seen before was strutting in and closing the door. She was writing on the whiteboard in red marker pen, mumbling each word as the nib screeched along: *What – Happens* she said, *– to – Girls –* I waited for the question mark, but it never came. We were left to glance at one another, waiting for her to tell us what we had to look forward to.

This woman wore a red summer dress, and her face smiled as though it was itching to tell us some exciting news. I watched different parts of her body beginning to fidget: her foot tapping, her hand scratching her ponytailed head, while a thumb screwed and unscrewed the lid of the pen in her other hand.

'Good morning, girls!' Her eyebrows raised and she managed to look directly at each one of us. 'I'm here to talk *with* you about some of the changes that happen to us as we approach adolescence. I'm not here to talk *at* you, so if you have any questions, feel free to raise your hands as we go along. We're here to put each other at ease today, that's what it's all about.'

Her other heel was tapping, and her red pen pointed towards a projected diagram of an adolescent girl who had shadows of hair under her arms and a dark triangle between the tops of her thighs. The girls giggled, and so did I.

'This is completely natural and can happen at different times for each person,' said the woman, quickly pointing at each shadow and swiftly lifting her finger away as though the shadows had electric pulses. 'It's the body's natural protection.' At the same time, I noticed that the woman had pinpricks all over her arms and legs because someone had plucked away every single strand.

The next image was a different type of stranger, and at first glance, appeared as the outline of a ram's head, the only difference being that the twirl at the end of each horn contained clusters of tiny little eggs. 'These are *generally* inside all of us,' said the woman, and it made me feel queasy; there was a whole creature I'd never seen. 'Four-hundred thousand eggs,' she said, and it made me think of each one as an insect waiting to hatch, crack open with a click before scuttling around the inside of my body where I couldn't get at it. It made my stomach twinge, so I crossed my arms over it and tried to sit upright. Then I was the one beginning to tap my feet, the one tilting each ankle from left to right. I hoped I wouldn't be sick.

I wasn't sure why but my thoughts strayed in a direction I wasn't fond of: Mam's funeral, the very moment the coffin went down towards the smoke. It must have been the idea of one thing becoming a cluster; one thing becoming lots and lots of the same. Mam as ashes. Mam without her eyes, her hair, her laugh. Dust, that if held in my hand, would want to escape through my fingers. And now all these eggs, resting like a rattling bag of marbles or the seeds of a pomegranate or tomato being ground up like the blood ants on Melody's fingertips as she pressed her garden wall. *Are you still a woman when you die? Or are you nothing at all?*

The next slide on the whiteboard was of an egg making its way along one of the fallopian tubes, right into the ram's ear canal! I could hear Mam. *Well, it's important that we discuss these things, Violet. It's important that you tell me if anything 'odd' or 'funny' happens, okay?*

'Unless it meets something while it's right here,' interrupted the woman, coughing down to her chest as though by 'something', she meant 'someone', 'it breaks down, and is released as a flow of blood.' Nobody had told me this and I'd never imagined it. It didn't sound romantic at all, certainly not like Romeo and Juliet!

I stopped looking again. I felt too dizzy. Besides, I didn't need to worry about it; dance was my only love. The only men I'd have anything to do with were ballet dancers, and Ms Madeline didn't teach a single one of them! My legs didn't want to keep still, so my feet *pas de bourréed* over and over again. They wanted to run away, far away, and so did my arms as they tried to untangle themselves. The woman was looking at me and smiling. *Focus, Violet. Black shoes. Need a polish. Should do laces more tightly if I don't want to trip over. Black skirt. Flatten pleats. White shirt, suddenly boiling. Try to sit up straight. Could the woman please stop staring?*

She was speaking again. '...while you're of legal age to consent...'

What did she say? Consent? My ears popped as though someone had changed the channel, just as they did whenever Dad drove us up over the mountains or when he opened the windows too abruptly, just so we could feel the fresh air upon our faces.

I wished I could have had fresh air right then. I was seeing less and less of the world, and the woman's voice was fading, slowly being left behind. There, I could see some of her, but she was entirely dotty, a person made of pixels. I felt myself sliding from the chair as I tried to keep focus on the words, 'What happens to Girls': they're still there, somewhere, aren't they? But I couldn't, it was too late: that woman's face was flickering in front of me and my body turned into air. The face disappeared.

'Violet's fainted,' I heard someone shout from a distance.

Dad hadn't prepared me for any of this. What does happen to girls that we can do absolutely nothing about? And why didn't we happen *to* it? In ballet, I happened as I pleased.

Someone dimmed the lights.

FREDERICK

Frederick was always at the school gate before me, smiling beneath his curls that blew around in the wind. He was always there, stepping from one foot to the other, waiting for me. So, as I walked towards that gate, I pictured his little face grinning about my episode the day before. I got ready for the nudge before he'd gently ask me if I was okay. I'd even brought my *pointe* shoes with me in a separate bag, so I could show him what being *en pointe* actually meant. But I couldn't see him anywhere. I hung on until the registration bell rang, just in case he was a little late, but he didn't show up.

When I finally ran to class and collapsed behind our usual table, a few of the popular girls turned my way.

'Aw, you alright after your fall, Vi?' This particular girl had brassy-yellow hair and ice-blue eyes that froze directly on me. I didn't trust them.

I wanted to say that it wasn't a fall, I'd just fainted, not that I understood why, I'd heard Bobbie talk about periods a million times, but I suppose it's different when you see the images. Technically, I had also fallen, so the girl was right.

I opted for a safe nod, followed by a shrug. It always confused me when people shortened your name even if they didn't really know you, but I also knew I ought to stay on this girl's side.

She gave me a thumbs-up and her face looked warmer than expected.

As she turned back to the whispering clique around her, I heard Frederick's chuckle erupting from the opposite side of the classroom. He was there after all, but instead of sitting alongside me, he was perched at the end of a desk of rowdy boys we'd never properly spoken to in our lives.

Looking at Frederick, I didn't know how he was managing any of it. He appeared as a bobblehead, the way his curls rolled back and forth with laughter as he rocked between chair legs, his eyes darting from one boy's cheeky grin to the next. It was hard to tell if it was nerves, excitement, or both. The boys were sliding Frederick's cartoons back and forth across the desk and taking turns to raise their hands and ask him to draw them. On this day, of all days, they'd requested his presence to be very much away from me.

'Now me, do me,' they were shouting, and Frederick's ecstatic face was turning bubble-gum pink as he raced to scribble each of the gangly boys fighting for the desk in front of him. It was funny to witness him as part of a crowd, it had always been just the two of us, but there, seeing how happy he was to watch his art come to life, it was clear he was in his element at the centre of those people.

My *pointe* shoes held their pose in my duffle bag. I so wanted to show them to Frederick, to tell him about the lady at the shop and its shelves of a thousand feet. I wanted to tell him how I'd felt, standing on top of the world, but I couldn't tell him right then, not after seeing him with all those boys. It would have meant drawing the curtain on his spotlight. Also, I wasn't sure if it would all sound quite dull compared to whatever was going on over there. At a distance, you begin to doubt things, everything. From just metres away, Frederick's hair looked longer than ever and slightly darker than his usual, bright yellow curls. *Has he really changed since yesterday? How many other things have changed without my noticing?*

At breaktime, Frederick became invisible.

At lunchtime, he returned, but disappeared long before I had the chance to catch up with him. He hadn't done that for years, not since we'd first met. Thankfully, I knew we'd see each other during last lesson because it was the class we most looked forward to. We had our own little corner table near the art cupboard, and Frederick's left arm took up our entire space with sketch after sketch after sketch. He lived through his drawings. He breathed everything into them, and I knew what that felt like. Most importantly, Art was where we'd catch up on each other's weekends. He'd ask me question after question, as full of wonder as ever with his widely animated face. *That's just Frederick, he'll never change.* I knew he'd have an explanation for what had happened during the morning. *Maybe he'd been pressured into sitting with those boys. They seemed like the type to do that.*

The problem was, Frederick didn't turn up at Art either.

Not ten minutes in, not half an hour in and not at the end. Our little desk remained quite empty. There was nobody to bang elbows with, nobody's charcoal, big-headed animals to burst into tears of laughter about, so, I decided he couldn't have been feeling well, in whatever way it was. In the meantime, I'd be sure to show Bobbie my new feet at our next dance lesson. If there was anyone I could rely on to get excited, it was her. She was ecstatic when she first went *en pointe*; she said it was when things became serious, when she finally got to grow up. Maybe that explained the sudden hollowness in my stomach. I wasn't feeling well either, now I thought about it.

For weeks, I waited in all the usual places to speak to Frederick: the dining hall, the old tennis courts, the music room. One breaktime, I thought I'd finally have the chance. There he was, walking right past me at our old meeting point in the English corridor.

'Fred,' I whispered, 'Where've you be —'

But he gave me a nod and just kept walking.

After that, his cornflower eyes stopped looking at me altogether.

Weeks began to feel like months, and months began to feel like years. I wondered if it had been something to do with the talk the boys had while we were told what happened to girls. *Why had we needed to be in separate rooms so much anyway? What had been said to them? That we couldn't be friends anymore?*

Unless it wasn't that at all. Maybe Frederick had finally realised that I wasn't the most entertaining person to be around. *Did I not make him feel like the centre of attention?* Until everything started to go wrong, I'd never really thought about the way Frederick and I interacted. I suppose part of our magic was that we didn't have to think about it; that's where all the comfort came from − or at least, I thought it was. The friendship was mutating into something so fast that I couldn't recognise it and I was worried that before long, I wouldn't recognise him. The truth was, he was the only one I gave my attention to. To me, there had never needed to be a centre.

The world slows down when you don't have your someone to spend it with. You end up thinking yourself into other places and sometimes, forgetting to come back. The extra *pointe* classes were leaving me exhausted. My toes ached, as did my calves; my back and my arms felt like pheasants while my eyes were beginning to droop.

There I was, sitting in Maths, the final class of the day, half gazing out the window, wondering about nothing extraordinary, when I felt two hands on my shoulders. I hadn't heard footsteps, or even a whisper, but there they were, two warm hands, very gently pressing me down, further and further into the earth as though I was being planted. It felt a little like hypnotism and I would have jumped if I hadn't immediately recognised the way she was absorbing my worries all at once, just like she used to when Melody and I had argued, or before I ran into a ballet exam. I felt her breath on the back of my neck and the flyaways of my ponytail as she stood behind me, protecting me without a single word. *If I turn around, will you disappear?* Just in case, I didn't dare. I closed my eyes and I let myself sink.

'Mam?' I mouthed, afraid to whisper her away, afraid to erase that sweet smell of moonberry, but she said nothing.

I only opened my eyes when the bell rang, and Mam's hands had disappeared. I slid my textbooks into my bag and ambled out of the classroom, letting everyone else barge past. I hoped

Mam couldn't see how I was at school these days. She would have been disappointed.

As I crossed the schoolyard, crowds quickly turned into stragglers. It was funny how a stage could transform in just a few seconds, and there I was, left behind like an odd prop. *Maybe I could transform in that time too. I'll show you one day.* I looked at everyone, on their way home, ready to discover their evenings. Mine was safely orchestrated to be the same as always, and I'd got to like it that way.

I'm not sure what made me turn around as I stepped through the school gate, but when I looked back, the yard was no longer as empty as I'd thought. Shadows were enclosing on something, and the shadows were being followed by figures, people who had crept out from behind the pillars of the new building. I watched them form a circle. Over the tops of their heads, I saw a backpack being flung back and forth, and as the circle shrunk and stretched, I saw, between the boisterous shoulders of gangly boys, dark blonde curls that I immediately recognised to be Frederick's.

I ran closer as fast as I could, but I was so far away that it was already happening, *had been* happening. I could hear him,

'Please, you don't want to do that, that's a special edition…'

'Oh, don't I?' The boy with the sickliest of grins was kicking and punching Frederick and whenever he fell back, the boy's friends bounced Frederick in one way, then the other, just like a wobble toy as he tried to rescue something from the ground.

'Leave him alone,' I shouted. 'He's my—' but my voice sounded much quieter than it had in my head. *Why does that always happen?* As I approached, the last punch was straight into Frederick's stomach. By the time I properly got to him, he was curled up in a ball on the gravel, cradling himself as his face twitched involuntarily like a puppet's.

'She's your what, Freddie? She's your *girlfriend?*' the grinning face asked, making eyes at me.

'No, she's not,' Frederick moaned.

The boy's friends forced a few laughs and punched each other's arms as they stepped back and eyed up what they'd done, the swelling that was already taking over Frederick's face. They traipsed away, easy as that, leaving just the two of us – finally – alone.

'*What?*' Frederick asked me. His face was screwed up beneath bits of gravel. I'd never seen him look like that before. I didn't know what to say. '*What*, Violet?' he asked again, but I wasn't sure, I just hated to see him in so much pain. It made me hurt too.

'Are you okay?' I whispered. I could see that his bag had been emptied and he was still spitting out shreds of comic strips. I tapped him on the back as he coughed, and then knelt, starting to pick up what I could salvage of the pages. They were his special Marvel ones, I could tell. I couldn't work out why he'd even risked bringing those to school. Perhaps to impress them?

His head drooped as he snatched his backpack from me.

'Get lost, Violet,' he moaned, his hair now a messy, weeping willow.

I carried on picking up the mess anyway.

'I mean it. Get *lost!*'

I looked up at him, and how angry he was – it was burning out of him, and I could tell he wanted to cry. If that had happened to me, I'd have been sobbing.

'Why aren't you going? Can't you take a hint?' he asked again. '*Go!* I don't want to see you. I mean it, *stop* being friends with me! It's about time we lived in the real world.'

The roll of comics fell from my hand as I stared at him, hoping he would take it all back. *Surely he doesn't mean any of it...*

'*Go!*' he shouted at the top of his shaky voice, and I could feel his breath on my face. I turned around and ran, as fast as I could while my sobs tried to catch up with me, making it difficult to breathe. *He couldn't have meant it. Frederick is kind. Frederick has always been kind.*

BEAUTY WAS PAIN

At ballet the same evening, I found myself in a toilet cubicle for longer than I'd hoped. I should have known my stomach pains didn't mean a dancer was trying to break free. My second self had nipped away at my insides for so long that she had to have an outburst, make a show of herself as blatant blotches of reddish brown upon my underwear, threatening to show through my whole leotard! It had happened, just like they said it would, the thing that happens only to girls.

I yanked as much toilet roll as I could from the holder on the wall, rolled it into a ball and laid it on top of the gusset. I recalled that there was a vending machine on the wall by the sinks, *if I can just creep out and come back as quickly as I can, I'll be okay.*

I jumped up, unlocked the cubicle door and spotted the machine. I searched my bag for coins at the same time as trying to yank my leotard back up to my waist, and because everything really does happen at once, Bobbie burst through the main toilet door.

'Vi, you in here? What's up? We're starting *barre* exerci—' Then she clocked the sanitary towel that had just landed in my hand like a sad gift. 'Oh,' she said. And I wanted to cry.

'Not you? Reeeeeeally?' Her smile was creeping wider and wider, and I couldn't bear it.

'Promise you won't tell anyone,' I managed to say, not

looking at her, until her hand flew up to her blood-red face and she burst with a cackle. Bobbie couldn't help doing things like that. Besides, I realised how ridiculous I must have looked, how ungraceful even compared to her, who was standing there unusually kempt, in an elegant, navy leotard and her hair scraped back in a bun.

'But, I haven't even started mine yet! That's not fair!' Without fail, Bobbie's breath smelled like apples. But her face was serious for a moment; she was right, she'd recently turned fifteen and nothing but tears had escaped her. I was still thirteen. *Lucky me.*

Yep, look how excited I am, I wanted to say; my second self was good at being sarcastic, but my mouth stayed shut. Bobbie, reading my mind, burst again.

'Okay, well, fair enough. Sort yourself out and get to class. I need to copy you.' She smirked, and a second after she ran out, I could hear the piano music playing the other side of the wall, which meant the usual line of girls were performing the sequence of *Battement Tendu*, *Port de Bras*, *Développé* and *Relevé en demi-pointe*, all clueless about what was happening to me in that cubicle, unless it had already happened to them, of course...

I tiptoed after Bobbie and stumbled into the dance studio. There was a line of certificates on the floor alongside the other girls' dance bags. Mine must have been the one that remained on Ms Madeline's table. As I walked closer to the table, Ms Madeline handed it to me and dropped her head with a wry sort of smile.

'Well done, Violet, dear,' she whispered, 'but you'd better make a start.'

I peeked at the certificate before placing it near my trainers.

Royal Academy of Dance
Grade 6 (ballet)
Violet Hart
DISTINCTION

I looked back up at Ms Madeline who put a finger to her lips, which I assumed meant not all the girls had done so well. Still, that was what I needed, even though the sanitary towel sitting like a flat ballet shoe between my legs, dampened any chance of me jumping around with excitement. *Come to think of it, how am I supposed to slip into the splits or yank my leg back into the perfect attitude without anyone noticing? How on earth do ballerinas deal with periods?* All the girls at the *barre* were beaming as though it never happened to any of them.

Next week, I'd wear a skirt. *Oh, don't be so silly, Violet,* I could hear Mam's voice. But I couldn't help it, everything was changing, things had started moving inside me and I'd begun to give away parts of myself without any say in the matter. *What kind of world is this? The one Frederick had been talking about?* Whatever it was, I wanted nothing to do with it.

At home, Dad was hunched upon a kitchen stool and trying to superglue a sole back onto one of his shoes. I threw down my dance bag, ran straight past him and straight up to the bathroom, where I slammed the door behind me, wishing the lock would magically fix itself. With a lock, a bathroom could be the most private place on earth. Even a quiet person needs privacy.

Aren't mothers supposed to be around for this day? Instead, I had to contend with a packet of pads that had mysteriously arrived in the cupboard under the sink. The purple packet looked years old but proud to be finally having its moment. Mam was supposed to be the one calming me down and telling me, 'We'll sort you out, don't you worry, love,' so I could be sure that everything would be okay, that my gurgling stomach wouldn't mean the end of dance or the end of me. Instead, I sat there wondering what else I wasn't prepared for.

'You okay, Vila?' Dad shouted up the stairs.

'Yes. Fine, Dad,' I yelled, still in a seated position. Looking down, I doubted pads could be put on Dad's compost heap.

'Vila?'

'I'm fine, okay!' I screamed at the top of my voice and immediately regretted it. There's nothing worse than someone talking to you while you're on the toilet.

I could hear Dad shuffling away while he muttered something about teenage girls. My second self seemed to be climbing out of me from all directions and I didn't know how to control her. Next, she slammed the cupboard door and the sound made us both jump.

She dragged my feet across the landing to my dance room, where Mist was already curled up in the corner, whispering behind her claw to each member of the dolls' house as though she'd known something all along. *The girl has fiiiinally caught ooooon,* I imagined her saying. And there I was once again, cross-legged in front of the tall mirror, staring past myself until something would happen. Nothing did, of course. It was always cooped up inside. I was a quiet story, pressed behind glass and framed by golden feathers; the same, skinny face above a recently different body.

My landscape was rapidly changing shape. A rough valley of excitement and pain laid under my skin as I felt partly desperate for change and partly terrified. Nobody else would see it, but there it was, bubbling inside me. Strange things would happen over time, I'd already witnessed some of them. They would try to get in the way of my dreams. My chest was beginning to swell on either side, my hips were trying to widen right there and then, and my hair was becoming darker and greasier at the centre of my fringe, which made it stick to my spotty forehead. *I should want change. Yes, I should invite it because from now on, it'll happen whether I like it or not.*

Be careful, Violet, be careful, I heard Mam say, and I told her, *I will, I will, Mam. I'll be careful not to waste my life and lose my dream!* It's true, you must work hard to hold on to yourself. You must be outstanding, so nothing can talk you down. Yes, I was the best ballerina in Ms Madeline's class, but I needed to be the best everywhere if I still wanted to be like Margot. I needed to give everything to ballet just as it had given everything to me. In ballet, I was in charge. I heard Dad whistling something as he traipsed across the landing. Just the sound of him was interrupting my focus.

I sat up on my knees and delved into Mam's vanity case while glancing between Margot and my own reflection. Right there, I began to paint myself, a reflection much better than the last. I saw little breaths of the one who had been trying to escape for a long time, maybe even since Melody had fled Secret Haven many years ago, and I knew I needed to decide who should stay.

This'll help you stand out in bright lights, Mam said, not wanting her little ghost to blend in with the background. So, in her place, I laid it on thick. I plastered foundation over my face like mud, then blended it all into one, solid mask, using Margot as my template.

Head back, Mam said, as I lined my eyes like a doll, smoothed white eyeshadow on my lids and brushed mascara along my top and bottom lashes. I swept powdery rouge along each cheek, carefully blending it to create some semblance of a bone structure, all while Mam was right there, pursing and pouting her lips until I did the same, *but where's the lipstick?* I rifled through the case and saw my mouth in the making of a blood-red stick. I drew it on, smiled to see the shock of it against my string of milky teeth, lingered for a moment and then kissed the old Violet goodbye.

Stop it, it hurts, I moaned at Mam, threatening to cry if she yanked my hair once more with the paddle brush. Now, I did it to myself, again and again; made sure I was groomed from roots to ends and head to toe, *no need for tears.* Beauty was pain. Or was pain beauty?

As I heard Dad shut his bedroom door, I plaited my hair on both sides and drew it into a bun at the back. If I wanted to be a dancer, I'd be a dancer every day, everywhere I went. I rested a black wrap-over cardigan and skirt over the radiator for next time, then gave my hair one last spray to keep it solid throughout my sleep. Violet would wake up as a true ballerina because dance was the only thing we could depend on. If I couldn't dance, I didn't know what I'd do.

I went over to the dolls' house and opened the part that revealed the attic space where two dolls lay on their backs on a patterned rug. There, alongside them, I placed the third, a young male doll, *Frederick,* before closing the roof again.

As I went to draw the curtains, I felt the Common glaring through the window at me. It was always there without question, but I was usually the spectator. Everything about it was eerily still. Lately, however, it seemed to stay awake longer into the nights, as though it didn't want to leave until it saw me fail, as though it wanted a story to smirk about.

As I pressed my nose up to the glass, closed my ears to Dad's snores on the other side of the house and looked further into the distance, I followed the line of leafy trees around the edge of the Common, one taking a slow bow and then the next, as though acknowledging their invisible applause. As dusk fell and the light changed, each tree grew larger, stealing more of the sky the closer to Secret Haven it got. The largest was taller than the stage, with sprawling roots and an ancient body, and as I watched its head drop, I thought I saw a strange silhouette beneath it, beckoning me to choreograph the rest.

I shut the curtains with both hands until the rail trembled. I needed to focus. Someday, I'd give the Common something worth watching, but nothing meaningful would come easy. It would have to wait a little longer.

Part Two

COPPÉLIA

With trepidation, I tiptoed between the wings. *If this doesn't work out, what then?* I brushed the thought away and looked at my world as it danced before me. I watched Bobbie play to the audience. Over the past four years, she'd grown from a girl into a young woman; an adult, who did adult things. I hovered somewhere in-between.

'Vi! Good luck!' Bobbie was the loudest whisperer I knew. When she kissed me, I wanted to rub her saliva away from my cheek, but I was afraid it would smudge my new face.

She giggled, always able to read me, and brushed it away with her fingertip. 'You're on next, aren't you?'

'Yes, Bob,' I was trying to keep calm. *How can she be confident even when she has a moustache drawn above her lip?* I'd been trying to run through the steps in my head, but I'd forgotten every single one of them!

'This is your big role!'

Her enthusiasm was making my chest hurt. I tried my best to ignore her, but she carried on.

'It's your *chance*. Your big *opportunity!*'

I gave her a long look. She'd had main parts before, but we couldn't all be so fearless. Plus, it meant much, much more to me. It always felt like my whole life was at stake.

'Okay, fine, I'll leave you alone,' she said, and ran away. I began to wonder why I'd put myself through this, the pressure to perform in front of so many people, and to feel so sick that I was dizzy, every single time. My head and body felt disconnected. I did some more stretches, felt my hamstrings lengthen as much as possible, and shook my arms and legs in front of me, watching the ankles and wrists roll around as though they didn't belong.

Within seconds, there was another whisper in my ear. 'You'll dance beautifully, dear!' Ms Madeline was standing at my side.

I was sure she'd been standing in the opposite wing just a second ago, I'd seen her face in the dark. *Never mind,* she kissed me and winked as though we both knew I had nothing to worry about. But it wasn't like that, not really. The combination of my solo still wasn't coming back to me; *glissade* here and there, *pirouette en dehors* or *en dedans*? Even if I remembered the steps, I couldn't remember the order or direction. Before I knew it, Ms Madeline was ushering a line of little girls offstage at the other side. She moved like lightning. If only I could remember the sequence, the dance would follow and so would the story... *Now, how does it begin?*

It was too late. The crowd applauded and the music was slowing down in readiness... I looked down at my white ankle socks and the petticoat of my dress, flickering around my calves, and I told them to run along, escape me somehow. Then, which one of us was ahead or behind, I had no idea, but I saw my body exiting the wings and fluttering across the stage with the grace of a broken bird that I hoped would soon find flight. A flute's melody led me behind a little house with a door and ivy-edged window that overlooked a garden. Only my face peered through it and out at the audience; I crossed my arms upon the sill, my head gliding from side to side as I eyed up the darkness, pointing at invisible people while the flute still tried to tease me outside, with its flouncy, quivering birdsong.

My face glowed as I stretched up and felt a circle of air just in front of me, then finally, glided from the window and opened the door to the steps. I peeked out and glanced across the audience while music hypnotised us all. Léo Delibes' *Valse Lente*, the waltz, needed me to join in with it, and I did, almost guessing as I went. I swung each leg up straight in front of me as I made my way down the steps, there was the *grand battement*, and another one, and then, well it didn't matter, I was beginning my sequence as Swanilda. The music was clicking, and I was remembering everything, or at least, my body was. These days, it did things without my mind's knowledge, and this time, I completely allowed it to. *Changement*, I thought, *entrechat*, and then just ballet, all in view of the beautiful girl in the window across the way. I was Swanilda, innocent, in love and close to getting married, if it wasn't for her, *but I can be like her too,* I thought. *I can be her if Franz wants me to.*

When the backdrop changed, I ran offstage to change – into a red *tutu* with blue stitching around the edge. After Bobbie rouged two circles of rosiness onto my cheeks, laughing as she did it, I ran back onstage and straight into position.

The music ticked and one of my legs lost its softness; began to swing back and forth like a pendulum, or the tongue of a bell; *grand battement en cloche! That was it!* There was nothing else to think about. The music continued to change because it was my medley; *I am Coppélia!* The flute music soothed alongside a jingle of piano keys that my arms followed like clockwork. Instead of the smooth stretch that ballet usually displayed, I felt all the sharp angles of it, the solid lines that I abruptly stopped upon. This time, I was the artist's mannequin and my torso tilted forward and back a little, connected by a spring. I eliminated any bend as I moved upon blocks, hearing my toes knock against the stage as I pivoted on one heel. I shrugged my shoulders up and down to the music, and blinked my eyes wide open to the beat, comfortable in my woodenness.

Next, I heard a new wall of scenery rolling down behind me, and someone, it must have been Ms Madeline, in the wings, draped a sash over my head. I folded my arms in front of me to do a Scottish dance and then lifted them into the shape of a W. Again, I moved away from the wings, someone dropped a fan in my hand, and I began to do a Spanish dance, I was someone else, then someone else, then someone else, keeping my face as fixed as porcelain throughout each transformation.

I was a doll brought to life, each step a chance to dance like something else, someone else. Why had I felt so uneasy? This was exactly who I wanted to be, feeling the bright stage lights so hot upon me, I turned and turned, and smiled and smiled with my glued-on smile.

The great thing about the pitch-black of the audience was that I could imagine anyone being in it, and in that lighting, with that music, I was alive and dead all at once, I felt the ground leaving me, *or was it me leaving the ground?* I drifted through air, magically interweaving with it, becoming it as I was drawn right up to the heavens! I tried to become Coppélia. All thought was sucked out of me through my enamel eyes, my painted nostrils. I only felt what she was supposed to feel. And I realised, that as long as I kept doing that, I could be wherever and whoever I wanted to be; dance was my language.

The dressing room reeked of vanity even after the girls had gone; of excess lipstick and skin-colour spilled onto the floor. It felt like famous dancers – a million Margots – and crying ballerinas, or the last-minute panic of being stitched into stage costumes. Ms Madeline must have been talking to the parents; she was usually around until the end, but then, Bobbie had disappeared too. Only minutes after the finale, the costume rail was bursting with zipped-up body bags. There, in the mirror, however, was Coppélia looking back at me.

I was slow to step out of her, gently loosening the back of the *tutu* and then sliding it down. There was my strange and girlish body, pale and ghostly compared to the more refined face of rich almond make-up that quivered upon the top. I found myself smiling, *but at which one of us? How do others really see me?* My pale torso had always been quite flat, but for a ballerina, that was ideal. I threaded my long legs – still sheathed in white tights – into my favourite purple knee-length skirt, and as I laced up my black ankle boots and wrapped my cardigan around me, I saw the two of us merge again, strange contradictions of one another. I hung my costume on the rail until the next performance, and pushed Coppélia to the back, so no one could lay a finger upon her.

After switching off the lights around the mirror, I grabbed my denim jacket, walked out of the dressing room and clicked the heavy door shut. Coppélia's home was in the dark. Still standing tall, I walked along the empty corridor and towards the foyer. There, I saw a little boy with curls who reminded me of Frederick years ago. He was bounding through the exit doors, his hair bouncing in the same way Frederick's always used to. I'd only ever seen him at a distance since that day when everything had changed.

There was a cluster of long-coated people standing in the foyer, swinging their heads back with laughter as I noticed Ms Madeline tearing herself away and disappearing down the long corridor to say even more thank yous and goodbyes. As I walked past the group and towards the arts centre's exit, one of the group called after me.

'Excuse me, sorry…'

Did I drop something? I turned around.

'Sorry, you're Coppélia, aren't you?' It was one of those subtle Welsh accents that only rears its head at the ends of sentences.

A tall, raven-haired man in a bottle-green overcoat was standing there smiling down at me. He held out a hand for me to shake.

Don't be rude, now, Violet, I heard Mam saying. The man laughed as if he could hear her too, and he held eye contact with me as I lifted my hand towards his.

Wow, to be touched.

His hands had that subtle ruggedness about them, the hair around the knuckles and the slightly dry palm; *what stories a hand could tell…* I'd felt safety course through my whole body within a single moment. *Just imagine a hug.* He looked as if he could have just stepped offstage himself. Then I realised that as of yet, I hadn't said a single word.

'Oh, yes, that was me,' I nodded, with a little extra enthusiasm to apologise for the pause.

His eyes were the colour of caramel, and they were full of awe as they danced from left to right, finding the most appropriate aspect of my face to focus on. It made my cheeks grin back.

'Well, I don't want to bother you on your way out, you must be exhausted, but I just wanted to say, well, wow... You were the star of the show this evening.'

'Oh,' I said, never sure how to respond to compliments. So far, I'd been carried away by my own thoughts and I was worried he'd read my mind.

One of his eyebrows stood much more proudly than the other.

'Without a doubt, the best,' he added with a single nod of the head.

It was impossible not to notice how attractive he was. If I'd seen each of his features individually; his slightly crooked teeth, perhaps, or his long-bridged nose, I might not have been so dazzled, but as a whole, his slightly *off* appearance made him seem more perfect, somehow.

'Seriously, all of us, here,' he gestured back at the long-coated group standing behind him, 'we were massively impressed by your performance. We enjoyed it immensely.' I looked at them all, so well-dressed as they laughed over tilted glasses of wine. Their expensive perfume filled the air between us.

A fallen feather of the man's wavy hair tried to kiss his temple and he kept tucking it behind his ear.

'You're completely gifted, you know – to have such an effect on people – to draw them in the way you do. I just wanted to say, *thank you*. You're the real deal.' He didn't know it, but the way he lit up on the outside was exactly how I felt on the inside right then. That was how dance made me feel.

He stepped back and bowed his head while holding a hand against the two lines of brass buttons on his coat. 'Ah, I've embarrassed you now, haven't I?'

For a second, I was worried I'd offended him with my reticence. *Silly Violet.*

His eyes were round with concern, and he laid a hand upon my shoulder. 'I know ballet is all about making it appear effortless,' and his thumb accidentally touched my neck before he returned both hands to his pockets, 'so I respect that there's a great deal of modesty that comes with that. You're good to hold on to it, Coppélia. Really wise,' he nodded, 'for now, I just have to say, well done! I'll definitely be looking out for your name in the headlines. Watch this space, right? Anyway, hope you're being treated to a glass of bubbly this evening.'

I shared my nervous laugh, an unconvincing saviour in high-stake scenarios. I hadn't even considered a celebration. *Bubbly, how mature. That would be nice… Perhaps I look older than seventeen with all this make-up?* He looked so sophisticated, the way his head turned and smiled above that black polo-neck.

I wanted to tell him my name – the one to look out for – was Violet, just in a friendly way, for awareness, but I was afraid he'd hear it as an ungrateful correction, especially after having complimented me so much.

Seeing his slightly nervous step from one foot to the other,

I began to think he might not be as old as I'd initially thought. *Look at that thick, inky hair; no greys to be seen. Maybe he's only in his late twenties.*

Thank you so much, the adult in my mind wanted to say, *that means the world*. Instead, I just smiled as he walked away; a stranger I'd never meet again.

As I stepped outside into the darkness, the cold air tried to bite. I wrapped my scarf more tightly around my neck. There was Bobbie, standing at the bus stop with her feet wide apart, and toes facing outwards as her mobile lit up her whole face. She looked so much like a ballet dancer, the way she stood so upright and thin as a board. It was rare to see her being so quiet, though. I waved but she was too engrossed in her phone to notice me. Then, she held it tightly against her ear and it looked like she was arguing with someone, the way she scowled and placed her other hand on her hip. The headlights of Dad's van lit up the rest of the car park and I ran over to jump in.

'That Bob over there?' Dad asked. 'She okay to get home?'

We watched as Bobbie's mother's car turned the corner and pulled up beside her.

'Ah, good stuff.' Dad turned on the engine. 'Well, how's my little star?' His eyes were twinkling behind his glasses in the dark.

'It actually went really well,' I said, turning the heater towards my feet.

'Ah, see, well, I've never doubted you, Vila *bach*, never doubted you. I only wish your mam could be here to see how you've turned out. We couldn't ask for a better daughter than you, you know. In all ways.'

I wondered why Dad had softened so much. It was true that it was the best I'd ever danced but he hadn't even been there to witness it.

'I'd like to see you dance one day if I could, you know, Vila. It only seems right that I see what you've been up to all these years.'

'Oh, it's fine, Dad,' I reassured him, wondering where all this was coming from. 'Not much to miss!'

He lifted the corner of his mouth and shrugged while he kept his eyes on the road. 'Well, maybe there's a lot, Vila, maybe there's a lot.'

I hadn't told Dad yet but I had my heart set on attending dance uni. I'd sent my application months ago. Dad had probably assumed I'd been following the more academic route, as he'd always drummed into me the importance of a good education and having options, but Ms Madeline had recommended The Welsh Dance College (WDC) to me because she understood my home situation. She'd told me in the past that most ballerinas aspire to go to London at an even earlier age, *it's the place to be,* she'd said, and tried to put my name forward for different things, but it had never seemed like the right time to leave Dad on his own like that.

Ms Madeline had helped me work out that the WDC was only about an hour away, so I could still live at home and catch the train back and forth each day whilst helping Dad at the shop. She said the uni had sent its fair share of dancers around the world over the years *but it's all down to you and your skill in the end.* She supported me with my personal statement and said that if I got in, she'd offer extra training to make sure I was meeting the required standard – all while Dad would hardly know I was gone. Not that any of it was important for a few more months.

I knew one thing; I could get addicted to the after-performance rush. Being centre stage really was everything I'd imagined, and for the first time, I felt noticed. I felt like Margot; happy and sorrowful, light and dark, weak but strong. I danced freely as though I was invisible and yet, I'd been seen. And then it struck me, *I'd like to see you dance one day,* Dad had said, so kindly, and yet, he'd said the word dance so softly, almost as though it could tiptoe out of my life just as easily as it had entered. *Perhaps I should include him more.* After all, it was a life-long dream, not a hobby... Since Mam and Melody, I hadn't told anyone how I truly felt about ballet; no one at all.

THEY'LL SOON SEE

On Monday, I became Quiet Violet again, a girl just trying to prepare for mind-numbing exams, so I kept my bunhead down. It was funny; I bet no one could have imagined me dancing in front of hundreds of people. I was beginning to enjoy that it was my delicious secret. *One day, they'll see.*

I was left to my own devices at school. It made life much easier. I floated in and out of English, French and Psychology, hoping I'd be summoned for an audition at the uni in a couple of months. I needed to spend more time on Psychology, but the teachers had predicted my final grades for everything would be As, which was more than I needed for the dance degree. Still, I channelled all my energy into ballet, studies and helping Dad at the shop.

Bobbie told me I fretted too much about school, but she'd catapulted out of there over a year before to have a gap year working in a shoe shop. God knows why. She said it was to find herself, but I think she was looking in all the wrong shoe boxes. Bobbie was a natural at ballet, it was wasteful not to share that effervescence with an audience, but she wouldn't see anything unless it was through her own eyes.

The excitement of the previous week's performances had left me lighter on my feet. As I walked along the corridor to go home, I noticed a boy in a bright red, baggy hoodie inside one of the empty classrooms and I'm not sure why but something made me pause. He was wearing giant headphones, holding a giant brush, and painting what looked like a whole wall, beginning with brilliant orange. I couldn't work out what the image was going to be as he crouched down in the bottom-left, properly in the zone as his eyes followed each line, but something about the way he did it intrigued me...

When he turned to add more paint to his brush, I could see his curled fringe was especially long and much darker at the roots than it had been before... The boy was Frederick, and he was happily engrossed in his own world! Part of me wondered if I could just knock and go in, revisit the old days when we used to nudge each other whenever Mrs Treadwell was asking one of us a question. But no, I couldn't do it. I felt as though I'd be disturbing a stranger, imposing upon a private landscape. No, I didn't want to risk it. Nobody likes to be interrupted while they're in the flow.

When I got home, there was another car parked alongside our rusty pick-up truck; a tiny, dusty-blue one. A stocky lady was carrying three brown paper bags in her arms and trying to open the car boot at the same time. There was one of our sweet potatoes, rolling along the ground behind her feet, so I bent to pick it up, shook off some of the dirt and handed it back to her before I walked on.

'Oh, thank you, Violet.'

She smiled as though nobody had ever picked anything up for her before, and I wondered how she knew my name...

In the garden, it was the birdhouse's moment again. Dad was hammering it to the fence since the previous nail had rusted away. That house had existed for as long as I could remember; we'd all watched it through the window on different occasions, hoping something would visit. Dad wouldn't give up on it until it had entirely given up on itself. He was like that. Over the years, he'd tried to fix almost everything around the house, including my sore ballet ankles and toes. He'd painted the birdhouse eggshell blue, just like my old Wendy House.

'That looks really lovely,' I told him as we slowly walked back to the house.

'Hm. It'll do. It's your mam's birthday today, you know; she'd be fifty-five.'

'Yeah. I bet she'd look exactly the same, though,' I said, thinking about the photo upon the mantelpiece. Those streaks of silver hair. She'd had them even when I was small, and she'd never dyed them; she just let her hair flow long down her back in whatever way it fancied. *Nature's nothing to be ashamed of*, she'd said.

'You're right.' He paused, taking his glasses off to clean the lenses on the bottom of his striped shirt. 'Probably best she can't see me like this, though.'

At first, I wasn't sure what he meant but then I took a proper look at him. There were no real wrinkles, apart from embedded crows' feet, probably from being out in the sun too often. Other than his beard, which had spread across his whole face, masking the edges of his mouth, little about him had changed. Maybe that was the problem.

We were back in our snow globe, needing to be shaken up. Everything looked fine from the outside, *but one day, eventually, I'll break out. How will that change the picture inside?*

'Dad?'

'Yes, *bach*?'

'What does it mean if I can't hear Mam's voice anymore? Does it mean she's gone, for good?'

Dad was silent for a while. He didn't look at me, just straight past me as he put his glasses back on.

'No, *bach*,' he said. 'Think about it. She can't be here all the time, can she now? She's got things to do up there.' He pointed up at the ceiling and smiled. 'And, you know what? I can't hear her voice all the time, either, otherwise I'd never get a thought in edgeways!' He laughed to himself. 'As long as we remember her, Vila, and who she was, and believe she's around us, we can have a chat with her whenever and wherever we like.'

Not that I couldn't hear her anymore. It was just that with everything going on lately, she was sometimes harder to tap into, and the thought of being somewhere and suddenly unable to recall the soothe of her words terrified me.

But Dad always had a way of rooting me to the ground.

THEO

Older ballerinas drop like flies. In the past two years, our class had more than halved, leaving only eight of us girls behind, as well as one boy – Luc – who had recently joined from another dance school.

As I slid into the splits, Ms Madeline announced,

'Unfortunately, Marie won't be returning to dance.'

We all looked at each other with stunned eyes. Nobody knew the reason, and nobody asked. *When the world tries to tempt you towards other interests, only the truly committed make it...*

When I looked up again, I saw Ms Madeline peering back at us in the wall-mirrors. Maybe she hoped the girls trapped inside would find their way out. We were all arms and legs but no faces.

We rose to our feet – the girls in the mirror accompanying us – and spread ourselves out along the *barre*, leaving extra space in case anyone else returned. *Ballet's supposed to be our whole lives, isn't it?* But once again, the room took longer to warm up as another girl entered Absentia.

At first, I hadn't understood how someone could one week be dancing so happily across the room, a pink smile across her face as she tilted her head to the music, and the next, become entirely indifferent, their bedrooms carpeted in abandoned tulle. *Where do they all go? What else could they possibly be doing?*

Bobbie wasn't there either, and for the first time ever, I didn't dance very well. I began behind the music, counted for too long between steps, held positions for so long that I fell out of them, and forgot where to put my arms. My hands wanted to stay stitched like pockets to my sides, and when I told them to move, they found all the wrong places to go. Coppélia hadn't left me alone.

'Violet, you're all over the place!'

'Violet, what *is* the matter with you?'

'Violet, who *are* you, today?'

But the truth was, I didn't know. Maybe I'd become too sure of myself as Coppélia when I was going to need to be hundreds of other characters going forward. *And where on earth is Bobbie?* I kept dancing anyway, and as I did, I felt a tightening in my chest; it was making my posture all wrong. I tried standing up straight, but my ribs stuck out and my back was beginning to ache because it was arching too much, not in the usual, good way, and my feet flopped and sickled. I began to understand what it felt like to want to escape. *Is that how Bobbie feels?* As soon as the last piece of music ended, and the piano slammed shut, I was the first to run through the door, without looking Ms Madeline in the eye.

Outside, I met the breath of winter. There was no sign of Dad, so, cold or not, I decided to start walking. Dusk had managed to hide the world away and January brought me back to reality. As I walked home after class, I glimpsed light's efforts to break through, but it couldn't help but gradually surrender. Soon, there would be me, the road that led towards the ivory house, and nothing else at all.

I followed what I could see of the edge of the Common, and once again realised how enormous it truly was, and how I'd appear as a speck of dust to anyone who looked at it from afar. The Common always gave me chills that were neither good nor bad, but a feeling I hadn't quite worked out yet. The glowing windows of houses became just a twinkle as I made my way further across. I gripped my phone as the blink of its screen led the way.

The wind tried to push me back.

The trees that armed the Common were flailing like my arms had at dance class. *Violet, what are you doing?*

I let the light dim – just for a second. *How easy would it be to disappear into the darkness? Would anyone even notice?* I could hear my footsteps picking up the pace.

A loud car horn shook the thought out of my head and I quickly turned, having to shield my eyes from the beam of approaching headlights. A car was pulling up alongside me and it reminded me of the Mercedes Melody's Dad had years ago! Its window opened slightly.

'Are you alright?' said the voice of the driver.

It was so dark that I couldn't quite make out the face inside.

'Is that you, Coppélia?' The voice had pronounced it properly: *Co-pail-ia*.

As I squinted, I saw a man's arm beckoning me from my daze and I finally recognised the strong shape of the hand waving, *and that well-formed wrist...* I felt so glad to hear a tender voice. *I exist!* It was the gentleman in the green overcoat – from the arts centre, the one I'd assumed I'd never see again. *Maybe this kind man has come to rescue me,* I wondered, *from my deepest and darkest thoughts.*

'Is everything okay?' he asked, stretching over the passenger seat and squinting. 'Hope I didn't startle you. I just didn't expect to see you there; it wouldn't have been right for me not to stop.' Even in discomfort, he found a suitable smile. I could make out his smooth, inky hair now too, more ruffled than before. I was glad my long, messy fringe was still pinned back since ballet.

I shook my head and smiled back.

'You know, you really shouldn't be walking along here alone. The Common is way too dangerous for someone like you; there aren't even any lights on this road, any other car might not have seen you, and well, I dread to think…'

I immediately became aware of my own ridiculousness, standing there in ballet tights and a skirt at the side of a dark and dangerous road. I was glad he'd spotted me. It was funny how someone's words, at the right place, at the right time, could bring you down from *bourréeing* into an inexplicable space in the universe, from a very wrong place at a very wrong time, and remind you that you had good feet once, and you could land on them again, if you tried.

'Would you like a lift – if you're heading home?' He nodded in a way that said, *better had,* so I did the same. Then, he gave me a smile as if to say, *that's better, isn't it? Best be safe.* He – *what was his name again?* – had a way of putting me at ease. It wasn't the words, but the way he said them, so soothingly, and his eyes were so genuinely attentive and kind. It was also very cold outside.

'Well, jump in, Coppélia.'

I opened the door and gently slid onto the passenger seat. *I suppose it only takes one meeting for someone to transform from a stranger to a friend.*

The heat of the car calmed me down a bit too. Still, I'd never sat so close to a man before, other than Dad, and yet, there I was, with my pair of pale knees only inches away from this particularly striking man's hand as it clenched the gearstick. He wasn't dressed as formally as before. He looked much younger, in jeans and a thin maroon jumper, *maybe twenty-five or so.* A striped scarf sat beneath his fashionably stubbled chin while he spoke.

'Sorry, you know, I just realised, I didn't properly introduce myself the other day, did I?' he asked, looking back at the road as the car pulled away. 'I'm Theodore Gamble. Well, just plain Theo, in most cases.' And, rather in the way Mist explored new people, I traced my mind around the sound, *The-o-doooore,* mapped it in my mind and pressed it into a neat space, from which I'd be able to draw it out again. There was certainly nothing plain about him. I quickly – while he wasn't looking – used the edges of my index fingers to swipe away any mascara smudges from under my eyes. 'Well, you do have to direct me, you know,' he said, laughing as he tapped the wheel with both hands.

I laughed out of embarrassment. I'd forgotten he had absolutely no idea where I lived.

'Oh, it's not far at all,' I said. 'Just after the end of the Common.' I was surprised by how comfortably the words rolled out.

He drummed the wheel with his fingertips, perhaps due to nerves. *Deep down, are we the same people? Is he an older version of me?*

'As you start to bend right at the end, it's just on the left,' I said.

'Nooo problem at all,' he said, and as we carried on, I couldn't help but notice that the Common looked glad to be left behind. *Go on Violet*, it said, *you shouldn't be spending time here, he's right.*

Theo turned on some music, I imagine, to make me feel a little more comfortable. And there was Tchaikovsky! Yes, *The Nutcracker: Dance of the Reed Flutes.* We'd performed *The Nutcracker* before Christmas and Bobbie was a Hoop, so perfect with her jumpy eyebrows and round eyes. That ballet was the only thing about Christmas that had remained the same since Mam.

'I danced in *The Nutcracker* last year,' I said, again surprising myself. It was the most I'd spoken to a new person for a long time. 'I love Tchaikovsky.'

He sent me a smile. 'Well, in that case, I'll turn it up. What part did you play?' The music belted out of the speakers around us.

'A flower,' I heard myself shouting over the music. *'Waltz of the Flowers.'* His head tipped back as he laughed at me shouting, so I laughed too. This little car journey was like a breath I hadn't taken in years.

Every now and then, I caught a hint of aftershave, and it reminded me of home at Christmas years ago; *mulled wine, maybe?* In the darkness of the car, I closed my eyes, just for a second, and hearing the festive music, saw Mam stirring in the ingredients, waiting for the syrup, cloves, cinnamon, and orange slices to consummate as the sweet aroma rose from the pan and I was offered a drop to taste. When I opened my eyes again, I noticed Theo quickly looking away, and blowing a strand of hair away from his forehead, like a little boy trying to act natural. I quickly turned my head to the window and wondered what he thought of me.

'Well, Waltzing Flower, where now?' His voice was deep even when he shouted, and it made me feel safe.

I giggled again, 'Oh, it's fine to drop me here,' I said, pointing at Melody's house, just three houses up from mine.

'Here? You sure?' There were those kind eyes looking at me again, checking. Then he turned down the music.

'Yep!' There we were, just outside Melody's house, the light of another family shining through the window. *Why does my voice sound so annoyingly young?*

'Ah, I love this area. The houses really have that charm,' he said as I undid my seatbelt. 'I looked for one here myself a few years back. I live just the other side of the Common. Right, well, glad that saved you. No walking across there on your own again, alright? Wouldn't even do that myself!' I didn't know if I could look directly into his eyes again just yet; the empathy in them made me smile too much. He didn't realise I'd walked that way for years, even if it was usually in the daylight…

'Okay, thanks so much!' I nodded. *Wow. He's driven in a direction he hadn't needed to, just for me…* I jumped out of the warmth of the car. I waved him off and then ran towards my ivory house where Mam's gold Christmas lights still glowed in the dark, years since she'd placed them there.

Back home, something felt different: I couldn't put my finger on it. It was as though our ivory house knew something, just by the way it ushered me inside and reminded me of how welcoming its rooms were, the softness of the carpet, the warmth of every radiator, the smell of the walls that kept me and Dad safe. *You can trust me,* it was saying, as I walked into the living room and saw the mouth of the fireplace wide open with shock and asking, *Violet, where have you been?* I felt myself blushing.

Dad was slumped at the kitchen table, which was scattered with paperwork. His large eyes looked poppy and exhausted behind his glasses while he sifted through the accounts. He was unknowingly creating enough silence for me to say all about my evening, and the house was goading me to say it, too, but the very same feeling stopped me.

Should I mention the music in the car, or how Theo's smile made me feel like a dizzy princess? All I really needed to say to Dad was that a kind man gave me a lift home, and Dad could say, *well, that was good of him, wasn't it?* Or, would he have said, *you should never get in a car with a stranger?* The thing was, I'd never mentioned Coppélia's previous meeting with Theo, at the arts centre, so it would have seemed strange to mention a second one.

I realised, that with all the silence between us, there must have been just as much that Dad wasn't telling me, that he must have experienced hours of those sorts of thoughts all day, just as everyone does, and he hadn't cared to relay even a fragment. *What's he done this evening? Where's he been? Who's he spoken to?* He would have probably answered me if I'd asked the right questions; only, I wasn't sure which questions to ask.

Instead, we both sat inside our different worlds. That's what made me decide to whisper, allow my words to shoot through the air and loosen our gravitational pull, just for a moment.

'Dad?'

'Yes love?' He was still looking down.

'I danced badly tonight.'

There it was, some of it at least. Out there. I'd needed to tell someone.

'Oh,' Dad said, and there was the surprise on his face that I needed to see; there was the depth in our atmospheres. 'Well, you couldn't help it, Vila *bach*. Everyone does things badly every now and then.' He said it as though he frequently fell from his *pirouettes*, 'we can't always be perfect. Look at my bees. I must've done something wrong,' he huffed, 'I kept checking the hive was up-to-scratch but perhaps that was the problem, I was fussing over them too much. They just packed their bags and left.'

It was true. Not everyone stayed at Secret Haven like us, and we didn't always know why.

'Oh,' Dad added, glancing at the window, 'it's really dark, Vila. Did Bobbie's mam give you a lift back in the end? Sorry, I should have thought, but then I assumed she would…'

'That's okay,' I said, 'Yeah, she did.' Dad seemed quite upset remembering how the bees had disappeared. It would have been wrong to give him more stress.

Mist followed me back to my room and we both curled up on my bed. I opened my laptop, logged into my socials and typed 'Theodore Gamble' into the search bar of each. I was looking for a photo, something, but nothing popped up. I supposed social media wasn't his thing. *What is it that he does for a living, anyway? It has to be something artistic.* I hoped I'd get to see him again. Mist jumped straight onto the laptop, and we were both comforted by the warmth. I plugged in my headphones and YouTubed *Waltz of the Flowers* to be my new night-time listen.

BEHIND CLOSED DOORS

On Saturday morning, I heard Dad's van leaving early and I wished I was still a lark, like him. Lately, my body seemed to grow through the night until it was too heavy to lift, and even when I tried to open my eyes, my bedroom felt journeys away. Still, an aching body was good; Ms Madeline always said *too much comfort means you haven't tried hard enough*.

When the afternoon finally greeted me, I was on the opposite end of time. Beyond my window, winter was still stalking me. Bony trees stood to attention, all raised in *relevé* as the wind swept the chorus line back and forth. And then, without warning, stillness.

The doorway to my dance room had lately – at the very time I most needed it – been filled with large boxes of miscellaneous things: batteries, old wires bent into unfathomable shapes, hats forgotten by heads, and an old telephone without its handset. I stacked them up, box by box, then slid them tightly against the wall on the landing. I had no idea what Dad's plan with anything was. Dusty Ana had even ended up in there, God knows how, so I rescued her and placed her back on the wicker chair in my bedroom, not that she ever displayed even a wink of gratitude.

I *chasséd* dust in thin lines along the floorboards with my bare feet, and I opened my eyes to the dolls' house, which was where it always had been, four storeys too fragile to be moved.

I remembered how each new person and piece had been a reward from Mam, for passing an exam, or finally managing to do the splits; for being good. And yet, there it was after all this time, another world, stopped in motion, the music prematurely ended; the women's arms mid-applause and some of their mouths wide open as if caught in conversation.

I hadn't bought a new piece since Mam had gone; it's difficult to reward yourself. Other than the attic, I hadn't even checked in and seen how things were with the family. *You never know what goes on behind closed doors,* Mam had said. Well, perhaps I preferred not knowing.

When I heard the staccato knock upon our front door, I immediately knew who it was. Dad shouted, 'I think Bobbie's here,' and I had no time to take my *pointe* shoes off before I ran downstairs, toes outwards. She couldn't start chatting to Dad! It would have been too much for him.

'I *missed* you,' she exclaimed, before I'd fully opened the door and Dad was backing out of the hallway. 'Wowsers, do I need to chop that fringe of yours or what?' There was Bobbie, much taller than usual, and dressed to the nines, her hair a halo of auburn, and her eyes shadowed with smoky turquoise.

'Bob, you're the one who hasn't been turning up at ballet… Where've you been? Ms Madeline…' I thought I saw her sliding one of our shop's beeswax and honey lip balms into her pocket, but I couldn't be sure enough to ask.

'Don't tell me you've been bloody practising again! Oh you *do* need to chill out!'

I could say the same thing about you, I wanted to say, but I didn't. I was surprised I even recognised her.

'Right! You're coming out with me,' she said, pushing past

me in the hallway, so I was left to shut the door behind her. She kicked her stilettos off and stomped upstairs lugging a black bag of what I could assume was another heap of her usually brand-new hand-me-downs, so I had no choice but to follow.

Seeing the light on in the dance room, and the door open, she ran in and stopped, directly in front of the doll's house. She stared, leaning forward as one of her hands reached out. I quickly jumped in front of it, facing her, and feeling the house tremble behind me.

'I'm only kidding. Don't you think I remember what *happened* years ago? I wouldn't do that to you again, Vi. Chill.' Bobbie sighed.

'Had a lot of time on your hands, have you?' she asked, looking around and noticing the old ballet CDs strewn across the floor. I shrugged, embarrassed. 'Yeah, I can tell,' Bobbie added, and I hated the approach she was taking, as though I was the one who needed help, as though *I* was the one seeing this boy after that one, then drinking it all away and vomiting it all back up just because I didn't go to school anymore. *Some gap year.*

Yes, that was her, the one marching us to my room like an older sister or a fussy aunt performing an intervention to get me out more. She was always telling me that. She tore various old clothes from my wardrobe, threw them onto my bed and then pulled a few faces before shortly returning them all. 'I'm not taking any of this crap,' said her stony expression. What she actually said wasn't that much different. 'Just get out of your fairy princess outfit, will you?'

I looked down at my clothes, realising how they must look, and I did as she said.

Bobbie pointed at Ana, sitting on her wicker chair.

'And by the way,' she said, 'hanging out with that misery guts isn't doing you any good.'

We looked at each other and burst out laughing. Then she opened the big black bag.

We left the house, both of us embellished in sequins, and my face, framed by a heavily lacquered and apparently 'retro' fringe that sat high and mighty above my eyebrows. Mam's red heels – the only heels she'd had – hugged my feet, finally free of their box at the bottom of the wardrobe. They'd been intended for something special, not for Bobbie's type of night out, but Bobbie had been adamant their square toes worked perfectly with the black and white check skirt she'd yanked in at my waist – not to mention the thick, red headband. *Timeless,* she'd said, fluttering her falsies as she strutted out in some kind of cobalt-blue kimono – but she carried it off. With that height, Bobbie could carry anything off.

I pronged my way through the gravel to tell Dad where we were going, but I could hear he was deep in conversation with someone at the barn shop.

'Oh, leave him to it. Don't want to interrupt, do we?' Bobbie insisted.

I waved to Dad and as he waved back, Bobbie grabbed my elbow and dragged me away. We trekked up past Melody's house, towards the village shop and within ten minutes, we were on a bus to the town centre.

I followed Bobbie as she strutted down the road and entered a lively little bar on the corner, with low ceiling-lamps, shabbily painted floorboards and a folk band tuning their instruments. She ordered us four fluorescent shots of some sour concoction – *each* – and then we moved on. She paid. It was the same at every bar, and since I'd never been out before, not properly, I let Bobbie play her game: she ordered, handed over the cash and we both drank until we were actually having fun, the town only tilting slightly as our heels wobbled upon it. Bobbie spat stories into my ear about everything she'd been up to lately; she'd been working extra hours, getting extra money and spending it all on nights out.

Our walk from venue to venue blurred with our dancing. Movement became our habit; everything was mercurial: the lights, the spilt drink on the shiny bar surfaces, from people's sweaty foreheads to the sticky floors we tripped on. The chaos made us feel like anything could happen; anything!

It was such a different sort of dancing to usual too. It seemed so animalistic at the time – so out of control, and I was always so used to being *in* control! Our bodies spun around each other, in this circle and that circle of people, arms gesticulating, heads swaying, hips twisting, all of us just letting loose, whoever we were, whether we were just stepping side-to-side or properly going for it. Bobbie's whole face lit up like Christmas when her favourite song came on, and when she started jumping to the chorus, everyone on the dance floor seemed to join in, with their arms around each other's shoulders or one hand in the air. I couldn't remember the last time I'd danced so ... impulsively. It felt good to be free of myself, somehow.

Then a boy wedged his way between me and Bobbie, so he could dance with only her while she was mid-lyric. And she obviously kept singing, not stopping him. Of course she could do both!

So, *no problem,* I just kept on dancing and dancing and dancing, breathing in the throat-burning aroma of Jack Daniel's, Captain Morgan – and mixing in all kinds of fruity daiquiris until someone nudged me with a big elbow that dug right into my side.

As I looked up, there was a bald man with a serpent tattoo around his neck and a nineties ring in his eyebrow – and he was looking straight down at me.

'Cheer up! It might never happen,' he said, drawing a finger either side of his mocking smile that reminded me of a shark's open jaw. I'd thought I was enjoying myself. *Didn't you see me dancing?* I wanted to ask. *Didn't you see me singing and laughing?* But it was no good. A switch had flicked inside my head that meant my whole image of the past few hours had collapsed around me. Instead, I just wanted to be swallowed and not even chewed on the way down. The man stopped looking at me, he was already walking away, and I suddenly realised how dark it was in the club. I noticed the grotty floor in the few flickers of light that popped right through us all, one mass of flesh – animals indeed. I also noticed how Bobbie had completely abandoned me, to continue dancing with someone she'd probably never see again. *How long has she even been gone for?*

How could I have been so convinced that I was enjoying myself? Theo wouldn't be seen dead in a place like this; he's far too sophisticated. What does that make me? I decided to check the toilets for Bobbie but there was no sign of her feet under any of the cubicle doors and she wasn't preening at the mirror either. Instead, in a cubicle that wouldn't lock properly, I crouched down, with my back closing the door behind me and I shut everything out.

All the spirits in me had changed from high to low and my sight was beginning to blur; my hearing too, as I cried as much as I wanted to. I'd lost control, alright. *Nobody outside knows. Nobody outside cares.* I wasn't sure where it was coming from, but I cried and cried and cried into my hands, burying my soggy face in my knees. I wasn't going anywhere, not like that. So, I closed my eyes and rocked back and forth.

I'd become no better than Ana, and someone was banging my back as though I was choking.

I woke up to what was actually someone knocking on the cubicle door behind me, but it wasn't Bobbie. *Where is she?* It was a man and he sounded angry. I scrambled up to open the door and felt the sting of those stilettos on my feet.

All the men in that place had the same bulldog faces that folded inwards. It must have been written on the job description.

'We closed half hour ago,' he said. 'You'd better get yourself sorted out – then leave.'

I wondered what it was that was suddenly allowing people to talk to me in that way. I was just me, just Violet. I wanted to cry again but I was too embarrassed, so I hid my eyes and walked as fast as my aching toes would allow.

As I entered the open air, it hit me; the solid but invisible wall I'd heard people boast about at school. My body wobbled as though boneless until I almost fell. Instead, I bent over, feet wide apart, and found my balance beneath the dirty, moonlit sky. I didn't like the feeling of yesterday blending into today. It felt like I was blending into a person I didn't recognise.

There weren't any buses so early in the morning, so I also had no idea what to do.

'Taxis that way, love,' a man shouted to me as he shut the doors to the club.

I wasn't supposed to have been there that long and I'd been told not to take taxis alone, but it was either that or walking all the way home in such a state.

The streetlights made my eyes squint, and my head hurt as I walked through the stubborn air. Regardless of all the fizzy liquid in my stomach, I was hollow like a Russian doll; I needed to fill my stomach with something. I was desperate to. I was also beginning to feel like Bobbie, and I wasn't used to it. *How does she manage to do this so often?* Bobbie shook her world upside down all the time, but I wasn't sure I could deal with the consequences.

There was no queue at the taxi rank, so I jumped straight into the back of the first one I saw. I clutched the door handle for dear life, just hoping to get home. I wished I was in Theo's car instead, safe upon the heated leather passenger seat. *Will I ever see him again?*

Home safe, as the taxi pulled away, I had a horrible feeling. I crossed my fingers in the hope that Dad had already gone to work. He was usually up early checking the greenhouses and stocking the barn shop for the day. The face of the kitchen clock said quarter to five in the morning. There on the sill, were a dozen jam jars that I was supposed to use for our homemade candles, ready for the shop Monday morning, but time seemed to have slipped away from me over the past twenty-four hours. My skin felt waxy, and I wished it would make me invisible too. *Seriously, how do people do this every week?* When I kicked my shoes off, one rolled off the mat and onto a kitchen tile. That's when I heard a cough in the living room.

As I crept in, there was Dad, lying on the sofa with his arm hanging over the side. His eyes were still closed, so I began to tiptoe past him to go upstairs. Another cough.

'I can hear you, young lady.' He sat up. 'Where on earth have you been?' He scratched his heap of messy hair.

I didn't know altogether.

'Is Bobbie home now too?' He was frowning at me.

Oh my god. 'I don't know,' I said, again remembering that I'd last seen her on the dance floor.

'Well.' He sat up, his eyes blinking again as fast as they could. When I saw how red and watery they were, I began to feel sick. 'You need to check on her right now, then get yourself to bed. We'll talk about this later. I was searching the streets for you, you know. The streets, Violet! I didn't think you were this type of girl!'

'Okay.' I found my head dropping down like Mist's when I told her off.

'Violet? Are you listening?' he asked, more sternly than I'd heard for a while – or ever.

'Yes!' I said, 'I am! Alright?'

I was angry, but I didn't really know why. I felt guilty already. And then, I felt scared. I looked behind me and saw Dad's face was still there, more tired and bedraggled than ever. I couldn't remember when I'd last seen him looking that bad.

'I'm sorry.' I looked away from him again, not moving.

'Please, Violet, not again,' he said, with the same tired face.

'Never,' I whispered, beginning to walk upstairs.

It didn't sound like our narrative, not one bit.

As I crawled into bed, I felt like an impostor, a lodger in my own home, a dirty face on a too-clean pillow. I knew I needed to check on Bobbie and I should have earlier on, but I wasn't sure why I didn't. I didn't want to be mean, but it had felt as though, during the night, nothing at all mattered. At some point on that dance floor, I'd become just a 'thing' in the large world I hadn't had to consider before. I'd felt no different to one of the sticky tables in the night club, or a beer mat, or an empty glass. It was just a night out, one of hundreds and thousands happening at the same time, growing out of control, just as they were supposed to. But it had struck me, the question, *what is the point?* And looking around me, I had no one to ask.

Hitting the mattress, I felt like a boat in water, only, the boat was dead still and the water was swooshing around me as I tried to steer. I unzipped my handbag and switched on my phone.

Seven text messages from Bobbie and eleven missed calls from Dad.

Bobbie's were all the same:

Hey Vi, sorry 'bout earlier, didn't mean to leave you.
So drunk and boy so fit.

Vi, where are you? Hope you got home okay x

Vi – answer me!

For God's sake, Vi, I said sorry – I'm home myself now!
Tell me you aren't dead.

How did Bobbie manage to make it sound like it was all about her?

Maybe it was, maybe I'd got it all wrong.

Even though I'd done almost the same as she had, I couldn't believe she'd consciously left without me. Saying that, I wasn't sure how conscious she would have been…

Vi, pleaaaaaaase! Answer!

And then there was Dad's answerphone message.

'Vila *bach*, where are you? It's gone half one – hope you're alright – starting to get worried now – oh – and – we lost our last hen, Sally, bless 'er – love you – uh – let me know.'

And hearing the panic flutter in his voice, hearing him say he loved me, made his face come to mind again. I heard the back door shut. Dad had gone to work completely exhausted, and I wanted to tell him I loved him back, that I'd never intended to give him a fright like that. *What if something had happened and I never got to tell him?*

I began to cry again, so much that I couldn't help but be loud. I shocked myself with how much I needed to pour out. Soon, my whimpering went on helplessly for what felt like hours, my body spasming as I bit my bottom lip, tugged on my hair and the bedsheets. My body curled into a ball, trying to stifle its noise, but the cries were still so loud above the duvet that they sounded like they belonged to someone else, maybe Ana, her sobs spiralling adrift and then throwing themselves up against me.

I didn't text Bobbie back. I couldn't. She wouldn't have understood such strangeness. *How could she?* I hadn't known there was so much to be sad about, so much in the world that was outside ballet; so much between me and Dad. The final wave swept right over me, capsizing my body and sending it sailing to a place not a soul had visited, me included.

I'll never be good enough, not for someone like Theo.

THE DETOUR

Luc, the new boy at ballet, gave me a nod before stepping away from the *barre* and walking to the opposite corner of the room. I took the opportunity to watch him while his back was turned. He was tall, but not too tall, and especially triangular from shoulders to waist. I couldn't help but notice the rise of his calf muscles as he walked. He was strong, and he walked in a strict, straight line, as though the tiniest tilt of his head could cause him to tumble from a tightrope.

I watched him change his white ballet shoes into a pair of pure white trainers, slide on a pair of loose jogging bottoms and throw a blue sweater over his ash blonde head, which was so fluffy that it reminded me of the chicks we always had on the farm. He looked clean and well put together. He took things seriously. I needed to be like him.

'Wow. An absolute beaut', right? I heard he's French.' Bobbie was obstructing my view with her mouth wide open, her eyes even wider.

I rolled mine.

'*What?* Are your rolly eyes blind? It's not every day you see a fine figure of a man doing ballet. Plus, he's a real good egg, hey, perfect for someone like you, Vi.' She nudged me and I rolled my eyes again. This was typical of us. *Someone like me… What an assumption to make. Besides, I'm sure Dad doesn't think so well of me right now.* Anyway, I'd always said I wouldn't let boys get in the way of ballet. She knew that. *Theo would be different, though. He's an experienced man.*

'Violet, come here a moment, please.'

Bobbie rolled her eyes this time, placing her hands on her hips as I ran over to Ms Madeline, who had sat down to lace up one of her shoes. Her hair was pulled back extra tight and revealing more grey around the parting.

'Have you started choreographing your audition piece yet?' Even the faint lines in her forehead and the elevens between her eyebrows looked smooth.

'Not yet, Ms Madeline,' I said, already panicking that I'd left it too late. 'Sorry, I…'

'Don't worry, Violet, but you mustn't leave this audition any later, okay? We ought to be working on it just in case the uni gets in touch with you. We'll book some extra time in for us to work on it together.'

She didn't give me a chance to interrupt and say that I'd been thinking about it a lot.

'You don't want to miss a good opportunity, do you darling?'

I shook my head. 'Definitely not, Ms Madeline,' I said.

Bobbie had crossed the room and was asking Luc question after question, so he couldn't leave.

'I couldn't want anything more than this.'

'I know, dear. I know. Just remember, put your *all* into it. Be fearless! That's what I'd like to think I teach you all the most.' She drew a fist to her chest and then rested the same hand on my shoulder; she spared one of her rationed smiles just for this inspirational moment; my mentor permitting me to depart.

Bobbie had already disappeared by the time I got to the foyer, and Luc must have gone around the same time. It didn't surprise me that she was already making a move. Bobbie couldn't leave anything alone. I needed to get home anyway. I didn't want Dad watching the clock again. So, I knew I had better start running if I was to avoid questions. I knew I should probably just text Dad, but I didn't want him to start picking me up from class all the time just because Bobbie was more unpredictable lately. I didn't want him to *always* be around, you know? So, I ran out of class, out of the building and into the dark. That was the downside of being independent, but the nights would hopefully start to draw out soon, and then, well, no questions asked.

'Hey you, what did I tell you about walking alone?'

Just as I was at the end of the road outside ballet, Theo, as if by magic, was driving by in his Benz. His window was down and he was smiling beneath a grey, cable-knit beanie, which accentuated his eyebrows and made him look even younger than before. I felt bad for promising I wouldn't walk like that again. I just hadn't wanted to bother Dad for a lift!

'Sorry,' I said, pausing for a breath.

'Well, don't be sorry,' he laughed, 'just get in, so you're safe and warm, miss. Don't you ever get a lift? I'm sure your parents wouldn't want you walking like this, right?'

'No, they wouldn't,' I said as I found myself climbing in – conversation already ran so smoothly with him. *Dad would be glad about me getting home safely; he'd prefer it to me walking across the Common.* 'I mean, Mam wouldn't have wanted me to, and Dad doesn't mean to. It's just that he gets busy and forgets the time, especially since Mam died. He does worry, though. I don't want to worry him.' *Whoa. Why did I just say all that? Violet, since when did you become such an oversharer?*

'So sorry to hear that. About your mum, I mean. I lost my Dad years ago, too. It's not easy, is it?'

'No,' I sighed, 'definitely not.' Theo and I really did seem like the same person.

'Oh, I hope you don't mind,' Theo said as we approached the Common, 'I just have to pick something up from the house *very* quickly. Won't be long.'

'No, that's fine,' I whispered, wondering what it was that he needed. A second later, I realised that it did happen to matter on this occasion. I needed to get home, or Dad *would* worry and that would defeat the whole point of me having a lift to begin with. I felt nervous but I couldn't share my panic because Theo would think I was such an immature girl, having to get home by a certain time because her Daddy said so. *Only children have curfews.*

Theo drove us along a sweet and well-lit street of bungalows that I found odd I hadn't seen close-up before since they were only the other side of the Common! I suppose I'd hemmed myself in since the beginning at Secret Haven. To think that those houses – that Theo – may have been there the whole time I was dancing away with Melody… Then again, he probably hadn't lived there all his life.

The bungalow we stopped outside looked fairly new, with stones that reminded me of a tortoise shell, and an asymmetrical roof.

'Won't be a sec.' Theo left the car and I was finally given the opportunity to examine him as he walked towards the front door. He was tall – just as I'd remembered – and slim but also robust, *athletic*, and the way he held himself; his neck and back perfectly aligned in a khaki jacket, and his frame so well-balanced, was kind of like a hiker... I imagined him with two trekking poles, a long backpack and boots laced high above the ankles that gripped curiously onto the earth.

Within seconds, I saw the door open again. Theo tapped the side pocket of his unyielding jeans and smiled before walking towards the car. As he sat alongside me, I could smell that aftershave whispering up my nose.

'Sorry I didn't invite you in just then, by the way,' he said, 'I don't want you to think I was being rude or anything, I just didn't want to make you uncomfortable, you know? And I knew I was going to be so quick, there was hardly any point...'

I should have known he'd be so considerate. *There he was*, I sighed, *just thinking of me*.

'Anyway, I was thinking,' he cleared his throat, 'again, I'd *hate* to make you feel uncomfortable in any capacity, but...' as we approached the Common again, he said, 'I'm usually around your ballet school *area* on Wednesdays anyway, so I may as well give you a lift whenever we're both there? You don't have to worry about bothering your Dad then, and you definitely won't be bothering me. I'll just be doing a favour as I pass. You can even come in for a cup of tea at mine next time if you like?'

We were reaching Melody's house and the seconds seems to be passing very quickly.

'No pressure or anything, and no worries if not, I just thought it might be nice. Always good to have a friend with similar interests, isn't it?'

It was safe to say, Theo had caught me completely off guard. Yes, I was glad he hadn't invited me in. *Next week, though… Why not?* Like he'd said, it was only a cup of tea. *I would actually love to.* I hadn't visited anyone 'for tea' since I was little. Also, it might have been just what I needed; to calm down, to let my mind relax before I refocused on my audition piece. Besides, Theo was all about ballet, so it wasn't off topic.

'Sound good?' he asked, smiling. How could I resist those warm, caramel eyes? He had chosen to pluck *me* from *Waltz of the Flowers.*

'Oh, I almost forgot,' Theo said, as he struggled to pull something from his side pocket, 'silly me, eh?' He threw something into my lap, and it fell down the side by the passenger door.

I picked it up. *A ball of wool? No…* I opened it. *A pair of gloves!*

'They're my sister's. She left them at the house. I'm sure she won't mind,' Theo explained, 'she has loads.' There was that adorable smile again.

I opened the fingers and saw that they were stripy and fruit-pastel coloured!

'Thought they'd be 'handy' while you appear to be so *determined* to brave the elements.'

He gave me a cheeky grin, raising one of his eyebrows. *Oh, Theo.*

'Oh my gosh. Thank you,' I said to him, looking right up at those eyes without any fear for the first time. I nestled each hand inside its new home and stretched my rainbowed digits out in front of me. They were so bright, so cosy, so *needed.*

'Life's about the simple things sometimes, right?' he said, reading my mind again.

'Definitely. Thanks so much. You're so thoughtful.'

His gloved hand held mine for a single second before it moved back to the gearstick.

Perhaps I'll prepare Dad that I'll be coming home a little later next week because of extra pointe work? Yes, for someone like Theo, perhaps that would be okay.

ON THE SAME PAGE

I was a nervous wreck at school. I just kept thinking of the visit to Theo's place. I kept wondering, *what will it be like inside? Will it be cosy and quaint? Or, sophisticated, full of his intellectual charm? Where will I sit? How should I sit? Is it really going to happen?* Theo had played it all down as something casual, but the truth was, I'd never been to a boy's house before – except Frederick's, only once – definitely not a *man's* house, and definitely not on my own, so I didn't know what to expect or what was expected of me. I wondered how Mam and Dad had met, where they went on a first date; not that I could ask Dad, he'd only wonder why I was suddenly interested. So, I found myself googling *What do you do on a first date?*

Seeing the search results pop up, I clicked on the top one and then clicked straight off it.

What on earth am I doing? I rested my head in my hands. *It's only a cup of tea…*

I tried to tell myself the nerves were excitement, just like those sickly ones before ballet exams, but by the time Wednesday came around, I wasn't so sure.

At first, I thought Theo hadn't turned up, but then I spotted his car parked at the end of the road. *Is he definitely waiting for me? How can I be sure? I haven't heard from him since last week.*

As I walked closer, I decided I could easily pass by if I needed to… I slowed down my pace, took my phone out of my pocket and began drafting an aimless text, just so I could look casual, preoccupied:

Hey Bob 😊
How's things? Haven't seen you for aaaages

When I looked back up, Theo's headlights flashed, *thank God for that,* and I felt myself smiling. I quickly jumped in alongside him.

For the first minute, I talked very little. I hadn't meant to be silent but the butterflies in my stomach had turned into sinking slugs thanks to all the anticipation. I hoped I wouldn't be sick.

'I've been so looking forward to this,' Theo said, pretending not to sense my nerves. He seemed happy to do the chatting for a while, and I was happy to listen while he told me he'd spent hours on the train that day and had come straight from the station to see me. *Wow.* With that, I relaxed into conversation, just like before.

The cul de sac felt familiar this time. I recognised the artful shape of each garden, the wholesome little green in the centre, and the cars parked on each driveway. There was Theo's place, with a few large plant pots placed outside the main window.

Theo pressed his hand very gently against my back.

'Ballerinas first.'

I felt my entire body tingle. It was overwhelming, tiptoeing over someone's threshold; you never know what unusual rituals you could be upsetting from your first step.

Theo stood behind me with arms ajar, ready for me to remove Mam's coat. So nerve-racking, I wasn't sure why, but I was eased by the way he so gently rested it over one elbow before hanging it so delicately on the coat hook next to his, as though it could breathe. It didn't smell of her these days, but over time, it had grown even softer than I remembered.

'Oh! Don't worry,' he said, seeing me slip off my shoes to join the polished wooden floor, 'you stay just as you are. Then again,' he paused, 'I imagine ballerinas' feet need to escape the restrictions of shoes as often as possible, am I right?'

I laughed in agreement while he clicked the door shut. I'd pinched a black Bardot top from Bobbie's most recent bag of goodies, so 'as I was' had at least involved more effort than usual when leaving class. At the same time, I suddenly felt a bit embarrassed letting my shoulders and leotard straps peek out when it was still so cold outside.

'Well,' he chuckled, 'I'd give you the grand tour, but as you can see, it's not the largest of homes. Still, it's got everything I need.' He stepped back with his hands in his pockets and cast his eye over the place as though he was putting himself in my shoes.

It was quite different to what I'd expected and much smaller than my house. Apart from what looked like a cosy room through the two sliding doors on the right, the rest was quite open plan; a living room with an olive-green feature wall and a large, maroon rug framed by two brown chesterfield sofas, rolling into a dining area, rolling into a kitchen, which had large French doors that led to the patio, where I could see a rusted white bistro table and chairs for two, more neglected than everything inside.

'Sorry,' Theo said, grabbing a few bulky books from the mosaic coffee table, 'I'll move these out of the way; just some reading. Most of the time, I work from home, freelancing here and there, you know how it is.'

I nodded, but his house looked so tidy compared to ours.

'I've got a few projects in the pipeline at the moment,' Theo sighed, 'so there's a lot of research involved.'

I felt self-conscious, exploring Theo's space while he watched. Everything seemed well placed, including a typewriter, which sat proudly on a small, wooden desk in the corner. A tall, peacock-backed chair filled the area by the main window, and a ceiling-high bookcase displayed its knowledge, leaving room for the odd leafy plant. There was proper wood flooring, the old stuff, a little scratched but polished. A closed piano sat against the wall near the dining area and a set of kitchen bar stools lined their granite island.

There were a few doors shut, and I could only assume that one of them was his bedroom... I began to question my home, with every corner and cupboard cluttered with long-forgotten items, but he didn't have to know about that. Anyway, Dad had recently been trying to sort things out.

'Would you like a drink?' Theo asked. 'Tea? Coffee? Water? Or, I have some elderflower cordial?'

'Oh, I love elderflower at home, so if that's okay...'

'Course it's okay or I wouldn't have asked.' He gave me a cheeky smile again. So down to earth.

He didn't only return with drinks, though. He was holding a little tray of two glasses and a platter of snacks: brie, cheddar, crackers, olives, bread and balsamic vinegar.

'Just a little something for us to share,' he smiled.

My stomach suddenly felt quite hungry after dance.

Theo leaned his long body forward, pulled the coffee table into the centre of the room and sat cross-legged on the floor to one side of it. He started to dig in, using a napkin to wipe his mouth and fingertips between bites. I remembered how much I loved seeing people enjoy their food. Frederick used to be the best for that.

'Aren't you gonna join me? Must be hungry after all that dance, right?' He pulled a cushion from the peacock chair and slid it along the floor for me to sit opposite him.

This is more perfect than I could have imagined. What on earth had I been panicking about? It was one of those moments you had to take a step back from and think, 'Is this really happening? Is this really happening to *me?*' I couldn't have pictured any of it an hour before.

'I can never get enough of nibbles. Can you?' He looked so endearing as he chewed, and so relaxed that it relaxed me too. 'Couldn't stop eating when I was in Italy,' he said. 'Everywhere I went, I was ordering a little dish of something.'

'You've been to Italy?' I asked. I would have loved to go, and Paris one day. Mam and Dad had been to Paris once.

'Oh, a billion times. You name one of those Italian cities and I've been there.'

That explained the bookshelf full of travel guides. I bet he could speak a few languages too. I felt self-conscious again because I'd only ever travelled from the ivory house, to school, ballet, town and back. That was my world. *How small of me, how ridiculous.*

'So, I've got to ask, what is it you love most about ballet?' He made sure to look up at me as he popped an olive into his mouth.

It was a big question, and I hadn't been asked it before.

'Ah, I completely understand if it's something too difficult to articulate,' he said.

I was worried I'd let loose one of my involuntary facial expressions. 'I can try...' I said, picking up a cracker with a slice of cheese. 'I guess, it expects everything and nothing from me all at the same time. It makes me feel in control and it makes me feel like anything is possible, y'know?'

He nodded, raising both eyebrows. 'Go on!'

'Well, I guess I love how I can be absolutely anything. Like reading a fairy tale and falling into the story. More than that, I *become* the story; sometimes, so much that I forget how to come out. It's addictive, you know? Yeah, maybe I'm addicted to ballet,' I laughed, 'it's my one dream, to be honest, to be a ballerina.'

'Ah, I see, but surely you already are one, aren't you? Don't you have other dreams too?'

'Not a proper ballerina. I guess I'm an amateur. I haven't reached my full potential yet.'

'Ah,' he said again as his chin lifted so he could assess me better.

'I mean, I do kind of well, I suppose, but I have a lot *more* I can do and be.'

'Definitely. I'm sure you do.' He gave a little smirk as he handed me another cracker, with a mixture of everything on it. 'Sure, it's important to remember that we're all at our best when we're multifaceted, right? That's humans for you.'

'Yeah, I guess. That's another thing. Whenever I'm sad, frustrated, angry or just completely happy,' I smiled at him, 'dance is the thing I can depend on the most. I suppose I *speak* through dance. I've done it for so long that I *am* dance. If dance was taken away from me, I'd be nothing.'

I was shocked by everything I was spouting. Theo seemed to do that to me, draw out my story without me realising I was telling it!

'Ah, Coppélia,' Theo's eyes lit up, 'I love hearing people talk about their passions. Don't you? It's when people are their most authentic. By the way, you seem to speak just fine with your voice too you know.'

I loved how he called me Coppélia. It gave me an unexpected buzz all over every time. *Why is that?*

'I mean, as you've probably guessed,'

I laughed in readiness.

'I'm in complete *awe* of what you ballet dancers do, which is why I spend half my *life* at the arts centre – or theatre, just as a spectator… You really push your bodies past the limits and that's what fascinates me most; the fact your minds *allow* you to do that.'

He moved his arms a lot when he spoke and pushed his neck forward when he did it. He was adorable to look at in animation.

'You are *literally* unbelievable, but Coppélia, I don't even know you and I one *hundred* per cent believe in you. Besides, I can always hook you up with a few of the theatre folk if you want to make sure your talent is appreciated more widely than myself and Margaret Madeline.'

Well, he must be okay if he knows Ms Madeline. She doesn't flippantly choose her company…

'A nudge in the right direction couldn't hurt anyone, right?'

I suppose that was the moment Theo truly made my heart *fondu* and I knew there was no going back…

Not everyone had the compassion that he did, and nobody understood me in that way, not anymore. Before, I hadn't cared if anyone believed in me other than Ms Madeline, but now, just knowing how it felt when someone else did, well, it made me feel invincible!

I was finally able to tell someone all the things I'd never told Dad. I heard myself speaking so loquaciously, and caught a glimpse of myself laughing in the black screen of the TV behind Theo. I began to feel more like Bobbie, talking more than *ever,* and a lot of it was about me! *What a luxurious mistake to be making.* He was so considerate, not even saying that much about himself, but just sitting there listening to *me!* *Why me?* And then I realised, it didn't matter. What stuck with me was the way he listened, how his head tilted to one side, making my heart swell up like a balloon.

'All that must have been difficult for you,' he said, 'when you were only nine. It happened to me when I was eighteen and that was difficult enough.' We shared a glance across the table, and I suddenly wanted to hold his hand. There, magically in my mind, he rested his palm on top of mine; didn't hold it, just rested it, for longer than he had before. *Did that really happen?* My heart did a *contretemps* inside my chest because I knew, if I wasn't careful, I could lose myself in seconds.

'You do have such a lovely voice. It's so sweet to listen to, you know how some voices are just naturally soothing? Yours is one of those, so gentle, and the way you word things, so articulate – and insightful.'

Nobody had ever said anything like that before. *Then again, not many people have heard me speak much in the last few years. Dad has quite a soothing voice when he speaks.*

'Well, I have to say, this evening was bloody delightful,' he smiled, and I couldn't help but laugh.

'You've been fantastic company and I just hope you join me again some time.'

I looked up at the iron clock to see that it was already half past eight. It was a shame it was already time to go home, and there I'd been, blabbering on about myself.

'Yes please,' I said, then covering my mouth, realising I hadn't hidden my excitement one bit. We both let out a laugh, just as Mam and Dad used to years ago. 'You're so sweet,' he said as his smiling eyes looked up and down my face as though *I* was some unfathomable creature. 'Glad we're on the same page.'

Glad we're on the same page...

As I laid on my bed with Mist after getting home, I wondered what page we *were* on. *Theo had originally said our meeting would mean very little, just a cup of tea, hadn't he?* But I wished it could mean a lot more... Just thinking about it, I had to catch my breath. What I would have missed if I'd said no to that invitation...

Some people are like journeys to a place you haven't yet visited. I could hear that expressed in Theo's low voice instead of my own. That night, it was as if I'd met myself for the first time and I really didn't want to leave her behind. I was thankful I'd come away feeling strong, like I could *sauté* right up to the moon and twirl around every star before landing softly in my bed to dream of the exciting things to come.

WHIRLWIND

Sunday afternoon meant helping Dad at the barn shop. Bobbie was my next customer, and she didn't look so good. Her bloodshot eyes struggled to blink at me, and her loose hair was as dry as a brush.

'Ugh, can we go inside?' she asked.

'You go, Vila,' Dad said, 'it's quiet here today.'

'I don't even know where to start,' Bobbie moaned with stale cider-breath as she marched us towards the house.

Me neither.

She collapsed on the sofa. 'So there's this guy. I may have told you about him – long hair, cool shoes, walks with his shoulders?' I nodded, not having a clue who she was talking about. 'Well, we're going out,' she added, 'only apparently, we aren't, or he doesn't think so. He acts like I'm mad, Vi, as though when someone kisses and does whatever they want with you, you aren't together. *Really?* Am I missing something here?'

As far as I could tell, she wasn't. If Theo had kissed me, I'd assume we were together too.

'Don't think so.'

'So apparently, he's the same with like a *million* other girls…'

I began drifting off, daydreaming about what a kiss with Theo would be like.

I tuned back in when Bobbie said, 'Wanna guess what I did?'

I shook my head, assuming she hadn't killed him.

'I told them all! Messaged every one of them online! Then, guess what?'

I made my face into one of shock.

'I was the only one who didn't already know!'

I rolled my eyes.

'Never knew I was such an idiot.'

'Oh Bob, you aren't an idiot,' I mumbled, seeing her sulky face sink right down alongside me, but she kept talking. Where did she acquire her energy, even when she felt like that? I didn't realise I'd tuned out again, surprised when she said,

'So anyway, now I'm going out with Liam, he's much cooler.' But she still looked miserable. 'You'd really like him,' she said, which she repeated every time she was with someone new, always forgetting how different we were. It didn't matter what I thought, anyway. I couldn't even count the number of occasions I'd given her advice and she just hadn't taken it; she never intended to.

Soon, Bobbie was smiling again.

'Wanna do something?' She was always the one with ideas. 'Let's go for a drive. Wherever we end up, it doesn't matter,' she said and, within moments, I was hopping into her mint-green Beetle. Bobbie's driving was as erratic as she was, kind of because she hadn't long passed her test and the car was so old that it apparently didn't matter what happened to it, and kind of because this is Bobbie we're talking about. Not that I minded, most of the time. Being with Bobbie was like being sucked into a whirlwind. I would have felt too guilty if it was the other way around; all that chaos, picking everyone up before dropping them straight back down and then sweeping them aside. I didn't know how she did it, but she was fun to be around; she made me more fun.

Bobbie stopped right on the top of a hill. There, she pulled a guitar from the backseat and climbed to the top of the car. I could tell it was a recent habit of hers from the dents in the roof.

'I didn't know you played,' I said, watching her handle it as easily as she did her own body at ballet.

'Oh, I do lately.' She smiled as though people could just become guitar-playing prodigies overnight. 'Come up, then.' She tapped the roof before beginning to tune the banged-up acoustic of hers.

'Oh yeah! What the hell was that text about the other day, Vi? Missed me, did you?' Bobbie was smirking at me. 'You'd only seen me a second before!'

'Oh, must have been an old draft or something?'

After some careful tiptoeing via the car bonnet, I sat alongside. Bobbie's hand was lifting and falling along the strings as softly as the air around us. She practised some chords and began to strike a little riff up and down the first few frets, smiling down at her hands and not once looking at me for some kind of appreciation as she sometimes did. *If Liam taught her all this, maybe he's not so bad after all.* We'd parked in a lay-by in the middle of where everything seemed to divide. I scanned the valley below, the farms, the green fields, and the grey sea beyond.

As the wind caught us, it brought a beautiful echo to whatever Bobbie was playing, a song I hadn't heard before, but it was haunting. It was in the high notes, all the black ones, and it was fragile, probably the most vulnerable thing I'd ever witnessed escaping her. It was only when she finished the song with a slower and higher repeat of the last pattern that she finally looked up at me, down, then up again; the first sign of embarrassment I'd ever seen upon her face. I couldn't help but smile.

'Wow, that was lovely, Bob,' I whispered, pulling my scarf tighter around my face. Did Liam teach you that?'

Her face changed completely. 'No! I taught myself.'

For about a minute, we stared out at the stretching landscape. I wasn't sure what Bobbie was thinking. The little car beneath us rattled like a boat close to water, and the breeze swept Bobbie's frazzled red hair along my shoulder. There, I noticed a pair of black, intricate wings inked onto the back of her inflamed neck. The sore feathers began around the top of her backbone and pointed right up to the backs of her freckled ears. They were kind of unsettling and kind of … free, just like Bobbie.

'Guess we should get back,' she said, already sliding down onto the bonnet.

'Oh, okay.' I jumped down, too.

Driving back, Bobbie was the quietest she'd ever been. I thought I liked stillness, but awkwardness was different. I wanted to ask about Liam, but I wasn't sure whether mentioning him had struck a chord somehow. I felt sure Bobbie never cared whenever she offended me; she probably just ended one day, then began a new one, but I couldn't do that, I'd never been able to; everything seemed to connect, just like the fields, the water, the sky. I continued to say nothing, but so did she and it became stranger and stranger. Soon, I felt as though I hadn't seen her for years, even though she was sitting alongside me; we could have been in different countries. She could have been as far away as Melody. *There's no way I'll have an opportunity to tell her about Theo, not like this.*

'See you when I see you,' she said, giving me a nod as soon as her car pulled up outside the ivory house.

'Don't you want to come in for a drink or snack or anything? It's only five,' I said.

'Nah. Stuff to do.'

'Oh.'

Stuff. Bobbie only elaborated when she wanted to. No one else could get away with that. And only a second after I slammed the door, her car whizzed off, blaring Guns 'n' Roses through the windows before I even reached the front of the house. She usually at least waved. Maybe I missed it.

Dad was in Secret Haven, bent over in the doorway of his shed and tossing different objects over his shoulder, one by one, in the same way a hamster determinedly throws straw out of its house.

'Want any help?' I asked, trying to ignore the knot in my stomach. He was in a strange mood, too, and recently, he'd been getting rid of a lot of things.

Finally, his dishevelled head emerged.

'I'm alright, Vila *bach*. Got it handled. Just having a clear-out.'

Dad was usually the type to hold on to everything, so I wondered what had changed, or what was about to. I knew Sally had gone, the loudest hen of them all, so it was even quieter without her. *Maybe this is good for him.* I walked through Secret Haven for the first time in ages. Something made me not want to settle in the house, not quite yet. Instead, I found myself strolling towards my old, lopsided swing. I sat down and gently pushed the world back and forth. The air smelled of the remnants of rotten greengages that not even the birds wanted to peck at. It also smelled of me, waiting for Melody all those years ago. For a moment, I caught a glimpse of her smiling face peeking around the Wendy House door. *Ready to start, Vi-vi?* And then it was gone.

I swung as high as I could, making sure Dad knew this wasn't something for him to get rid of. It may only have been a rope and a plank of wood, but things like this, just the movement, they kept me going.

MY SECOND SELF

I'd told Dad to expect me home later from ballet on Wednesday evenings because of *pointe* practice. That was nearly two weeks ago, and I hadn't seen Theo since. For some reason, he'd just never showed up and instead, he'd left an imprint, so I couldn't stop thinking about him every day at school.

Maybe I need to grow up. Is that the issue? He'd have had a good point; who has a dolls' house when they're seventeen? Maybe I hadn't smiled or talked enough during our time together. Maybe, unexpectedly, I'd got carried away and talked too much. Whatever it was, I wasn't feeling good about myself; I started panicking that I'd lost my special someone after only just finding him, someone who seemed to understand me. I hoped I could fix it; I *had* seen an article online that was all about how people can improve themselves...

I wore my new gloves while I waited outside Ms Madeline's; interlocked my fingers and pretended they were the warmth of his hands. I wished I could have texted him, just to ask how he was, where he was or where he'd been, or just to say hi. But he'd never given me his number, not yet, anyway. *Why is that?*

I waited over an hour, but no car pulled up. *Perhaps he's on a late train?* The sinking feeling in my stomach grew larger as the rain ran down the back of my neck. I messaged Dad.

Sorry, Dad, only ever text you if I'm really stuck – Bobbie
isn't here tonight. Any chance you can give me a lift please?

When we finally got home, I draped my poor, dripping coat over the hook and let my bag slouch against the kitchen wall. *What an evening.*

'There's some *cawl* on the cooker if you fancy it, *bach,*' Dad mumbled, pulling his chair under the table, 'someone brought it over for us this afternoon.'

It smelled good but that sinking feeling in my stomach just wasn't hunger. 'Thanks. Think I'll take it up with me. Gotta dry off a bit.' I ladled some into a bowl, wandered up to my room and set it down on my bedside.

I wrapped my wet hair in a towel and collapsed onto the duvet.

Ana stared at me.

'Don't *you* say anything,' I whispered.

Just as I closed my eyes to have a moment, my phone pinged and its screen lit up the whole room. I sat up, thinking, *what if it's Theo? What if, somehow, he's found my number?*

Not Theo. My thumb followed its usual path around my phone screen: texts, social media, emails... There at the top of my mailbox was an email from the uni. *How could I have missed this?* It said my audition would be in March! *This'll help me focus.* I imagined my life through Theo's eyes. How confident I must have appeared onstage, how passionate. *She deserves praise*, he must have thought. And I found myself secretly agreeing.

Over the next week – into the half-term holidays – I threw myself into dance, into choreographing the piece I wanted to

187

startle the panel with. Starting with my dance room, I cleared the floor of any abandoned leotards or tights to give me the ultimate space and pushed aside any of Dad's boxes that had wriggled their way back into the room.

After trawling through Spotify for the perfect song, I finally chose one I'd kept returning to over the past week or so and began playing it on loop. It was an old one; 'Communication' by The Cardigans, but it was *the* one. The melody was so moving. *A couple of minutes of this track would be perfect.* I set my alarm as if every day was a school day, so I could start my warm-up straight after a healthy breakfast of poached eggs on brown toast, or porridge with berries.

After ten minutes of stretches, I was ready to begin.

My piece started off slow and lyrical on the floor, then, as I bloomed and flowered, I gained a little strength and dared to move more. Then, my movements became faster and choppier as I burst out of my shell into a more modern world where I was even taller and bendier and sassier. By the end, nothing moved in straight lines and nothing was as black and white as it always had been. It was just the music for me; I felt it in my toes. I called the dance, *My Second Self*. It would end in an untraditional pose. That was the purpose, expressing originality. To the audition, I would wear a long-sleeved black leotard and chiffon wrap-over skirt with my *Coppélia pointe* shoes. They had worked so well for me before.

After days of finding the right arrangement, and capturing the best mood and narrative, I paused for breath. I wondered if Theo would still be in awe of my commitment. Soon, spring would start to show itself through the window. The Common would be decorated with golden gorse and I would wish to leap over it all, and yet there I was, in my dance room with the dolls' house, always dreaming. But I hoped it would all be worth it in the end. *This evening, I'll show Ms Madeline everything I've prepared.*

PRETTY INTOXICATING

The ballerinas didn't look like humans when I walked into class. They were sea-creatures folded up on the floor; heads leaning all the way back to touch the tips of their toes and hands holding on to their ankles. Some of them looked so vulnerable, and yet, the strength that it took to stay that way, in the oddest positions, as slaves to their passion...

'Dance is a labour of love,' Ms Madeline said with a sadistic grin as I joined those creatures and folded myself at the end of the line. With one arm, she scooped each of us up like baskets, just inches off the floor, to test how strong we were.

'No Bobbie, again?' she asked the room, but she was really asking me.

It wasn't the first time it had been mentioned, either. A group of girls had asked me at school a few days ago, 'How's your friend?' and I'd just shrugged and walked away. I wasn't sure how they even knew her; she'd left school ages ago. 'We heard she's a druggie,' they'd shouted after me, as though they expected me to turn around and charge at them.

But it was too sad, I felt pretty helpless about it all. She hadn't been answering my texts. I'd phoned her, too, just once, even though that wasn't what we usually did, but when she answered, I heard a scream, and panicked. That was before I heard a sickening giggle straight afterwards, and the heavy breath of a boy, before she disconnected. For a change, I guess I took the hint and stopped trying.

But Bobbie caused problems even when she wasn't around. None of our dance sequences made sense without her, the shape was spoiled by unsightly gaps, and this particular evening, after weeks of waiting for change, Ms Madeline finally replaced her with a worried-looking girl.

'There you go, Lily, you stand in Bobbie's place.'

But Lily was pocket-sized and lacked Bobbie's range of facial expressions. I could hear Bobbie's voice in my head: *look at her; she only looks about ten! Nothing like me!* In my head, I told her to shut up; the fact she thought she even had a right to complain about anything, even when she wasn't there…

At the end of class, after everyone squirrelled away, Ms Madeline asked, 'So, have you started yet?'

I assumed she meant the choreography. So, without even saying a word, I ran to the centre and began my new piece – without music.

She stood and watched, hands on her hips, as I held my final position. She was the true judge.

I felt my back burning up with nerves about her reaction. She pouted as though she was trying not to let go of a smile.

'Violet, where on earth did that come from? And why on earth haven't you done this sort of thing before? I love it, dear. Absolutely love it, and I'm so relieved.' Her hand was on her heart and some lines reappeared alongside her eyes. 'I knew you had that creativity in you, it was just a matter of time before you'd express it in your work.'

I liked that she'd called it work, as though I was a

professional. That was the aim. The relief glided through my body.

'The only thing I'd change,' she looked to the ceiling for inspiration, 'purely as an improvement upon what you've already got, is that the final position should be more open, as though the story you're telling isn't as final as you make out. So, to choose a position that could hypothetically *enable* another one fairly soon after would be ideal. The incomplete journey of adolescence. Yes. Bravo, Violet. Really, bravo.'

'I understand,' I said. 'Thanks, Ms Madeline. I really appreciate your guidance.'

Even though I'd begun to realise I was unlikely to see Theo ever again, I waited outside Ms Madeline's, just as I had every week lately, just in case he turned up. Even when I left, I made sure to move away slowly in case he was late. I would have been even more annoyed at myself if I'd missed him. After a while, still, no Theo, so I started my walk towards the Common, alone once again.

As I strolled, somewhere inside my head, Theo and I were having conversations about ballet. There we were, swinging our heads back as we laughed at how perfectly we understood each other's passion, like nobody else ever had, and we were saying how odd it was that *some people just click*, fit together like jigsaw pieces, light up when they find their fuse. We were authentic together, and with him, I was bubbling with everything I'd wanted to say for so long, all those feelings I'd kept locked up for seventeen years, the Violet I hadn't met until recently.

The Common was becoming almost invisible to me again

as I walked along it. It soon appeared as a yellowy-green blurred line while I thought of Theo, while I got carried away by things that weren't there, in the breath of real life, and I felt Mam's presence. *Make sure you're careful now,* she said, seeing me at the side of the road.

'Knew I'd find you here!'

A voice was shouting from a car window, just like before, and I'd wondered if I was still imagining things. Had Theo been looking after me on my journey after all?

Yes. There he was. Just as Mam had always kept me in the corner of her eye, he had too. He pushed the passenger door open, and I jumped in without hesitation.

'Sadly, I've been a bit caught up the last few weeks, *Coppélia,*' he said. Maybe he knew how much I'd missed him. 'Hope you can forgive me for that? Anyway, how have you been? Are you doing okay?'

I wanted to know what he'd been doing, and if *he* was okay, but I didn't want to pry. After all, he had so many important things to do, and much more life experience than I could ever imagine...

'I'm great, thanks,' I said, smiling as much as I could. *Today's going so well.* Theo was dressed less casually than before, in a navy jacket and gold tie. I imagined him speaking at a conference where the audience hung on to his every word.

'Ah, I'm so glad you're alright. Are you rushing anywhere this evening? How about you come back to mine again? Just for a while? I've missed you, Coppy...'

My heart *sissonned.* Of course I wasn't rushing, I'd been moving more slowly than usual. *Does he really want more time in my company, of all the people he could choose from?* I could hear Ms Madeline's voice. *Fondu*, she'd said, meant '*to melt*', and I truly did.

*

'I've tidied up a bit since you last visited,' Theo said.

He tapped the sofa alongside him and I shuffled into my space.

As we shared a hug, and I let my body press into him a little more than before, I looked over Theo's shoulder and something on a shelf in the far corner caught my eye. A colourful array of paper ballerinas – and what looked like swans?

'Oh, have you spotted something?' Theo asked as we let go of one another.

I gestured towards the shelf.

'Ah,' he paused, with faint dimples appearing in his cheeks. 'You'll think I'm bloody mad, won't you? Hey guys, my boyfriend makes paper ballerinas!' He nudged me.

'Well, I didn't want to say anything...'

We both burst out laughing.

I raised my eyebrows, wanting to hear more. I could have listened to *my boyfriend* for hours.

'Well, not for you to think I spend all my time doing it, it's just that I learnt origami while I was in Japan; it's very therapeutic. I'll show you how to make something sometime if you like?'

I quickly nodded.

He wandered over to the shelf and delicately lifted one or two of them to show me.

'Japan was an amazing experience. Have you been there?'

I shook my head. I hadn't been anywhere.

Standing at my shoulder, he was smiling down at each figure in such a gentle way that I couldn't help but laugh at him. Anyone who didn't know him would have thought he was a bit weird.

'Oh, well, it was such an experience.' He looked back up at me. 'Well, it all was: China, Japan, France, and so many other places in Europe. It's just so interesting how different the people are, isn't it?'

I nodded, not really knowing enough to share thoughts.

'It gives you such an insight, you know, into what makes an individual unique and just how original we all are, depending on our upbringings – our cultures – even our food, I suppose. It all says so much about our personalities and how they grow, you know?'

'Definitely!'

'Oh yes. The different styles of dance, too, wow, you'd have enjoyed it all *so* much; it's all so different, everywhere, which I'm sure you know a lot about, so tell me if I'm boring you.'

'No, you really aren't!' I widened my eyes as much as I could.

'Your scene in *Coppélia* actually brought up those memories; the Japanese geisha dance, so strange and, well, strategically *impressive*. It makes you think how dance finds a way of shaping *life*, and vice versa, of course – how people's bodies move differently just as their minds do – it's when their souls come out to play. Sorry if I'm going on a bit...' he laughed, 'so feel free to...'

I shook my head. 'No, not at all. Carry on, please...' *You're perfect,* I wanted to say. *I can't talk about dance like this with anyone.*

'Don't you worry, I know we're in the present, now, Coppélia.' His neck craned towards me. 'A place where you've gotta *remember* to live. In fact, if you're already *remembering*, you're doing it all wrong, right?'

I nodded. 'Definitely!'

'*More feeling and less thought.* That's my mantra. As a dancer, you probably agree, don't you? Excessive thought ruins the dancer – so to speak – package her up in a costume and make-up, a body that has been taught but is purely lifeless. But you can't be taught how to *feel*, can you? That's where the magic is – the illusion that makes ordinary people like me so fascinated with *you*.'

He was right. Passion couldn't be wrong, and thoughts could definitely ruin too many things, it could take away from life itself. I knew I should try to think less, but that made me think of Bobbie, who – it was true – was a spectacular dancer mainly because she was the least inhibited.

I couldn't help but wonder what it was that kept Theo there, with me, in some irrelevant present, which might only become a forgettable past. *More feeling and less thought, Coppélia.* There was so much meaning to his stories, to the places he'd been, that at first, it felt embarrassing to think of my little world, of Secret Haven, the birdhouse, the beehive, our ivory house and its fireplace, my dance room; all the small places with enormous meaning, to me, and, reading my mind, Theo said,

'But I have done all of that, now. It's gone, and now I'm here, right where I should be.' He was smiling at me again and looking concerned. 'Gosh, you really don't realise, do you? You're so special, and so unaware of it. That's what makes you ballerinas even more beautiful. And your silence speaks volumes because you have so much soul.'

Us ballerinas. I could feel myself falling into a safe pocket of his mind, both of us locked away from the world.

He stood up. 'I take it, being a dancer, you like a lot of music?'

'Oh, loads,' I said, then watched him walk over to put a record on.

'Then you'll like this.'

And I already knew I did; the guitar, the strange notes. I was sent spinning back into the past. Dad used to play Simon and Garfunkel in the van when I was little. 'The Sound of Silence' filled the room.

His arm was soon around me and it felt perfect.

'I love how quiet you can be sometimes,' he murmured, as one whispers into the cradle of a sleeping baby, and it made me nestle into the crook of his arm. 'You can tell people are at peace when they can be quiet like you. So many people are afraid of silence, but being a ballerina, you understand the unspeakable beauty of dance, where, to speak would be to ruin it. You know, *Pythagoras* said, "be silent or let thy words be worth more than silence".'

By this point, any pressure had completely melted away. I'd finally got used to the scent of Theo's aftershave and I felt deeply comfortable. It was funny, the more he accepted my quietness, the more I wanted to speak. He knew me so well already, knew how to perfectly adjust the air between us. He was right, I was at peace!

I'd never thought of quietness as such a beautiful thing until right then. I hadn't realised that a lot of how you feel about yourself is due to how you think you ought to. Theo expressed so many wonderful things and he made me feel so at home.

'Oh! Just so I don't forget, and while we're talking about talking,' he did a nervous laugh, 'Do you have a mobile? I didn't want to be presumptuous before, but it might be handy to exchange numbers. Would that be okay? Unless you don't like tech—'

'Oh, I do. I'm always on my phone! I mean, I use it a lot, you know?'

I handed mine over for him to type in his contact details, noticing when he handed it back that he'd put a little heart alongside his name. It was safe to say, I'd fallen head over *pointe* for him.

On the sofa, I followed Theo's lead. I squashed the doubts that had recently troubled me. *He's too old, I'm too young. What would Dad say? It feels wrong.* You can't judge people like that. *Older could be good, and what's age, anyway? A number. Who's counting?* I kept counting, though, subtracting seventeen from what? *Thirty-five? Twenty-nine? Twenty-seven?* Besides, Theo often seemed, in a strange way, younger than me. I repeated the mantra: *don't think, feel.* And what I felt was – happy, a grown-up kind of happiness, or one that would lead to growth; to insight, as Theo would say. I was only now realising that for so many years, I must have expected the opposite of happiness, to be this surprised by someone wanting to be close to me. That's what made me realise just how sad I must have been, until that moment, and just how happy I was going to be!

We stayed stitched together under the starry skylight for so long – just chatting and laughing – that we ended up sinking further into each other, and soon, he drew me on top of him until our feet touched, his much bigger than mine. It was there that I noticed just how small I was compared to Theo: *if anything or anyone were to attack us during this moment, I'd be kept safe by his body.* I listened to his heartbeat, heard it telling me, *I'm here, I'm here, I'm here,* and I felt my own racing alongside. This skylight was our very own Aurora Borealis, but Theo instead chose to gaze into my eyes, gently thumbing my fringe out of the way. 'You know,' he whispered, and I felt his breath mingling with mine, 'these beautiful green planets of yours – are – pretty – intoxicating… There must be all kinds of landscapes in there…'

My eyes scrunched into a smile just as his did. I felt dizzy with warmth, as though the sofa was about to melt beneath us and send us floating into space.

'Well, it could take me a lifetime to see them all,' Theo added, before he kissed me, properly, for the very first time

and my whole body turned to dust.

THE AUDITION

'Could number twenty-two please report to studio two? Please report to studio two!'

That was me.

From the moment the audition room doors opened, I held my posture, *shoulders down, chin up, bum in, ribs in, hips turned out*, as – all in black – I ran to the centre of the room and smiled serenely to greet the panel. *I am not just a number.* I gave them everything I was advised to; showcased my flexibility, my strength, my creativity, my discipline and not just my work ethic, but – I felt sure – my whole ballet ethic. I curtsied and ran back out feeling confident that I'd done everything possible. I couldn't wait to tell Theo how the day had gone. He'd told me to text him a while before I was about to arrive back at the station, so he'd be there to pick me up.

In fact, as soon as Theo knew I had an audition, and that I'd be attending extra ballet classes with Ms Madeline, on Mondays and Fridays, he'd insisted on picking me up after those too, so of course I was delighted. 'Let's make the most of all that time together,' he'd said, so, there he would be after every class, parked in the same spot without fail, and leaning over to kiss me as soon as I jumped in. Then, he'd take me back to his and I'd show him any new inclusions for my audition piece. 'Such beautiful lines,' he'd say, as well as advising me if he thought something should be 'just a little gentler, that's it,' or 'now, fierce, passionate!' He really was the most supportive partner I could have asked for.

Seeing each other more often meant everything flowed so naturally and so comfortably, like a dance that's been danced a hundred times before, as we submerged into kisses for longer – never wanting them to end – and missed each other during every day in-between.

So, of course, after the audition, as promised, there he was, smiling at me from the train station car park.

Don't ever let me lose you.

When we got to his bungalow, he said,

'Give me five minutes,' pressing my shoulders, and I noticed how smart his trousers were as he jaunted away; grey herringbone this time, with a skinny belt that matched the brown brogues on the mat.

I waited there on the doorstep, still in my audition outfit, trying not to hear whatever he was shuffling back and forth between rooms.

'Okay, ready,' he eventually announced from a distance.

His face was beaming as I walked into the living room, which was lit up by what felt like a hundred candles, flickering like little stars.

'Thought we should celebrate,' he said, with that adorable smile as he took my hand to lead me towards the kitchen. 'There! Romantic with a capital R, right?' He pulled my chair out to sit me down at the neatly laid dining table. 'There you go, my sweetness,' he said, slowly pouring white wine into my glass. 'Don't worry, it's just a small amount. Don't want to be a bad influence now, do I?' He raised one of his handsome eyebrows again.

I'd only ever drank wine at Christmas when Dad had been given bottles by customers. That's what the taste reminded me of, the dry grape of Boxing Day, when Dad fell asleep on the sofa.

Theo checked on the pizza in the oven, then began making a bowl of salad for us. 'So, tell me how it all went, Coppy!'

I took a second sip. 'Uhm, well, I guess I couldn't have done any better,' I said, worried about sounding boastful, but also feeling the smile spread across my face.

'Ah, I'm not one bit surprised. You don't have to act modest around me, you deserve to feel good about it. You put everything into your dance, I know you do.' He was right, I really did.

I welcomed his eye contact lately, learnt to appreciate how much he liked to absorb.

'Hey, so, you know I love you, right?'

'Oh,' he'd caught me completely off guard. 'Maybe? Yes?' I said, looking up at him, so cultivated in his black polo neck. 'I suppose I know now,' I forced a laugh.

'Maybe? Don't be silly. I bloody worship you, Coppélia.'

I felt myself coyly looking away and immediately regretting my timidness. *Don't be so immature, Violet.*

'So,' he said, as he placed the food on the table, 'do you have anything to say to me? No worries if not, but I guess I'm checking in, you know?'

'Oh,' I said, 'I mean, definitely. I – really – love you. That's probably been obvious…'

'Not at all, actually,' he held both my hands as he sat down, 'I mean, I'd love us to make it *more* obvious, though. Would you? I'd like to show you...'

There, my mouth must have bobbed open like a goldfish. *This is it. Already.* So soon, and yet, it was exactly what I wanted, wasn't it? I wanted him to love me, and he did. He wanted me to love him, and I did. So, what else was there to wait for? *This is what it's like to be grown-up about life, about relationships, and Theo is – and will be – the love of my life. I just didn't expect this part so soon!*

'Don't worry, my sweet,' his thumbs stroked my fingers, 'I completely understand how you must feel, like it's all a bit quick, but when two people like us are meant to be, it's meant to be. I just think you're out of this world.' He gave me such a reassuring smile, with a little nod of his head, so I'd nod back.

I suppose I wasn't doing him justice; the effort he'd gone to, all those candles around the living room and along the kitchen windowsill. His home looked magnificent. He'd made such an enormous gesture, and all to celebrate my audition. *He has so much faith in me. Now, it's my turn to have faith in him.*

'Well,' Theo gestured, 'best eat this food before it goes cold, hadn't we? Then we can just relax. As always, no pressure, anyway, okay, Coppélia? That's the last thing I want. I just want you to be happy, and then I'll be happy too.'

I was trying to bite the corner of my pizza, but a slice of pepperoni kept falling off the edge. I looked up again, embarrassed, but there was his face, looking at mine as though I'd done the cutest thing. *Why am I suddenly so nervous? I trust my feelings, don't I? So, what right do I have to not trust his?*

Besides, according to movies, people always feel nervous about this. It's what makes it even more special!

We continued to talk about my day, what the university had looked like, and if I'd got to meet many of the other dancers. He seemed to be making it all about me, and I was happy to oblige, still giddy from it all.

As we curled up on the sofa, Theo handed me the fluffiest pair of white socks, with little rubber grips on the bottom, which I assumed were so I wouldn't slip on the wooden floor at his place.

'For my little duckling,' he whispered, kissing me on the temple. 'We've gotta protect those delicate feet of yours, haven't we?' Some of the other girls sometimes wore those socks over their *pointe* shoes at the beginning of class and I'd never got around to buying any for myself. I knew I'd never meet anyone who thought of me as much as he did.

'Here, let me.' He turned me towards him, laid my two feet across his lap, and noticing the holes at the soles of my feet, as was always the case with transition tights, 'ah,' he said, revealing a mischievous smirk, 'I'd forgotten about this, access especially for me.' He then very slowly unrolled my tights over my sore toes, up over my insteps and ankles until my toes wiggled free in both his hands.

There they were, bare before him and I felt self-conscious of the bruises, blisters and blackened toenails. But the way he held them, just for a moment, and sighed, his skin against the balls of my feet and my toes resting inside his big fingers, I felt soothed all over. And when he looked up at me with that glint in his eye, I couldn't help but smile back. People underestimate the power of comfort and contentment among two people.

Theo pecked my little toes with a kiss, then took the roll of socks from my hand and placed it beside him.

'We'll have to make sure to not leave these little ones out, won't we?' He said, almost doctor-like in the way he held one foot and leant across to pick something up from the side-table. There, he squirted soft, lavender-scented cream from a little tube, into his hands, rubbed both hands together and spread it across both my feet, using his thumbs to press all the right points under the arch, moving in circular motions around the balls of my feet and slowly stroking each toe between thumb and forefinger, then stretching them into a backward bend, before curling the toes forwards and back inside his fist again. 'These poor little things work so hard. They deserve some special treatment, right?'

It made my feet tingle and become one with his hands, as though we were moving together, backwards, and forwards, so fluid, it was euphoric having my feet treated with such care. They felt so soft and almost left behind at the ends of my legs once he was done with them. When Theo looked up at me again, he laughed, seeing how drowsy I must have appeared.

'I've found something else you like, then? That's good. We'll always look after these.'

I yawned as he unrolled the pair of white, fluffy socks I'd almost forgotten about, and softly slid them over my toes, heels and ankles; one and then the other.

Theo stood up and held out his hand,

which I accepted, letting him lead the way.

For the first time, we found ourselves lying on his bed. We were on top of his duvet of midnight blue, in the glow of a solitary candle on the windowsill.

I was afraid of the moment that approached, but I was also comfortable as we both rested on our backs and just held each other's hands. Recently, the importance of hands had become clearer, the strength of his, the softness of mine. Delicious food had weighed me down, and it made me sink cosily into the mattress. Theo, maybe feeling the same, reeled me in alongside him until I curled up, his large arm around me, his clothed body as dark as the duvet. For moments, we just laid there, hearing each other breathe, in that place that can so easily drift into dreams.

Then Theo began to move again; first, just a stroke, down from my shoulder to my elbow as I laid on one side, then back up again, so slowly that it could have sent me to sleep. The comfort brought a new feeling I couldn't explain, but it made me pull myself closer to him until I could feel his heart racing. Growth doesn't come if you aren't willing to be scared sometimes.

Soon, he'd pulled me on top of him again, then spun us around, so my head sank into one of the pillows where all his final thoughts ran through his mind at night... His scent surrounded me, *mmm, just like that mulled wine,* his face touched mine and my eyes closed. I allowed his lips to lead mine. We were learning a new dance, a slow *waltz,* the same pattern, forward, then back, to the side, and repeat and repeat and repeat. *So this is what it feels like to have someone's warmth upon you, breathing their love into you.* I'd brought a grown man to love me this much, made him almost infantile in his compulsive need for more of me. I had no need to worry, *this is proof: we're the same.*

Any initial awkwardness crumbled as our tongues met: the same, the same, the same.

'Are you sure?' Theo asked, whispering through quick breaths, 'We can always wait if you need more time.' He was so attentive, but his eyes were desperate as he rolled his black jumper up over his body and threw it onto the floor, leaving just a bare chest, with a spray of dark hair at the centre. That sweet – so sweet – smell of mulled wine suddenly filled the room. *He was just a handsome man in the foyer and now here we are.* I nodded, telling myself there was no reason not to be sure – not that I could think of. *Because what would Bobbie do? As soon as she wants something, she goes out to get it, with no doubts at all, and I could be like that too; I've been doing well enough so far!* He was removing those grey trousers too… *This is what everyone else does, so why shouldn't I be entitled to the same experience?* But he seemed so different without all his smart attire… *Maybe I need to get to know him again.* But I was thinking too much, and as Theo began to slide his hand underneath my skirt, and then my leotard, I ceased to think altogether. *I can do it, I can do it.* It was only right when I felt so strongly about this man, and so from that moment, I thought nothing else at all, I only *felt.*

Nothing good comes without pain, Coppélia. And it was true, as all the hurt shot through me. Together, we pushed past it.

When I woke up, Theo's arms were still around me but he was awake and looking right into my eyes again.

'Well, I have to say, I feel … rhapsodic,' he said. 'Hope I'm speaking for both of us,' and then I saw a glimpse of his shyness again as he glanced towards his bedroom floor, strewn with our feeble clothes.

And he was speaking for both of us. He always was. We were both still there, as happy as we had been hours before. *Nothing had been spoilt, had it?* Not like in the movies. Nothing had drastically altered … *What on earth had I been so afraid of?*

I could tell from the light in the room that it had been dark outside for a while; the atmosphere had changed colour around us, and I probably should have been home hours ago. I checked my phone and I saw that it was 1am. And it was a weekday. There were missed calls, too, from Dad, a list as long as the screen, which made my stomach twinge. I shouldn't have done that to him again.

'Oh, dear, sorry, Coppy, I didn't realise it was so late,' Theo said, and I wondered how long he'd been awake, watching me with those soft, caramel eyes that looked even more buttery than before. 'I hope you won't be in any trouble. You know, if you ever need more time, for schoolwork or anything, you never need to explain. It goes without saying, I'll understand. You can always do work or study here.'

Theo couldn't be more perfect if he tried. Since Mam had left, I'd never believed someone caring about me that much was humanly possible, but I was starting to realise it was all I'd ever wanted.

'Come on, my love, I'll drop you back.'

*

When I walked into the living room, Dad was sitting on the edge of the armchair, and his face was tipped forward, dwarfed by his enormous hands.

'I've been worried sick, Vila,' he said, 'why didn't you phone or something? We've been through this before.' Looking around me, I realised how messy our house was: there were pots and pans piled up in the kitchen, and a week's worth of newspapers had been left in the hallway as though Dad had done nothing but work. If Theo had been with me, I'd have wanted the kitchen tiles to swallow me whole.

I would have called if I hadn't fallen asleep, I really would have, but that wasn't a good enough explanation. What could I possibly have said? I couldn't tell him *that*.

'I phoned Bobbie and she said she hasn't seen you.' His eyes met mine.

I was stumped, but words came from nowhere as I found a flowery spot on the gold carpet to focus on.

'Well, because Bobbie wasn't at ballet, I had a lift with one of the other girls, and she asked if we could practise our *barre* exercises tonight because we have another exam coming up soon. We ordered a takeaway, and I lost track of time.'

By 'soon', I meant months away, but Dad wouldn't know the difference.

That felt like the first real lie I'd ever told Dad, not counting the major audition I'd failed to mention... *Maybe I'll tell him if I get in.* I was surprised by how easy the lies came, but I also hated it. What did it say about me?

'Oh,' Dad said, studying my face as though it was someone

he hadn't seen before. He looked into my eyes again. His looked even larger than usual behind his glasses as they blinked very slowly and tiredly. 'Well, you have to let me know; I've told you before and I don't want to have to go through this again, you're seventeen, I know, but you're not an adult yet. I mean look, it's two o'clock and you have school tomorrow. You mustn't lose perspective, Violet.'

'I know,' I said, 'you're right, but I'm doing great, thanks. Better than ever.'

If only he knew that sometimes, perspectives could change for the better. Mine had changed a lot since I'd met Theo. I wished I could tell him how happy I was, but there weren't any other words that could articulate it, so I just added a smile.

'Is everything alright at school though, Vila? I know I'm not up on everything,' he looked at the kitchen floor as he said it, 'but a friend of mine's been asking me if you're doing okay, and sayin' about her nieces having to prepare for a whole heap of exams and all that. They're about the same age as you. Is it stressful, love? Alongside all your dance? She also said you seem to have shrunk lately, and if you ask me, I think so too. Just lookin' at you now, well…'

Can he tell that tonight, I'm different?

I pressed the top of my head to check I'd pinned my fringe back properly since leaving, and wondered who on earth this woman was, to have aired such close observations of me without me even knowing.

'Oh, it's just the extra rehearsals, Dad.'

'You sure, Vila? Because I do worry about you, you know.' I nodded.

'Okay, well,' Dad dragged his hand through his dry bale of

210

hair, 'you let me know if you need to have a chat with someone, whether it's me or not, I don't mind – I know I'm not always the best – but heck, you could even talk to my friend if you like; she'll happily talk a glass eye to sleep...'

'Dad?'

'Yes, love?'

'Which friend?'

'Oh,' he laughed, 'she's just from up the road, up there,' he pointed, but I still had no idea, 'you know her, she comes to the barn shop now and again.'

'Oh, okay.' I traipsed up to bed, still unable to picture who Dad was talking about.

'Alright, my Vila,' he shouted after me, 'well, there's always plenty of grub here, so don't be afraid of tucking in. We don't need you wasting away.'

Just as I was about to doze off, my phone pinged. It was a small text and all it said was:

Love you, Coppélia x

I immediately replied:

I love you too x x

EVERYTHING IS PERFECT

The following week passed by in a complete daze. Each day, I zoomed out to properly look at myself. I watched her put clothes on for school, and wondered if she really looked any different, if her hair was shining more, or her skin was glowing, since we'd discovered a new experience, entered the part of life that people keep quiet about. *Will everyone know?* I saw no visible signs, only my usual paleness before I painted over her. My mind constantly drifted towards Theo. *Everything is perfect, now,* he'd said, or had I been the one to whisper it?

And yet, how perfect had it really been? It hurt, didn't it? Have you already forgotten? It was excruciating, as though he was inviting himself to a place where nobody was supposed to go, not yet, maybe not ever, and you just kept your eyes closed and smiled in the dark, now and again watching the shadows of the candles flickering on the ceiling, and then the flickering you who had pretended not to flinch. But it was beautiful, too, wasn't it? Just like pointe: with more practise, you'll hardly notice the pain. That's what the lady in the dance shop had said years ago, and she was right. *Then*, it would all be perfect, and worth it. Everything would be.

My week was bookended by thoughts of Theo. I took my time to walk home from school, relishing in my happiness and looking forward to walking along the Common, where I had

212

the freedom to think about him even more. *How has work been for him?* I wondered, as I saw the hover of a skylark, heard its persistent song, *has he been thinking about me?* The skylark parachuted down. *When will I see him again?* The confusing thing was, Theo hadn't texted at all since the other night, and he hadn't turned up outside Ms Madeline's at all either. I wasn't sure why that was. *Does he not want to come on too strong?*

I decided to text him a smiley face. It was Friday after all. It had been a whole week since seeing him! What did I have to lose?

☺

I waited for a response, checking my phone from the top pocket of my school bag every minute or two and swiping away any notifications. I just wanted Theo's name to pop up. I could see that he'd read my message but obviously chosen not to respond. He must have been busy at work.

As I passed the bus stop, I saw Bobbie waiting there – on her way to work, I assumed. I made eye contact with her, but it didn't look like she was going to play ball. I didn't know what was up with her lately. She gave me a scowl, so I walked on.

'So, who's the secret guy?'

I carried on walking.

'Who *is* he?' she shouted again.

I quickly turned around to Bobbie's face, right there, her hair looking more fluorescent than ever in the light. It felt like ages since I'd last seen her.

'Bob, what's the prob—'

'Violet, tell me who he is, now!' Bobbie grabbed onto my arm, her thumb and fingers clawing like pincers. She looked skinnier too, and so pale that even her freckles had disappeared. Blue veins showed themselves in the bags beneath her eyes whenever she smiled, so she was as translucent as a jellyfish. Somehow, it wasn't a happy smile, it was paining her face as she did it, just as much as she was paining my arm, for she still hadn't let go.

'Okay, okay,' I said, 'well, he's called Theo, and he's well, he's perfect if you must know.' I felt uncomfortable telling her his name; it meant she could use it to wedge her way into our world.

'How come your Dad doesn't know about him, then? If he's so wonderful?' Bobbie's bottom teeth were showing. They were slightly stained, ginger with tobacco.

I couldn't understand why she was choosing to be so vitriolic, and so out of the blue. 'Vi, I just care, that's all. I'm sorry, this just isn't like you!'

I could feel the blood rising in my body; *how dare she start judging me after being off the radar for so long!*

'*What?* So it's okay for *you* to be a certain way but as soon as someone else starts having fun, as soon as I feel *happy* for once, you hate it?' There, I'd said it, and I was saying more, too. 'You don't even know me anymore, anyway. Maybe you never did.'

From Bobbie, I expected nothing less than a slap in the face, but I didn't care. Not that it came. Instead, she just stood there, staring back at me, with a similar expression to the one Dad had held the other day, only there were tears in her eyes; what was wrong with her? It was like she was made of mush, her strength all washed away with the tide. That painful smile reappeared, and she spoke through it.

'Vi, you don't want to be like me, I'm telling you!' The tears were still in her eyes, and I could see she was trying not to blink in case they fell down her cheeks, 'but if you're happy – I'm sorry – and I'm really glad.' Then she turned around and walked away.

'What? You expected me to hang around for someone who never even turns up?'

But she didn't hear me. My voice would never be as loud as hers.

Never mind, I wasn't going to let any guilt get to me; I was fed up of her having that sort of power. I thought of Theo again; *he* wasn't trying to make me feel guilty about anything. I wanted to see him, right then, at that moment, but I knew I couldn't, not until my next dance class.

You don't even know me anymore, anyway, I'd said to Bobbie, shouted at her, in fact, and the sound of my own voice made me queasy. It was sure of itself, yes, I should have been proud of that, but it was also razor-sharp and may have left a wound. *If you're happy, I'm sorry,* she'd said, but why were there tears in her eyes?

Within an hour of getting home, I received an email from the uni and my stomach wanted to collapse while I tore into the envelope.

'We would like to provide you with a conditional offer...' I continued to read. I needed three Bs and I'd be in! It was great. However, the other feedback they provided strangely hurt, and I needed to tell someone about it... I walked to the nearest bus stop, needing to see Theo.

I knocked on the door a few times. His car was parked outside but there was no response. I began to doubt what on earth I was doing there, but then, as I turned to leave, the door opened. Theo was standing there in his bathrobe, with tussled hair.

'Oh!' His face looked startled. 'I was just in the shower. Wasn't expecting you. Everything alright?'

I fell into his arms. There, I could feel his wet hair against my face, and I suddenly felt ridiculous for calling on him without having text first...

'Ah, tell me, love. What's the matter?'

I showed him the email on my phone. He took it out of my hand and squinted at the screen.

'Ah, it's the bit about having more to give, I take it?'

'Yes,' I cried. He already knew me so well. 'I tried so hard. Really, I did.'

'Oh, I know you did, my Coppélia. I know you did. Come here and sit down a sec. We'll sort this out. Look, it says here that all you need to do is continue doing well with your studies and they'll take you. You can't ask for more than that, surely?'

I shrugged.

'Ah, Coppy, you expect far too much of yourself. You're seventeen, not twenty-seven. We all have so much to learn. Even me.'

He did seem older all of a sudden, but in a good way, a reassuring way. I could trust the wise words of someone more experienced; I needed them. If he was twenty-seven right then, I was glad.

'If you're that worried,' Theo continued 'I know plenty of people in the business who could give you some advice, but I do think you're doing just fine.'

216

It bothered me that when I'd been asked to explain my reasons for wanting a career in dance, as usual, I'd stood there, clamming up, searching for the words. But they didn't come. I'd always thought dance spoke for itself if it was orchestrated well enough. What if it didn't?

Theo took hold of both my hands and looked me in the eyes.

'It's not always about trying, you see, Coppy. Sometimes, it's just about feeling. That's the main thing. If you dance how you feel, you can never go wrong.'

That's so true, I thought, *so true.*

He pulled me closer and we kissed; a long, lasting kiss that made me think of our first night together and hopefully, another night together.

My head slipped onto his shoulder and then he held me tightly against his chest. There, I heard his heart beating – strong, fast, sure, and I wanted him to hold on to me like that forever.

'Right,' he said, as he held my shoulders and gently slid away, 'I'd best get dressed and then drop you home.'

Have I been too awkward this evening? Too vulnerable? I hoped not, but perhaps that was why nothing more was happening between us…

While I waited, I took a closer look at the paintings above Theo's piano, hating that I knew so little, even about ballet! I'd always assumed I knew so much. *Perhaps I could learn from him? Yes, I could learn a lot.*

I felt Theo's chin rest on the top of my head as he whispered, seeing my eyes linger on the painting of the girl in the white *tutu* and long black plaits.

'I'm in love with Degas,' he said, 'I really am. That one's called *Dancer on the Stage*. See how the stage blends into the wings behind her?'

I nodded. I suddenly felt a little embarrassed about my Margot picture at home. It wasn't a painting, after all, just a large fold-out poster taken from one of Mam's magazines so many years ago.

'She's the focal point, see? She's in the limelight. Call me insane but that totally reminds me of you all those weeks ago, Coppélia. Everyone was watching you like that. Look at her, so lost in her world, just like you were.'

SWAN LAKE

At the end of my next ballet lesson, Ms Madeline took me aside.

'I'm surprised at that sullen face of yours, Violet,' she said when I showed her my email from the uni.

I felt the disappointment wash over me again.

'You've basically been accepted, my dear! Did you *really* expect to be a perfect dancer at *this* age?'

I looked up at her and saw her smirking at me. 'Because if you did, you know a lot less about dance than I thought. At seventeen, even Fonteyn had a long way to go. You do *realise* that don't you?'

I nodded.

'Besides, all of us are learning, no matter how old we are. That goes for life as well as ballet! So, tell me, what makes you think *you'd* be any different?'

'I don't know,' I shrugged, 'I suppose I just try so hard...'

'Don't we all, dear. Don't we all,' she shrugged. 'Did you know I suffered a horrific spinal injury when I was young? Yes, right before my starring role in *La Sylphide* at The Royal Albert Hall – and once they saw how well my understudy did, do you think anyone came searching for me—? Well, I can tell you they certainly did not. It took many, *many* months to get my strength and movement back to its original state, and it's had its limitations ever since.' She rested the back of her

219

hand on her lower back. 'So, let me tell you, there's an awful lot that comes into play as well as hard work, my dear. Hard work and good timing – and even then, you need the grit to keep going if you stand a chance of holding on to it all! It's important to be prepared for that, Violet. Tremendously important.'

I suddenly felt like a fool for having taken the feedback to heart over the past few days. It was frightening to think of one incident putting a pin in everything you've ever imagined.

'Anyway, now, what to work on next?' Ms Madeline added, looking me up and down. 'Ah, yes, that's it. Right then, chin up and chop chop.' She clapped her hands together. 'It's *finally* time for us to begin *Swan Lake*.'

I couldn't believe it. I'd always wanted to dance *Swan Lake*! It was one of the most challenging and emotive ballet performances. Ms Madeline had always said we'd need to mature before we could learn to appreciate it in the right way, that tension between light and dark, that shade.

I wondered what it was that had made Ms Madeline think I was ready… I looked in the wall mirrors to see if anything had changed about me. Could *she* tell? Ms Madeline knew more than she was letting on, about a lot of things. After all, she had her own partner who we hadn't heard a whisper about for all those years.

*

As soon as we got inside, Theo was opening a bottle of wine,
    'Just a little *Châteauneuf-du-Pape*, my favourite. You like?'
He was pouring me a very small glass before I could answer.

'We're celebrating,' he announced, 'My Swan Queen,' and clinked his glass against mine.

He always knew how to make something feel extra special. I sat comfily cross-legged on the sofa and watched him as glass-in-hand, he took centre stage.

'Now, *Swan Lake*, one of the most timeless and romantic stories … but how does it begin? Let's see,' Theo shrugged and rolled up his shirt sleeves, 'there's a prince – Prince Siegfried – who is sick of people trying to coerce him into marrying someone he doesn't love. So, he escapes to go hunting one night.' Theo placed his glass on the side-table, so he had two hands free for his performance.

I'd seen recordings of *Swan Lake* performed by Margot and Nureyev a long time ago, so I knew the story, of course, but I decided not to let on… There was Theo, a tall and slim animation; his teal, patterned shirt peeled open slightly at the top to reveal the subtle hair of his chest, that warmth. I smiled encouragement back at him.

'There in the forest, Siegfried spots a group of beautiful swans, so he decides to very carefully follow them,' Theo continued. 'Now, one of these swans, there by the lakeside, turns into the most beautiful young woman,' he pointed directly at me, and bowed, so I laughed as I got up to curtsy before quickly sitting down again.

'So, he approaches this *beautiful* woman, just gently, reaching out a hand,' Theo reached his hand out to me and stroked the inside of my wrist, 'to make her feel safe, and she finally introduces herself as…'

'Odette!' I shouted from the audience as Theo stood back in his place. I remembered this part of the story well.

'That's you,' Theo nodded. 'So, Odette explains that a *terrible* curse was placed upon their group by a wicked man with the name Von Rothbart! A curse that meant they were all turned into swans and could only turn back into humans for brief moments when darkness fell. Now, this curse, Odette insisted, could only be broken by a man who fell *truly* and *deeply* in love with her and promised, of course, to marry and be loyal to her forever.' Theo pointed from himself and then back to me before pointing at himself again. My heart leapt.

'So what happens next, eh?' Theo reeled me back into the story. 'Well, of course, Prince Siegfried knew what love at first sight was, just as I do,' Theo coughed for dramatic effect, before winking at me, 'soooo, he declared his love right there and then! You see, through Prince Siegfried's love, Odette feels like she might *finally* experience the freedom she's desired for so long – because his love will break the wicked sorcerer's spell that entraps her as a swan.'

I could relate. I'd felt that freedom. Since I'd met Theo, it was like he'd opened a music box and out I'd popped, spinning and spinning and spinning for as long as he encouraged me to. That was me, learning to spread my wings and soon, I would fly out of that box completely, I was sure of it. So yes, I could understand Odette. I could become her. I was her.

'So, all was well, you think? Happily ever after, right?'

I shook my head, knowing it was never that simple.

'You're right! Sadly, Von Rothbart turned up in the forest right after Siegfried declared his love, and do you know what Siegfried did?'

I shook my head.

'He aimed straight at Von Rothbart with his crossbow!'

Theo set his arms into position, aiming at the window of the living room.

'And Odette strangely, defended him. Why?'

I wasn't sure.

'Ah, well, you see. If Von Rothbart had been killed, just like that, his curse would have died along with him, meaning Odette would be trapped as a swan forever! Just imagine being imprisoned like that, unable to ever be your true self again!'

There was so much I'd have to consider while dancing on stage, to be able to bring Odette to life again.

'So, Odette runs away, Siegfried follows her, and they spend some magical time together, but sadly, their love feels doomed because Odette is to turn back into a swan before dawn.'

'What next?' I asked, needing to know soon, 'I can't remember what happens next.'

'Well,' Theo gave me a look of warning, 'there's a beautiful ball, set up just for the prince to find his bride. But don't worry, no one there will catch his attention as much as Odette… However,' Theo coughed, 'a magnificent vision appears – Odette has returned – or so he thinks. And of course, once again, he's completely entranced by her, not realising it isn't actually her at all…'

'Who was it?' Deep down, I'd remembered, but I didn't want to hear the truth, and besides, I was playing along.

'Von Rothbart's daughter!'

'His daughter? Nooooo…'

Theo laughed at me. 'Yes, it's the black swan, Odile…'

'That's awful!'

'It is, isn't it? – He even proposes to her!'

'Oh no…'

223

The palm of Theo's hand pressed his forehead as he narrated the rest, 'so when Siegfried realises what he's done, it's too late. Far too late. He spots a very upset Odette running away, so he chases after her. When he finds her once again at the lake, he begs for her forgiveness,' Theo fell to his knees before me, reaching his hand out once again, which I kissed before he stole it back, 'and she does forgive him,' he announced, loudly and triumphantly, 'there is that, at least, but as we know, he has already broken his vow and there's absolutely nothing he can do about it. So…'

'What? What then?' I asked, loudly, looking down at Theo who was slumped on the rug before me, head down on his knees, only picking it up to tell me the ending.

'They throw themselves into the lake,'

I gasped.

'…and they die, together.' Theo rolled onto his back, legs limp and eyes closed; one arm across his head in true suffering, and the other splayed alongside, so he took up almost the whole rug.

And he kept them closed.

'Aren't you going to check I'm alive?' he asked, pretending to be annoyed. 'Come and kiss me or something,' he moaned, still with his eyes closed, and I burst out laughing, seeing his lips twitching as they tried their best not to.

So, I joined him on the floor, checked his pulse and kissed him on the forehead, joking with him.

'You can do better than that,' he said, opening one eye and then quickly closing it.

He was hilarious. I gave him a warm, long kiss on his wine-stained lips until he smiled. I stretched my legs beside him and there we laid together, rolling onto one side and then the other, just kissing for a while.

When we finally took a shared breath, Theo, panting, pressed his forehead tightly against mine, looked deep into my eyes, and brushed my bottom lip with his thumb.

'That story, you know it doesn't have to happen to us, right? Sure, we're timeless, but we definitely aren't doomed. I see you for who you truly are, and you see me, for who I am, I hope?'

I felt myself nodding. How did he do it? Manage to say everything I'd always wished someone would say to me? Everything I needed to hear?

As I laid with my back turned into the shape of Theo's chest, just feeling his breath in my ear, he slowly began to remove each hair pin from the lacquered bun on the top of my head, one and then the next, placing each in his trouser pocket. *Ah, the relief* as he pulled loose the tightly wound band and let my hair tumble free. 'My little chestnut,' he whispered, kissing strands of me in his hand, 'Mm, you're so silky,' he whispered, kissing my neck, 'look at your feathers; so beautiful, so alive.'

I caught my reflection in the tall mirror by the front door; a waist-length spray of hair that was a much richer brown than it used to be. He was right. I couldn't remember when I'd last looked at my hair like that; what was always knotted above my neck was now cloaking my entire back. It might have even been longer than Mam's.

Theo pushed down the top of my leotard over both shoulders, slowly rolled it down over my chest and then turned me towards him.

'Together, we'll be real, we'll prevail,' he added, combing

his hand through my hair, 'and show the world what love is all about. Besides, these days, ballets are full of alternative endings. Let's be one of those.'

When he talked like that, it just made me want to kiss him again and again until we got tired of it – not that we ever could.

'When you're on that stage,' he said, stroking the side of my bare hip, running his finger up and down the curve, 'you need to show it. *We* know how true love feels and what it's like when you have the courage to act on it. So, show them that courage.'

Theo began to strum my whole body with his fingertips; my ribs became his harp as he caressed each of them, up and back down, faster and then more slowly between kissing me deeply. *What would our music sound like?* With Theo, it was strange, I could hear it. It would express so much longing, so much desire, as Theo's body pressed so tightly against mine and I could feel every rise and contour of his love, every breath in and out until we weren't sure whose breath belonged to who. Every time I turned away because of the intensity, he gently coaxed me back to him, stroking my feathers.

My chorus of swans would have encouraged it; anyone would have. I could imagine them, fellow dancers, arms wide apart in *port de bras*, fanning the hot, passionate air of the room. At the theatre, there were moments I'd always thought could never be matched, where you become so immersed in the story, that your surroundings disappear somewhere in the stage smoke, and you forget you're performing altogether. You're at your most primitive. Dance was the only thing that had ever done that to me, but now, I felt like I was beginning to lose myself in Theo too, and it felt … fantastic.

There came the gentle moan of the violin trying to escape as our bodies met again after only seconds apart.

I allowed my back to bend and my head to fall with it.

I opened one leg, with a pointed foot he kissed, and he lifted my chin to face him.

'My ballerina,' he whispered, 'my love.'

All at once, as the feeling inside me grew, Odette's feathers broke through my skin.

I looked into his eyes, and it was already happening; the room disappeared as we both held a note for what felt like a sweet forever.

THE SELF-PORTRAIT

I felt kind of bad, lying about it, but I still told Dad I had some busy weeks ahead because of *Swan Lake*. I'd be late coming home from dance practice some nights, occasionally stopping over at one of the other girl's houses and heading to school straight from there.

'Well, as long as you don't let things slip, Vila,' he said, resting his hand on my shoulder and repeating, 'don't let things slip, now.'

'Uhh, I might not be free to cover the barn shop as often,' I told him.

'Oh, don't worry about me,' he said, 'Faith'll help out if she can,' while putting his shoes on to head into the garden.

'Who's Faith?' I asked. He'd said her name as though everyone knew her…

'Remember the lady who brought us the soup? And those nice candles?'

Vaguely. Soup, yes, but I couldn't recall any candles. I nodded all the same.

'Well, she's been helping me out every now and then, just when she can, you know, when you can't make it.' He brushed the dust off his knees.

I felt my stomach tighten.

'Anyway, don't you worry,' Dad was already halfway out the door. 'You just make sure all that schoolwork is up to scratch, alright?'

I nodded as he ambled away.

It was true that there were more dance rehearsals, anyway; even more than I'd anticipated: three evenings a week as well as tiresomely long Saturdays and Sundays. Still, every one of those classes would end with me being picked up by Theo. Over the weeks I got used to watching the clock tick behind Ms Madeline's head. I counted down until it reached the hour and felt my smile widen during those last few minutes.

We got to spend so many nights together that weeks felt like months, and I wondered how there had ever been a day that we didn't know the other existed. In-between evenings, Theo normally texted to ask if I was okay, so I'd often tell him how exhausted I was from all the ballet, and he'd say things like, *ah, I wish you could twirl around in my life forever,* and of course, my face would light up more than my phone. It didn't take much. Every conversation was a version of us madly missing each other. If it wasn't for the fact I could hardly keep my eyes open at school anymore, I would have seen Theo all the time, just as he wanted, but my yawns were catching up with me, and I was afraid Dad would catch up with me too.

I'd become so comfortable at Theo's home, so familiar with our bed, our sofa, our table, where we held hands, shared food and thoughts; looked into each other's eyes and out at the view – through the glass doors – of the little bistro table in the garden where we hadn't yet sat.

While Theo took a shower, I threw on one of his shirts and thought I'd get some ballet practice in. I could see the sliding doors to the second room were open, so I kicked my leg out to test the space. It was a cosy room but just big enough to do my *fouettés*, so I began to spin.

As I found my focus point, I noticed an easel leaning nonchalantly against the wall, and a ukulele resting on a desk alongside a pile of leather journals. Some looked quite wrinkled, and I imagined Theo cradling one on his lap under lamplight, inking profound outpourings from all his experiences over the years.

I would have loved to hear Theo play, or to watch him paint. He'd mentioned his talents a few times, but I hadn't got to see them for myself yet. I felt guilty that everything had been so much about me lately, so much about dance – and he was the rescuer I'd been waiting for, my Siegfried to Odette; the best person to help me let myself go. But what about *him?*

As I slid into the splits and began stretching towards my left foot and then my right, I noticed a photo album on the floor under the desk – quite old, with an unglued spine that meant its insides were beginning to fall out. I moved it closer to me, excited to see Theo's baby photos – or perhaps his mam…

'One day, we'll go through those, if you like?' Theo's voice made me jump. He was standing in the doorway. 'They're just some of my travel photos,' he said, snatching the album away and taking my hand to help me up. 'I have *hundreds,* so I'd like to show you them in order. When it comes to family photos, I'd prefer you to meet them in person first, you know?' His hands were on his hips as his head nodded. 'Everyone thinks they're so 'connected' through social media etcetera these days,' his hands became quotation marks, 'but I'd like to hang on to some *real* connection, you know?' He had a convincing smile. 'Plus, I know my sister would *adore* you. You'll be such a lovely gift to her in person. You're just her style. Trust me.'

That was probably one of the things I loved most about Theo. He was so authentic.

'I totally, understand,' I said. 'It should probably be the same for you and my Dad – in person, you know, whenever the time comes.' I smiled, only then realising that I didn't want them to meet too soon, or it could all go wrong. Dad needed to be ready.

'Yeah? Oh, good. We're always on the same page, aren't we?'

We both smiled but his expression faded as papers fell straight from the easel. Among the blank sheets was a picture. The face, made of charcoal, had the hollowest of eyes, with the long nose and broad chin of Theo – only, it was dark, so dark, with jagged edges. Within seconds, Theo had gathered the papers and slid them into his desk drawer. Self-portraits probably bring back images you'd rather forget, the little ghosts that haunt you even during a good day.

'Well, Coppy! Back to work,' Theo led me into the living room and closed the sliding doors. 'By the way,' he looked me up and down, bare legs poking out the bottom of his teal shirt, 'I look good on you.'

I gazed up at him, his wise face one that was always worth abiding by, and as always, I returned to dance in the fullest way possible. His confidence in me was relentless, so I became relentless. He'd asked me to dance for him so many times that I assumed he wanted to see every new, even minor accomplishment, so I'd tell him about my better extension or stronger elevation. *Look, look!*

'That's it,' Theo said, 'Now, listen to the music, close your eyes, and lose yourself. Tell me something emotional, something meaningful.'

So, I told him about Mam – properly, this time; about the fact I never got to say goodbye – the image of her lying there in that hospital bed, like one of her plants, beautiful but uprooted, fallen on its back and nowhere to go from there. I tried to remember the last things we'd ever said to each other. *Was it about school? Melody? Dance?*

And then Theo interrupted, which startled me at first.

'Use dance to speak to her,' Theo said, not letting my mind drift again. 'Dance can take you to a higher place. Haven't you ever wondered how you manage to do something so miraculous? You're a *goddess* and goddesses have power. Use it. Also, you're a woman. Don't be afraid.'

There was my artistic partner at his brightest, with fire in his eyes.

'One of the most important things to remember is that while you're Odette,' Theo continued, 'you aren't only Odette; you're Odile too. You're awkward and delicate as a bird, but also a *human,* with all these human passions and emotions. We can't take our eyes off *either* of you. So, just remember, you need to learn to love your dark side just as much as your light, okay?'

'Okay,' I said, immediately thinking of Bobbie. She would have been perfect as Odile. *Where has she been, lately?* I'd been so used to her disappearing before popping up when I least expected her, but it didn't seem like she was coming back to dance anytime soon. She was probably up to something that in her mind, was much more exciting.

PAS DE DEUX

Everything had changed so quickly. Some of the biggest things in life were happening to me all at once.

'Do you want me to pick you up at the same place, or—?'

'No, it's fine, thanks, Dad. I've got it sorted,' I said, putting my vanity case over one arm and grabbing my costume bag.

'Oh, right. Okay then. Well, opening night, eh? Break a leg – I've heard that's what they say – but please, not *really*,' he said, smiling down to his chest. 'We need you in working order.'

I forced a laugh. He was a good man, Dad was. He made the world a lighter colour.

Just the thought of Theo being there comforted me while I waited in the wings. He knew I'd be nervous. That's why he'd booked a seat in the front row.

'Dance as if it's just for me, my duckling,' he'd whispered the night before. 'You'll be fine.'

Still, it was hard not to forget the vastness of the theatre, the heat of the spotlights, the hundreds of eyes, all on me.

A crowd of ballerinas in ballgowns *piqued* past me, one taunting herself about how she'd landed too soon. Another smiled and whispered *merde* to me as she looked my white, feathery *tutu* up and down. *Good luck*. My head repeated it: *merde, merde, merde*.

The others said, 'Shhh,' in unison as they linked arms to escape backstage. The bitter smell of hairspray and stale sweat lingered.

I peeped around the curtain to find the first few rows, but I could only see figures, not faces. I stood back and rotated my ankles ten times on each side, rose *en pointe* five times, rolled my shoulders five times forward and five times back, stood up straight and smiled three times to check my facial muscles were working; the taste of beeswax honey balm covered my lips to stop them drying out, something Mam had told me dancers sometimes did. Bobbie and I hadn't performed without it for years.

'Impressive, isn't he?' Ms Madeline rested both her hands on my shoulders just as I thought I spotted Theo's silhouette in the audience, and then she turned me a little to the left.

The stage backdrop had changed to a moonlit lake as Luc – almost unrecognisable – took to the stage from the opposite wing, in white leggings and a black and gold blazer; his strong arms held a crossbow as he pointed a long, muscular leg behind him and looked straight ahead – at me.

'You two are just perfect together,' she whispered as his eyes pierced into mine.

It was funny. Luc had always felt like a stranger, no matter how much we'd trained together for this very week. Even when we'd looked into each other's eyes – as part of the act – we'd seen straight past each other. Here, he was even more of a stranger, but an impressive Siegfried nonetheless.

'*Merde*, my love.' Ms Madeline took another step back.

There was the chase of music I'd been waiting for.

Luc lowered his crossbow as he saw me join him onstage,

glissade

        grand jeté

I am here.

The audience applauded as Odette, crowned with white feathers, took to the stage, my testing ground.

Now I had people's attention, I just had to hold on to it.

A slow and sorrowful tune followed my every move. The passion poured from every finger and toe as I began – like Margot – to let my eyes tell Siegfried my story, head dipping towards a pointed foot, arms fluttering like wings at the edges of my frosted *tutu*. I imagined this to be my first meeting with Theo, and as I warmed to Luc, I warmed to the performance. I told him of the curse and the chance that it could all change, while my hands curved over at the ends, pushing away any hardness from the air, testing it with both bewildering arms. I bent forwards, then backwards, all with the grace of a swan, just a gentle teasing of Siegfried, *I am pure, I am vulnerable, I could be yours – but only if…*

I let Siegfried approach. There in the spotlight, I could see the intensity in Luc's eyes, something I understood. In class, yes, we'd been looking straight past each other but at the same dream. *I trust you*, I thought, and maybe he could tell. So, we began our duet, partners in passion, reaching out to the audience's hearts – through each other. He was Siegfried now, so I beckoned him towards me with my soft wings. *That's right*, Theo would have said, *just like that, my love,* and so I had the courage to continue, to welcome my freedom.

There, I felt what it was like to dance with a man in a real ballet performance; what it was like to twirl, slide and fall within the safety of a body I believed in, all before Theo's eyes, but I didn't look for him in the audience this time; I didn't want to lose the power he had given me. In a way, he was my puppeteer, allowing every one of my mercurial movements to manoeuvre around Luc – who used both large hands to rotate me from the waist. Everything we'd all practised came to life right there – until Von Rothbart arrived.

The audience gasped and I ran to stage exit.

Quick change

and then it was time

for the black swan maiden to appear.

I'd never dressed in such an exquisitely dark costume. I entered the stage ballroom, a seductress with a sweet taste of slyness in my smile, and Siegfried looked satisfied by the sight. Our steps were synchronised, each one brimming with boundless adventure. I smiled *dance with me* at him, at us, a power couple in the making, me, not needing to be saved but confident in my own safety; him, a saviour no longer weighed down by the need to save. My arms and legs were lengthless, our symmetry was unsurpassable, our energy was contagious – because Odile was a force to be reckoned with, an opportunity not to be missed. *I can be dark and daring.*

Siegfried could hold on to me but not for too long – unless...

But I only suggested the rest.

How would I impress him further? Well, I committed *fouetté* after *fouetté* after *fouetté*, seeing his adoration from the corner of my eye as he became dizzied by my spins.

Theo will be proud, I thought, as I found my focal point, imagined those kind eyes, and the audience clapped in approval of our love. I felt the strength of Siegfried's lust as Luc remained close, wanting to be the only one to see me spin like that.

And then he spun too.

My shoulder blades opened and closed before Siegfried, and my black-feathered wings let me fly. He lifted me right up, right over his head and held me there, allowing me to rise above him, his prize, Odette. He was unaware that I was actually the dark Odile. The music was gentle, soulful, and I felt angelic as I landed to a Siegfried who swore he would love me forever. *This is a pure, ideal love,* don't you see? I smiled, thinking of Theo. *It's unique and magical. I am your Swan Queen!* Isn't it funny how one *pas de deux* can be so different from the last?

Quick change

I returned as Odette, soft and sad, *bourréeing* since Siegfried's betrayal. I felt the loss, felt my world going up in feathers.

The rest of the performance happened without much thought at all. *Feel, feel, feel,* Theo had reminded me, and if there was any pain, Siegfried and I experienced it through entangled hands. The music had become sorrowful and yearning. I tiptoed *en pointe* away from Siegfried, I spun and swayed, he twirled me to one side and then the other, and I gently touched the floor with my fingertips, whilst lifting one leg right up into the splits behind me. *Just one more kiss of the stage.*

Siegfried elevated my limp body.

We had reached our *coda*.

Siegfried knelt down before me and kissed my hand.

I forgive you, I forgive you. As Theo said, we are only mere humans.

We celebrated that we had found each other, even though we knew it couldn't last. We gently spun away from each other and then spun back; back and forth until he lifted me over his head, and I curved outwards to the earth once more, blowing a kiss to the audience, and picturing Theo's face, his eyebrow raised, his hands clapping above his head. In my final high

238

arabesque, Prince Siegfried gazed up at me, and I did exactly as Theo had said; I let myself shine.

We embraced, shared a single kiss and then…

Theo was right. This story is a masterpiece. It's better to be free in death than trapped in life.

I took a leap into the stage smoke – all before a chorus of waving swans

and Siegfried followed.

As we ran into the wings, Luc and I held hands ready for the finale, but we didn't look at each other; we just kept in character until the end of the performance, as true dancers do.

*

'Well done, Vi! You rocked,' said a voice in my ear as the girls took turns to come over to me while I leant down to untie my ribbons.

'Yeah, you totally stole the stage,' said another.

'Woah, you and Luc really have something,' said one more from the other side of the dressing room, winking as she wiped her other eye away with a cotton pad.

'Oh! Thanks! Well done to you, too,' I said back, again and again, hoping they could hear me through all the noise. Mums congested the dressing room even more as they swiped their younger daughters from the surfaces they were perched upon and blew kisses until 'the same again tomorrow.'

'Oh, love!' One mother had noticed that I was still completely in costume. She rushed to unhook the back of my *tutu* before escorting her family away. 'There you go,' she mimed, as the room slowly emptied and its hustle and bustle moved outside.

Inside, it was quiet; just me rising from white feathers.

As I stepped out of my *tutu* and slipped a jumper-dress over my head, Theo was standing there.

He crept his arms around me for a gentle hug, as though mine were still fragile wings. When the door to the dressing room screeched open again, we both jumped, and Theo let go completely.

'Oh!' Ms Madeline's face was a shape of horror. 'The girls said you were still in here, Violet... And this is—?' But she didn't look at Theo for the answer, she looked at me.

'Um—' My face was burning up.

Theo, thankfully, took a step towards her, his arm outstretched before him.

'I'm Theodore Gamble.' He nodded. 'It's wonderful to finally meet you.'

I wondered what he meant by 'finally.' I'd always assumed they knew each other. That's how it had seemed at the Coppélia show, when everyone had been standing in the foyer. *Hadn't he called her Margaret just weeks ago?* I must have misunderstood. Ms Madeline's eyebrows drew together as they did when she choreographed a dance and something didn't quite sit right. I suppose it was an unspoken rule that no men were allowed in there, and I had broken it.

'And who is *Theo*?'

I was surprised to also be interested in this answer.

'Well,' Theo laughed, 'I'm actually an *aficionado* of ballet, and I have to say, your dance school, well, it's the perfect example of beauty and discipline. But I suppose you hear this all the time, after such a successful venture…'

'No, no,' Ms Madeline interrupted with a condescending laugh, 'I assure you I do not… Well, Violet, I came in because I'd forgotten something!' Her eyes searched the room around us. 'Ah, yes, there it is!' She stretched an arm towards the mirror behind Theo, 'Excuse me! *If* you don't mind,' she said, so he had to shuffle away from me, to let her squeeze past.

Theo awkwardly shifted his weight from one foot to the other, as Ms Madeline snatched any items left behind as though they were children playing up in public.

'By the way, Violet,' she said, 'you were startling, tonight. Absolutely startling. You've truly blossomed since you were a little one. I couldn't have felt prouder, and you should believe me when I say that.'

As always, that frown accompanied every one of her words, but there was something softer about it, wasn't there? Something younger, and for a moment, she looked closer to Theo's age than I'd initially thought, or was he closer to hers? Still, as she strode backwards towards the door, I smiled at her over Theo's shoulder, and when she didn't smile back, I felt something pecking at my chest.

'Well, don't dawdle now, Violet. It's getting late. You need to make your way home.'

Ms Madeline left the door wedged open, strange for her – she was usually adamant about closing it while us dancers were inside.

'Your teacher was right, you know. I've never seen you glow so brightly,' Theo said on the car journey back, and I couldn't help but smile. 'See,' he said, with that smile again, 'look at you,' and he brushed his thumb across my cheek before his hand dropped towards my knee. He squeezed it as normal – or was it a bit more tightly than normal?

He kept looking to his left, his eyes squinting as though I was exuding a light that he was struggling to see through. The noise of other cars passing filled the silence.

I said nothing, still on a high after the concert. Eventually, Theo stammered out, 'It's great that you can be so comfortable around the opposite sex.'

It was a compliment really, but something felt backhanded about it. I looked at him and saw his eyebrows raised, his eyes focused on the road and his hands gripping the steering wheel. I nodded and smiled as he looked at me.

'Why do you think that is?' he asked.

I didn't know how to answer.

'Do you think it's a good thing?' His eyebrows raised again, but I still wasn't sure what to say. 'Oh, sorry, I just can't help but find it interesting, it's such a talent that you have; it must feel like you're in your own, magical world.'

Of course he knew of my world! Since Melody, he was the only one I'd spoken to about dreams. Here, however, in the dark car, he was making me feel uneasy, as though I was being watched before I had a chance to stumble. I let out a gentle laugh, but it sounded false.

'Well, do you?' he asked again.

'Um, I guess so?' I eventually responded.

'Do you *enjoy* that part of it, then?' He was determined.

'Uh, I don't know.' I wanted him to answer instead.

'How can you not know? You're the one doing the dancing.'

I shrugged and knew it wasn't going to be good enough.

'Well, does it *feel* enjoyable? It's okay if it does.'

'I don't know,' I said.

'Well, I suppose you'd say no if it didn't, wouldn't you?'

This time, I said nothing at all. It was getting confusing. Theo knew I'd been training with Luc for the *pas de deux* for weeks. What made this evening any different?

'It's always best to be honest, you know. I would understand.'

It was true that Theo understood most things. But it was funny, hearing him without looking him in the eye, he sounded as young as I was. The word 'immature' hovered and I rejected it. Childish was how he sounded.

My phone buzzed. I'd recently started to keep it on silent not to interrupt our dates, but it buzzed loudly against the hairbrush in my dance bag.

'You're in demand, aren't you?' Theo laughed, but I didn't pick it up.

It buzzed again, making the silence in the car even more obvious.

'If it's that girl, Bobbie, you know there's nothing wrong

with telling her how tired you're feeling if you don't feel like talking. A true friend understands that. I know you always like to be polite but being direct can often be best.'

I didn't peek but it probably was Bobbie.

After this, the silence continued until we arrived at Theo's. There, we sat on the living room sofa without talking. I wanted him to put music on, anything, but he didn't. And he didn't seem to have any intention of speaking. I wondered if I should leave; he clearly didn't want me there anymore. But something kept me rooted to the sofa. I looked from the piano to the paintings, to the bookcase and back again.

The room became smaller. *This isn't how I thought it would be after my performance went so well.* Theo's arm wrapped around me, and his head began to dip towards my chest, asking me to cradle it. As it trembled, I had no choice.

He was crying. I'd never imagined a grown man sobbing in my arms and even though I loved him and only wanted him to feel better, whatever *this* meant, it frightened me.

Holding him tightly, I managed a whisper.

'I love you,' I said into the nearest ear, but as soon as I said it, Theo's body stiffened.

'Do you?' he asked, still whimpering and looking up at me. I nodded. But his body didn't soften, and he felt too large for me to hold. Sensing my awkwardness, he sat up, his face no longer sad, but angry, aggressive. 'Do you enjoy your time with me as much as you do onstage, with *him*?'

He was talking about Luc, who I still hardly knew. Onstage, it was true, I'd felt luminous; it was everything I'd wanted it to be, and I was everything I thought Theo had wanted me to be.

There he was, those fierce eyes, staring, darkening, and he may as well have been pointing his finger because every word he pronounced pierced straight through me.

'Oh, Coppélia, it must be easy to be beautiful. It must be easy to forget what people mean to you when everyone loves you. How do you think it makes *me* feel?'

It was obvious how it all made him feel, but I couldn't seem to do very much about it. Theo's voice was ringing in my ears. I noticed the tower of books on the side-table, and how they hadn't shifted since he first knocked them into order.

'…I'm feeling so worthless right now. Can't you say just how *much* you love me? How much I really mean to you?'

There were five books about ballet, two about Spain, one about Japan, and another about all kinds of dances across Europe. Such knowledge, and yet…

'Are you even listening? Do you want to lose me? Is that it? I'm speaking to you! Don't you care?'

My phone buzzed on the coffee table in front of us. I would have done anything to talk to Bobbie at that moment.

'*Is* that Bobbie? You ought to watch your reputation, hanging around with someone like her. She isn't the classiest. My friends are much more on your level. Why aren't you trying to make me feel better? Why aren't you saying anything? Speak!'

'I…' My voice cracked.

'What? Spit it out.' He looked all teeth.

'I just, I love you,' I said. 'I do. I really love you.'

He rolled his eyes and sighed, still angry, but in a way that made me feel like he was giving up. I couldn't understand why he was so frustrated with me.

'Show it, then! For my sake! You looked like you were besotted with *him* up *there*, in front of hundreds of people.'

Soon, his hands were gripping my shoulders with some force, but I still didn't understand what I'd done that was so wrong. He no longer wanted me to speak. He yanked at my clothes, peeling my dress away, and then my tights, as though it was my very outfit that made him so angry. His nails dug into me and his kisses were different: more tooth than lip as they bit into my neck.

'You must have practised that *pas de deux* with him an awful lot to get it so perfect.'

Then, right there, without even removing every item of clothing, he did it, used his passion to remind me of what I was; who I belonged to.

There on the sofa, I did what Ms Madeline said to do years ago when I was first learning how to *pirouette*. She said to find a sticker on the wall and focus on it, so I could keep balance. There, I found – not a sticker – but a prominent shape in the Artexed ceiling and kept my eyes on it without even blinking. It was the outline of a little ballerina. Yes, she was in a strong *arabesque*. And then I saw another and another, all dancing away. *How beautiful.*

'Who's a bad girl?' Theo whispered into my ear. As a tear escaped my eye, I said, 'I am,' and his face responded with a smile.

I looked at my ballerinas, all the girls in the ceiling. *Yes, one pas de deux – even with the same partner – really can be so different from the last.*

Afterwards, I laid in his arms with my head against his chest, and I felt my own racing with panic. It swelled so big that it was almost up in my mouth, telling me, *this is what you're capable of, Violet. No more than this.* I felt safer while his eyes were shut tight. *We'll slow down, now. This won't have to happen again.*

The following morning, Theo's eyes still looked tormented, and I knew it was because of me. Were relationships supposed to be this difficult? I wasn't sure what to say or do. Without a word or a look, Theo slipped out of bed and walked to the kitchen. A creep of light showed itself through the gap in the blinds, and the stillness told me it was way past ten o'clock. Time had run even further away and left me completely behind.

FAITH

I was far too late for Psychology but, thankfully, I got to double English just as Miss Allsop was shutting the door. I slouched in the back corner by the radiator and felt my eyelids drooping. She was talking a lot, about poetry and stories meaning different things depending on people's interpretations, and her round, freckled face kept shaking me awake. All we had to do was listen and nod, but I couldn't pay much attention. Instead, I allowed each lid to land for as long as possible, and I closed in on myself.

'Who's *Theeeeeeeeeeeeeeeoooooooooo?*'

Instead of Miss Allsop, I could hear a girl's voice in the distance, and when I managed to open my eyes again, I saw her rubbing a tear of laughter from her face and smiling right at me as though she was in awe of something I'd said. Another girl was looking at me and frowning, with a pen hanging from the corner of her mouth.

'That's the most we've ever heard Violet speak,' she said, still looking right at me, as though I couldn't hear her, as though her voice was knocking against me, but there was nobody inside. It was the first time she'd ever said my name, and everyone was laughing.

'Stop it, Theo. Stop it,' one of the boys said, as he pursed his lips and squinted his eyes towards me.

I was beginning to panic. *What else have I told them?*

248

Everyone's face was happy, except Miss Allsop's. She was standing still at the front of the class, leaning forward a little as though I was still talking. Her full face looked ready to burst. I'd never seen her so angry before.

'Everyone, be quiet!'

There was a hush, and heads turned away from me.

'Violet, come with me.' Miss Allsop stood up and pointed towards the door. 'Everyone talk amongst yourselves for a while, please.'

When she shut the door, her voice softened and I followed her bouffant of highlights along the corridor towards an empty classroom. There, she pulled out a chair for me to sit down, and I collapsed into it, hunched over from all the humiliation.

She sat opposite me. 'I think we need to have a chat,' she said, sitting opposite.

'Now, this isn't you,' she said, looking down at me, 'what's going on? I've seen that your grades aren't as good lately, when you hand your work in, that is, and you can – clearly – hardly stay awake in class!'

I looked up at Miss Allsop's face. It was properly concerned.

And then the tears came.

I couldn't say exactly what was wrong. It may have been that I'd been hiding so much that it was overwhelming. She couldn't possibly understand mine and Theo's relationship, even if I attempted to explain.

'Oh dear, Violet, what is it?' She shifted her chair closer alongside and put one arm around me. She thought we were really putting our heads together on this one. 'You can tell me,

Violet, I'm your teacher, and if there's anything worrying you this much, I really ought to know.'

As I opened my mouth, I felt the tears in there, too, and as one note left my tongue, my stomach came to life and provided me with a thousand breaths. *Hu – hu – hmff, hu – hu – hmff,* faster and faster, and the embarrassment made me feel worse. It was no use, I wasn't even sure why I couldn't answer her. Tiredness? It would have sounded so ridiculous, especially after all the drama.

Miss Allsop's arm was still around me, her hand resting lightly upon my shoulder, which only made me cry more. 'Oh, Violet, what is it?'

I shook my head, giving up on even trying to pronounce any words in such a state.

'Are you being bullied? Is that it? Is it anyone in your class?'

Then the '*hmmff*' of my cries grew even louder; I couldn't cope with it anymore, all the build-up, I was trying to explode into speech but there was something constricting my breath.

I thought about Frederick all those years ago, the tears in his eyes as he'd picked up the pieces of his comic books all ripped into shreds. It made me feel awful. I shook and shook my head. It definitely wasn't bullying, it wasn't like that. I didn't deserve such attention.

'Violet, if that's not it, why are you so upset? Is it the dance? Is it all too much?'

Sobbing, I managed to shrug my shoulders. I looked up at her concerned face. She really did want it to be the two of us against the world; she was only young, herself, perhaps she would have understood more than I expected her to.

But there was nothing more that could be said. Her hand patted my arm and she sat up.

'Would it help if you had someone else to talk to?'

I shook my head.

'Okay, dear, well, would you like to stay here for a while?'

I nodded, still trying to get my breath back.

'Alright,' she said, her eyebrow raised with questions that made me feel painfully self-conscious. There really was nothing I could tell her. Theo didn't look at me that way; he understood everything.

As Miss Allsop slid her chair back to where she'd found it, she said, 'Actually, Violet, perhaps you'd best take the rest of the day off. You look like you need some sleep. Are you okay to get home?'

She smiled and I managed to nod back as I picked up my bag to leave. *Sleep?* I thought. *How on earth? I have so many more performances to do and so much schoolwork to catch up with.*

At home, I collapsed on my bed without even taking my jacket off. My body felt twice its usual weight, as though someone had filled it up with sand, and my head felt too heavy for my neck to hold up. I was a toy after its batteries had run out, but I was in no rush for anyone to replace them.

At the same time, my head throbbed like toothache as it tried to make sense of everything that had happened. I'd been on pins since leaving Theo that morning. Everything had felt so wrong in the car. Neither of us had spoken: he'd breathed, and I'd breathed, he'd sighed and I'd sighed; not even our silences had been in time with one another. And he hadn't been in touch since. Still, I clung to my phone, hoping for a pulse.

I logged into my socials and typed 'Theodore Gamble' hoping for different results to the first time. Not that I even knew why I wanted to see him. I just needed … something.

Nothing.

'Theo Gamble'

Still nothing.

'Theo'

Hundreds of profiles were listed, all the opposite of him. So young, so tacky. Maybe – somewhere within the social media world, there were wall posts between Theo and his theatre friends, saying, 'Oh darling, it was fabulous that you got to see my performance in The Big Smoke!'

As I scrolled down the list, I saw my notifications increasing.

Grace has tagged you in a photo.
Leigh Chan has commented on a photo of you.
Maria has commented on a photo of you.
So many names.

I clicked on the photo. There we all were, swans and cygnets, smiling from the dressing room. For a moment, I felt so happy, so proud, and then, when I looked more closely, as though I was a complete outsider, I noticed Luc's arm was wrapped tightly around my shoulders. Him and me. Me and him. Odette and Prince Siegfried, entwined again. I wished I could prise Luc's fingers away. *Please, let go!* Even though I couldn't find Theo on there, what if he found me and this brought it all back up?

Luc has mentioned you in a photo.

I panicked and definitely didn't want to read whatever Luc had said

but the comment was right there at the top of them all!

Violet Hart *we were on fire tonight.*

That was when I untagged myself from the photo and deactivated my Facebook account.

I considered that I may have been cruelly ignorant around Theo the night before. Maybe a little off-balance, too defensive, perhaps? *I should have been more sympathetic. I'd said how I felt about him quietly, I know, but that wasn't good enough. It wasn't like Theo to act that way, so vulnerable. It must be easy to be beautiful.* For more than a moment onstage, I admit, I had felt like someone else; I was supposed to, I was Odette and Odile, *but I'd possibly become too caught up in my characters, felt my feathers in the air, seen my beak as it pointed up to the beaming stars;* dance had always allowed me to lose myself like that. I could hear Ms Madeline's voice: *We have to become entirely impressionable, change like captivating chameleons! He'd probably only said that mean stuff about Bobbie because he felt he hadn't seen his own friends for a while* – because he'd prioritised me.

I read Theo's last text.

18:03, one hour before last night's performance:
Good luck, my little duckling. Let them see those feet
patter. All my love. x

His words had made me feel so fuzzy all over, and now, they
made my stomach feel swollen with guilt. He must have typed
them not long before leaving his house to find his seat in the
front row, just to see me. *He knew I was nervous and he'd given
me extra confidence before stepping onstage. But where had his
love been last night? And why were yesterday's texts – so perfect,
so loveable – the only ones there to refer to? Where is he right now?*

I must have read that text about fifty times, just hoping it would
somehow teleport me back to the day before, when nothing had
gone wrong. I would have chosen nervous happiness over restless
anxiety any day… Still, those words did nothing but torture me,
and no new texts arrived to replace them.

While I waited – not knowing what for – I saw that there
were a few unread messages from Bobbie. *It had been her
causing my phone to buzz last night.* There were five messages
in total, but as usual, equivalent to one. Bobbie spoke as she
thought.

22:31
Hey Swanny, saw your show. Bloody amazeballs…

22:32
Also saw your guy! Looked alright from the back. Good
on ya, girl!

22:32
Didn't see the front, mind

22:33
Anyway, sorrynotsorry I had to run. Didn't want Ms Madeline spotting me. Ms Mad-at-me, more like. I'll be the death of that one!!!

22:52
P.S. Did I say you rocked? You can be my bird ANY day. Xxxxx

Bobbie always managed to coax a laugh out of me. For a minute, I almost forgot anything strange had happened. We hadn't spoken properly for weeks, not since I'd seen her at the bus stop and we'd said all those awful things. Now, I wanted to send some emojis, the ones crying with laughter, ask how she was doing lately, how she was *really* doing. It would have felt so good to just talk to her. Still, I knew I couldn't. *What if she asks more about Theo?*

Instead, I replied:

☺ Thanks, so glad you enjoyed.

I put my phone down on the windowsill, suddenly feeling quite alone.

'Well, if I can't talk to Bob, you'll have to do.' I turned to Ana, who was just sitting there, no sign of a smile on her face.

'Anything to say?'

As usual, nothing. *Useless.*

*

Mist was curled up on my chest. Her eyes looked up at me as they struggled to stay open. *Do you have to go to another performance tonight?* I didn't have the energy. Her fluffy head butted my chin. We could have just as easily stayed exactly as we were. I turned on my side as her warm body clung to me; just what I needed.

A faint knock on the door made me open my eyes again.

'Alright, Vila?' Dad's face had appeared in the gap, almost as dozy-looking as mine felt.

I nodded.

'Ah, that's where that darn cat is. She always pops up when you least expect it, doesn't she? Always making me jump, she is.'

Mist's head turned to look at him. *How insulting.*

'Anyway, love, just thought I'd give you a heads up, Faith and I will be coming to see you dance on Saturday – the last show. She picked us up two tickets yesterday. Couldn't believe I wasn't seeing your show, so she'd gone to get them before I could say anything. Hope that's alright? You'll hardly know we're there!'

I wasn't sure what to say. Why was this woman's name popping up all the time all of a sudden? I didn't even want to perform again.

'Still, she is right. I should see my own daughter's show… I know it's important to you – all that practice you've been putting in!' Dad had opened the door a bit wider.

'I guess so…' *But why now?*

'Right, that answers that, then. I've always thought of it as more of a 'Mam's thing' and I know Bob's mother has often helped out, but I think your mam would be turning in her grave if she thought I wasn't supporting our ballerina.'

I sat up. It didn't feel right that Faith and Mam were being mentioned in the same conversation…

'Anyhow, let me know when you're ready later and I'll give you a lift, okay?' He looked so hopeful, so oblivious to what he'd just done.

I nodded, biting my bottom lip as Dad clicked the door shut. Then the tears rolled.

THE AFTER PARTY

By Saturday morning, I'd decided to stop checking my phone every thirty seconds. Theo hadn't texted all week and neither had he turned up at the arts centre. I suppose Bobbie would have called it *ghosting* if it were happening to her. It felt like it, as though all our memories together had become hazy, crossed further into the past, gossamer nights.

Still, these things take time.

When I sat to eat my peanut butter and banana on toast at the kitchen table, I returned to the last night we saw each other, the way he had touched me, the sharpness in his tone; *you must have practised that pas de deux with him an awful lot to get it so perfect*. By the time I filled up my flask with hot chocolate and jumped into the truck with Dad, I was convinced the end of Theo and Violet was for the best. When I got to the arts centre early and eager for the performance, and as I walked through the foyer with my dance bag over my shoulder, I recalled everything I'd been waiting for – for years – and finally began to feel strong again. *Ballet is my true love* I reminded myself. I'd have been foolish to let anything else take priority.

So, when I heard my phone buzz against the dressing room mirror and I saw Theo's name pop up on the screen, I was annoyed; at myself because of the excitement that ran through my whole body all at once, that made me drop my powdered rouge on the floor, leaving one side of my face blood-red.

Hey Coppy, good luck for later. I'll meet you after your final performance for a little celebration, if you're willing? I've been thinking about you. x

He was like the hot chocolate that calmed me down before a performance, and his kiss at the end was the warm sweetness of the last drop.

*

It had been more difficult to dance while everything was on my mind. I'd got used to the eyes of strangers the last few evenings, but during the *matinée*, my nerves of the first night had returned in readiness for the evening performance. *Dad, Faith, Theo.* Still, I'd managed it —and Luc, perhaps having sensed the anxiety in my eyes as he passed me doing my stretches in the corridor, whispered,

'You don't have to prove anything, you know? Dance is just part of you,' he said, 'you're just being ... honest. It wouldn't be good to lie, right?'

I'd never thought of it that way, but it explained Luc's confidence, in class and on stage; the way he glided without question, posed without a pardon. *I am here for you to see, and if you do not see me, I'll be here anyway.* Dance was part of him too.

After that, the performance had actually gone quite well. Luc and I had grown so familiar with the stage, the audience's response to our positions, and of course, with each other; the speed of a *pirouette*, the shake of a thigh held in position for almost too long, a secret pause to catch a breath. We worked together, knowing that without the other one, a *pas de deux* would be pointless. A new path had formed, between each other and across the stage; a curtsy and bow to the audience after the finale, a run back into the wings, and then the obligatory group hug with all the dancers backstage until next time. For a week, it had been our lives, and now there was only one performance left before we entered reality again.

'Violet, would you like to come for lunch with us?'

Grace spoke to me through the spotlit mirror, flattening any stray black hairs around her temples and quickly rolling extra deodorant under each arm. Two accompanying cygnets fluttered their thick eyelashes as they checked nothing had smudged, then turned from side to side, smoothing their bony hips and tummies as though to banish any weight for good. I remembered the warm ham sandwich in my bag, probably sweating alongside one of the bulbs. *Why hadn't I brought something better?*

One of the cygnets squawked something about Luc being outside, and I could see the tops of her ears turning red. These girls were in the class below me – the class from years ago, and we hadn't spoken much since then, not even throughout rehearsals. Even though we were the same age, they seemed so much younger, the way they ruffled their feathers about a boy. Still, as it was the last day of the show, I said,

'Sure,' zipping my bag up tight in case the ham sandwich crept out before us all. 'Where are you going?'

As I slid my phone into my pocket, it buzzed in my hand. Theo. *Is he cancelling? Do I need to prepare for an evening of sadness again?*

'Meet us in the café if you like?' Grace smiled and the cygnets were at her side by the dressing room door.

'Okay, see you in a bit,' I said, beginning to read the text while quickly zipping up my dance jacket.

Hey Coppy, think you can get away for an hour? I'm outside. x

OUTSIDE? Again, I was confused. I knew he was coming to the last performance but I didn't expect to see him so soon. *Is something wrong?*

Theo was online.

I began typing.

Ok, see you in 5 ☺ x

Then, I removed the ☺ not to appear overeager.

I had a sinking feeling in my stomach because I'd always thought we weren't one of those couples who played games.

He replied – immediately. Maybe we didn't have to be one of those couples. Maybe it wasn't too late.

I'm so glad, Coppy. I'll be waiting at the entrance for you. x

It didn't sound like he wanted to break up. Nothing like what Bobbie had sent people, anyway.

As I walked along the corridor, I picked up the pace, hoping none of the other girls would notice me. I could see Grace and the cygnets through the centre's café window, giggling with Luc in the queue. I doubted they knew what they were getting into, with someone who wore dance right down to the bone.

Luckily, the foyer was empty while everyone lunched – not a receptionist in sight – and there he was, *Theo*. I mouthed it as I walked towards him, *my Theo*, in his black polo neck, waiting where we'd first met. Hadn't he been the beginning of everything?

Theo wrapped his arm around me and escorted me out to the car park. *My gentleman.* He opened the passenger door of his car, just as before, and I found myself climbing in.

'Can I?' he asked, as he joined me from the other side and leant over to kiss my cheek as I buckled up.

I nodded, timid once again, as though we had rewound many weeks, right back to the shyness that had shielded me at the start. *Come back, confidence.* But there was also something exciting about our newness. Just the touch of his hand – and that woody, fruit-spice smell of his hair; the low calmness of his voice alongside me again was the angel on my shoulder to balance everything out. Here was the charming Theo who'd approached me in the foyer all those weeks before. And we were finally together again.

Theo pulled out of the car park and drove along the road Dad would usually take, which made me wonder if he was taking me back to the Common, but then he took a different turning altogether and I suddenly realised I had no idea what he had planned.

Is that a flicker of blue in the distance? The sea? Are we heading to the beach? Surely Theo knew I needed to be back in time before the final performance? Plus, I couldn't let my hair or make-up get messy before the big night. I'd need time to stretch, and my before-performance routine had become so important lately, especially the past week; holding on to my little patterns had kept me sane. I suppose I'd need to explain that to Theo – in time.

As we approached the coastal wall, he opened the car windows. There was the gentle breeze on my cheeks. The sea was loud and so alive, just metres below us as Theo joined the line of cars parked along the edge. Water had its patterns too. It drifted in and out, always in conflict, always leaving, always returning. So soothing, so powerful and yet, well within its right to take up such a large part of the world, it never left that familiar, sandy bed.

The couple in the car alongside us were sharing a tray of chips. I could almost smell those chips, soaked with vinegar and – I bet – smothered in salt. On what felt like a summer's day, couples were strolling along the promenade, so many couples, hands in each other's jean pockets, kissing between licks of ice cream, one girl letting go of her boyfriend's hand to jump onto the sea wall; both of them dizzy with sea-air smiles. And there we were, as happy as all of them, weren't we? And, for the first time, as public as all of them.

'Look, my love,' Theo rested his hand on top of mine, 'I'm very sorry about the other night. I think I must have been in shock. All these weeks and months, you've felt like you just belonged to me,' he stroked his thumb over mine, 'so when I saw you out there in the world, so *unbelievably* beautiful, and I suddenly realised I had to share you, I panicked. I felt like I was losing part of you, all of you, and ... us. I know we'd talked about it a bit, but I was surprised by how it actually felt when I saw you with someone else.' He looked me straight in the eyes. They were sorry, sad eyes. 'Do you ever feel like that? Like you just want to keep something secret, so other people won't see how good it is and smash it into the smallest of pieces?'

I thought of Mam. I hadn't told a soul about her since she'd passed. I suppose that was because I wanted to preserve the memories in the exact way I chose to; the way she could change the energy of a room or a whole house in less than a second, that smell of moonberry in her hair, or her soothing whisper when I couldn't sleep. I missed that.

Yes, I understood what Theo meant. It was strange how alike we were. Those days when I thought I'd lost him, I'd felt like all my pieces were missing.

'I do sometimes wish I didn't have to share you with everyone, but don't worry, I know that's irrational – love makes us all that way sometimes, right?'

I nodded. If anyone had witnessed me checking my phone like it was my lifeline...

'And, I know I can't be selfish. You're so talented. Let's face it, it would be a crime to hide you from the world.' His thumb stroked my wrist and I looked away. I still hadn't learnt how to respond to compliments. 'Still, isn't private love the truest of all? Anyway, I don't want to bore you with my anxieties, I just wanted to apologise – face-to-face, not through a screen. Can you forgive me?'

I looked into his eyes – they'd become buttery again – but as I was about to speak, Theo pressed his finger to my lips.

'Actually, no… Too soon. You need time to think about this after I've been so…'

I thought I saw his chin wobble – just slightly.

'There's no need to do anything hasty. Promise me you'll just … think about us? Just in case you change your mind.'

I nodded, wanting to say something that would alleviate his worries. *What decision does he think I'll make?* After him not contacting me, I hadn't realised this was my choice. *How lonely must he have been, sitting in his little bungalow, giving me the time and space he'd thought I needed?*

'Right, you wait here,' Theo added, tapping me on the knee before he got out of the car, 'won't be long.'

I risked a smile at the couple alongside us. *We're a couple too,* I wanted to say. *We're on our first date. We aren't a secret! Maybe we'll take a walk along the promenade. Maybe one day, we'll go swimming together, have a picnic on a large rock and lie on our sides on the sand, whispering between kisses, not caring who will see.*

But I did care if Dad saw. Luc's words haunted me. No, it wasn't good to lie.

Never mind, Theo's smiling face turned up at the car, half hidden by a giant tub of vanilla ice cream and two spoons.

'Thought you deserved a treat after all that dancing,' he whispered, plonking the tub into both my hands, and then snatching one of the spoons away, 'go on, then, my love, dig in.'

I shouldn't have really, not on a dance day, but I didn't want to offend him… *Just a few spoonfuls.*

Together, we looked out at the sea, one of Theo's arms

265

around my shoulders as we shared the sweetness. Theo didn't know yet, but I'd already forgiven him. In fact, everything that had happened made me believe in us even more. We were no longer too good to be true. We were real.

'Nothing like ice cream on a warm day,' Theo said, 'ya think?'

I nodded. Contrast was often good. It made you appreciate things.

*

As I joined Luc onstage for the final performance, I noticed that he had a certain sparkle in his eye while we danced. He'd always had an air about him, but this was different. His eyes were wider, slightly amused, pleased with themselves as they looked through me at something – no, at someone else in the wings. Grace. That was it. She clapped for him. Luc didn't just look passionate, he looked … happy. I knew how that felt, glad to be back in that familiar place again.

The audience welcomed us back to life with a song of applause as a curtain of cygnets swept across the stage and confetti of feathers fell. This, at the end of *Swan Lake* was not a death but a very particular reawakening within both of us; swans reborn and burning as brightly as phoenixes. We did not fall. We flew.

After the performance, I felt the exhilaration of it all, not just the ballet, but the feeling of finally having everything perfectly aligned; so enormously that I already missed it, in the knowledge that one day, it would all disappear again, just as it always did.

This is it.

The foyer was buzzing with ballerinas; mums hugging daughters, dancers hugging dancers, coats draped over shoulders and costume bags dragging along the floor, dancers spinning with excitement before their music box would be shut again.

Dad gave me a wave as he made his way towards me from the other side of the crowd. Alongside him, a lady's face lit up, trying to draw a smile out of me. *That must be Faith.* I sort of recognised her ... Usually, I'd feel all smiled out, but thanks to Theo, happiness came easily this time. *Isn't she the woman who dropped those vegetables outside Secret Haven a while back? The one with the blue car?*

'Here you go,' Dad said, handing me a single red rose. 'We're heading off now, so we'll leave you celebrate with your friends, but well, we just wanted to say how wonderful you were in the show. Really wonderful.'

Since when did they become a 'we'?

Faith gave me a farewell wink and whispered something in Dad's ear. He nodded, she tugged his sleeve and together, they shuffled away.

'Ah! Violet!' Luc approached with a wide smile and gave me a sweaty hug.

'Well done for this week,' I said, 'you were amazing. Everyone was.'

As Grace walked over, 'Catch you both at the after-party,' I mumbled,

and slipped away.

The lies were expanding like plump caterpillars in my stomach.

The truth is, I would have gone to the after-party – especially after the success of the show – and I may have enjoyed it, but when it came to choosing the party or Theo, there was no competition. I rested my head on the car window as we drove home in the dark, just like old times. As I listened to the drizzle of rain, each drop like a tiny firework, popping just for us, I dragged my fingertip across the foggy glass.

Violet ♥ *Theo*

It helped the caterpillars stay still for a while.

Theo reached for my hand.

As I looked straight ahead at the dark Common, almost falling asleep, I noticed something in the middle of the road; a figure, crouched over in the distance. *A girl?* There were arms, draped so delicately over her head, frozen into position with such discipline. *No, it can't be a girl.* I rubbed my eyes, afraid I was hallucinating. *Am I that tired after the show?*

'What – on – earth?' Theo muttered under his breath, as he squinted over the dashboard and slowed the car down. I noticed how curved the girl's back was, how damp her clothes were, and how much smaller she was than I'd expected. She was ghostly pale and still bent over, unmoving, even in the breeze. *Is she crying?*

Theo pulled the car to one side and we both got out. The

girl was just feet away, but I could see that it actually wasn't a girl at all. Her hair was feathers, her sullen face, which I'd thought was the hood of a coat, was a beaked one. Her arms were in fact, a large pair of wings.

'Oh, you poor thing,' I heard Theo whisper alongside me. Patches of blood had flowered along her coat. She made no sound, just laid there, the long neck of her bowed right down to the tarmac road, praying to survive. No prayer would work, though; her flesh-pink beak was pinched perfectly closed. She wasn't moving because she was dead – had been for – perhaps – a few hours. Dad had brought home dead pheasants before, but this was different.

I looked up to see the guilty pylon staring down at us, giving none of its spark away. It must have felt the thud while it stood there, wired up to the dark sky around it. I felt my eyes tearing up just thinking about the shock, the head-first hit, the neck threatening to break.

I turned to Theo and saw the same concern in his eyes.

'Just a moment,' he said, gently pressing my shoulder.

I watched him walk to the car and return with a black bag.

'I wouldn't look, my love. You don't need to see anymore.'

I turned away but in the car's wing mirror, I saw Theo sliding the bird into its body bag, a black bin liner, before tying the end where any air would have got in.

'It's best we move her from here,' he whispered, as though she could hear, 'you know, out of any more danger,' he added as he lifted her into the boot of the car. Next, he slammed it shut. We both looked at each other, doing something good – I thought – but I couldn't help feeling like an accomplice as we drove away with a corpse behind us.

When we got to Theo's house, he got out first. He walked to the back of the car and carried the fallen angel across the threshold. It reminded me of when he'd first found me walking along the Common that night many months ago. What would have happened if he hadn't? It wasn't a pleasant thought... I waited in the living room while Theo transported the goose through the kitchen, then disposed of her in what I assumed to be a dustbin in the back garden.

'So sad,' he bellowed from the kitchen sink, 'beauty just isn't safe these days, is it?'

Before I could answer, he carried on, 'pure beauty needs to be looked after,' he said, joining me in the living room. 'People are so unappreciative, don't you think?'

'Definitely,' I said. Everything could feel perfect again, now he was by my side. It was just us, with no interruptions.

'Anyway,' he sighed, 'now, back to you, my ballerina!' again gazing at me as he dried his hands with a towel. 'Would you like some water? Oh! Your socks! I've warmed them ready!' He ran to collect them from the radiator. His urgency to please was adorable.

'Thanks,' I laughed, glad to be once again curled up on the sofa. Our rhythm was already returning, I could feel it.

'I've missed you, Coppy,' Theo said, holding up my chin so I could look him in the eyes, 'so, so much.'

'Me too,' I said. 'I mean,' another awkward laugh escaped me – I wished that laugh would disappear forever, 'I've missed you too.'

'Well, no matter, we're here, now, both of us,' Theo whispered in my ear before kissing the side of my neck. I felt so grateful that after everything, I was still allowed to love him.

Within minutes of kissing, Theo led me to his bedroom, and I did nothing but let him. *No thought, just feelings.* As our faces remained interlocked and he kicked the door shut with his foot, we fell sideways onto his bed, toes looking for toes, fingers feeling for fingers, both catching up with all the time we'd lost. *Love is something to be fully absorbed,* I thought, *now, let it absorb you.*

DIGGING IN

The whole night had passed, and I had a feeling most of the morning had too. It was definitely Sunday. I could smell a roast in the oven, something I hadn't experienced since Mam was at home; carrots sliced into coins and those crunchy roast potatoes, honey-covered parsnip and lamb gravy covering everything...

My body felt hollow since the night before, and my stomach grumbled. Different to usual, the bedroom door was ajar, and I could see the blur of Theo, floating back and forth.

'Hey, sleepyhead! Dinner is *served!*' Theo swung the door open with a wide smile that said he was proud of his creation.

I slid my fluffy socks back on and tiptoed out to the kitchen, where each plate was piled high with vegetables, topped with a crunchy Yorkshire pudding and lashings of gravy. I hadn't eaten much all week, so my stomach was desperate to catch up. It was just the feast I needed.

'Now, I hope you know how much time I've spent on this,' he said with a glint in his tired eyes. 'Please – dig in.' He nudged the air with his fork until I embarked on the hefty breast of chicken before me.

'Oh, sorry, I prefer the dark meat, I shouldn't have assumed you'd be the same,' Theo said as he saw me searching for something a little lighter beneath the gravy. 'We can't be the same in all ways, can we?' He was already gorging as though he hadn't eaten for days.

I managed to load some meat onto my fork and finally sank my teeth into it. It tasted like beef at first, but sweet, almost, and definitely very rich. Still, I was famished, so I quickly scooped up a potato – greasy from the meat – followed by a crunch of Yorkshire.

'So, do you like it?' Theo slowly chewed what was left of his mouthful.

I watched him, savouring every part of it as it paddled over his tongue.

'Tell me you love it.'

He swilled it down with some elderflower cordial, and I used this as an opportunity to do the same.

'Go on then, tuck in.' He watched every morsel pass my lips until I picked up another piece of chewy chicken, trying to pretend that something didn't taste wrong.

'I'm still waiting,' he said, with that sensual smile of his.

When I swallowed, his smile became more mischievous.

'There we are. Good girl. Do you like it?'

I nodded before quickly drinking more cordial. Something tasted off. Had he left the chicken out for too long in the heat? I watched Theo as he gobbled everything up. *Doesn't he realise something isn't right with the chicken?* His plate was almost empty, whereas I teased the cutlery around mine, nipping at the potato, picking up a carrot every now and then as my stomach growled 'no' to accepting anything else.

When I looked up again, I glanced towards the French doors leading to the back garden. It was then I noticed it. A pink webbed foot, all alone on the patio, like an abandoned ballet shoe. And there! Alongside the kitchen sink, was the droopy goose's head! It had been there watching us eat the whole time.

I placed my cutlery together and felt something grow inside me. It lengthened its neck, flapped its wings and sunk its head deep into the pit of my stomach. I saw Theo staring back at me as though he was about to burst with laughter, and there were traces of gravy around the corners of his lips.

'Sorry,' I mumbled, 'I'm already full,' and I took flight to the bathroom feeling as though I could throw up everything, feeling *mad*.

Theo wouldn't do that sort of thing, surely? I knew Theo hadn't killed the wild goose. It was already dead. *Still, shouldn't you treat a body with respect?* Mam had looked so calm at the hospital all those years ago. She was also taken away much too soon, with no idea of what to expect, gently collected from the side of the road.

From the bathroom, I could hear the clink of cutlery and plates in the sink, and the running of water. He was carrying on as normal out there, while I was wiping vomit from my chin. As I opened the door, he shouted from the kitchen,

'Are you okay, my love? Some sort of intolerance?'

I groaned but he didn't seem to hear. He was humming a tune, a classic I couldn't put my finger on. Yes, I had an intolerance...

I'm not sure how the afternoon dragged into the evening. I think we sat on the sofa and talked – if I got any words out. Every so often, my brain seemed to pause and rewind back to the kitchen table and the poor goose on the road – not that I wanted Theo to know what I was thinking. I tried to listen to him, but I just couldn't focus – I don't think he could tell. The bungalow seemed small and large, all at the same time. I felt small. Sunlight beamed through the living room window and yet, there we were, cooped up inside, skulked in shadow and the stench of a cooked goose.

We soon relocated to his bedroom; it was just the natural order of things and by that stage, I felt completely weak from my ordeal.

'Let's get you comfortable,' Theo said, plumping a pillow for my head. I fell spread-eagle on top of the duvet cover, just content with the comfort for a while.

Until then, with my sudden lack of energy, I hadn't questioned how often we made love, but I wondered, was it excessive? Then again, I had little to compare it to. Did love excuse everything?

I wanted him to get his hands off me as he stroked my collarbone. *Leave me alone. Let me be!* He went on and on about religion – that was his latest topic – ignorant of my distress. *Did* love excuse everything? Did it really?

I knew I shouldn't be fickle, letting my actions – or my words – be affected by every whim of a new mood, but it would have been so easy to fall asleep while Theo banged on and on about how God was an illusion; to an extent, everything was, he seemed sure, but I began to imagine that he was an illusion, too. That was a more interesting thought. He may also have been the most deluded of all.

Yes, he was sure of every word, and yet, I was for the first time, thinking: *I'm bored, how selfish of me.* And I wanted to laugh, but nothing was funny, only ridiculous. Still, I opened my wings wider and listened out for the something I supposed I must have been missing.

'You know, any religion is just man's creation for the purpose of rules, guidelines to maintain some kind of order upon life. I mean, how could you possibly believe in something there are so many versions of?' Even though he was asking a question, he didn't seem to be asking me. He was looking at his own shadow on the ceiling.

The shadow reminded me of a crow that I'd once seen. I'd been sitting in the garden when I was little and there had been a small bird splashing around in the bird bath. I hadn't noticed the crow until it was swiping at the sparrow, and then I'd heard a kind of keening. *Too late.* Thankfully, Theo wasn't looking for answers. I wondered – as I stared at that ceiling and noticed the crow growing hair in the spiralling Artex if – ironically – he was asking someone above.

Still, I let him talk. I did like how he made it seem as though we had the same qualms, as though I was on his intellectual wavelength, but I also felt guilty that I really wasn't. From a young age, I'd always believed in many things that weren't visible. It was what brought life to everything, the mystery. Even so, Theo made sense most of the time, and he had a point. *How could something apparently true be so optional?*

'No, I believe in none of it,' he continued. 'I believe in man, and man only,' and I assumed he meant women, too. I reminded myself that he'd thought about everything in great depth, and my puny thoughts were far behind his.

At the same time, I found myself irritated by him. I wanted to go home and dance, or read a book, or walk to the beach and split-leap over the waves. *What time is it? Around six? There's still time for me to have a real evening if I leave this second…*

I hadn't realised Theo was looking at me...

The guilt.

Then, he turned me around, his knees were either side of me, and he had those hungry eyes again.

'Look.' He clasped his hands around my ears without warning, parted my lips with his and plugged his tongue down my throat. As I was about to catch my breath, he pulled away. He looked down at the heat I could feel rising in my cheeks. 'Only I can make you feel this way, no one else. Am I right?'

I nodded. Of course I nodded.

Theo quickly got to his feet and put a record on. He returned, smiling at me with one eyebrow raised. Yes, I recognised it. Tchaikovsky. *Swan Lake*. It was the one called *The Dying Swan*. Tremendously beautiful but terribly sad.

Theo lifted the duvet over us and began to whisper things in my ear, so close that I couldn't make out what he was saying. *Should I be speaking too?*

He bit my ear – just a tickle – and then broke away to say,

'Lovely, you don't have to say a thing. You mustn't ever feel under any pressure, okay? I know I've said it before but I do really mean it.'

So, of course I said nothing, did nothing but lie there, feeling rather than thinking, just as we'd agreed.

'Keep those eyes open, though, darling, so I can look at you,' Theo said, smoothing back my eyelids with his thumbs. 'That's right, yes,' he murmured, 'just so beautiful,' he was panting. 'No, don't blink. That's right, now then, give me a smile.'

Things were different to before. The music wasn't calming, it was so loud that it filled the whole house, and it occurred to me that the neighbours wouldn't hear my screams if I was to even try to make a sound. Nevertheless, my rescuer covered my smiling mouth as he stared right into me, with dizzy eyes as his urgency continued

and continued

and continued

until nothing seemed good enough and nothing seemed fast enough.

Here I am, I realised, *like the goose, being dug into with a sharp knife*

but he no longer looked at me, only through me; far through me to someplace dark, and with nothing to stop him, he kept going,

again and again and again,

until I was afraid I would soon disappear beneath him

and so, when the real pain came, my whole body taken over with no room left to say, 'No! Please, STOP,'

I did disappear.

There I was, back at Secret Haven, where only the smell of Mam's lavender and the blue sky could wash away everything that hurt, the place where a bruised knee was gently kissed better and every blade of grass was handled with the care of a mayfly. There I was, sitting on bare knees, making daisy chains opposite Melody in the middle of the thirsty green lawn – both of us in our summer dresses, white petals in our hair, each moment a willing world of its own. That lavender, so sweet, so calming

and then – as he gave a final groan – with the dead weight upon me,

Melody asked me something. 'Vi-vi, are you okay?' she mimed,

and I shook my head. 'Don't go,'

'What?' she asked, giggling,

but there I was again, lying in the bedroom, searching for the crow on the ceiling, bewildered by the space inside me, one I'd never considered being trespassed upon.

A STRANGER

Something looked different about the ivory house. Perhaps it was the first time I'd looked at it properly for a while, but the grass looked longer from the recent sun, and some of the wall paint had flaked away. Dad didn't usually allow it to get like that. I watched the sun *fonduing* deeper into the sky. My body had felt pain after dance, but this was different, it was all over... Every muscle had been pressed to the surface with thumbs and fingernails and such rehearsed rhythm, not a role I would have chosen, and the stage exit didn't seem to be an option at the time. *Why has so much changed?* Soon, the same sun had fallen, and the sky had bruised way past purple as the light in the garden turned an aching grey.

When I peered through the kitchen window, there Dad was, but his clothes were different. Compared to Secret Haven, he looked reasonably well-kept. His jeans were new, slightly darker, maybe, and his hair had been trimmed, so it spread more evenly over the top.

He'd been somewhere that evening, I could tell – his eyes had that look of recent discovery about them. Since Mam had left, he'd seemed to prefer his bees to people. If only they hadn't gone away too. After that, he'd become a bit restless, I suppose, but continued to use the last of the wax and the honey when the hive was left entirely empty. After a while, it was as though we'd only ever imagined the swarm.

I'd remembered the gentle way he'd handed over the last bar of lemongrass soap made from the remnants, one hand laying over the top and the other underneath, as though it was still alive. He hadn't told me, but I knew not to use it; instead, I'd placed it at the back of my sock drawer. The last candle he'd made was a stumpy little thing that we'd watched burn away in no time, the wick not even having a chance to frazzle the way they usually do. Both our heads bowed towards the shrinking wax as it left its mark in a little china saucer between us. Dad said nothing about the room being darker, he just ran straight to the window, pushing it open to let the smoke out. Then he stood there for a while, just watching it blow away as though it was alive.

Now, he was standing there, with his mind on other things.

For a moment, I assumed he was talking to himself, that he had held everything inside for so long that the madness was about to tear him apart, but there was a stranger at our ivory house, and Dad had given me no warning. There she was, just a shadow, at first, standing right by the back door, in a pair of jeans and a baggy blue blouse. As she came into focus, I could see it was the woman who'd been standing next to Dad the night before; Faith. This time, she was a bit closer, so I got the chance to properly take a look. I could see that she was middle-aged, about the age Mam would have been if she'd continued to live; maybe a little older. This time, I didn't feel so happy to see her.

When Dad finally saw me, he gestured for me to go in.

'Oh, alright, Vila?' Did you have a nice time with your friends? Bet you could do with some food right now, too.'

This time, I couldn't find my words, not even with Dad. I wondered how I'd become a *too*.

I had no idea what *she* was doing there, standing in the corner of the kitchen with her feet apart and a long-empty mug in her hand. Her thick, ash brown hair curved like a helmet beneath her round chin. She didn't look surprised by me at all, which bothered me.

'Why don't we all sit down?' she said, placing her hand gently on Dad's arm, and then turning to me to say, 'we weren't properly introduced the other night, love…' With scrunched-up eyes, she smiled and said, 'I'm Faith.'

Faith didn't fidget, or comment on anything; she didn't even readjust her jeans or push her hair behind her ear; she just sat watching Dad, and I wondered what she was looking for. Mam would have been standing alongside him, already knowing his every move and every word. They were in it together. But Mam had her own path, now, wherever she was until we could finally catch up.

Mist appeared and began to trace the outline of this woman's body with her own. Faith laughed down at her and I sat there and tried to imagine the future, but it was too difficult. The picture was changing and I couldn't keep up. I tried telling myself, *things happen when you least expect them to*, but I began to lose my breath.

Soon, the three of us were eating together but everything was going down in lumps. I felt as though I was acting in the wrong performance.

'Bobbie called earlier,' Dad said, finally breaking the sound of us all chewing.

'Did she?' I didn't even pretend to sound interested.

'She did. Wanted to know where you were again.' He looked at me.

'What did you tell her?' I snapped, though it wasn't him who I was angry with.

'Said you were at one of your ballet friends' houses,' he frowned.

Well, that wasn't an exact lie.

The rest of the meal was filled with the idlest conversation. Faith said she thought I'd danced brilliantly the night before; she made some joke about her not even being able to touch her toes and had told me she'd look forward to seeing me dance the next time. All I could think when she said that was, *clearly, you aren't going anywhere soon, then.*

Faith began to stack our plates.

'Thanks Faith but you don't have to do that. I suppose it's getting late now, so I'd best see you to your car. And you,' Dad gave me a look, 'had best try and get back a bit earlier these days if you plan on staying awake at school. Those exams don't pass themselves.'

Doesn't Dad know next week is Whitsun Week? There is no school... He stood up and stretched, puffed air out of his mouth and then walked towards the door, letting Faith go first. He had a way of acting older than he was, I hated it.

I slammed the kitchen door behind me, not caring that Faith may have heard. 'She's the one imposing on my home after all,' I mumbled as I stomped upstairs. *How come I hadn't even noticed her car outside?*

'What?' I exclaimed at Ana who was sitting there eyeballing me from her chair. 'Don't judge me! I didn't lie to him if that's what you mean! Stop it! You're just a doll, and you're supposed

to help me,' but she kept staring. 'I didn't lie!' I threw my jacket over her and got into bed just as I was, clothes and all.

I rubbed the tears from my eyes, much too riled up to even think about closing them, so I just laid there for a while, listening to all the little sounds of Dad, pottering around the kitchen. There he was, closing a cupboard, opening the fridge, locking the back door, switching things off in the living room, back and forth, back and forth until he eventually began to walk up our creaky stairs, huffing and puffing as he did so.

Maybe if he knocks on the door. Maybe if he knocks on the door and asks, 'Vila, you alright, love?' Maybe then, I'll tell him, 'No, I'm not actually feeling so great.' Not that I was sure what I'd say, but I knew I wouldn't tell him if he didn't ask. *Please ask! Dad, please ask.*

Dad stepped foot on the landing, checked the dance room for something, and I heard him closing the curtains to the Common. Then, he walked towards my bedroom and paused for a moment on the other side of the door.

'Night, Vila,' he said, a bit more abruptly than usual.

I took a few seconds and as I heard him creaking across the landing towards his room, I felt a lump rising in my throat.

'Night, Dad,' I managed to say, but so quietly that he probably didn't hear.

My whole body boiled up as the tears left my eyes, but I still didn't remove my clothes. I couldn't right then, not again—

Even in the dark, I could feel Ana staring from the chair alongside me.

'You don't even know what you're talking about,' I whispered, with a broken voice, 'you literally have no idea.'

I was sweating all over now, but still, I held the covers close to me.

Just metres away, Dad's bedroom door clicked shut.

*

Sleep had been long and discombobulating. My mouth was as dry as talc and my legs were as floppy as a ragdoll, but I didn't budge. I could still smell Theo; that aftershave, right there in my room.

Dreams and nightmares had competed as much as Odette and Odile, and I couldn't remember who claimed the victory. My brain felt filled with feathers, my fringe was stuck to my forehead, and I was far too tired for details. *But his hair, the way it had fallen onto your face when he was above you.* I closed my eyes again. *Ballet isn't for a while yet. Teenagers sleep. I'm only seventeen. Just seventeen... It's an extra class, just because dance exams are coming up.*

I curled up on one side and imagined I was a child again. Mam would call me for school soon. I could smell the toast about to pop up. There was the sound of Dad turning on the shower. I'd soon see Melody in the afternoon, and we'd be able to play. I felt myself smiling as I began to drift away to somewhere else.

Scratch scratch.

Melody's giggling face disappeared; for a second, replaced by Theo's. Those eyes. *Yesterday, it was different between us. Something was different.*

Maybe it's a mouse – in the attic?

Tap-tap. Tap-tap.

There's the smell of him again, all over the bedclothes. Theo.

Relentless. I squinted through aching eyes.

A breeze blew the curtains back and forth, and through a small gap in the window, I saw Mist piercing back at me; her body tall and hunched over as she used her back feet to balance on the windowsill. Her panicked, grey face pressed against the glass as she knocked with a battered paw.

Meow. Let me iiiiIiIiiiiin.

I hoisted my body up and swung the window open.

MeeeoooooOOOOWW!

Mist leapt across me and landed on the carpet, her nose flat against it as though there was prey buried underneath. She strutted over to me, nestled her face against my calf and weaved around my legs in a figure of eight, just as she had when we'd first met. This time, she did it over and over, as though I was some stranger she couldn't get used to. She'd been acting strange recently. So needy.

'Mist, it's me,' I whispered, resting my back against the headboard, 'it's me,' and finally, satisfied by my stroke of her neck, Mist strutted away, to find a resting place upon Ana's lap instead. *Fine, be like that.* Mist dragged a claw back and forth, plucking the hem of Ana's skirt.

I felt irritated by Ms Madeline having scheduled a class the first day of half term. Some people had lives and I needed to … recover. On the other hand, perhaps the only way I could shake off that strange feeling – and blow all the feathers away – was if I went along with everything as normal. I sat on the edge of my bed and looked down at my toes, their chipped nails and ripped skin wanting to peel me right down to the bone. For me, normal meant dance, but my thighs sank back into the mattress; all that goose, all that—

I stumbled into the shower and let the hot water run over me. I watched the soap fall to my feet as the tiled walls held me up and I saw yesterday swirl down the drain.

Where are those ballet clothes? With a towel around me, I rifled through my top drawer and slid some tights on while Mist – no help at all – purred in her dreams, calm at first, until a loud *hissssss escaped her.* Then, she was back to purring, with one ear pricked up as I left the room.

After a while of searching, I found my skirt in my dance room, draped like a veil over the dolls' house! I quickly wrapped it around me, needing to tug the belt a little tighter around my waist than normal, and looked at myself in the tall mirror.

There stood a skinny girl in an outfit that had previously fit like a second skin. Now, her tights wrinkled around the knees and the V-neck of her leotard hung low between her breastbone. There appeared to be much less of her than before – almost hollow in the middle where her ribs poked out, and something of *him* staring out of her poppy eyes. I tried to make her smile, to change what I saw, but then I heard his voice in my head; *that's right, yes; just so beautiful*. I shielded my face.

*

At class, I tried not to think about anything. *You're only seventeen, remember?* So, I slid into the splits, curved into a hundred different shapes at the *barre*, and shared the spotlight at the centre, ready for exams, where I would be anything they wanted me to be. All of us did as we were told, stayed smartly in lines, with smiles and eyes wide open, eyebrows raised, ribs in, tummies in, bums tensed, turned out, shoulders back.

So, was it really that different, with him?

'Grace, don't let those arms flop like chicken wings,' Ms Madeline shouted.

Yes. Much different. He's supposed to love you.

'Amy, your ankles are rolling.'

I saw Amy's ankles immediately adjust.

'Livvy, no spider fingers!'

'Perfect, Luc!'

Am I the only one who feels so strange? I seemed to zoom out as though I was a drone filming the room. I could see everything from above and it was all beginning to echo as it does when you're about to faint. The glass mirrors shrunk – as did my reflection within them – but we all kept dancing.

The classroom kept spinning and spinning in the mirror until I was such a blur that I was close to disappearing. Then, I saw the image of the goose again; Theo's face as he'd waited for me to tuck in, lay the first morsel upon my tongue and then swallow it – and I wobbled.

'That's it, Violet, *smile* through your mistakes,' Ms Madeline said, with her blinkers still on me. If only she knew...

Then I saw Bobbie.

I didn't know whether she'd turned up late – as always – or if the time had finally come for me to lose my mind. She looked even more dishevelled than usual, *unintentionally* mismatched, her new pair of wings were very much on show beneath her messy bun, and she had a distant look about her – almost no look – the way she caught up with every dance move a second later; so unlike the real Bobbie who could have improvised a whole show of her own in the past, no direction required.

I sank to the back of the room, trying to avoid Bobbie's arms and legs, so unpredictable and suddenly erratic as they took turns to chop through the air, not caring who was around her – especially me. When the eyes of our reflections met, I *chasséd* to the outside. Bobbie was a storm I didn't want to be stuck at the centre of. And I was feeling less equipped than usual.

'Bobbie, if you want to make a scene, how about turning up to dance a little more often?' Ms Madeline said, as Bobbie tore through the air in some sort of dance tantrum. The other girls gasped, shifting to the side where I stood, as Bobbie's performance escalated even further, her arms spinning like a hurricane, her legs doing who-knows-what as she jumped, eventually doing anything but ballet

until the music stopped.

There was Ms Madeline, holding the remote control in her hand.

'Well, girls, Bobbie definitely caught our attention, but you're not the only ones who have exam practice today, so hurry on out, please. And keep working hard!'

In the corner of my eye, I saw Bobbie's face turning beetroot.

As Grace and the other dancers began to walk around her and towards the door, I followed, but I could feel the heat of Bobbie's fire on my tail.

'Hey, Vi!' Her tone was intimidating, so I didn't dare turn around. 'Oi,' she exclaimed, looking for a battle, but I didn't bite. Even though Bobbie meant a lot to me, I could see why others – why Theo – would think she wasn't the most discreet... *I can't do this right now,* I wanted to say, *not right now, Bob, please.*

As I picked up my trainers and bag, Bobbie, with her hands on her hips, stood in my way, still panting from her scene.

'What, Bob?' I asked, sounding more irritated than I'd intended.

She flinched. 'Aren't you even going to *ask* me about anything?'
I must have looked so clueless.

'Haven't you even been wondering how I *am* lately?' This
was fiery Bobbie. I was used to her spark but now, I couldn't
quench it.

I shrugged. So much had happened lately. A bit of time can
change your whole world. She'd stopped showing up. The
world doesn't stop spinning just because you don't show up,
but maybe she'd wanted it to.

Not that I had the energy to say any of this out loud.

'What is it? Cat got your tongue?' Bobbie still blocked my
pathway, and her big blue eyes marbled me.

My mouth opened, but I wasn't sure where to begin, or
whether I should tell her anything anyway.

'Oh, don't give me that,' she said, snarling. 'Come on,' she
said, staring at my goldfish lips as I tried to find my words.
'Come on,' and I tried my very best to squeeze some clarity
out of my mind, to find *something* that would escape, enough
to explain, but I couldn't.

That's why the tears came. I looked at the shiny tiled floor,
ashamed and beginning to despise myself. I could feel Bobbie
looking down at me.

'Yeah, that's right. Make it all about you.' She sighed,
slinging her backpack over her shoulder, and then turning on
her heel, as stroppy as ever. Before the door swung shut in my
face, she shouted,

'Guess what?'

I was already out of guesses.

'My mother's ill, *really* ill. Just thought you – of all people
– would understand that.'

After she'd gone, my stomach plummeted deeper than an iceberg, and I decided I'd walk straight to where I needed to be; home.

I spent almost the entire walk thinking of everything I should have said to Bobbie. Mam had been taken away completely without warning and if I'd known beforehand that her days were numbered, I would have missed her even sooner. It made sense that Bobbie looked like a ghost. She was right. I'd been so focused on feeling sorry for myself that I hadn't noticed how other people had their own issues to contend with. How long had Dad been spending time with Faith? How long had it really been since I'd seen Bobbie? Or tried to call her? Perhaps it was even longer than I realised... No wonder everyone was angry with me.

I considered how Dad must have felt, having to introduce another woman into our home, Mam's home. I bet he'd felt concerned about how I would react to it all. How must Faith have felt, intruding on our untouchable landscape, our special snow globe, moving all our dusty memories around? My reaction had probably been everything Dad had dreaded; that of a typical teenager.

So, it wasn't all about me.

In fact, compared to Bobbie's situation, the issues between Theo and I were nothing. *I bet any experienced person would tell me that relationships weren't all plain sailing, especially when it comes to the physical expression of it all, something so unique to each relationship, right?* There were so many layers we

292

probably hadn't discovered yet. I imagined we'd only scratched the surface, and yet, I didn't like it – whatever it was I couldn't explain. It's not as though people usually have full conversations during sex, so did it matter that he'd asked me not to speak? The way he'd looked at me, with such intense eyes…

Theo had texted me as if everything was normal, but I decided I'd wait until I got home before replying. I needed some time to hear myself think. Yes, maybe with a little time, those unsettling feelings I had would calm themselves down and I'd laugh about how disturbed I felt way back when there was so much I didn't understand. After all, everything I'd thought was bad last time had ended up completely fine. I was probably blowing things out of proportion yet again and would soon feel embarrassed about it.

At home, I found a spot to lie down and write my message. There I was, on the floor in my dance room, deliberating over how many kisses to include, if any. Everything felt safe there on the old, woollen rug while the dolls in the dolls' house whispered, *don't worry, Violet. Any good man would wait for you.* So, it took me twenty minutes before I typed a word.

Just got home from ballet. Got studying to do today x

Theo would have to be okay with that for the time being.

'Vila, love! Want tea?' Dad shouted from the bottom of the stairs.

'Yes please. I'll be there now,' I said as I heard him already plonking the kettle down.

I pressed 'send,' nervous about how Theo would take it.

As I sat with Dad in the living room, both of us with mugs in our hands, I felt my phone buzz in my pocket, but I didn't check the screen. *Time,* I reminded myself, *just a little bit of time.*

Dad lifted his chin to his top lip, his version of a smile. Until then, I'd never even imagined a day I wouldn't want to see Theo. It was a frightening feeling, and I had no idea what it meant.

Part Three

MORNING, SUNSHINE

Since I'd decided not to visit Theo over the half term, Dad and I had found our own little routines together, and our ivory house felt more like a home than it had for years.

Each morning would start with the sound of Motown playing from the kitchen, and the smell of bacon or sausages sizzling on the grill. We'd eat breakfast together at the table while the sun blazed through the window, and then I'd wash the dishes and Dad would go outside to check all the crops around the back of Secret Haven. Feeling like there was a world of possibility ahead of me, I'd open my revision books right there at the kitchen table.

That's where I'd stay until early evening, other than the odd stroll through our village, and an hour of dance practice after lunch, with only Mist's company as she curled up on the seat cushion closest to the sun. Dad would pop his head in every now and then to offer me snacks or a doorstop sandwich, and eventually, Mist would leap onto my lap, yawning and tugging at my T-shirt. Each night ended with us having our mugs of hot chocolate or honey tea before an early night. While I was with Dad, it was easier not to think of Theo. This was how days were supposed to be done when you had exams. This was how you felt in control of your life.

By Wednesday, Dad knew exactly how many rashers of bacon I preferred and how I liked my egg – usually scrambled. We wouldn't talk a lot in the morning, but sometimes, Dad told me about things like bees; how fascinated he was by them. *Did you know bees love to dance too, Vila? They do, y'know. They wiggle to show the direction of the food.* He definitely missed his hive.

Dad seemed to have sprung to life a bit more since I was around the place, and it was lovely to see. *You'll ace those exams, you will,* he'd say, whenever he bounced back into the kitchen to refill his flask for the day. *Don't go exhausting yourself, mind, Vila. Remember you've gotta look after my girl.*

He didn't know I wasn't able to concentrate on a single word; that every time I reached the end of a page of *Twelfth Night*, I had to revisit the first line; that I did this at least a dozen times, not wanting to give up but eventually moving to a new book, a new subject.

The same thing happened again and again. My eyes read thousands of words, but my brain absorbed none of them. I still felt guilty about all the people I hadn't paid attention to recently. Spending more time with Dad had made such a difference to both of us – even if my schoolwork hadn't improved – but it was only the start of so many repairs. Theo kept popping up in my head too. I hadn't been ignoring him completely – that was impossible. We still texted. I just took hours to reply. Everything felt more … detached? A little like our last evening together. He'd normally have picked me up after ballet on Wednesdays but because of the holidays, my usual class had been switched to Thursdays. Not that I'd told him that…

As each day went by, the more my stomach felt full of emotions in a constant tug of war. I'd wait for Dad to venture out to Secret Haven before I'd scrape more of my breakfast into the bin. The scrambled egg looking back at me made me want to be sick.

When Thursday evening came, I closed my books on the same page I'd opened them on Monday morning. Instead of staying indoors, I decided to follow Dad out into the sunshine to Secret Haven. I couldn't see him at first, so I took a stroll towards the Wendy House and then back to my old swing. Since my last visit, its seat had split in so many places. The rope had been gripped so tightly over the years that it had blackened and frayed from all its twisting, so I didn't dare to go very high. I sat down and allowed myself to spin in one direction and then the other, like spaghetti unfolding, all my grudges and worries ready to be released.

I remembered the simpler times of Secret Haven, where dreams were lived daily, and dance was enjoyed regardless of who was watching.

Tea will be ready soon. Melody's already gone home, but we'll have tomorrow. There's Mam, strolling through Secret Haven, cutting off the dead heads of the hydrangeas, and me chasing after her, grabbing onto her cotton dress, slightly faded from the sun. I gather as many of the heads in my arms as I can and try to stick them back onto their stems.

'What are we going to do with you?' Mam laughs as I crouch in dismay at each one that falls again. Her clammy hand grabs mine as I look up for her comforting smile, the one I've held onto ever since.

And there I saw her again.

In one of her floral dresses walking around the side of our ivory house. Just a flicker of her through my tired eyes. She'd

299

never left, not properly. An excited panic ran through my whole body as I spun more slowly, eventually coming to a stop. *This week couldn't feel more perfect. Our family – whole – again.* Sometimes, I was convinced that going back in time was the easiest way. *Home again.* I would have stayed with Melody and Mam in Secret Haven forever if I could have.

But when I saw Dad following Mam, I knew my dream was coming to an abrupt end.

I could tell he was smiling by the way his words widened. He was nervously stepping from one foot to the other, with his hands in his pockets. Only, as I listened more closely, that wasn't Mam's voice at all. Still, Dad was as happy as he'd been the past few days… Faith was in a long dress that was a similar mossy green to one of Mam's, only, the pattern was made of feathers rather than leaves – *how dare she.*

Secret Haven suddenly didn't feel so good.

The whole place needed trimming back. One plant blended into another, climbers had lost themselves within the hedge and the lilac and lavender – although sweet – became stifling when left to roam. What happens when your dreams are overgrown? Or when you outgrow them? Perhaps with all my thoughts, I weighed too much for the broken swing. Mam had been gone for a long time and so had Melody. As I watched Dad and Faith together, I remembered the other night with Theo but also all the other times. It was funny, regardless of our last few days in our ivory house, which had been the loveliest in a long time, Dad still needed someone. And don't get me wrong, I did too.

And I suppose we can't trust our minds with anything while our hearts want something so badly.

As I curled up in bed that night, browsing Bobbie's social media – strangely silent for her – I started to doubt anything had ever been wrong with mine and Theo's last time together. Of course, I didn't think everything had been perfect but none of it seemed particularly bad anymore. If I'd said it out loud to someone, it would have sounded like the most trivial thing. I suppose time had helped as I'd wanted it to, but soon, a whole week would have gone by without seeing him. I reread his last message:

08:45
Morning, Sunshine… x

I'd sent a waving emoji back at lunchtime…

Since then, nothing. Absolutely nothing. He'd read it – I could see – and obviously chosen not to respond.

So, I began to worry if a week had been far too long.

REMEMBER TO SMILE

I didn't want the love to be missing any longer.

By Friday morning, my hand was sweaty from holding my phone for so long. I threw it across the room, hoping something would shake it into making a sound, but it did nothing but lie there, useless. Ana looked at me as though she knew so much.

'What? For God's sake, what?'

'Are you saying he's not going to text? Is that what you're saying? You think I should j-just get over it?'

I was struggling to breathe.

'It's – not, it's – not – that e – easy!'

I cried while Ana looked blankly at me.

I sat on the edge of my bed, wrapping my arms around me as I rocked back and forth, trying to stop it. Then, something inside me – my second self – seemed to take over in a single second and pushed the whole chair over on its side, including Ana. There she was, sprawled across the carpet, arms above her head and legs wide like a starfish.

I joined her, face-down on the floor and let my tears seep into the carpet as it indented itself in my forehead.

'Look,' I mumbled into the soggy weave. 'Look how much of a mess we are without him.'

I missed being able to talk to him, to anyone *properly*. I had

Dad, but on Thursday evening after dance, he'd gone to see Faith and as a result, I didn't know what to do with myself. I'd started to panic again, that I may have been wrong all along and expected too much. That I'd not appreciated something I would never find again for the rest of my life, not with anyone else.

'Vila, food's ready,' Dad shouted from the bottom of the stairs.

There was no way I could catch my breath, never mind eat. I continued to whimper out of frustration.

'Vila?'

How come the whole world is so oblivious when I'm this upset? My breaths came back in closer proximity. I lifted my head and knelt on all fours. My room was too bright for such sadness. I wrapped my dressing gown around me, pulled its rope tight around my waist and double-knotted it. I wiped the tears away with my sleeves and then trudged downstairs.

By the time I sat down at the kitchen table, Dad was already on his way out the door.

'Thanks, Dad,' I said, looking down, so he couldn't see my puffy eyes.

'Not a problem, love. Hey, see you in a bit,' and he was gone.

Diana Ross and The Supremes were singing their hearts out on the radio as I stirred the scrambled egg around the plate, watched it dry up and break into smaller pieces the more I stabbed at it. *Shut up,* I wanted to say. *Just shut up!* It was always a mystery how one day could be so different from the last.

By lunchtime, even my usual morning message from Theo wasn't there to mull over, just my very dull and very scratched reflection on screen. *Maybe it really is too late. Maybe I've blown it.* I left the phone where it was on the other side of the room and resorted to lying on my bed for a while. There, I wished I could fall asleep for weeks.

At three in the afternoon, my phone pinged. Still alert, I ran over to it, quickly swiped away any meaningless notifications and opened the message:

> Hi Coppélia … I'm up the road where I usually drop you off. X

The relief that ran through my whole body almost made me feel sick.

Oh my god, Theo's outside Melody's house. Right now!

I knew it was an enormous risk for him to take in broad daylight. He could have been seen by anyone; Dad, Faith, anyone! And that didn't even take me into account. He knew I'd have to jump straight into the car without making a peep because what if Dad saw him and I hadn't explained yet? Was that romantic or was it … I don't know? Maybe he wasn't afraid at all. Maybe he was just being mature, ready to stand up for us – unlike me.

Lately, I was afraid of everything. I was afraid of *him* just days ago, but now I was more scared of never seeing him again, and if I didn't get into that car soon, all my opportunities would cease to exist!

I shed my dressing gown, threw on some creased jeans and a T-shirt from my chair, and dragged a brush through my sloppy hair before tying it back in a chaotic ponytail at least three times to achieve no better result… Next, while Dad was chatting in the barn shop, and I was close to hyperventilating, I snuck around the side of the house.

Then I saw him, hard to believe at first, as any image you long for tends to be – my Theo – sitting in the driver's seat right outside Melody's, with the window down and his arm resting above the glass.

I slowly opened the passenger door, but Theo's head didn't turn towards me. Neither was he smiling as he had been on all the other occasions, and strangely, he didn't seem to be encouraging me to get in. I sat alongside him without buckling up.

Theo continued to stare straight ahead through the windscreen and towards our ivory house. I hoped Dad would be in the barn shop for a while and not walk around the front of the house for anything, otherwise I'd have to duck, and Theo would finally have confirmation that I was completely ridiculous.

'Coppy, do you not want to see me anymore?' He still didn't look at me. 'Because if you don't, you can just say.'

His eyes were filled with tears.

'Oh,' I said, 'I didn't mean to make you feel like this…'

'I've been wondering what on earth's going on and why you've been avoiding me.'

He took a deep breath to stop his voice trembling. Theo looked down at the steering wheel and I thought I could – for the first time – see some grease in the crown of his hair. *What a terrible time he must have had.* 'You think I haven't noticed?'

I kept an eye out for Dad. 'I'm so sorry, I really am, I—'

'Never mind being sorry, Coppy. Do you want us to be together or not?'

I turned to look over my shoulder in case anyone was nearby.

'Or, do you want to leave us behind? It's completely up to you.'

Maybe I'd hesitated for too long. Theo's back was straighter and he was still looking straight ahead, focusing on the special place that belonged to Dad and me. I tried to picture him stepping across the threshold at the back door, walking through our rustic living room, drinking from an old, faded mug and putting his feet up on one of our peeling pouffes. I almost wanted to laugh, it was so hard to picture, as though Theo was a caricature!

But he wanted us to be real.

'Because I'm sure I would survive, Coppy. But I have to be honest, I would be extremely sad for a long time, and I don't think I could ever forget you. But I would survive, so don't worry about hurting me as I wouldn't want that to be the thread keeping us together. What are you smiling about? This isn't a joke...'

I hadn't realised he was looking properly into my eyes, his pupils as big as cocoa beans. Now, I was worrying. He was talking about us breaking up. The end, right there as we sat in the car for the last time, where couples often break up in films and TV shows. He'd said he'd survive but I didn't feel sure that I would.

'Sorry,' I whispered.

Theo took my hand in his, which felt more comforting than ever before. 'I just, I've been out of my mind without you,

Sugarplum.' He dragged his hand through his hair and then rubbed his temples. 'You know you can be honest with me, don't you?' His finger ran up and down my chin. His hand was so warm as I rested my cheek in his palm.

I nodded. As always, I nodded.

I considered everything I'd do without Theo; pictured my bedroom with Mist, my dance room with Margot, dance lessons, school... Yes, my life would be busy, but it certainly wouldn't be full.

'I want us to be together, I do,' I said, suddenly conscious I didn't look my best to be making such a case.

'You're absolutely positive, Coppy? On your Dad's life?'

I nodded again.

Theo smiled. 'I'm so relieved to hear you say that,' his hand pressed his chest. 'There we are then, my love. Let's get ourselves back to normal, shall we?'

His eyes twinkled with so much happiness, I couldn't help but feel I must have done the right thing.

That's how I ended up back at Theo's house again. Just like last time I turned up after a brief reprieve, everything felt the same but very slightly different, like a place that's been tidied just before you got there.

We slotted together like spoons on the sofa, glad to be in each other's arms again. I suppose you appreciate something even more when it's so close to death, so each of our kisses, reminded of its own sweetness, was hungrier than before. For a change, it was Theo who slowed things down.

'Now now, Sweetness! There's no rush. Besides, I hope you aren't with me just for my out-of-this-world lovemaking?'

I let out a laugh and gave his neck one more kiss.

'You're not? Oh, well, that's a shame…' Theo turned me onto my side in front of him and stroked up and down my arm, from shoulder to fingertips and back. 'Right then, let's catch up properly. Let's *talk*.'

I curled up as small as I could in his arms and just for a moment, closed my eyes. *So comfy.*

'So, tell me about ballet, Coppélia. What's happened recently?' His eyes widened like those of a little bear, and I could tell he really was wracked with guilt. I knew how bad that felt.

'Uhm, Ms Madeline said there's a Prima Ballerina coming to see us Saturday after next. Well, she used to be one anyway.'

'Oh, really?'

'Yeah, from a top ballet school in London.'

'That's bloody brilliant. Why's she visiting? Is she going to show you all her dance moves? What's her name?'

'I think so. I mean, I imagine so!' I couldn't help but smile, just thinking about it.

'See, this is exactly what I mean. I know how much these things mean to my little Coppélia. I know it's not your fault, it's mine, but people start to disconnect when they stop sharing their dreams.'

'Sorry I didn't say. I just didn't want to make a big deal out of it, or I'd get nervous, you know how I…'

'Aw, you worry too much. You'll be just like her one day, you know? Margot. Out there in the spotlight, just like when I met you, only on the big stage! You just need to find your confidence again, that's all.'

Have I lost my confidence in dance? I didn't realise. Does it show? Ms Madeline hasn't said so.

I felt Theo's very slight stubble against my cheek as he leant over and gave me the gentlest of kisses on both my eyelids. 'Look, I can't control myself around you. Why do I even try?'

I giggled, beneath him once again as his fingers interlocked with mine and he lifted my hands above my head. Today, Theo had listened, and now, we listened to each other; speaking without words and letting our bodies sing.

'Can I tell you a secret? It bothers me when I have to keep everything inside.' Theo's fingertips were cool and unexpectedly soothing as he played with my fringe.

I nodded, but I felt the empty room in my mind, not willing to let anything in.

'I trust you won't tell anyone.' He kissed my forehead to seal my promise. Love can hush everything away.

'Well, I know you won't judge me,' he said, 'and I'll feel better if I tell you. We can tell each other things like this.'

I found myself nodding again.

'Okay, well, here it is.' He looked at the ceiling as though he'd never confessed whatever it was in his whole life. I'd never seen him so shaken up. 'I had a wife,' he said, 'for a time, anyway.'

A wife? So, he's loved someone else before me?

Theo carried on, 'but well, she died.'

And immediately, I understood. He had pain, just like me. Pain can cause strange behaviour too.

'She became a different woman after she was ill, you know? Literally, almost half the size.'

I thought of Bobbie's mam, of Bobbie.

'She didn't look like my wife anymore. She used to be a

wonderful painter at the beginning, you know? Best I'd ever seen – in real life, at least. Really, quite admirable, but she couldn't seem to stick it. Such a waste. She could never seem to focus. Strange. Such a terrible waste to have a gift and then, *poof!*' Theo's fists burst open as his lips puffed imaginary smoke. 'Ungrateful, really.' He hadn't finished. 'In the end, she was a stranger.' Theo flinched and shook his head as though to get rid of the image.

I thought of Mam all those years ago, lying in that hospital bed. Sometimes, I still wondered if it hadn't been Mam at all, and imagined my real Mam, still alive somewhere, just waiting for the perfect moment to stride back home because it had all been a mix-up and no one would ever need to explain if we carried on as normal.

'But it was she who let herself go that way,' Theo said, 'she must have wanted to leave me. She must have planned it. I'd heard some women could be calculating but I'd never thought she was one of them, wanting to escape at the first opportunity. You'd never do such a thing. I know you wouldn't.'

His face was crimson. *Is he serious? He thinks this woman was responsible for her own illness?* He didn't understand that we can't know why we come or why we go.

His fingertips curled around my forearm, and I tried my best to sympathise. Then, he pulled me closer.

'I'd never tell anyone else things like this. You know that my love, don't you? I can trust you more than anyone in this whole universe.' His breath in my ear made me shiver.

My love. Had he called his wife the same thing?

'I can trust you to never leave me in the same way, don't worry.'

The sofa suddenly seemed so much smaller. The room had closed in around us. Every piece of furniture was twisted; each face of every ornament, tormented.

His eyes were on the ceiling, again. I must have risen up there, too, and goosebumps lined each of my arms, opening me to more darkness, allowing it deeper into the stuffy room inside my mind.

'Her story was that *I* had gnawed away at her just as much as the illness. Can you imagine the nightmares that thought has left me with? The dying just never think of the living. It's *all* about them, you know?'

I could feel Theo's mind twisting and turning.

'It only took a few hours for her eyes to completely close. Can you believe that? No hanging around, not even for the man who'd tried to do his very best for her.'

Again, words didn't come to me. They had all gone.

'I'll never forget that long gasp when she went out cold – my little china doll, who I kept in that bed for as long as I could.' He gestured towards the bedroom. 'Loyal until the end, that's me, even if she didn't appreciate it.'

The room inside my head was packed to the brim.

I'd left my body again. *Here I am, huddled against something monstrous, and we're knotted together by secrets.*

He'd said his wife was a painter, hadn't he? So, was it her easel in the other room? I felt myself gasp. *That grotesque portrait of Theo… The one that had fallen out, right in front of me! Was that actually hers?*

When I looked up at Theo's face, I expected to see tears. Instead, I saw something had reignited within him. His eyes were ablaze, full of life.

For me, the room became icy and I froze.

'How about we have our first photo together, my love?'

I hoped Theo couldn't tell how stiff my body was as he held it against him and held his phone at arms-length to capture our faces.

'Now, remember to smile,' he whispered, 'maybe it would be nice to frame this one, eh?'

STRANGE SHAPES OF DESPERATION

A large, solitary moth kept throwing itself against my bedroom window, itching to follow the dusky light through the gap. When I knelt on my bed to shut the window, I thought I saw a figure – perhaps a man – there on the Common, just standing and looking back at me. *It couldn't have been, Violet, you're losing it. Don't let the thoughts take over.* I yanked the curtains shut.

Desperate to speak to someone, someone who might help me snap out of it all, I picked up my phone. *Please don't let me lose the whole weekend like this.*

Hey Bob, just checkin' in... How's your mam?

It felt better just texting her.

Message delivered.

I watched until I saw the delivery tick turn blue to show she'd read my message. Then, I waited for the response. *What a relief.* I held on to my phone, ready to say sorry for the other day, but at the same time, deciding against it. I definitely didn't want to make it about me again.

The phone didn't light up. I thumbed across to Bobbie's face, her frizzy red hair. She still had her old display picture

313

of us both. Her arm was wrapped around my shoulders, but I looked so shy, even with her. Always so shy.

Still no reply.

I decided to crawl under the covers again, this time with my laptop on the end of my bed. Thanks to the vivid colours on screen, the door of my bedroom shut tight and the calming Tchaikovsky waltz, I began to feel small again. That's what I wanted, to feel young, to feel safe. I was a little ballerina in a cosy music box that had never been opened. I was a little ballerina who hadn't popped out into the enormous world of dark things waiting to greet me.

Thank God there's no ballet today.

*

I dissolved into such a deep sleep, that just as I was drifting away, I suspected I'd never return. When I tried to lift my limbs, gravity dragged me down to the mattress. *My abraded body is Theo's temple now.*

As the air rippled around me, Theo's living room and bedroom grew larger and smaller, and so did I, but my eyes remained open, and began to bear witness to different things. All around me, the chair and table legs were shaped like women's legs; the calves and thighs in an elegant bend, and within moments, the lampshade was a woman's head, screaming as it flickered, its mouth opening and closing as it puffed smoke. The rug was made from hair, as it slid from beneath my feet. *How did I not see this before? Have the women turned into furniture, or has the furniture turned into women?*

That door in the kitchen: I'd never seen that before either... I stood up and walked towards it. Under the spell of my nightmare, I opened it without question. I was over the threshold. The door slammed behind me. I fell forward. The floor was lined with ... what? ... Mattresses. Most of us were born in a bed and would end our days there, too.

This room was dark, all walls and no windows, and just as everything could appear larger in dreams, here, it was helped by the mirrors along each of the four walls. There were a dozen of me. I was stretched and distorted into strange shapes of desperation. *Violet,* mouthed the bun-headed faces, *Violet,* but their voices were trapped behind the same glass that confined their bodies.

There were others. *Look at them.*

Three women. They sat like mannequins in the corner: one, with hair the colour of copper, and two, completely identical, with lemony wigs dropping way past their chests. Their mouths hung open, knees ajar, mannequins without any costumes at all. *What dead eyes.* If a doctor shone a torch right into them, they would never blink, and yet, their skin looked so soft ... *Perhaps they were real, once, before they became dolls.* I wanted to, needed to ask them, *how did this happen?*

All my selves shook their heads in all the mirrors. Our breasts were bee stings, smooth straight down to the hip bones, apart from the overbite of our ribs. The mirrors showed stiff wire beginning to poke out of each limb, breaking the skin. No blood though. A scream wanted to come. The glass didn't let it.

A dozen mouths, all mine, were agape around me. They closed again. We all looked at each other as a large, gruesome face – that painting from the easel – appeared in the doorway and filled the room.

I woke up crouched over with my head in my hands. I could only just see my meagre feet in the shade of twilight. *How do you bear the weight of all this, every day?* I felt myself rocking back and forth, cradling my pointy elbows on my lap, in time with the tick of a hidden clock. Of course, I knew there wasn't really a secret room filled with dolls or mirrors, but the feeling stayed with me.

Ana was my only company, there exactly where I'd left her on the floor. *At least she has no disturbing secrets to tell.* I spotted each layer of myself around my bed: a fleshy pair of tights rolled down mid-motion, a leotard, silver as sealskin, a transparent skirt and some flimsy plimsolls, and I let the thinness of the silk and satin drape against my fingers as though I'd never truly felt them before, never sensed how little there was of me to be pieced back together.

There was a time I had only dreamt about being Margot.

IT'S THE BALLET THAT KEEPS ME SANE

On the first day back at school, the school counsellor told me to take a seat. She was more glamorous than I'd expected, with a mass of oyster-grey curls that fell flatteringly against her dark complexion. Her fuchsia lips said my name as if we'd spoken a hundred times, only, we'd never actually met.

I stared over her shoulder at the purple door, where my reflection was a moving shadow within the thick paint. It had previously been just another door out of hundreds dotted around the building. Isn't it funny what you miss when you don't need to see it?

'Feel free to call me Gina, by the way,' the counsellor said, giving a smile that meant I should smile back with immediate effect.

I made sure my face flickered a little, and then, embarrassed, looked down at my twiddling thumbs. I'd never understood nail-biting until recently. Now, every fingertip looked bloated with injury.

'So, tell me, Violet,' she said, sitting across from me and leaning back as though we were going to be a while, 'how are you – in general?'

I shrugged, having no idea why I was even there, never mind what kind of answer she was looking for. *Is this career-counselling? Or some routine meeting all students get before uni?*

'Okay, well, just in case you're wondering why we're here...'

She was good.

'... I thought it would be nice for us to have a little chat because it's been brought to my attention that you've missed quite a few lessons lately, okay, Violet?' She lifted a pair of thick-rimmed, polka dot glasses from her desk and gently slid them onto her nose.

My heart sank. I'd always thought of myself as quite invisible at school. Just the idea that I'd been noticed mortified me. *I wonder what else they know...*

'Your grades have dropped,' she continued, 'I'm told you don't seem at all yourself at the moment, and that you've lost some weight, okay?' she said – or asked. There were so many 'okays' that I wasn't sure if she wanted my response. 'I know we've never met but it looks like we need to get to know each other a bit now, okay?'

I nodded back at the last 'okay' – it was difficult not to. She was really building the atmosphere.

'While some of the classes you've missed are revision classes, I know,' she nodded, looking me right in the eyes, 'they're still *very* important, *especially* if you aren't doing the revision, okay Violet? Now, I know this is *very* unlike you and that's why we're here. You see, it really stands out when one of our top pupils is having to be chased for coursework and especially when their performance has dropped by two or in this case, three grades.' Her concerned voice was starting to make my chest feel tight.

'Am I in trouble?' I took a big gulp.

'No, no, you aren't in trouble, okay, but we're quite

318

concerned about what will happen if you don't catch up in time. As you know, exams are very, very soon, so you need to try extra hard right now to improve. We're also concerned about you, sweetheart, and how you're feeling right now. That's the main thing. How are things at home?'

I shrugged.

'Life isn't easy as a teenager, God only knows, so you don't need to feel self-conscious or silly about whatever's going on right now. It's a chaotic time for you all. So, are you having any problems?'

'No, not really,' I whispered.

'Not really?' she probed, drumming her fuscia fingernails on the desktop. They looked ready to spike through anything. 'Is there something going on at home, perhaps?'

'No, not at all.' That wasn't technically a lie as far as I was aware.

'Hm, right, okay. Is anything else going on that's been distracting you?'

I paused, perhaps for too long because Gina's head seemed to lean right over the desk, and her eyes were squinting as though they knew there was something I wasn't letting on. She was on to me, but at the same time, she did seem like she wanted to help. *What if I told her? Gina isn't so bad. She must have heard so much crazy stuff from schoolkids, so she probably wouldn't judge me. But what would she do with everything I'd told her? Would she tell the other teachers?*

'Hmm, okay, Violet, well, how do you feel, generally? Tell me, in *whatever* way you like.'

Without me even needing to try, a word floated to the top of a dark and heavy cloud that was ready to burst.

Lonely.

And to be honest, it surprised me. I was so close to Theo, how on earth could I have felt lonely? Without him, yes, but surely not with him?

I squirmed in my seat, hoping Gina couldn't read my body language, the clenching and unclenching of my fists, the dip and lift of my head, the biting of my lip as my mouth wrestled with everything my brain was trying to put out there.

'Uh – w-well – well, I feel,' the best I could do was use Gina's word, the one she liked so much, 'I feel, uh—' I took a deep breath, 'I feel okay,' I shrugged, giving up on myself.

Gina didn't look convinced. I saw her picturing a tower of *Jenga*, trying to pull out one block at a time to see what was hiding in-between before the rest tumbled.

'I hear you're marvellous at ballet?' she asked, still trying to build some rapport. 'Do you dance quite a bit throughout the week, Violet?'

I nodded. It was strange she had to say my name so often.

'How many times per week, would you say?'

'Maybe three times,' I mumbled. I didn't tell her that sometimes I danced more than that for different occasions.

'Ah, yes, well, that's quite a lot isn't it … especially alongside school, Violet. Perhaps you should concentrate on your schoolwork instead for a while? Give yourself a break. Everyone needs a rest sometimes. It's important…'

I shielded my eyes. *Please don't take it away from me,* I wanted to say. I could feel the tears trying to come out.

'No. Please,' I managed to whisper through my fingers, 'it makes me feel better.' My voice was trying to crack as I tried to speak louder. A full-on panic was coming on. *It's the ballet that keeps me sane,* I wanted to add. *It's what keeps me going. It's literally e-v-e-r-y-thing.*

Gina's eyebrows pulled together. 'I'll ask you again, okay, Violet, and remember, this is all confidential if you want it to be... Is anything going on at home that you'd like to talk about? Anything that's making you feel ... bad?'

I shook my head again, even though I was sure Gina could see my eyelids twitching as they tried to stop the tears pouring out.

'Hmm, okay, well, in that case, Violet, all I'm going to say is that you really need to knuckle down with your revision and make those classes, otherwise you won't be able to get the grades you need to get into the university you've chosen. Unfortunately, it all depends on these grades and none of us want to see you fail, so something's got to give. So, if you ever need any support, you need to come straight to us, but if you don't, we can't help you, okay?'

I nodded but felt like shaking my head over and over.

I somehow hadn't realised it was possible to fail. It never had been before...

It had started off as just one day off school because I was feeling so drained, and then another. I just thought nobody would notice *me* missing.

It sounds ridiculous, I know, but I didn't realise what impact any of it would have on my plans. I'd always done so well that I thought it was a given that it would keep happening.

Please give me a chance, I wanted to shout, scream, yell at Gina. *If I'd known, I would have...*

What would I have done?

For the first time since Mam was taken away, the whole world folded around me. *Without my dream,* I thought, *what am I?*

WHAT A MESS

Sometimes, the person who comforts you is the same one who inflicts the pain, but what are you supposed to do once they've become your whole life? Once it's become hard to imagine your world looking any different? Some people are just drawn to each other no matter what. That's why a week later, as usual on Saturday morning, I was at Theo's place. The truth was, whatever had happened between us, he was always there, my only constant.

I'd been so exhausted lately that one day *chasséd* into the next, not involving much routine at all. My legs felt like tree trunks and my eyelids struggled to stay open. *Live for the good moments,* I told myself, as I turned the opposite way to go back to sleep. *Just one more moment,* I promised, hugging the pillow.

'Oh no,' I groaned, remembering what the afternoon meant, 'oh no, no, no. What's the time?'

'Just coming up to twenty to twelve. You okay, Sleepyhead?' Theo was fully dressed and standing at the end of the bed while he scrolled through his phone, probably doing research.

'No,' I mumbled, 'I'm late. Really late,' while crouching to grab my dance bag when I hadn't even dressed yet. 'Class starts in twenty minutes!' I panicked as I searched the room for my clothes, unable to find anything. 'Why can I *never* find my stuff in here?' I never understood it; the tidiest house I'd ever been in was the easiest place to lose things!

Theo looked over at me with dozy eyes, 'Aren't these yours?' smiling as he held my dance jacket at arm's length.

I snatched them from him. It wasn't just my clothes. I was embarrassed. *Am I losing my mind?*

Theo smirked. 'Oh, I'm sorry, lovely. I would've woken you if I'd realised you were definitely going today. You just looked so cosy and peaceful, you know? I didn't want to disturb my Sleeping Beauty.'

I bit my lip. *Why on earth wouldn't I be going to something so important? A visit from a Prima Ballerina?* I hadn't missed an entire class since I'd met Theo, and not many in my whole life. He knew that better than anyone.

'Well, don't worry, my love,' Theo said as he was slipping his shoes on. 'You know I'll get you there – but you're right, you'd better hurry up.' He was already standing keys-in-hand at the door.

My body began to sweat as I slid my tights over my knobbly knees. I couldn't move any faster. I wished I had time for a shower to wash away all the grime of the night and all the anxiety of the moment, but I suppose that was only possible for the ideal versions of me.

'I know I set my phone alarm, though. I remember doing it,' I mumbled, as I slipped my shoes half-on and stumbled after Theo as he made his way to the car. No breakfast. No shower. Not even time for a wee. 'I even double-checked that I'd done it,' I said, putting my seatbelt on, 'triple-checked, actually! I really don't understand.'

'Oh dear,' he sighed, 'maybe you checked it so many times that you *un*set it?' He turned on the engine.

I shook my head, 'I don't know,' I rolled some deodorant

under each arm, stuffed a handful of mints into my mouth and started piling my hair into a makeshift bun on the top of my head.

'Ah, well don't worry about it now. We just need to get you there in time, okay?'

I knew that Theo was right, but the realisation that I wouldn't even have a chance to warm up before such an important class... I flipped the visor down and rubbed crusted tears from the corners of my eyes. *What a mess.* Yesterday's make-up showed all the cracks.

*

A stranger stood at the front of the class, balancing on the toes of her black dance boots, elbows resting against the wall behind her. She was taller than most ballerinas, especially with her high ponytail; so elegant in her lilac leotard, grey parachute trousers rolled down below her long waist and her hands resting on her hips. What it must have been like to be so confident.

'Glad you could make it today, Violet,' she said, as I scurried towards the *barre*. Ms Madeline pulled a face, perched upon her umpire seat.

I never would have been late for something like this before. *What's wrong with me recently?*

'Violet, girls and boys, this is Julia, and as I explained to you a few weeks ago, she has kindly visited us – all the way from *London,* can you believe? – to share some advice and experience from her time at The Royal Ballet. So, we're very lucky to have her here.'

I heard excited whispers around me, and we all started clapping as Julia came down from her boots and gave us a curtsy, not something Ms Madeline ever did for us.

'It's a genuine pleasure to spend an hour with you this afternoon, girls. I'm sure it will remind me of how much I enjoyed my classes at your age. So, I do hope you gain as much from it as I do.' She beamed as her eyes found each of us, welcoming our smiles in return.

Barre work was the same as normal. Ms Madeline hit the music and we began. Then, we heard Julia striding across the tiles, whispering in one girl's ear and then another's, nothing I could decipher, but I could tell from the tone and the girls' nervous laughs in reply that she was altering their positions, maybe gently pulling their shoulders back, lifting their chins up, pushing their diaphragms in or raising their sunken arms from the elbow.

Next, I heard her footsteps approaching me from behind. I was the last one at the *barre* and so standing right at the front, relying only on myself and the music to remember the steps. Luc was in control of the other end of the *barre*. *Please don't come near, Julia,* I wanted to say. *Please don't touch me, I'm repulsive right now.*

As I turned before repeating the exercise on the other side, Julia waited on my left, but she wasn't smiling as I was sure she must have with the other girls. Instead, her face was scrunched up in concentration and her arms were folded. *I've ruined it all, sabotaged it. Since I was late, she thinks I don't care, that there's no point wasting her energy on me.*

'Right, dancers,' Julia announced, clapping her hands together and strutting towards the centre of the room, 'take off your shoes, we're going to do something a little different to what you're probably used to and see how you find it...' She eyed us all up, 'yes,' she smiled again, 'right, so, for our *allegro*, let's do something *modern*, shall we?' She didn't wait for an answer, and I could see a smirk on Ms Madeline's face as she stood behind her. There was a murmur from the other girls as we untied our ribbons, left our second skins at the side beneath the tall wall-mirrors and felt our naked feet on the icy floor. I could hardly remember the last time they'd been out like this.

Julia looked over her shoulder for Ms Madeline to press play on the remote she held in her hand, and as the music poured out, my underarms began to sweat. All I could do was dance as my instinct told me, and without my tiredness letting me down. I smiled through my yawns and stretched into each *port de bras*.

Julia asked us to do different variations of traditional ballet moves: *attitude, arabesque, pas de chat*, just to see how we coped with new sequences.

'More,' she shouted, 'stronger,' she yelled, 'faster,' and then, using me as a guinea pig, again, probably because I'd been late, she ushered the girls and Luc to the other side, took up their space alongside me and told me to continue with the latest sequence while she danced alongside, adding a more modern feel to it all, softening her arms, letting them sway, flexing her hands and feet. Everyone gasped. I'd seen ballet like it on TV but to be able to actually do it... My audition had been nowhere near as modern as this.

'Feel free, not restrained. Ballet is freeing,' she announced, 'let those toes feel the floor, let them ground you, let yourself reach up and grow,' while pulling off all these moves, and while I somehow got to dance *alongside* her, mirroring a Prima Ballerina! I began to feel glad I was so tired, or I may not have been able to glide along with this dream so gracefully and without question.

'Thank you, Violet. Now, all of you please join us,' Julia nodded at the rest of the group.

Luc strutted to the front, looking so focused that his eyes were almost completely hidden beneath his brows. I could see him from the corner of my eye, fighting the air with his arms. He was so passionate that he almost looked angry. That air was nothing to him and he wanted it all.

'Yes, yes, that's it,' Julia told Luc, turning to Ms Madeline every now and then to whisper something. I understood, completely. You could watch Luc do the same dance a hundred times and he'd bring something entrancing to it the next time. His fierce confidence, that 'Look at me!' So, we did. It helped that none of us knew him outside ballet or even spoke to him much during class. Nobody other than Bobbie had anyway, but that mystery, that Luc-ends-when-class-ends, felt almost like Luc-ends-when-ballet-ends. It gave him that otherworldliness that was required of ballet.

For the last part of the class, Ms Madeline stood up and said, 'Now, girls and boys...'

We all nodded in unison whilst trying to catch our breath.

'It's time for us to do some improv.' As Julia said, it's all about feeling free.'

'Of course,' Julia said, 'this is the best part of dance, isn't it? Using all that skill, strength and imagination and really putting it into practice? Let yourselves go!'

For the last time, Ms Madeline pressed play. Even though

we were supposedly free, we all felt that we were being tested… I jumped, I twirled, I spun, I flexed my hands, spread my fingers and toes, kept my hips turned in for a change, held positions fiercely and for just-that-second-longer. 'This is mine,' I imagined myself saying, 'this is all mine,' ignoring the expressions of anyone around me, even Luc, as I felt dizzy yet in control of the floor as I *chasséd* along it, as the sweat left my every pore, I ignored it; even when that makeshift bun collapsed from the top of my head and left my greasy hair to cascade down my back, I was still spinning, still dancing, still – thank God – me.

When the class ended, Ms Madeline mouthed something to me while Julia answered a call outside. I picked up my hair bobble from where it had flown across the floor, and I yanked my hair back into a ponytail.

'Violet, now, I didn't want to tell you earlier as I know how nervous you get; also, I didn't think it would be kind to say it in front of the other girls who have worked so hard, but this whole class wasn't just about meeting Julia. It was about her seeing you dance.'

'Oh,' I said. 'Well, we've all enjoy—'

'No, mainly *you*, Violet,' she interrupted. 'Julia was adamant that she saw something raw in you, something nobody can fake through dance. She thinks you're malleable, clearly naturally resilient and can adapt to absolutely anything, and I'm inclined to agree! That's just what they need; dancers who can learn anything, be anything and truly have a passion for it!'

'Well, anyhow, Julia couldn't take her eyes off you the

whole time, and I'm not sure if you realised it, but you danced particularly well just now, thank goodness. So, she's asked if you would like to be in their show at The Mercury Theatre this summer. I assume you know all about it, yes?'

I shook my head, feeling a little self-conscious about seeming so ignorant. The truth was, I hadn't been to The Mercury since Mam was around. We'd seen *The Nutcracker* there for the first time. The building had been so grand, so elaborate, so majestic, with its stone pillars, and arched, leaded windows. At the time, it felt titanic compared to me. I remembered thinking every dancer there must have been famous to be able to dance on that stage and have over one thousand people watching them. I was in complete awe! The arts centre had been the largest venue I'd ever danced at, but soon, I was going to be there at The Mercury, as one of those dancers… *I'll have to get the bus there. How long will it take? About forty minutes? An hour? May have to get two buses…*

'Ah, well, it's a wonderful showcase of *all* the very best dancers in South Wales, one from each of the top dance schools, I'm obviously *delighted* to say. So, the lucky one representing our dance school is you! Isn't that wonderful?'

I heard a rustling at the back of the studio behind me. I'd thought I was the only one left, but Luc was walking quite briskly towards the door.

'Oh dear,' Ms Madeline said. 'He'll be so disappointed. You know, it's one of the reasons he joined this dance school last year. He was extremely close to being chosen; you know. And this was nothing to do with me. You'd better make sure you hold on to this good fortune. Dancers are quite used to nipping at each other's heels.' She gave me a wink.

'I will, don't worry,' I nodded. 'I'll practise so much. Can't believe it!' I thought about what the school counsellor said, about cutting down on the dance… *She just doesn't understand what it takes.*

'Yes, well, sometimes that's the best way, isn't it dear? And you can adapt, just like you always do!'

After class, when I saw Theo sitting in the car, I felt my smile fade a little. It dawned on me how he might feel about the show, especially after everything that had happened after *Swan Lake*…

'Let's get you home, shall we?'

I collapsed in the passenger side; my fringe stuck to my sweaty head; my old make-up even older. I was so conscious of how I looked, seeing him with his clean hair and his creaseless summer shirt. He always smelled delectable too.

'Yes please,' I mumbled, channelling the grumpy girl he'd left just over an hour ago, 'I need to revise for my exams… Actually,' I puffed some air from my lips, 'I'm gonna need more time to focus on my revision over the next few weeks… Hope that's okay… It's just, the school counsellor warned me that my grades…'

'The counsellor?' Theo interjected, 'oh dear. Of course!' I heard his fingers drumming against the steering wheel.

'Well, as I've always said, you take all the time you need, Coppy. I don't want a talented girl like you flunking out because of me. I want to support you – with anything – so, you just tell me whenever you need the time, okay? And I mean that.' His jaw tightened with concern.

I nodded. He'd always cared about school, so I knew he'd

understand – and besides, it was the truth. I could tell the truth. That was easy.

It ended up being even easier from there. I knew Theo hadn't forgotten about the drama that had started the day, the rush to see Julia – not that he knew her name – and the state I had left his house in – but he didn't ask how it went. I waited a few minutes for him to bring it up, I didn't even have the energy to fill the air with a different subject – but I had some words ready – all the right ones – to explain everything in the best way possible.

Maybe he was just being polite, not wanting me to dwell on the negatives, recount each awful step and fuel my embarrassment after a class that could surely have only ended badly after how it had begun. But Theo didn't ask, and so I decided it would be safest not to tell him.

THE MERCURY

The first rehearsal at The Mercury Theatre was a real eye-opener. I turned up extra early but everyone else was already there, dotted around the largest studio backstage. *Ah, my refuge,* I thought, as I placed my dance bag next to the heap in the corner and slid onto some free floorspace nearby. *Finally, a chance to breathe.*

Different to Ms Madeline's class, nobody spoke, not even a whisper. Instead, there seemed to be an air of silent but brutal competition. Nobody moaned about the icepacks strapped to their ankles or the supports around their knees. Instead, everyone's weakness seemed to somehow be their strength. Another difference: around a third of the group were boys, and all adorned in narrow vests or tight T-shirts, so Luc would have looked at home there after all.

The door swung loudly through the atmosphere when, yet another ballet dancer tiptoed upon our icy landscape. Julia spoke ballet with her tongue and we translated every French word into a new movement. The dancers pointed their toes to eternity and beat their feet together without caution during every *changement*. Everyone raised their hands to speak. *Where were they all these years while I'd thought I was top of the class (other than maybe Bobbie)?* It was scary; the exciting kind of scary, to know that we all had the same dream but we had no idea who it would come true for.

An instructor used the sweep of his arm to guide us into a semi-circle in front of him, nodding his head of slicked-back silver hair as though to speed us up. He was very sleek, dressed head-to-toe in black, with matching lace-up jazz shoes.

'Welcome, all. I'm Gabriele,' he announced, upright, with a muscular frame that gave him a strong balletic posture. 'Welcome to our workshop for our special performance at the extravagant *Mercury* Theatre. As I'm sure you all are aware, you've been especially chosen as the *crème de la crème* from your current dance schools, to work together to showcase the best talent across South Wales!' He coughed. 'Do not take this opportunity lightly. It means you have exceptional capabilities, but it does *not* mean you have the right to take it easy. Far from it— We want you to come out of this experience with much more than what you came in with. There will be lots of rehearsals and you are expected to turn up to all of them. So, continue to work hard, and most importantly, get lost in that dance!' Then, he swept away into the wings.

Every one of his words buzzed through my whole body. Discipline, hard work, exceptional skills. It was exactly what I'd been made for, to dance.

*

After two weeks of rehearsals, I'd become used to my new bus journey, used to finding my window seat where I'd unwrap my sandwiches and just dream for a while until I spotted the sublime Mercury approaching. There, I'd run straight to the studio, entering a world even bigger than Secret Haven and Ms Madeline's... It made me feel bigger, made everything feel so much more real, more adult, more possible. I was growing up in so many ways lately, even if some ways had been unexpected – and it was exciting!

Things with Theo had been going surprisingly well too. It was just like our first dates again, when we met just a couple of times a week, after ballet. Maybe Theo thought my new contentment was due to him rather than dance rehearsals, but was there really any harm in letting him think that? It just felt so good to have something that was all my own.

*

I decided I *would* tell Dad about the show. That was different.

But it would have to be at the right time.

I needed things to improve more at home first. Not that it had been terrible, but me and Dad weren't as close as we used to be. We seemed to be on pause. It wasn't just because I hadn't been there very much, but Faith had been there a lot. It was a busy time of year for the barn shop, so they were together all-hours.

I didn't like Dad and Faith being a 'thing' at first. Of course I didn't. It made me miss Mam more than ever – but as I saw Theo less and spent more time at home, the more I started to become accustomed to Faith being around. There she would be, sloping through the living room and kitchen in her same-old pea-green cardigan with the brown button hanging loose, and pottering in and out of the barn shop with Dad – always smiling.

The first time I'd noticed Faith sitting in the living room with a mug of tea in her hand, I'd smelled her first. An aura of peppermint radiated from the woman, who had a constant supply of hard-boiled sweets in her pocket. She looked older than she must have been, the way she sat, so sunken in the corner of our sofa, that I panicked, suddenly not knowing what to say. I'd completely forgotten what I'd even gone downstairs for and ended up running back up, trapped in my room for the rest of the evening. But it wasn't too bad. Neither Dad nor Faith seemed to sit for very long and not often together, it was more about 'having a breather,' so I suppose I had some time to adjust, to catch my own breath.

I'd tell Dad about the show once I knew I wasn't going to fall flat on my face.

'Fair play, Vila *bach*,' Dad said when he found me revising at the kitchen table at 7am on a Saturday, 'you're firing on all cylinders. Don't know how you do it.'

Dad fished his bread from the toaster. He was the hard-worker I probably got it from. Both him and Mam were like that, they never gave up on something until it was done, *bees, happiest at work*.

Dad held out a plate of thickly buttered toast. 'We'll have to get some meat on those bones once your exams are over,' he added, 'gotta watch you aren't doing too much, mind.'

'No need to worry, Dad,' I said, 'it's just all the dancing. Got a show coming up.'

I mean, of course I was tired, but in a different way to before. Instead of being worn out like I had been a few weeks ago, this new level of dance was so exciting that it was fuelling me from deep inside. *Exhaust yourself, go on, exhaust yourself,* it was saying, *and it'll all get done. You've come this far; you just need to keep going!* So, as the days went on, I had a tired, almost manic energy about me, while on the inside, I was a single shoe-ribbon away from collapsing.

'Oh? Another show?' Dad had finally heard what I'd said and his eyebrows were raised, 'I didn't realise. We'll have to come and see that!' The lilt in his voice made me feel like I could have told him sooner, *should* have told him sooner.

Dad pulled up a chair and sat down, taking gulps from his mug of milky tea. 'So, tell me more then,' he said, clearing the tiredness from his throat.

When I explained, he let out a sigh.

'God, to think I've spent so many nights worrying about you, Vila, and you sound like you're doing blimmin' brilliant. Just look at all this. Nobody could work any harder.' He rested his hand on my shoulder. It was warm from the tea, and rough from all the gardening. 'Proud of you, I am,' he whispered.

I'd forgotten how large Dad's hands were, the shovels that had scooped up all the earth in Secret Haven many years ago. *How had I forgotten that?* There must have been a time when two of those palms had been able to cradle my whole body while I yawned and scrunched my face up in just the beginnings of all those dreams... And he would have just held me throughout all of them. It hurt to think I may have given him sleepless nights, made those bags cling under his eyes. *Is that all me?* I couldn't let that happen again.

Dad sat there continuing to drink his tea, and I crunched at the corners of a piece of toast even though my stomach felt full of worries: yesterday, today, tomorrow, next year... But there at the kitchen table, in those few moments, our ivory house almost felt like before; the walls became thicker, the ground became stronger, summer showed its glowing cheeks through the window, and the tiny birds were beginning to sing on the other side of the glass.

Without our words, we heard the clock's *tick-tock, tick-tock,* but instead of leading us somewhere far away from where we were, it measured the warmth, the comfort, the calm. It measured the time we had left. And it was funny, I only realised when I heard it, but I couldn't remember Dad ever saying he was proud of me, not out loud. Yes, there was the time he'd said Mam would be, a long time ago, but he hadn't said it himself. I'd forgotten how much I needed to hear it.

Faith's face turned up at the kitchen window just before 8am, and Dad joined her on the other side of the glass. I watched them wandering around Secret Haven together, Dad carrying flowerpots and Faith carrying a box of marmalade jars that she was trying her very best not to drop.

A few hours later, as I walked through the living room on my way upstairs, I noticed the photo of Mam had been moved to the centre of the mantelpiece. There she was, looking younger than ever, smiling coyly at Dad who was the other side of the lens.

It reminded me of the last time I'd visited Theo. That photo of us both, framed on his bedside – the only one in his whole home. Unlike Mam's, my smile was forced and higher on one side, but nobody else would have spotted it. I imagined Theo gazing at that single photo he'd taken of us – every night before he went to sleep, while he texted me to say that he missed me. The secret I was keeping from him pinched at my stomach, but I felt sure it would be worth it.

He doesn't need to know, I told myself as I walked across the landing towards my room. There, I found Ana – someone else I needed to make peace with – sitting with her back against the wall.

'Come on, you,' I mumbled, picking her up and carrying her towards my dance room. 'You know you like to watch me practise. Well, I hope you're ready for weeks of it!' I propped her right on the top of Mam's dolls' house and could have sworn that as I turned to get into position, she had a smile on her face.

MERDE

I was alight and I didn't want the flame to go out. I'd managed to keep the big show a secret from Theo and even completed my Psychology exams.

It wasn't a big secret, more of a white lie. Not even a lie. Theo hadn't asked about it, so I simply hadn't said anything. It made everything easier – no drama – and I became more confident that I was doing the right thing.

The final week of rehearsals was even more exciting. Our feet sketched out where to dance on the vast, taped stage, which wings to run in and out of and which stage curtains we could creep behind. Then we looked out at the theatre's four levels of plush, red velvet seats and elaborate gold balconies, knowing we were only days away from performing to an audience.

'And remember,' Julia shouted as dancers filtered offstage to go home, 'the dress rehearsal won't be about perfecting the moves! Everything needs to be perfect already!'

But it was okay. Julia had drilled the fear of failing into us since the first frightening session. We knew it wasn't an option. By now, after all the weeks of sheer adrenaline-driven exhaustion, we'd done it. I'd done it! I was ready.

As I stepped outside to make my way to the bus stop just around the corner, I heard footsteps behind me. *Strange. I'm usually the last one.*

'Violet,' said a low voice, and even though I knew someone was there, I jumped out of my skin.

I'd seen Adrian dance a lot during rehearsals, but I was surprised he even knew my name. There he was, zipping up his shoulder bag and pulling a hood over his head, which kept falling back down thanks to the breeze. It was cooler than normal that evening and I was conscious of my fringe blowing all over the place.

'Sorry, didn't mean to scare you,' he laughed, 'only wanted to say *merde* for the big performance, not that you'll need it.'

I felt the colour rising in my cheeks. I was surprised he'd even noticed me.

'I know I'll see you before then,' he said, 'but y'know what it's like when we're all rushing around before the show... It's hard to actually ... talk.'

He wasn't wrong about that. I hadn't really spoken to any of the dancers. We were all so focused.

'Oh! It has been a really busy time... Well, *merde* to you too, Adrian.'

'Yeah. Thanks, Violet. Speaking of talking, would you like to catch up properly some time?'

Adrian's long, dark eyelashes blinked at me like quills.

I stood there blinking blankly back at him.

'No worries,' he laughed again, 'well, I've gotta go, but have a think.'

His hair reminded me of chocolate truffles. I liked the way it curled a little behind his ears and at the nape of his neck.

He handed me what looked like a clothing tag, with his name and number written on it, 'message me if you like,' he said, giving me another smile, and then he turned to walk away, very much with his shoulders, as Bobbie would say.

Bobbie would have said to just go out with him anyway, but I could never do something like that, I never understood how anyone could. *No harm in a drink,* she'd say. *It doesn't have to go anywhere! Nothing wrong with having a male 'friend'.* I could see her fingers flying in quotation marks above her head, but my mind and heart were so painfully full. I folded the clothes tag and pushed it into the front pocket of my bag. Everything had been more peaceful the last few weeks and I wanted to keep it that way.

As soon as I found a seat on the bus to go home, I took out my phone. About to text Dad, I saw that Theo had sent a message. *Strange.* He hadn't inundated me with his texts the last few weeks because he hadn't wanted to interrupt my revision. I wondered what was up. There on the screen, sat three messages from two hours ago, unanswered…

Uh oh.

There was a voicemail lingering above too. *33 minutes ago. 34 minutes ago. What must he be thinking? Nothing good. 36 minutes ago.* I played the voicemail.

'Hi lovely, I'm worried about you. How come you didn't respond? I know you, always glued to that phone of yours, so I had a feeling something must be off. Are you unwell? You've seemed so tired lately, I thought perhaps you were coming down with something.'

I felt the guilt fill my stomach. *Why hadn't I just told him where I was going?* Now it would seem like a bigger deal than it was.

I opened the text to read it, but the phone started vibrating. Afraid to answer, I left it ring for many seconds while the people around me all watched. *Perhaps I could just leave it ring?* But then I remembered he would see that I'd just opened his text message, so he'd know that I was very much available!

'Hello,' I said in a low voice, 'how are you?'

'I'm good, thanks, lovely. Are you feeling okay, my Coppélia? You sound a little fragile.'

The guilt yanked at me again.

'Oh, I'm fine, thanks yes, I am a bit tired.' It wasn't a lie. I was always tired in some way or another. This time, I was mainly overworked.

'Aw, bless you. Did I wake you up?'

'No, no, I wasn't sleeping,' I said. A woman from the opposite seat gave me a smirk. She probably thought I was a pathological liar…

'Do you need me to bring you something? You don't sound yourself.'

A boy at the back of the bus began playing loud hip-hop music on his phone and an older man in front of him told him to shhhh. Now, I was stuck.

'What's that? Where are you? Are you not at home?'

'Oh, no, I'm on the bus,' I said. 'I just had to catch the bus home.'

'Home from where?' he asked.

Now, I was sweating so profusely that my back was beginning to stick to the seat. I was repulsive right now, in more ways than one.

'Home from dance,' I said, dreading the rest.

'Dance? It's Tuesday, dear, are you feeling alright?'

'Yeah, it's a different dance thing, not a big deal, just something else.'

'Right, I see,' Theo said, sounding like he'd just finished putting a jigsaw together but couldn't find the final piece. Then there was a long pause. 'Well, I'll tell you what. I'll pick you up from the bus stop, so you aren't walking alone again, and then drop you home safely. You can tell me all about it. Does that sound okay to you?'

I just wanted to sleep but I thought I'd better agree on this occasion. It would probably be easier in the long run.

'Sure,' I said.

'Just tell me where and when. Okay?'

He had a warm look on his face when he picked me up, but as soon as I belted up, I heard all four doors lock. That's when I knew he wasn't taking me home straightaway. I prepared myself for a blurry evening of a one-sided argument. *How long have you been going for? You lied to me for that long? After I specifically and kindly requested that you share things with me? You've made me feel like such an idiot. So, someone else is touching you now? Someone else since that slimy swan prince? Are you happy to just give yourself to everyone now? Do you have no self-respect? Do you even know how lucky you are?*

Theo had a talent for remoulding a perfectly good day into something hellish. By the end of it, I felt guilty, unbelievably guilty. Yes, I'd been the bearer of awful news. I *was* the bad news. It was true, I'd never been a liar before.

What happened?
How foolish of me.
Thank you, Theo, for enlightening me.

A MATTER OF TIME

Stage make-up had been a loyal acquaintance over the past few years. It had hidden every imperfection and allowed me to blend in each flaw with a single brushstroke. This time, I tapped the unscarred part of my colour palette: swept some green across my cheekbone to calm down the redness of each of his finger-marks, combined it with some skin-tone concealer, and smoothed a final layer of foundation across my whole face, so all the pain could balance out. White shadow and a brighter blusher would hopefully pinch the rest back to life.

Maybe Dad didn't know I'd already started my exams. I couldn't blame him. He'd been spending even more time with Faith the last couple of weeks, so our mornings with each other were either brief or non-existent. On this morning, I deliberately hid in my room until I heard him close the back door after him, so he wouldn't see the impression Theo had left on my face. I was hurting – everything hurt – but I dragged myself towards school a little after eleven. The Literature exam was at half past.

I felt like an intruder on the drizzly, deserted yard where children had been replaced by seagulls – but I noticed a figure in the distance. *Why is there always a figure?* Just in case, I kept to the opposite side. *You've already gone mad, Violet. That can't be Theo, not at your school.*

345

It didn't help that the figure seemed to walk at exactly the same pace as me and seemed to really keep an eye on me. From far away, I could see he had an especially concerned face. Yes, it was definitely one I recognised.

Thank God. Frederick. Probably going to his own exam.

After all this time.

Think fast, Violet.

I shielded my throbbing face as Frederick gave me a thumbs-up, pouting his lip just like he would have after one of our trivial disagreements in the good old days – not that there were many, and when our eyes connected, just as we approached the school, he started crossing the yard towards me.

I panicked, not wanting him to see me while I was in such a state, so I gave him a thumbs-up and my heart seemed to explode. *No, I definitely can't do this right now!* That's why I power-walked behind one of the school demountables and took a shortcut back home.

My body and brain kept moaning to me on the way home. I was in a black hole, and I knew it was all my own fault. *Ballet is just a skill I've learnt, anyone can do it with a lot of time and little life, there are plenty out there much better than me and many more could fill my space. What would even be the point in me going to the show now? I've ruined everything. Exams, zero. Dance, zero. Violet, zero. And what else is there? I inflict dullness, darkness and frustration upon those around me. I wonder if I was never supposed to be here.*

I tried telling myself, *this is ridiculous, Violet, listen to yourself,* but I was listening, that was the problem, I could hear myself more loudly than ever, speaking what felt like the truth, the deep dark secret I was able to ignore on happy days.

But that was the thing, ignorance wasn't actually bliss, it was just dishonest, unconstructive, and waiting to creep out. When it made its appearance, it was bigger and darker than ever.

But it can't be the truth, Violet. What makes you so much less important than anyone else? Why you? Isn't that too fitting, too convenient?

Maybe, I said, *but the truth never lies,* and as I laid there on my bed, even my tears started to give up on me.

It won't be long, Violet said to me, whispering. So, I accepted her, my second self. We merged and I let her overpower me.

It won't be long before you've calmly disappeared, she said.

She was right. There's only so much control any of us have over ourselves. Bobbie was a perfect example of that. She was amazing but at the same time, ruining everything for herself; maybe that was what she was always supposed to do. I just wished I had the power to help; the energy, but the truth was, I was more exhausted than I'd ever thought was possible.

I picked up my phone and typed:

Always thinking of you, Bob. Sorry about everything. Hope your mam's doing ok x

But what about Dad? I asked. *Won't he at least be sad?*

He will, Violet said, *of course he will.*

And there, I began to cry again. My whole body sobbed, imagining him pottering around outside, in the garden, hammering planks of wood back into the broken fence or raking loose grass into a bag, unaware of my life drifting away inside. I felt guilty that I couldn't complete my job as his daughter, whatever that meant, to just watch over him, make sure he didn't drift too far from his safe path, lose his grip. But he had Faith now.

But he'll get used to it, too, won't he? It will be like after Mam; it took him a while, but he found a way to move forward, even if it was at his own, slow pace. He's good at accepting things, Dad is. He can think profound things, accept that there are no reasons, and he can stop asking questions. It's all about acceptance, and you can't do that, can you, Violet?

No. It was right there that I stopped asking. Instead, I nodded and walked to the bathroom. I watched the water run. I could feel that I was detached, I could sense it, I was my own shadow, but I didn't mind, it would make everything easier. I could hear more than I could see, but even the sounds were far away. The water running would be the last sound, no cry, no scream. I felt numb, I'd never had a story to tell because I'd never been a real person.

No sounds, see. No one is listening out for you. No one knows you.

I climbed into the hot water, but it didn't wake me from my conscious sleep. I fell back, looked up at the fading white ceiling, and thought, *maybe it doesn't matter so much, not to be part of this life. There isn't much good about it, not really. Maybe it doesn't matter that I don't matter.*

And at that moment, I accepted the existence of nothing beautiful. It had all been an act, and I was opting out of the performance. I thought of what people would say when they found me, limp in the bathtub. People in the houses up the road

348

were probably having tea. They would do the same, day after day. Their children would grow up, turn themselves into adults, who would have children of their own, and they would do the same. Dad would age and not realise, oblivious to the wrinkles, just as he was with the apples in our fruit bowl. I must have grown rotten before I could ripen.

Maybe that's what they'll say. 'She was always a quiet girl, it's a shame she couldn't come out of herself. We always tried, but there's only so much you can do. I suppose some people just prefer their own company, prefer to be alone.'

They'd nod and lower their heads at the funeral, and the kids from school would come. Maybe Melody would. Dad would cry, but in a different way to before, he would look at me as though he could have predicted it, as though it was inevitable – because he did see things, didn't he? He did know. Bobbie would probably be hysterical, for a while, but she would rub her red, puffy eyes and be laughing again a few weeks later.

It was inevitable, Violet. It was only a matter of time.

And then months would pass, a year would pass, and for their own sakes, people would move on with their lives. *There's only so much you can do.*

It was always downwards that I felt the pull. There was something heavy pressing upon me. Lying there in the clear water, my body was boiling, it felt as light as air as I rested my life upon my elbows. I began to feel dizzy as I tilted my head backwards below the water, tried to let it sink, but guess what? I couldn't even do that. My body floated, weightless upon the top, kicking its feet above the surface. This was ballet; one last dance, perhaps.

Violet, we are trapped.

And I realised I might be under the power of someone's magic forever.

But that was all that happened. I looked at Violet in the mirror, her body lobster pink but the face much paler than before. Her mascara had run, leaving shadows beneath her eyes, her foundation was nowhere to be seen and her lips were a little blue, just like the grab marks around her arms. It made me wonder whether I had died a long time ago. Yes, maybe that was why I could neither live nor kill myself. I was in a strange purgatory between worlds that no one could save me from. If you have no dream, you have no hope and there is nothing to look forward to in life. *Please let me dream.*

THE CRACKS UNDERNEATH

I wasn't sure how it happened, but there was a doctor sitting in front of me.

It was just the two of us in her small, stifling room at the surgery. Dad was waiting in the pick-up truck. He'd told me – just calmly – that we needed to go somewhere, and I wasn't up to questioning things anymore. Everything since he'd found the drenched towels on the bathroom floor and the blue vase that had smashed when I'd accidentally knocked it onto the tiles was a complete blur. I couldn't tell you why Violet hadn't picked any of it up, why I hadn't.

The doctor was leaning forward as her soothing voice chose every word scrupulously. I hoped she wasn't close enough to notice the bruise that was threatening to smoke through the skin. Today, I'd chosen yellow to hide it. She spoke steadily – too steadily – as if too-high a peak of intonation could pierce right through my jellied head and cause me to have a jeopardous wobble. It made me just as scared of myself.

'So, Violet, you probably know that your dad spoke to me on the phone when he booked this appointment…'

I hadn't known but it made sense. I pictured him rubbing his forehead behind the dusty windscreen. *Poor Dad.*

Her sallow face inched closer. 'From what I can gather, you've been a little overworked with school and other things.

How would you say you've been feeling, lately?' Her droopy eyes found mine and waited.

I looked through the window and then looked down at my shaky hands, saw how bony they were, with those blue veins, so prominent you could pull at them. Even though Dad wasn't aware of the entire bathtub episode – and what could have happened – even if he'd been busy lately, he wasn't blind. 'This isn't her,' I remembered him mumbling from the bathroom as he cleared everything away, 'this isn't my Vila.' Plus, my teachers had probably told him I'd missed that exam... I crossed my arms and considered my world.

But I didn't know which world to choose. They all blend, don't they? *How have I been feeling?*

'I don't know,' I mumbled, 'exhausted.' It was the truth. I didn't have the energy to lie.

'Okay,' the doctor produced a gentle smile as well as a piece of paper and pen, 'and why do you think that is?'

'Overwhelmed,' I said, giving her something. 'Revision, exams, everything else...'

'Right,' she said, nodding but looking at me for more.

But I didn't know what to say. I knew seeing a doctor was serious, everything was serious lately, but where would I begin? I looked at the floor instead.

The doctor tried again. 'Well, it's obvious you're into ballet, how's that been going?' she said, fishing. *Had Dad gone into all that too?* I realised I was sitting with my bun in place, and my usual dance jacket that had *The Ms Madeline School of Ballet* embroidered across its front pocket, with an outline of ballet shoes as the logo.

'I guess I've been busy,' I said.

'Right, okay,' she nodded again, 'I'd like to check your weight. Would you step on the scale please?'

The doctor stood alongside me, and we both watched the glowing number alter and then commit to its final answer. It did surprise me. I'd never paid much attention to weighing myself, but I'd assumed I was heavier than that. Lately, my whole body had felt like it weighed a ton. *With everything that's been going on, food hasn't exactly been top of my priority list, but I wasn't doing it intentionally, if that's what she's wondering…*

'Your BMI is quite a bit under what we'd regard to be healthy,' the doctor said, feigning concern, 'so we'll keep an eye on that.'

'Oh, I've never been big, though—'

'—Well, we need you to be healthy. So, how have you been on a day-to-day basis, would you say?' she asked, sitting down with one leg crossed over the other. 'Have you been getting everything done that you would ordinarily want to?'

My head was sent into a spin again. Seemingly simple questions and yet…

'I guess I've been a bit stressed, trying to fit everything around dance, with the big show coming up.'

'Right, I see,' she kept nodding as though it was her way of winding me up, so all the words would come out, 'and what is your "everything"?'

My usual daily activities had become so intertwined with Theo, going to his house, eating with him, listening to him and everything else…

But I can't tell her that part!

It was unsettling, sitting there, trying to talk about everything that I knew, deep down, was already broken. Once something's broken, you can't fix it, you just have to learn to live with it in a different way. Even if you use glue or tape, all the cracks are there underneath, threatening to splinter, just like they had before, and you know they can do it so well…

Maybe it had started when Melody left, when things first began to change, when Mam left, when Dad became distant? If feelings were ever light, they had been dark for a while, but I didn't know whether it was the way I was seeing things. *Can you project darkness, or only light?*

I'd been silent for too long again. 'Sorry,' I coughed as one tear tried to escape, 'I'm just tired. So tired.' I needed to cry but I couldn't. *If my make-up runs, it'll definitely uncover the bruises!* This was all supposed to be helping Dad, I guess, and my teachers, but I couldn't help it, I had no answers. I'd wished for answers for a long time, so I suppose they were all going to be disappointed.

'Don't apologise.' The doctor had turned to her computer, scrolled down the screen and clicked on a few icons. 'Right, we wouldn't normally do this straightaway but as there's such a long waiting list for counselling, and you're almost eighteen, in the meantime, I'm going to prescribe you a very small dose of an anti-depressant,' she said, slowly blinking at me as though I'd visited her with the common cold. She said it with such finality, like she'd found the antidote in a space of ten, mostly silent, minutes. 'I'd like to see you back here in a month's time to check how things are. If there are any issues, give the surgery a ring. And try your best not to skip meals, even when you're busy.'

I looked at the clock above her desk. Yes, our appointment was almost over. She was all for time management.

Maybe she knew something I didn't, but I wondered what her database could have possibly told her about me. She knew nothing of Dad other than a single phone call, and nothing of how we'd coped together since Mam, and nothing of school, not really. She knew nothing about my life, nothing about how my mind worked and what should be *my* 'normal'. Not even I knew what that was. But never mind all that. I just carried the slip of paper out of the surgery and down to the pharmacy. Dad, at least, needed me to return to the car with some hope…

It wasn't deliberate that I didn't take them. Not that I told Dad I couldn't. My throat had closed up, just like my voice had again lately. I'd tried and tried, rolling the tablet around on my tongue, hoping for it to rocket its way to the back with a good gulp of water, afraid it would eventually melt on my tongue, leaving its vile, chalky taste. But it was as difficult as I imagined swallowing marbles to be. I felt them stocking up inside my brain, trying to break through my skull. So, I leant over the bathroom sink and spat it all back out, feeling even more disappointed with myself.

'Vila, love,' Dad had said, his voice making me jump from the other side of the bathroom door, 'just for you to know, I, uh, fixed that swing of yours.' I could hear some confidence creeping back to him, thank God.

'Thanks, Dad,' I'd managed to splutter between coughs, somehow without choking. *Why can't I just swallow a little happiness?*

POINTELESS

I didn't go back to school for the final exams. What would have been the point? I didn't go to ballet. I didn't go to Theo's place either. I spent most of Thursday and Friday tiptoeing between my dance room and my bedroom, trying to practise for Saturday's show. Different to previous occasions where I'd forgotten the steps; this time, I knew every step from all the rehearsals, but my body couldn't summon the strength to stand up for longer than a few minutes, never mind dance.

My body slid down the wall and slumped beneath the *barre*. *Useless Coppélia, useless,* I said to myself. *After all those years, what a failure.*

But I felt dreadful for the brand-new pair of *pointe* shoes on the windowsill. They'd laid there in waiting for the past two years, ready to be worn during the perfect moment; originally, my first day at uni. We all knew that wouldn't be happening now. I stared at them, now absolutely *pointeless,* just like me. *What a waste of a dream. If only I could wear them to The Mercury tomorrow. If only I could muster up some energy. Perhaps if I considered this my final performance in life – but it would have to be a great one. Yes, this could be it.* It was the least I could do for myself, but I would need to bring those shoes back to life somehow. *After that, whatever happens, happens.*

I gently placed them on the floor in front of me before throwing a tea towel over them. I stamped on top of both blocks a few times until they widened, and then opened the inner shoes back out to their original shape. *Love is pain*. They would understand. Next, I used both hands to bend each shank forwards and backwards, hearing the satisfying crunch and crackle whilst being extra careful not to snap it at the centre. Those shoes needed to be shaped perfectly to my feet, no room for error or I could collapse. I bent each shank just a little bit at the *demi-pointe*, then loudly banged and slammed the tops of both shoes together, so I would land as lightly as a ghost. This was important, being the last sound I would ever make.

Eventually, I slid my *pointe* shoes on, squashed my plastered bunions inside the gels and cotton wool, and rose as tall as I could on the very tips of my toes. Then, I walked on *demi-pointe* to the bathroom, where I held each heel under the tap, so my shoes would be able to have a tight grip on me.

Back in my dance room, I sank onto one knee and dug the other into the back of the shank of the opposite heel, before alternating to improve my foot's bend. *That's it,* Margot said from the poster. *That's it*. Finally, I squatted on the floor, still *en pointe* for a couple of minutes just to feel flexible, then stood up again, rolling through to a full *pointe* and then back to demi. Now, my feet and I were shaped up for the challenge. This was the moment I'd been waiting for. If it went wrong, my shoes would just be morbid mouldings of me for afterwards.

A PROP IN THE STORYLINE

It's strange what can change in a single hour. I was relieved that I'd made the right decision, that I was standing in that red-carpeted theatre foyer, with my bag in hand. Nobody there would ever have pictured me slumped against a wall. Why would they? At the theatre, I was supposed to be somebody else, I was supposed to perform.

The air felt different the night before the show, in the same way it does before Christmas or Halloween. I looked towards the double doors of the foyer entrance. One dancer. Another. Another. Adrian. And another. Almost all of us, all in our individual dance school jackets or T-shirts, topped by faces layered with vibrant make-up, the eyeshadow widening our eyes. We filed into our dressing rooms, everyone rifling for the costume bag with their name on it.

There was mine.

Violet Hart.

But who really is she?

I yanked my bag off the rail, determined to quickly step into one of the many selves on its hanger, hardly recognising any of them. We'd been measured for the costumes before, and at some point, a woman with a mouthful of pins had held satin against our bodies. She'd poked and prodded at us while we'd stood in a long queue, and she'd mumbled and spat things like, 'right, yes, *in* a bit here,' while yanking the fabric around our waists, but we weren't allowed to take the finished pieces home. *Of course not.* They'd been passed down over the years, just as the pin-woman probably had. Besides, we knew they shouldn't be revealed to anyone other than Julia and the dancers before the show.

But we weren't just dancers. In the bulbed mirror, searching for space, I saw characters in chaos; sharp elbows adding extra blush to cheeks, blending in birthmarks, and giant cans of spray cascading over faces, all of us solidifying more every second, cracking final lipsticked smiles before we filed into the backstage corridor.

I'd forgotten how difficult it would be to distinguish everyone in costume. At Ms Madeline's, we always wore glamorous outfits, but these were of such high quality – a million sequins sparkled all over us, giving everyone that *this is real* glint in their eye as we waited in our very particular order.

The theatre we'd been in for many weeks was stunned in silence. The rows of seats were taken by ghosts as the stage was thumped like a drum by *pointe* shoes marking their places. But we weren't to focus on the audience now. Instead, we absorbed the magic before anyone else could; the damp smell of stage smoke where our feet disappeared, the blinding stage lighting, the fast-changing backdrops, the invisible curtain-puller, the gate and window props that opened and closed to our next scenes, and we did it all while gracefully making sure our wigs didn't fall off and our costumes didn't fall apart before and during the quick changes, where backstage strangers greeted us and helped us to undress, redress, undress, redress – sometimes in less than a minute; different costumes, different hair, different selves – again.

Soon, everything was a flowing tapestry of colour, back and forth across the stage. No more questions. Just all the answers. *To think, I could have let this go.* I became a prop in the storyline, happily lost, like a tree in a dark forest, kind of in a nightmare and kind of in a dream. We had no idea who would be watching, or how many seats would be filled the following night but that didn't matter anymore. All that mattered was the story being told in the best way possible, so that onlookers would believe we weren't ballet dancers, but something magical.

And it was our chance to believe in our own illusion.

We only followed orders that evening. It was a relief to me, knowing not only where I stood but where and how to move. We were all ready. We were all nervous.

When the music stopped and we took our final curtsies, Julia warned us all,

'Please be early tomorrow evening. You'll need to be warmed up before the show or your stand-ins will take your places.'

Just the idea gave our warm bodies the shivers. I remembered poor Ms Madeline.

And as we all stood there, nodding, I realised how much I would miss it all: Julia's harsh voice, her intimidating frown and her clipped pronunciation. I would miss the clapping and the counting, the music being stopped and then restarted for us to try again and again and again. I would miss the smile Julia produced when she was surprisingly impressed, and I would miss how she'd say she would keep us there dancing until we got it right – because I never wanted to leave.

But at the drop of a prop, the rehearsals were over.

*

The bus I'd just got off flew in the opposite direction, all its light, warmth and noise a distant memory. The Common seemed eerier since dusk had disappeared. I picked up the pace as the cars zipped past, their headlights casting a drifting shadow of me and then snatching it away. As I walked along the edge, scared of my own breath and chasing my own footsteps, I realised I'd already managed to get quite far, much further than expected *only around ten minutes until home,* so maybe I'd get my sleep that night after all.

I continued to walk. *Just another seven minutes. Only around five minutes, now.* I was close to the end of the Common, not far from our cosy, ivory house, really. *It won't be long. It's all worth it.*

And then I heard a car slowing down beside me but not quite stopping. I didn't dare look, but I felt my whole body stiffen. *You may be imagining it.*

'Weren't gonna leave me standing tonight, were you?'

There was no getting away from it. Just the sound of that voice made me shudder. I closed my eyes for a moment. *Breathe. Just breathe. You're so close. You're almost home.* I tried not to look towards his face again, those eyes that always drew me in.

It was my big night soon; it was unbelievably important, and my only chance to claim back the small part of me that might be salvageable. *Please leave me be. Please.*

'You've got your show tomorrow,' said the voice, 'you don't

want to wear yourself out with any extra walking, do you? Your poor little feet. How about I rustle us up some warm food and you can have a rest at mine? Really, my love. You look exhausted.'

How did he even know about the show? I hadn't told him when it would be, had I?

Don't do it, Violet. Don't go.

What happens if I don't go? I looked across the deserted Common. *What if... What then?* I felt the tingle of the fading bruise on my face, remembered the hand that had covered my mouth and dragged nails along the skin of my ribs, and I decided it would be best not to contest anything Theo said.

Instead, I found my hand reaching towards the car door just as before and saw myself climbing into the passenger seat in the same way I had that very first evening many months ago. This time, I said nothing at all. I looked down at my worn-out feet in the familiar footwell, those bony legs attached to them just flopped outwards. They had done so much, worked so hard and yet, there I was again...

So, this is the path I'm supposed to follow? Really? Is this it for me? The big love story? The dream? It was strange, all those times I'd pictured everything, it had never looked quite like this...

'There we are, my love. You're alright,' Theo said, resting his hand on my thigh, which made me flinch as I plugged in my seatbelt. *Does it look like I'm alright?* Instead of turning, he drove past Secret Haven, where I could see light glowing so warmly through the windows, and then spun the car around and went back over the Common. *Where are you going?* I thought. *Where on earth are you taking me this time?*

It was strange, but the evening at Theo's wasn't how you might expect.

'I just want to treat you this evening, Coppy. You deserve it,' he said.

And he did. He really did.

First, he served my favourite pizza. I watched him make sure he added extra cheese to the top. Once it was done, he cut it into extra thin slices, just as he'd noticed I'd liked it the first time. Next, he was offering me every drink from the cupboard or fridge, asking if I was hot or cold, paying close attention to the open windows and radiators, as well as to me. As we eventually bit into the nauseating silence between us and I began to find it too painful to bear, he raised his eyebrows above the floppy, tomatoey slice he was holding to his lips, and I couldn't help but send a smile. Our whispers – between gulps of ham and pineapple – slowly grew into words that soon became scrumptious sentences. Later, he was holding my feet in his hands – as before – and gently massaging all our tension away until I melted like mozzarella, and then, just as we were set to snuggle on the sofa, he wrapped a blanket around me before handing me a steaming mug of hot chocolate brimming with mini marshmallows.

With each sip, a little more warmth came back to me.

That was when I decided I'd better text Dad. He was bound to start worrying after getting home to an empty house; understandably a lot more on edge about me lately, and he'd have expected me to come back the night before the show:

Hey Dad, a group of us are staying at a dance friend's house tonight. Will catch bus home in the morning. x

He replied within seconds:

Right, ok, love. You be careful. Love you x

And that helped me breathe a little easier while Theo made proper love to me for the first time in a while; real love. He was so gentle. He whispered, left soft kisses along my collarbone and my ribs, and we just cuddled on our sides, just like the old days I'd pictured us always having – if you can imagine the past.

Had I worried too much? Catastrophised everything? Perhaps I'd put him in a box too soon, just like I'd never wanted him to do to me just because I was quiet. Everyone has their good sides and their bad sides. He loves all of mine, just as I should love all of his.

YOU USE OTHERS TO FEEL ALIVE

'Sleep well, my love?'

'Oh my gosh, perfectly,' I said, stretching and smiling up at my handsome Theo in his long dressing gown.

He slid a tray onto my lap: a swirling glass of orange juice accompanied a plate of eggs Benedict. Theo had just wanted to look after me from the start. He'd taken me under his wing and taught me how to navigate both ballet and life. Lately, I tended to jump from extreme to extreme and I suddenly felt like a different girl to the Violet I was the day before. *Every serious relationship has some rocky patches.*

I just hoped Theo would forgive me for creating a distance between us. I felt glad that he'd come looking for me, rather than waiting for me to find my way back to him. Now I knew everything was right between us, my mind would be at ease during the performance. He was my strong foundation, and I could dance happily and freely without any worries at all.

I pulled on the previous night's leggings and T-shirt and tiptoed towards my dance bag to do some yoga ready for the evening.

'Where ya going, Coppy?' He laughed.

Crouching down by my bag, I looked over my shoulder at him.

'You're not still going to that show, are you?' he asked. His chin came forward and his smile was exaggerated, as though I had told the most unbelievably funny joke.

'Of course,' I whispered, 'It's my...'

'Oh, Violet, you're so young and naïve sometimes, honestly.'

I froze. He'd never called me Violet, not once.

'You don't need to do any of that *dance* stuff anymore. You're my little ballerina and nobody will appreciate you like I do, you know that. You can dance just for me – wouldn't that be wonderful? – and we'll be *so, so* happy here, okay?'

It wasn't okay, and I was worrying. In fact, my heart was racing. Dance *stuff? Little* ballerina? *Who is this man?* The sight of him standing there in his dressing gown suddenly repulsed me. He looked older, much older, and like he hadn't shaved in days. He could even have been in his forties because what had previously looked like laughter lines around his eyes, now just looked like ingrained crow's feet to me.

'Oh come on, Coppélia, it's the least you could do for me after all your lying lately. Didn't you expect me to find that boy's number, scribbled in such juvenile handwriting? Do you think I'm a mug? I don't deserve this kind of treatment.' His smile was fading by the second. *This was how he expected me to redeem myself? What number? Oh... Adrian's... Maybe that was wrong of me, but why's he been looking through my bag?*

'I think I need to go now,' I said, still on the floor. 'Please, will you take me home?' I was rifling through my bag. *Where on earth are my ballet shoes?*

'Don't spoil everything for us, lovely. I understand that at the moment, you think it's your dream, but it's just because you haven't known happiness before. There's a whole world out there. This is happiness, isn't it? Think of last night, and all our special moments together. Are you saying dance means more than *that?* Are you really going to be that greedy?'

Tears were building in my eyes, and I was trying to blink them away. He didn't understand and I'd always thought he had. I couldn't comprehend why I suddenly had to choose between Theo and ballet. My dream of becoming a dancer was the biggest dream I'd ever had, and he knew that. *Where on earth are my shoes? I really need them. I need them now.*

'What *are* you looking for, Sugarplum?'

I said nothing as I kept looking.

'*These,* by any chance?' I turned around again to see that Theo was holding both of my ballet shoes, one in each hand. 'Don't know what you're worrying about. You won't be requiring them.'

I leapt forward to snatch them from him, but he dodged my every move, smirking at me while he teased the air with their ribbons.

'I wonder how easily they could break, Coppélia? Do you know? Maybe we ought to find out…'

I felt my heart doing a hundred *entrechats.* It was him who'd tried to sabotage me getting to my ballet class before. *It must have been him who'd been messing with my alarms,* and I was afraid he'd try to ruin this for me too. *Why on earth did I get back in that car?* If I didn't turn up at the show, it would be disastrous. *Please don't do this now!*

Theo stood there, provoking me with my own shoes, squeezing the toes between his fingers and thumbs, and biting his lip as he did so.

'You know,' he said, 'everything about a ballerina is so

delicate. I've always admired that. The arms,' he said, as he broke the shank of one foot in half and I heard the crack, 'the legs,' he continued, as he snapped the other, 'what else, I wonder?' behind gritted teeth.

I jumped back. My stomach had departed me, and I crouched back down on the floor. The shoes wouldn't function now. I wouldn't function. I felt like my backbone had snapped along with them. *Was this the way he'd treated his wife?*

'Too many emotions, that's the thing with you ballerinas. If only you realised you'd be even better dancers if you left all those emotions behind,' he sent me an aggravated smile as he walked towards the kitchen area, carrying my broken feet with him. I had no idea what he'd do next and then – *unbelievable* – I saw it, right before my eyes, he drizzled some oil and dropped both feet into a frying pan. I stood up in protest as he relished in watching them sizzle. My feet were burning right there; all hope of dance and becoming Margot, disappearing in smoke!

I'd never have believed he'd do that to me, and for a moment, my mind took me elsewhere, back to the moment years ago, right after Melody had left, when the dolls' house had been thrown on the floor. But this man was from a different planet to Bobbie. Bobbie's heart was warm. This man was a monster. *Why on earth did I let him in?*

I heard Mam's voice. *You have to look after your own life, Violet. You have to be responsible and look after yourself. Believe me, nobody else will.* And then Bobbie's. *Nobody can tell me what to do!*

I found myself looking Theo straight in the eyes, eyes that had lost all their softness. Then, I channelled both Mam and Bobbie to say what I really needed to.

'You know, you absolutely disgust me. You're the vilest creature I have ever known, and yes, I feel bad about myself right now, but not for the reasons you think. I feel bad that I could have ever been around someone as repulsive as you for longer than a second.'

Theo was beginning to fidget.

'You have no heart, you know nothing about dance, you know nothing about love, and you certainly know nothing about me.'

I saw his face drop, but I was determined to continue, realising, all at once as I looked around his bungalow, that after so many months, I hadn't heard Theo pluck a single ukulele string, hadn't seen him pick up a paintbrush, and nor had he shown me any of his many published articles – online or in books. I'd initially assumed it was just his humble nature, to keep me as his focus, which I'd thought was endearing at the time, but maybe I'd just been stupid to believe anything he'd uttered.

I ran into the other room, looking for something. *That photo album,* I needed to see it – properly! As I pushed Theo's laptop aside, I spotted it sitting at the back of his desk, discreetly placed beneath a tall pile of travel books I'd once been impressed by. I rifled through the thick, linen pages, desperately searching for an image, just something to prove me wrong, *please, just one, of his mother or sister,* but every page was as empty as him, other than the transparent pockets where memories should go. I grabbed one of his journals, to pore over his worldly writings but again, nothing but blank pages looked back at me.

Theo was standing in the doorway, sustaining a sickening smile as the smoke alarm came on. Dread consumed me. *Will I even survive this nightmare?*

'You aren't a person,' I shouted above the sound, 'you're a parasite and you try to chip away at people who you think are more likely to crack, which makes you the weaker one. I don't care what you've done to my shoes; you won't stop me dancing for the rest of my life if I want to. Even if I can't dance tonight, I'll just be glad I won't have to be with you.'

'Oh, I see, so, this is what it takes to get some volume from you? Are you done?' Theo asked, loudly laughing, which made me boil up again. 'Have you said enough?'

'No, I haven't actually,' I added. 'This is my turn to speak, and I'd wish you were dead if you weren't already so…'

'Oh dear, Coppélia,' Theo said as he calmly walked through the smoke, 'you think you suddenly know it all, don't you?' He soaked a hand towel under the tap and gently draped it over my ballet shoes. 'There, there, Coppy,' he said to them and then turned back to me. 'The sad thing is you won't be anything without me. I created you, helped you to be who you are right now.'

'You can't create something that already exists,' I shouted. 'Besides, you're just a plagiarism; a collage of all the bits you've dreamed to be but never bothered to become. You use others to feel alive.'

I heard Bobbie's voice in my head, spouting whatever we wanted to at this man, and it didn't want to stop. She would have been proud of me here, regardless of our arguments, I knew she would have. *You go, girl!*

Theo – on the other hand – was quiet for a moment. His eyes were turning to glass and his skin was pale as candlewax. For a second, I almost felt bad for him.

'So, Coppélia, you're really sure you want to leave all this behind? Never see me again? Never *properly* talk to anyone or share delicious food with anyone, or make passionate *love* to anyone ever again?' He stood there, with his hands in his pockets, less sure of himself than ever before.

'Because we both know you have a very lonely life,' he said, gaining some confidence again. 'And, you do know you've always been here of your own accord. I never once held you captive or made you do anything you didn't want to. In fact, I always told you there was no pressure, don't you remember? Don't you think you're being a little ungrateful and dramatic?'

Even during my outburst, it was difficult not to be convinced by him; that I wasn't good, that I should stay quiet, that he would always know more than me. I began to picture my future without anyone and that frightened me just as much as he did.

I looked over at the coffee table we'd once sat either side of, to the sofa where we had shared our first kiss under the stars, and the record player that had played *Waltz of the Flowers* for us to dance to, but they were all onces, weren't they? Yes, there were so many bad things, too many to even recall…

I slowly stepped backwards, making my way to the front door, afraid that he'd locked it. The door, however, clicked open quite magically; my escape, clear ahead of me, as easy as that. I suppose, in his head, he knew I always came back…

But the open door made me question things, made me stop and linger. Was I being overdramatic? Paranoid? Misunderstanding things beyond my intellectual ability? *It was true, he had never detained me, had he?* Yes, he'd hit me, but it was after I'd lied to him. He could have hit me just moments before when I'd raised my voice, but he hadn't. The door had been open all along… Had he ever really forced me to stay?

In sudden conflict, I looked down at myself, at my skinny wrists, fingers, and elbows, so small, so frail, and I saw that I was gradually disappearing. If I stayed with him, he would finish me off for good. He would erase my whole identity. If I stayed, I would have nothing to live for. I saw the anxious look in his eyes. I glanced towards the ballet shoes, no longer sizzling, then back at him.

I heard a voice in my head. It wasn't Mam or Bobbie. It must have been my second self. *Violet, make a choice.*

'Coppélia?' Theo called from what felt like miles away. I opened my eyes and could see he was panicking about me being full of thought. I'd never seen him panic before.

As I turned towards the front door, Theo stood behind me, using his arms like brackets to hold me there.

'No,' he said, 'please don't, Coppy. Please…' And then he slid down to his knees, right there in the doorway. With his head in his hands, he began to whimper.

What now, Violet?

I remembered our first meeting, and how I'd considered afterwards what he did for a living. One thing I'd imagined him to be was an actor.

But this seems real, Violet. You can tell he's not pretending. Don't be cruel!

Theo looked up with those dark eyes, filled with tears but

narrowing in on me. I considered the other occasions he'd been like that. The time on the sofa after *Swan Lake*, and how angry he'd become when he'd told me about his wife. But there was that portrait too... It had been awful. Terrifying, now I reflected on the hollow eyes, the darkness...

'You really don't want to spend,' Theo cried, 'your life with me? You just want to—' he kept whimpering, 'you just want to,' he finally caught his breath, '*leave?*' He was wiping tears from his eyes and his face had turned blood red.

This poor man, I thought for a moment. Just a boy, really...

Then I saw that disgusting glint reappear in his eyes, just as he reached up to stop me opening the door, just as he tried his best to wrap his hand around my ankle.

That was when I yanked the door open against him, grabbed my trainers,

leapt across the threshold

and ran.

PLEASE DON'T COME AFTER ME

I ran without looking back even once. As soon as I got to the edge of the estate, I slid my trainers on and then continued to run as fast as I could towards the Common, fighting against the wind and the rain as though they were Theo's arms trying to pull me back.

I ran so fast that I couldn't think about the fact my shoes had been burnt alive, and they were the ones I needed for the show. I couldn't think about what Theo's face was like as I left; how angry it had looked, how frightening; the way his two sets of teeth had showed themselves like those of a large black dog, the way his eyes had stopped blinking and just stared as if he had nothing to lose. *Had he been close to snapping?*

I ran until I no longer knew what breath was. My poor feet, where the blisters were already raw on my heels and toes. When I reached the Common, I ran in a straight line along the edge of it, the opposite direction to before and *oh God,* I hoped he wouldn't follow me! *Please don't come after me,* I cried out loud, catching rain in my mouth.

And then I heard the car. I heard it beep, I heard it pull over and I heard the engine turn off.

But I had completely run out of breath, again so close to the other end of the Common.

I'd got so far but I could no longer push forward.

My legs were so exhausted, they were running on the spot,

and I had to stop completely, almost throwing up. *This is it*, I thought. *This is the end, my end* that I was too late to do anything about, that I had been too stupid to take control of while I'd had the chance to leave, to be free, to grow up and be the dancer I'd always wanted to be, to make Mam proud, and to apologise to Dad for all the lies. Right there, my head dropped as I heard a car door open and then shut, and feet crunching on the gravel at the edge of the Common. *I've asked for this. I've asked for it all. How could I have been so stupid?* I fell to my knees, surrendering to the Common's theatrical tragedy.

'Violet?'

I began to shake my head and I began to sob. Too much air and too little breath had all caught up with me. I couldn't do it anymore. I tried my very best, but I just couldn't do it.

'Violet! Is that you?'

'Please, no. Please, don't,' I shouted without opening my eyes, and then I muttered it again and again and again. 'Please, no, no. Don't. Stop it.' All those things I wished I'd said a hundred times before in a hundred different situations, while we were together and hidden away, but I couldn't because I had no voice.

'Violet, dear.'

The voice was closer now, right behind me. He couldn't convince me he was a good man now, no matter what he did. I knew I'd never see him that way. A hand dropped on my shoulder and made me jump out of my soaking skin.

'It's okay, dear. Aw, it's okay. What's up love? Whatever's the matter?'

But I was still far too scared to look up as I hugged my knees to my chest, hiding from everything that was to come.

'It's me, Faith, love. It's only me. You know me, you don't need to worry. Who are you afraid of?'

I looked up to check and there was Faith's round, smiley-eyed face, concerned but comforting.

'A – man,' I whimpered, with broken words between tears. 'I've–been–seeing someone,' I cried, 'older. A lot older. And he…' Now, I couldn't stop crying. 'I've–done–things but I didn't want to do the–things. I didn't want–to. Not–those things.' Then I burst into full-on tears again.

I didn't see Faith's eyes as she listened, but I could hear in the change of her tone – from softness to strictness – and in the firm cradle of her arm, that she meant what she said next.

'Right. It's okay, love. You haven't done anything wrong. Nothing at all. Don't you worry about this.' She squeezed me harder. 'Listen to me. You haven't done *anything* wrong. Nothing whatsoever. You leave this with me. Your dad and I will sort it out.'

My whimpering paused for a second.

'And you don't have to think about this ever again, okay? Whatever this man has done is wrong and he'll get what's coming to him.'

Then, she held me so tightly while we both sat on the wet grass. I let her. Oh, how I'd longed for that sort of hug; needed it, forgotten it was there to be had.

'Here, sweetheart,' she took off her green, woollen cardigan and draped it around my shoulders. My fringe had stuck to my eyebrows and my feet were soaked inside my trainers.

'Come on now, *blodyn*.' Faith patted the back of my sopping T-shirt, then shepherded me across the gravel towards her little car. 'You're alright, love, come on,' she said, as though she were Mam speaking to Mist when she was a kitten. Every move made me want to cry again from all kinds of pain and I was past the point of embarrassment.

I only paid attention to Faith as we sat in her car. I couldn't even bear to look at the Common anymore. I just listened to Faith's breath, her thoughts, rather than my own, of what she was going to cook for food later, all the cleaning she needed to get done at home before the week started, how she needed to give the dogs a good wash, how her morning had passed by so quickly, and how she had found me, like a drenched stray, with frightened hair.

'Now, let's get you home,' she said, as my head fell back against the window and I closed my eyes not to gaze at the passing Common, wondering what it thought of me now, after everything, and wondering if it was saying, *I told you so.* Nothing was safe outside Secret Haven.

BACK TO SECRET HAVEN

Even though Faith had opened the gate to Secret Haven many times before, as we approached it, I still whispered, too quietly for her to hear,

'Go on then. It's alright, just for today.'

When I heard the squeaky hinge, Mist meowed at my return, as though I was a bad spirit waiting to enter. Maybe, after everything, I was.

'I'd better fetch you a towel,' Faith said, but first, Mist nuzzled her cheek against Faith's calf. 'Oh, you're a soppy thing, aren't you?' Right in front of me, *my* cat's eyes drank up her strokes as though they were the sun itself.

I felt homesick. *How is that possible?* There was our ivory house, as it always had been, just metres away, with the same hairline cracks. And there was that shadow along the lawn, where two little girls used to sit and play the other side of that dark line. Why was it that everything was so much more mesmerising while it was adorned with the sky's teardrops? The flowers had opened their eyelids, and there was the twitter and wheeze of our resident greenfinches. Yet, all of it, altogether, still made me want to cry.

There was Dad in the distance, with a sweeping brush in hand. The sound of Faith slamming the door and stumbling towards me with a towel over her arm, woke him from his reverie. When he turned around, he looked astonished to see us.

'They came back,' he shouted, 'they came back!'

He ran towards one of the fields and thumbed the air, so we knew we were supposed to follow. I could see Faith rolling her eyes. He wasn't talking about us, but still, we followed.

Sure enough, it had happened, the sound that at first, we thought was in our heads, but it went on for far too long. It was a dull drone, a mad drone, a passionate, workaholic drone, and as I opened my eyes, I saw Dad pointing and gazing with wonder at his hive, as though the love of his life had finally returned. Inside, were all his bees. Can you believe it? After a long absence, there they were, resuming their occupations as though nothing had ever changed. Of course, they weren't the same ones, we knew that, really – nothing could ever be the same – and yet, not one of us said it out loud.

Faith gave Dad a squeeze and I was tempted to hate her, but for some reason, seeing her there with the sun stroking the many lines on her face and the same on Dad's, I decided to reserve judgement. I stood, shivering beneath a towel, with Mist turning her nose up as she tiptoed around me. Faith nudged Dad in the ribs, knocking on his shell, I suppose, and inviting him to crawl out as often as he could, to see all of us.

At Secret Haven, everything had always seemed perfect, even when it wasn't. It was the one place I could always rely on to be there. Lately, though, I hadn't appreciated it, and I felt ashamed to be walking through there while I looked the way I did. Dad turned to me.

'Isn't it marvellous, Violet?'

But then he properly caught sight of me, half-dressed, drenched and with a face full of smudged make-up, probably revealing the greening bruise across my cheekbone.

'Oh my God, Violet, what's the matter? What's happened?'

Faith wrapped her arm around him before pulling him to one side. She sent a simple nod in my direction, and I could see her whispering. Dad looked concerned, about to walk over but Faith stopped him again. After a few moments, they both came towards me with linked arms and gentle smiles.

'How are those feet of yours, Violet? Got that show tonight, haven't you? At The Mercury?' Dad asked, spritelier than I'd imagined if he'd heard even bits of the truth. *Surely, Faith told him she'd found me running across the Common? What must he think of his daughter?* I couldn't imagine what horrible scenes were playing through his head at that moment. I didn't want to recall the reality myself. *What a disappointment I am. What a revolting disappointment.*

'She doesn't have to go if she doesn't feel up to it, do you love?' Faith said, as softly as she could.

'Oh, she'll be going, won't you, Vila? She doesn't let anyone stop her from dancing. Do you?' His hands moved from his pockets to his hips. It was the first time I'd heard him challenge Faith… It was good.

I shook my head. 'I don't think I can, Dad. My feet – and my – oh god, my shoes. He has my shoes. I ran away from my shoes. He has them, Faith. He has everything.' The tears were trying to rise again. If Dad previously had no clue what had happened, he definitely did now… His face looked plagued with … guilt?

'It's okay, love, we'll sort it out,' Faith said, patting me again.

They seemed to work well together, and I – for some reason – so weak and tired, didn't seem to mind. Mam and Dad had worked well together.

Faith guided us all back to the house and into the kitchen.

My feet were aching, really aching, and the blisters were stinging too. Faith, seeing me twinge with pain as I sat down, went to the sink to fill up a large bowl of warm water, and added some sweet-smelling bubbles.

Dad sidled out of the kitchen. 'Just gonna shut shop. I'll be back, now,' while Faith rested the bubbling bowl on the floor in front of me.

'Lift up,' she said, as I lowered my feet very slowly into the hot water. What a feeling, for my feet to be nurtured in that way, after I'd worked them so hard so many times and for so long. What it felt like to be properly cared for. I saw the steam rising from them, smelled the lavender and it made me drowsy. I just wanted to sleep.

As I sat there, my eyes drooping closed, Dad returned and pottered around as normal. He didn't make a fuss or say anything about what had happened, which was just what I needed. Faith did the same, following his lead, just looking at me and smiling gently every now and then, as though I was a baby who hadn't been cuddled enough.

'She'll be alright. Won't you love? I'll give you whatever help you need,' Dad muttered.

I managed to provide a drowsy nod.

After a while, Faith gently lifted my feet out of the cooled water and patted them dry with a fluffy towel. Again, I let her, and shortly after, as I was dozing off in the chair, Dad did something he hadn't done since I was little. With both arms, he picked me up and gently placed me on the sofa.

'She weighs hardly anything,' I heard him whisper to Faith.

'I can tell', she said, draping a woollen blanket over me.

When I woke up, Dad was still excited about the bees. I could hear his voice, louder than ever. There was a rightful buzz around the house just as there now was outside it. As my eyes focused, I noticed something on the cushion alongside me. *How strange.*

A pair of *pointe* shoes.

At first, I panicked. *How did they get here? How have they come back? Surely, he hasn't been here? Not to Secret Haven!* Then I realised that of course he hadn't, he couldn't have. Those shoes had been burnt. Well and truly burnt. These, I realised as I examined them with my fingers, weren't even mine. I only had one other pair and they'd been used every week at class, far too old for a show. These ones looked only slightly worn, and not quite the right colour, but hopefully, it would go unnoticed. They also had the shapes of toes already in them. I turned them over and saw no initials, but when I tried them on, although they were very slightly too big, they were the perfect support for my swollen feet.

'Ouch,' Faith said, as she saw me limping from the bathroom. 'That reminds me, I got you something for those earlier.' She was talking about my feet as though they were pets, and it reminded me of how Theo saw ballet dancers, those beautiful creatures that people were in awe of, as though they were something magical that ought to be adored. Only, he'd never truly adored me. Faith, however, was holding gel toe pockets! Just what I needed. *How on earth did she know that?*

'Got these at the dance shop in town. They recommended these or *these?*' She also had a rolled-up bandage in her hand, 'for wrapping around your toes…'

I laughed.

'…And plenty of these!'

The box of plasters tumbled from her other hand, and I couldn't help but give her a proper smile. She really was trying. I let her hold each foot on her lap and gently press plasters around them, just hoping they would both wake up in time for the evening.

GIVE ME TIME

I always loved and feared the moment just before a performance, when I could easily fly away. Everything was magnified. A peculiar breeze blew through the theatre; the curtain fingered the stage; I could hear the murmur of the audience becoming whispers behind the velvet, and the smell of costumes fidgeted in the air. The dance group and I, competitors for many weeks, now hugged each other, mimed kisses, and whispered, *merde*. In just minutes, we'd become one. We'd take turns to tell our stories, a contemporary medley of the classics: *Giselle*, *Sleeping Beauty*, *Romeo and Juliet* and finally, *Cinderella*.

The violins soon stopped scraping themselves into tune, the whispers died down, and there, finally, as the curtain rose, was silence.

The floor creaked beneath us and we tiptoed into our places.

I wanted a trap door to open – *please, there is still time* – but when the music played and light bore down on my forehead, I was home again.

We were part of a relay, exchanging feet in the wings. I joined the chorus in awe as I watched a dark-haired girl steal the stage in a peasant outfit – as Giselle – our first lead of the evening. I envied her unfaltering focus as she committed all her strength to every playful pirouette. From the back, you could sometimes catch a ballerina's lick of the lips or blink of an eye – but not her, not this dancer, on her way to becoming a professional. One stumble and all the magic would disappear.

Applause.

Mischievous Giselle had already disappeared, and then there was the first quick change.

Sleeping Beauty next – in a rose *tutu*, russet hair and a smile that opened as gently as petals – stole everyone's hearts as soon as she *bourréed* into place.

We were a carnival of fairy tales with a modern twist, and every chorus we were part of supported each lead. We switched and swapped places, flowing freely through sequences and variations around the stage. Only now, seeing our performance in full, with no pauses for corrections, did I realise how amazing it felt to see and be part of all the ballets I'd watched so compulsively on a laptop screen over the years.

Each lead was different, but when it came to the *pas de deux*, I couldn't take my eyes off the next pair. It was hard not to notice – while I stood in the wings – how graceful Adrian was with his Juliet; the way he lifted her so gently from the waist; the way he let her take the limelight, no better Romeo.

But I had become too drawn in, as though I was one of the audience, something I would always struggle not to be, so taken in by the orchestra. I almost forgot why Adrian whispered *merde* in my ear as he ran past. Then the fear came back, accompanied by the haunting score by Prokofiev.

The backdrop became a fireplace and a little kitchen window between old castle bricks.

I tiptoed towards the hearth and knelt.

It was my turn to take the lead

as the audience awaited

Cinderella.

Being the last one in the show was either a blessing or a curse.

In rags, I started slowly, trying to block out everything that had happened, what I must have looked like on the Common earlier that day; the rain, my feet, my wailing, but at the same time, I harnessed it. I thought of Cinderella. She had lost people too, and had things taken away. She also had a dream to dance – just for one night, at the ball.

I saw the theatre as everything I'd once had; Secret Haven, the very beginning, with Mam and Dad and the safe pasture they'd built for us, filled with beautiful colours and the green palladium that Melody and I had danced upon.

My patterns and paths returned to me. I stood up and step by step, extended each arm and leg, curved with motive, gaining energy, feeling the music taking over me as I began to feel the world.

As I became more aware of the gentle sounds and the tremble of music around me, I tingled at everything new, fascinated by my own movement as I grew into its shape. This was me – and I could be anything I wanted to be! I looked around, my hands unveiling the world as though it was a picture of wonder, hard to believe such beauty, such grand possibility. Anyone could be beautiful. Anyone could be someone. Anyone could go to the ball.

My rags didn't wear me, I wore them. I pointed my leg in front of me and let it guide my body forward. I followed my hands as they reached towards the audience, and I felt my way through the air towards that dream that sat somewhere behind the camera in the distance. *This belongs to me. It all belongs to me.*

And then it happened. That feeling again, the one I'd been afraid I would one day lose, the feeling I had never had from anything else – other than Theo. *But don't think about him. Don't think about him now.* When someone abuses your dream, they abuse you.

But it was more difficult than it sounded; not thinking about him.

I slowly danced away the pain, felt the softness of silk cloth as I spun with it against my skin

and then The Ugly Sisters, John and Louie snatched it from me, taking my dream of going to the ball along with it.

I pictured all the people I'd once had and then lost. Me and Dad were almost lost to each other.

And then I wept, playing my part.

I heard the twinkling of bells. *If stars could sing, this would be their music.* I looked up to see a sequin-covered Zuri as Fairy Godmother, with flowing black locs that twirled around me until smoke erupted from the stage and I leapt into the wings.

It was time.

There, someone placed a tiara in my hair, someone else yanked at my ragged skirt, and as I spun back out of the wings, in a straight line, right across the stage, each rag spun away with it, leaving me in a shining pale-blue and silver *tutu*.

Alongside men dressed as mice, and a pumpkin carriage,

I would go to the ball.

I danced until my legs felt like air and I no longer needed to catch my breath; it needed to catch me. One thing Theo was right about was that ballet is a miracle. I was higher than the stage, higher than anything, up there with the Gods, speaking to something, someone else.

Mam, can you see me? Please, Mam, look.

And I felt the smile take over my face as though she was pulling it from inside.

It was Mam who had smiled at me when she'd stitched my elastics on my first pair of ballet shoes, it was Mam who had smiled at me when she'd fastened my hair into a bun, it was Mam who had smiled at me through the dance room door and watched me do my first *plié*, and it felt like she was smiling at me now.

Beautiful gowns waltzed around me with their partners, impressing each other and the onlookers. The Ugly Sisters looked towards the Prince for approval but only gained the audience's laughter. Then the court jester tumbled down the steps onto the stage, and with such strong elevation, leap-frogged and side-split into the air, committing cartwheels and high split-runs, making the audience giggle again.

A roar of applause.

Any dancer usually forms a silent but deep connection with their partner during duet rehearsals. Oliver and I, however, had only obeyed Julia, never questioned each other, but let her move our bodies together and apart in a precise way that the tender flute had led us to believe. From week one, to me, he wasn't Oliver but the Prince, and I, to him, was Cinderella, in full character. Now, I looked him in the eyes as the music wooed us and pulled its violin strings. I saw the blend of sorrow and happiness in his expression just as mine had blended in dance, finally at the ball, finally free from being a slave to someone else's happiness – *Theo's.*

In our modern retelling, the part we danced together was a shorter *pas de deux* than normal. It was regal, it was suspenseful, synchronised as Melody and I had always been, and alluring like many romantic first meetings, but within moments after our final lift, just as the trumpets introduced themselves, just as we realised our innate comfort with one another, our bodies speaking every language as we both united in our desperate longing for meaning, I let go of the handsome prince

give me time

because I wanted to dance

and Cinderella wasn't going to fall for him so soon.

As Oliver watched with the rest of the ballroom dancers, I began my gentle *grand jeté* variation around the stage, speeding up as the music did beneath the giant ballroom chandeliers,

and then the clock started to tick, loudly, warning me of midnight.

It sent me into a spin in the same direction as its hands;

one leg whipping the air, the other, rooting me to the spot,

fouetté after *fouetté* after *fouetté*

fearing my riches would turn back into rags, for the performance I had waited so long for would have to reach its end. *What does it mean – for me – when this dance is over?*

I continued to spin,

around and around and around

as Prokofiev's clock continued to

tick-tock, tick-tock, tick-tock, tick-tock.

I spun and spun over thirty-two times, just like the ballerina in the music box in my dance room, not for Theo's eyes this time but for mine, and the whole ballroom – including the handsome prince – who looked on in wonder

as the giant clock behind us struck midnight.

But there was no need to be afraid. I saw my own world, just as I wanted it to look and I just kept going, smiling at the furthest point in the audience, spinning on one leg as though I never needed to pause because I danced on my own watch.

The audience was convinced I would spin forever, like some magical creature, long after they had all disappeared, and they roared with applause; an applause that built and built

until I finally came to a stop.

There, as I looked out, I saw that people were on their feet.

The curtain fell and Oliver and I were joined by the three lead couples of *Giselle*, *Sleeping Beauty*, and *Romeo and Juliet*. It lifted again, and as the lighting changed, applause came once more and I looked over at the crowd, taking everything in. I could see Dad and Faith were right there in the front row. Dad was clapping and wiping tears from his eyes as everyone stood up.

In the row behind them, there was that kind face I hadn't long encountered; Frederick, standing alongside a boy of similar age who had his arm draped around Frederick's shoulders. Their hands interlocked and they lifted each other's fists into the air. Frederick whistled twice and then waved frantically at me, so I couldn't help but smile. There was so much I hadn't known for all those years, but now, there we all were, out in the open.

As the curtain rose for the last time, the rest of the dancers joined us. The crowd roared and I could see a theatre lit up by faces. We walked forward to take our curtsies and bows. The first few rows were the only ones out of darkness, but I noticed in the front row, on the opposite side of Dad and Faith, that a single seat was empty. Even though he wasn't there, I could still sense the shadow of him.

THE TRUTH

Backstage is where everything becomes clear for a dancer. It's where you find out how you really did out there, regardless of any standing ovations. It's where your inner critic asks, 'Was that the *best* I could do? For me? *Definitely?* Or, have I done better before?' You don't need words to answer. It's something you instinctively feel, either as an inner silence, a hateful, impending darkness or a euphoric high that makes you feel like you can do absolutely anything – because you just have. You either rip away your eyelashes or you pause and keep your face on for a little longer, just to hold on to that dream.

As I sat down, Ms Madeline walked in, excusing her way past half-dressed dancers. She was wearing her out-of-dance clothes; a long, soft black coat, with tan high heels and smart jeans, her elegant ebony hair slunk straight down to her hips. I'd never seen it down before. Nobody had! She leaned right over me and planted a kiss on both my cheeks.

'Violet. Now, let me tell you, I have never – in all the years you've been dancing at my school – seen you dance as beautifully as you did tonight. I won't go on too much with the praise,' her hands were on my shoulders as she looked straight at me, 'but you should be so, *so* proud of yourself. Your passion, your *gift*. The crowd out there was in absolute awe and let me tell you, Violet, that takes some doing.' Her smile stretched wider than I'd ever seen it.

She left just before there was a knock at the door.

At first, I felt afraid. *Please don't be Theo, please don't spoil this for me now. Surely you wouldn't come in here, not with all the other girls. Maybe it's one of the other dancers. Adrian, perhaps?*

I watched the door handle sink. Someone peeped through a little gap, and *what a relief,* there she was, Bobbie.

She strode in, tall and slim, with her freckly smile and red hair in a long plait, *oh* and – *what's that?* A hint of a bump where her narrow tummy would have ordinarily been! *My gosh, Bobbie.*

'At least one of us made it then, eh?' She gave me her cheeky smile.

'Oh, Bob, I had no idea—'

'Come here, you,' she said, pulling me into a big hug. I gave her a gentle squeeze back. Her baby would be a tough and fiery one. That was a nice idea, a little Bobbie again.

'I am *seriously* proud of you, girl! As proud of you as I would be if it was me!' Without fail, she made me laugh. I'd missed that.

'Besides nobody knew, Vi. Nobody. How would you? I know you're special but you ain't bloody magical. Anyway, don't judge a ballerina until you've danced in her shoes, eh?'

I looked down at my feet and then back at her, gasping. 'Really? These are your shoes?'

'Yep, so I get some credit now, right?' She nudged me in the ribs.

'Definitely, Bob.' She was a funny one. Always there when you least expected her to be. If she only knew everything that had happened with me lately. *How could I judge anyone?*

'Thank God you're okay,' she said. 'I could tell you weren't yourself when I got that text from you the other day. What did you think you needed to be sorry about anyway, you daft thing?'

'Oh, lots of stuff,' I mumbled. 'But you didn't reply, Bob...' I felt myself fidgeting.

'Eh? Course I did.' Her eyes popped. 'A bit late yeah, but look!' Bobbie took her phone out of her pocket and showed me the screen. 'Anyway, talk about pot kettle! There's tons of messages here that you totally ignored!' She continued to scroll. There were pages of emojis, GIFs and her trademark bursts of witty one-liners.

'Oh God! Sorry, Bob. I haven't seen any of those, I swear. Nothing... I really don't understand.'

'I could make a guess...' She pulled her sarcastic face and mouthed with a loud whisper, 'it's that man. I knew he was a weirdo from the get-go but you were obviously too in love to see it. We all do it...' She wrapped her arm around me. 'Anyway, shit happens.'

Tell me about it...

'Look at me. Got myself in a right pickle, but could be worse...' She stroked her stomach. 'If this is a girl, Vi, I'll probably name it after Mum. She's so much better now. She's really on the mend.'

I felt the air puff out of my lungs. 'I'm so glad she's doing alright, Bob. Really, I am...'

As I lifted a foot onto the chair alongside us and began undoing my shoe ribbons, Bobbie unhooked me from my tutu, so I could quickly get dressed. I definitely hadn't seen any replies to my texts... In fact, now I thought about it, I'd received less texts in general recently. I'd assumed it was because I'd potentially annoyed people by being more distant, but now, I was definitely beginning to wonder…

'God, look at you,' Bobbie said as I zipped up my vanity case, 'you really can be anything in dance, can't you?'

I stood back and looked at myself in the mirror again. Out of habit at first, I only glimpsed Coppélia. Then, I saw Odette, Odile, Cinderella…

'How do you *do* that? I mean, become other people so easily?' Bobbie had always been so good at being herself.

I shrugged, considering everyone I'd been the past few months: *Coppy, Sugarplum, My love*… In a way, cooped up in that little bungalow, could you say I'd become *him* too?

'You know what? You look just like her, Vi.'

Then, I saw who she meant.

Mam – with her most defining features.

There was her full smile as if by magic, as though she'd been hiding amongst my make-up the whole time, since I was nine years old, then popped out like a genie. And there were her high cheekbones that only brought more attention to the fire in her eyes. How often had I disguised her in powder, then dusted her away?

Bobbie hung my costume on the rail and dragged me, still heavily made-up into the bursting foyer. Clusters of dancers, parents and teachers took turns to gasp at yet another person joining their circle before more hugs and more air-kisses were blown left and right across a foyer full of fluttering falsies.

But no matter where I looked, I saw him, like a ghost who was yet to pass over. There he was, leaning against the wall after shaking people's hands or raising his eyebrows at a passer-by he somehow recognised, and still wearing that charismatic smile of our first encounter at the arts centre.

'C'mon, Vi!' Bobbie tightened her grip as we pushed our way through the crowd, where we found Dad and Faith in a quiet conversation with both Ms Madeline and Julia. *Oh God, what could Dad possibly be saying? And Faith? I dread to think…* Julia was beaming, though, so it couldn't have been anything about what had happened that morning.

But why was Dad on pins? It was making me nervous; the way he was biting his bottom lip and nodding, with his hands back in his pockets as Julia's arm gestures dominated the space between them. There he was with a freshly shaved chin and a brown corduroy jacket. As I stood alongside him, there I could smell the familiar scent of lemongrass soap we used to make from the beeswax.

The shouty man from the first rehearsals – Gabriele – stood at the opposite side of the foyer, not speaking to anyone. Instead, he kept his nose up in the air and shoulders back as he assessed the crowd, eyes scanning from left to right – for what, I couldn't be sure.

'Oh!' Julia clocked me. 'It's been so lovely to meet your dad here, Violet. I've just been telling him how talented you are and how tonight was just that extra … sparkle on the tiara!' She clutched one of my cold hands while she continued to speak with the most ecstatic eyes, but I couldn't help but keep looking past her. *What if he's here somewhere after all?*

'Now, I've spoken to Ms Madeline here,' Julia turned to her and then back to me, before ushering us all a little closer to the wall, into a space beneath the stairwell and continuing, 'and

I'm sure she'd be very sorry to lose you, but … also delighted for you to be offered a scholarship with … us – at our ballet school in London – if you would like that?'

This time, she took both my hands and looked at me face-on as though to capture how stunned I was. 'I know this might be a lot to take in straightaway, but you're the real deal.'

She let go of me as though waiting for the news to sink in.

My hands searched for each other behind my back to hold me steady.

The foyer was slowly emptying. There were stragglers throwing their dance bags over their shoulders and making sure to eyeball us as they walked past. Adrian was one of them, giving a little wave. I felt guilty at their curiosity.

'All the best, darlings,' Julia exclaimed and then carried on speaking to just me, 'now, your strength, skill and expression is beyond what it usually is for any young lady at this level, and that's without our further training. With our help, you could have a *big* future ahead of you…'

Julia was smiling in anticipation as she held such intense eye contact that I could see the speckles of brown – strange but alluring – in such pale grey eyes.

'*Well*, Violet,' Ms Madeline interjected, 'what do you think? Would you *like* to join this *elite* dance school?' She held her chin up in anticipation.

I wanted to shout, 'of course I would like to!' To finally achieve what I'd been working hard for my whole life; to dance on stages that dancers like Margot Fonteyn had danced upon, and mostly, my whole dream coming true to such an extent that I could touch it, live it, breathe it, and tell myself, *Violet, you weren't crazy after all!*

But while I stood there – with all of them looking at me – my mind was smothered with questions.

What about Secret Haven? All its colour and comfort? I thought of how I'd danced with Melody there all those years ago, twirled and split-ran before I knew it would become *pirouettes, pas de chats* or a *pas de deux. How could I possibly leave all that behind? The beginning of everything? At the same time, would it ever truly be comfortable again without my big dream?*

I looked over at Dad and my stomach sank. Those kind eyes. How they'd clouded over after Mam had left…

Then I pictured myself in a little dorm room in London; train and bus-distance away from home, lying on a single bed, without Mist's warm body curled up alongside me, or the Common to peer out at. *Because we both know you have a very lonely life*, Theo had said to me just that morning. And he wasn't wrong.

If Julia and everyone else knew about the past few months, I bet they'd feel differently, I'm sure of it. What terrified me the most was that somewhere inside me, there would always be a space that allowed something to fit so snugly that it could take over my whole life.

Alongside Dad, I saw the reason for his happiness having returned – not just my ballet, but the hand clinging to his arm, rubbing it with her other palm as if to say, 'Come on, now, you.' This woman had been so tender when she'd found me; so nurturing. So different to Theo, where love had become pain.

Dad stepped forward and his hand felt stronger on my shoulder than I'd expected.

This one was the hand that had lifted me onto my swing after attaching the rope to the big greengage tree; it was the hand that supported my nervous waist while I first rode my bike without stablisers, and then let go. This was the hand that would have caught the whole sun and brought it to me if he'd thought it would brighten my day. And when my swing broke years later, it was one of the same hands that fixed it, that fixed my ballet *barre* onto my wall without me needing to ask; that shaped the little birdhouse and put his whole heart into those bees.

He'd never wanted me to be broken.

The foyer was silent since every other dancer had disappeared.

'Go on, love,' Dad said, without wobbling, 'you're made of tough stuff,' as though I was one of the baby sparrows he'd supported with the edge of his knuckles.

'But Dad, I'll worry about you…'

'Isn't meant to work that way round, Vila.' Dad said as he looked back at Faith. 'Besides, you've got nothing to worry about and you'd be mad not to give this a go after what I saw up there on that stage tonight.' There was nothing guarded about Dad and Faith, now, just warmth in their eyes.

And as the hand pressing down on my shoulder let go, I decided I would fly, just like the bees, knowing I could come back whenever I liked.

Bobbie was standing behind everyone, giving me the most unsubtle thumbs-up; her eyebrows raised like question marks.

'Sooo, should I take that as a yes?' Julia squinted as she pressed her ear forward with one hand. Her eyes were darting between me and Dad.

'Yes,' I said, with a laugh of relief, 'yes, please, definitely. Thank you so much!'

'Well,' Julia said, 'we're lucky to have you, Violet. You're a name to watch out for. I really couldn't leave this evening without telling you.' She gave me a peck on the cheek and then pulled her satchel over her shoulder. 'It's been lovely to meet you all. We'll be in touch to make it all official, of course, and we'll look forward to seeing you soon!'

Julia and Gabriele – joined by Ms Madeline – exited the theatre, and I saw Bobbie mime, 'YeeeeeEEEESSS,' with a fist in the air.

'It's fab news, love,' Faith said, 'absolutely fantastic.'

Bobbie tried to gather us all in one, giant hug but I went to Dad separately.

He whispered in my ear, 'Would have expected nothing less, Vila *bach*. Nothing less. Your mam would be over the moon.'

As we walked down the steps to leave the theatre, I couldn't help but cast my eye across the moonlit car park to check no one else was watching, listening, waiting…

'You doing okay, *blodyn*?' Faith asked me with a knowing look.

'I think so, but it's kind of like, everything, all at once…'

How strange that regardless of all the hugs and all the congratulations, I could still clearly picture the excitement that would have been in Theo's eyes, the animation in his arms as he'd ask me about all the next steps, and I could even smell the aftershave on his neck as he'd draw me into his chest – that mulled wine. *But that was the old Theo.*

Every time I thought of the bad aspects of him, I sooner thought of the good ones … But I needed to spin it around. Even though I hated the idea of him hurting someone else, I hated the idea of him loving them first. It was all too much to think about…

I love how quiet you can be, he'd said before, knowing – so well – that I'd speak in my own time and in my own way.

His words from that morning replayed in my head: *You won't be anything without me. I created you, helped you to be who you are,* and it made me wonder, was there anyone else I could tell about all this, without it all becoming *his* story? Without him being in the spotlight? After all the hard work *I'd* done?

The truth is, right there, right then, I was finally Violet Hart again, just as Mam had named me, and I had never felt so alive.

NOTES

Myfanwy Haycock's poem 'Taskmaster', from her 1937 collection *Fantasy*, is quoted at the front of this book with thanks to the *Western Mail*.

In 'Pretty intoxicating' Theo quotes Pythagoras:

'You know, *Pythagoras* said, "be silent or let thy words be worth more than silence".'

This quote is taken from Ballou, Maturin Murray. *Treasury of Thought: Forming an Encyclopædia of Quotations from Ancient and Modern Authors*. United States: J. R. Osgood and Company, 1872.

ACKNOWLEDGEMENTS

A big thank you:

To anyone reading this.

To my editor, Susie Wildsmith, and to everyone at Parthian for giving my debut novel – and Violet – a chance to share her voice with the world. It's something I'll always be grateful for.

To Professor Stevie Davies, who witnessed the book from its very conception. Her mentorship and wisdom throughout my PhD were helpful beyond words.

To Dr Alan Bilton, Menna Elfyn, Professor Caroline Franklyn and Jon Gower who provided me with thoughtful and optimistic feedback, as well as the confidence that this book would find a home.

To all my Swansea University creative writing peers who continually inspired and strengthened me, and all involved with the Literature Wales Writers at Work Scheme at the Hay Festival back in 2019. It was an experience that will always stay with me.

A heartfelt thank you:

To Mam and Dad for always supporting my writing endeavours. Without you, my perseverance would have no foundation and this novel wouldn't exist. My mother's scrupulous eye and dependable honesty were ineffable and won't be forgotten.

To all my close family for their patience, and for never questioning the project I was always working on.

To my adorable baby girl – who gave me just enough time to complete the last big edits before she arrived in the world.

And lastly, to my husband, for having unshakeable faith in me from the very beginning – just because – and for always understanding how much it all means.